WINNING A WIFE

WINNING A WIFE

Annie Wilkinson

This first world edition published in Great Britain 2005 by
SEVERN HOUSE PUBLISHERS LTD of
9–15 High Street, Sutton, Surrey SM1 1DF,
by arrangement with Simon & Schuster UK Ltd.
This first world edition published in the USA 2005 by
SEVERN HOUSE PUBLISHERS INC of
595 Madison Avenue, New York, N.Y. 10022.

British Library Cataloguing in Publication Data

Wilkinson, Annie
    Winning a wife
    1.   Suffragists - England, North East - Fiction
    2.   England, North East - Social life and customs - 20th century - Fiction
    3.   Love stories
    I.   Title
    823.9'2 [F]

    ISBN 0-7278-6199-9

Typeset by Palimpsest Book Production Ltd.,
Polmont, Stirlingshire, Scotland.
Printed and bound in Great Britain by
MPG Books Ltd., Bodmin, Cornwall.

Acknowledgements

My thanks to all my family and friends for their encouragement and pleasure in my recent success, to Rilba and William Jones for help with research and the loan of books, to Paula and Murtagh MacDonnell for advice on veterinary and other matters, to Maureen and Leslie Sanderson, to Terry O'Riorden, and to all at Hornsea Writers, especially Linda Acaster and Karen Whitchurch, Penny Grub for advice on computers, Madeleine McDonald-Ullyat for a snippet, retired miner Rick Sumner for sound information, and Pippa Ireland, who 'fell orf'.

Thanks also to all writers on women's suffrage, especially David Neville for his thesis on the women's suffrage movement in the North East of England, to the redoubtable Pankhursts (of course); to all writers on the history of coalmining communities in Britain, particularly John Threlkeld for *Pits – A Pictorial Record of Mining*, Norman Emery for *The Coalminers of Durham*, to Lewis Jones for *Cwmardy*, to William Stuart Howard for his unpublished PhD Thesis 'Miners' Autobiography 1790–1945', to Huw Benyon and Terry Austrin for *Masters and Servants*; to the late George Dangerfield for that fascinating account of British politics between 1910 and 1914 entitled *The Strange Death of Liberal England*, to Dr Robert Colls of Leicester University for recommending the last two books named, to Dr Bill Lancaster and Graham Soult of Northumbria Universities for their recommendations for reading, to Anita Thompson and all at Durham Clayport Library, to the staff at Barnsley Central Library, Hull Central Library, Hull Greenwood Library, and Newcastle Library; and last but not least to Judith Murdoch, literary agent, and to Kate Lyall Grant, editor, for all their help and patience.

Prologue

There was an officious rap-tap on the door, and no doubt about who it was. The butcher and the butcher's daughter. John opened the door as wide as it would go and stared this bristling, self-important little man full in the eye before transferring his gaze to Elsie. She flushed and looked away. He gave a mock bow and stood aside for them, sweeping his arm in the direction of that holy of holies, the front room. 'Come in.'

Hartley ignored the invitation. 'Where's your brother, and when's he expected home? Only there's a bit of business here he ought to attend to, and before much longer.'

'Why, come in,' John repeated, looking him up and down, for once feeling the advantage of a full three inches extra height.

'I wouldn't set foot in your house, but she'd better come in. He got her in this mess, and he can take her and the consequences.' Hartley attempted to push Elsie into the house, but she broke from his grasp and walked a few paces down the street. 'All right, stand there and wait for him,' he called after her.

'She cannot stand there,' said John, 'and we've no idea when Arthur'll be back. He might not be back for another year or more.'

'He knew what he was doing, didn't he? Run off and leave her to face the music on her own. He ought to have been jailed, out of the way of hurting anybody. I don't know which is worse, having her not married at all, or having her married to that hooligan. That's if he ever does marry her. You'd better see to it that he does. Make him do right by her.'

'How am I going to do that, even supposing he ever does

1

come back? He's a grown man. And it's got nothing to do with me.'

'It's something to do with your family, and you're at the head of it, so it is something to do with you, whether you like it or not. If you'd been any sort of a man you'd have come to see me yourself. That clever madam you sent round to do your dirty work made it clear enough the bairn's not yours, and if it's not yours it's your brother's. Bloody suffragettes. Bloody meddling destructive interfering bitches of hell, making a bloody nuisance of themselves everywhere they go. I'd give them the vote, I'd vote them all a bloody good horsewhipping.' Hartley stared at John for a moment or two, his expression a mixture of revulsion and impotent fury. His pale, protruding eyes suddenly moistened, but his voice was full of anger. 'My daughter. She's insane. She must be to have anything to do with you people. I'll have her certified. I'll get her locked up out of the way, where she cannot cause any more trouble. That's what people have to do with cases like her. Moral defectives.'

Shaken by the man's sheer malevolence, John lowered his voice and insisted, 'Shut up. Shut up, man, and come inside, instead of trumpeting your business for the whole bloody street to hear. Come in, and we'll talk about it.'

'There's nothing to talk about. She's pregnant, and your brother's the one that's responsible for it.' His lip quivered, there was a catch in his voice, and for one awful moment John believed he would start weeping. 'She was promised to the parson's son. Did you know that?'

'Why, there's nothing to stop the parson's son having her, if he loves her. She's not married to anybody else.'

Hartley gave a short bark of a laugh. 'Are you mad?'

'No, just trained in Christian principles, like the parson's son ought to be. Love God and love your neighbour? Love your enemy, even? Remember that one? He'll mind what St Paul said, "Love suffereth long and is kind." If he loves her, this shouldn't be an obstacle to him. He'll want to protect her, just like St Joseph protected Jesus' mother by marrying her. That's his example.'

Hartley drew back, his face a picture of contempt. 'You're

2

making bloody game of me. Want to protect her? Now she's pregnant by a pitman? He might have some doubts about what kind of girl she is, to lower herself so far. Him? Marry her now? You're as mad as she is; you make a pair. This is the Church of England I'm talking about, and it's got principles – not like the bloody Jack's Chapels that spring up everywhere you people go. The Church of England! I don't wonder it will have nothing to do with pitmen. You people. This was a good place to live until you came here with your filth and your rioting, destroying the countryside, using other people's daughters. I wish you'd get back where you came from, the lot of you, and take her with you. She's one of you now. You look after her.'

Eyes tear-filled, and face almost puce, evidently not trusting himself to say any more, the butcher abruptly turned heel and walked away. Elsie moved swiftly towards him, attempting to catch his jacket sleeve as he climbed back into his cart but he jerked it free. He took up the reins and looked down on her. 'You! You're a disgrace, and the people that helped you disgrace yourself can either take you in or leave you in the gutter, where you belong.' He gee'd up the horse and drove away, shouting at her not to follow him home.

So there she stood, some distance away and alone, and John leaned against the door jamb watching her. Her once shapely figure was now beginning to look just a little ungainly, her clothes stretched too tight round her expanding girth. Her face looked thinner and older, her shoulders were bowed. She was looking helplessly round, but avoiding looking at him, making no move towards either her home or his. The perfect little Venus who was so far beyond his reach a few short months ago had been hurled at him, whether he wanted her or not. Now a sullied goddess with feet of clay, she could so easily be taken, that she was no longer wanted. Because he knew that in her lying little heart of hearts she was Arthur's lass, and her belly was the proof of it. Arthur! How does he manage it? John thought. And why did I have to meddle with things?

His mother took hold of his waistcoat, dragged him inside and shut the door. He made no protest, but walked into the front room, snatched up the paper and sat down. It was nothing

3

to do with him. Nothing. It might have been different if she'd ever shown any interest in him, any liking even, but there was none. And he was courting strong now, and Alice was the best lass in the north. He felt his sister Sally's eyes on him.

'Her father'll be back for her.' His words were curt, final, and he knew he lied as he uttered them. He fixed his attention on the paper, determined to obliterate the thought of the butcher shaking off his daughter's hand, and the words he'd shouted at her as he drove away. But the print might as well have been hieroglyphics for all the capacity he had to take it in. At last, unable to resist, he got up to look through the window and see her sitting at the foot of the market cross, head bowed and hugging her knees, looking like a bundle of unsold rags after market day. All the fire and pride in her, all the promise of sensual delight, everything about her that had attracted him was extinguished; his heat for her was as cold as yesterday's ashes. He refused to care about her pain and her humiliation. Why should he? He was nothing to her. Why should she be anything to him?

One

'Oh, there's naught like hunting! Nothing like it! To be up and out on a morning like this, moist and still, and perfect for the chase – why, man, it's heaven!'

The pale sun was rising in a grey eastern sky presaging a fine day, its dullness enlivened by the scarlet coats of the riders waiting at the edge of the gorse bushes. The two men in black were sitting on a pair of hunters, smoking cigars and conferring as they waited with the rest of the crowd for the fox to break from the covert. Black-coated herself, and wearing the unmarried woman's veiled bowler, Elsie watched through narrowed eyes, detecting too much condescension in the smile the rector gave her father.

'A pleasure to have your company, Hartley. Any man as enthusiastic about the sport as you are makes a very welcome guest, I assure you.' The booming heartiness of his response set her teeth on edge, and the hunting clergyman's eye fell on her, as if it were appraising a bitch or a mare. 'And Elsie, damned fine girl she is, what? Not very big, but damned fine all the same. First time you've ridden to hounds, Elsie! I charge Rupert with making sure you enjoy it.'

With all the assurance of seventeen years and a perfect knowledge of her own flawless beauty, Elsie coolly turned her face towards Rupert, who was a few yards distant. A younger version of his father, he sat astride a fine black stallion with the appearance, as he returned her gaze, of being the master of all he surveyed.

My God! The arrogance of him, she thought, not deflecting her eyes for an instant. If he were as rich as Croesus, or as handsome as Arthur Wilde, it might be justified, but he's neither!

'On you go, Elsie, my girl. Go to Rupert, and he'll explain the ins and outs of riding to hounds,' the rector urged her.

Her father nodded her to obey. 'Go on, Elsie. You'll enjoy it all the more with a good teacher, a fine horseman like Rupert.'

His voice was loud enough to carry to Rupert, and ingratiating enough to puff that self-important young man to bursting point. Elsie gave her father a look, and reluctantly urged Love me Long, her young chestnut mare, in Rupert's direction; catching as she went, the words: 'Of course, we're only *tradespeople* . . .' Two bright spots of fury rose to her cheeks, and under her breath she muttered, 'Has he no pride at all?' If only her father would not abase himself so, especially before that – clergyman. If he thought she was going to demean herself to the son, he was mistaken.

'I've seen you ride.' Rupert's smile contained a strong taint of his father's condescension. 'You ride well. But do you ride well enough to keep up with me?'

'I should ride better than you if I had your advantages.'

Rupert raised his thick, sandy eyebrows, and his eyes widened. 'Oh, and what are those?'

'I should think it's obvious. You ride a massive stallion, and you straddle him.'

His fleshy lips stretched in a grin that revealed large yellow teeth. 'And you perch side-saddle on your little mare, and very prettily too. But you've thrown down the gauntlet, and I shall see that we have matched horses at the next meet, though I doubt you'd manage this one. No woman's son would be his master, if he could help it, far less a daughter. He's not called Tempest for nothing.'

She held his stare, though a shiver ran through her. 'I like my gentle mare. Don't trouble to choose any horses for me.'

He laughed. 'I'd take any amount of trouble to test your brag.' He opened his mouth as if to say something more, but checked himself and smiled.

Another inward shudder, and she was mercifully saved from making any reply. A red fox broke from a clump of gorse, and a cry of 'Lui in, lads, yoi over!' accompanied the wail of the hunting horn, and a shout of 'Forrard, forrard, forrard!'

6

as twenty couple of frantic hounds gave tongue and flew as fast as hawks after it.

'Keep up with me – if you can!' With a feverish glance back at her, Rupert drove his spurs into the stallion's flanks and was gone, tearing after the fox.

The rest went in his wake. 'Come on, Elsie, come on, get after him,' her father shouted as he passed her, picking up speed. He rode well for a man of over forty who, until recently, had spent every waking moment of his adult life tending his business, and had never sat astride a horse until a couple of years ago.

She sat stock-still on Love me Long and watched him go. Hunting had become his passion. He was ambitious to get his scarlet coat, and to be in with these people he would once have called his betters. His butcher's business now had branches in twenty villages, and he supplied the Co-op, giving him an income that surpassed that of many a finer friend, and he was having a large house built, just outside the village. He was proud of his wealth, made lavish contributions towards the expenses of the hunt and imagined that earned him the right to be in among the gentry. They tolerated him, but Elsie saw the looks on their faces whenever he opened his mouth, and heard the sneering tones in their voices when they spoke to him, and wondered how he could endure it.

'I haven't done much hunting, but I've done plenty of reading about it, and talking about it. You know you've got to give way to the Master, and the Huntsman, and the rest of the hunt servants, and you've got to do what the Field Master tells you, but after that, the first thing you've got to understand is, you're not chasing a fox. You're riding to hounds. The hounds chase the fox, and dogs are like men, Elsie. Some of them are like your dad, as keen as mustard; they never let a chance slip by. Others are only followers.' Her father had told her all this on the way to the meet in Old Annsdale that morning. 'Watch the hounds that are out in front, and mark the one that turns before the others turn. He's the one that's hot on the scent. Ride alongside him, if the Huntsman will let you, and keep just wide enough not to get in his way or the hounds'.'

7

In the heat of the moment her father seemed to have forgotten his own sage counsel, for she saw him haring after the black coat-tails of his friend the rector, quite oblivious of the hounds. She began to fear his ambition, and to have misgivings about his familiarity with the rector. Did he mean her to pursue the fox, or Rupert, Elsie wondered – or was she herself the quarry? The rector might tolerate a match between a butcher's daughter and his son, if the butcher were willing to put enough money in his hand. A little snort of derision escaped her. If that was their scheme, they were reckoning without the daughter. She could twist her father round her little finger. He'd never been able to make her do anything she didn't want to do. Never had, and never would; and if he tried, she'd elope with Arthur, to Scotland.

Her keen eyes searched beyond the bobbing scarlet coats towards the maddened, running hounds. 'So, go for the *first* dog in the hunt,' she murmured, 'or at least keep the Huntsman in sight. He'll be onto it.' She marked the likeliest hound now, not running directly away from her, but separating from the pack and making an oblique turn to her left. The rest followed him. She inhaled the wintry air, scented with field and wood, and her spirits lifted. If she were cunning enough, she might get to the fox before Rupert, and prick that bubble of self-satisfied superiority; show him she was not the inferior, submissive female he imagined. And even if she could not, the day was fine, and she would have a glorious ride. Her canter became a gallop as she raced to catch the leader of the pack.

They were hot on the scent and the going was fast, the ground heavy. Elsie began to fear for Love me Long. She had ridden her too hard. The game little mare had given everything, and was almost spent. Three-quarters of the way across a ploughed field she stumbled and staggered, and Elsie just managed to throw herself out of her side saddle before she fell. Plastered in plough, Elsie was struggling to her feet when the rector's wife brought her horse to a halt beside her.

'Have you fallen orf?' the voice boomed, sounding mightily amused. Elsie raised her eyes to the woman who leaned towards her, taking in the black habit, the enamelled fox head that pinned her silk stock, the ruddy, mannish, mocking face under the top hat. Really, the question was too stupid to merit an answer. Not deigning to reply, Elsie staggered towards Love me Long, her habit and boots heavy with mud, her sole concern to catch her frightened little mare's reins, to soothe and calm her.

With resolute eye, the rector's wife urged her brown steed forward. 'I'll soon have the horse!' she cried.

'No!' Elsie protested, and watched helplessly at the sight of the little mare's alarm as the massive horse and rider bore down on her. With a fresh spurt of energy she made her escape, then galloped away towards a hedge and tried to leap over it at the very moment that Rupert was taking it. She caught Tempest at an angle, bringing horse and rider down with her.

'Oh, no!' Elsie shrieked, moving as fast as she could towards her animal, fearing she may have broken a leg. But Love me Long was up, and moving towards her mistress, apart from her fear none the worse for the mishap. The rector's wife was watching her son with an expression of some concern as he and his stallion struggled out of the mire.

Elsie caught her little horse's reins, and began to laugh as she approached them. 'Oh, poor Rupert,' she called, her voice full of mock solicitude, 'have you fallen orf?'

With three other deputies, John squared up to a horde of hostile strikers. One of them stood at the back of the crowd, a head taller than the rest and unmistakable with his mop of black curls and his pristine white shirt. Arthur. Deathly silent, strikers and deputies stared at each other for breath-holding seconds, then a voice bellowed and a bolt of pure fear shot through John.

'Bloody blacklegs! Bosses' men! Get the bastards!' A shower of stones, bricks and bottles hurtled towards them, and the rattle of boots on the concrete and shouted insults and obscenities accompanied the advance. Outwardly calm, the deputies stood their ground, until the man next to John was felled with a pickaxe handle and the other two were swept off their feet by the surge of men.

9

John threw a punch in self-defence, and would have got the best of a fair fight but two men held his arms while a third punched him in the stomach, knocking the wind out of him. A severe mauling seemed a certainty, and then another shout went up: 'Run for it, lads! They've got the cavalry out!'

The missiles were dropped. The mob turned and ran, with nineteen-year-old Arthur now conspicuously, victoriously at the head of it.

He stood at the kitchen sink, bathing his bruised face, with his mother hovering at his elbow. 'Never bother, Mam. We had to stand a bit of pushing and shoving, but there's no damage done, nothing broken. You might know, our Arthur was with them, playing the bloody Byronic hero. Anywhere there's any trouble, he's got to be at the front of it.' He caught hold of a rough towel, and started dabbing his bruised eye and mouth. 'You'd think he'd know better. He knows we've got to go down, strike or no strike. If we don't keep doing the safety checks they'll not have a pit to go back to.'

There was a knock at the door. 'Is Arthur in, John?' Seventeen-year-old Elsie Hartley stood before him dressed in the latest fashion, and immaculate, her mahogany curls glinting in the low February sun. Eyes the colour of bitter chocolate stared out at him from thick fringes of lashes the same hue as her hair. They, and the dark ivory of her skin with its flush of deep rose across her cheekbones almost stopped the breath in his throat.

'Go home, Elsie,' he said. 'You know very well your dad doesn't like you coming round here.'

'He doesn't mind,' she lied. 'Anyway, Arthur told me to come round. He's going to take me for a walk.'

'Arthur's gone on a walk of his own, and he'll walk into the lock-up before he's finished. Do as your dad's told you, and get off home.'

'It's nothing to do with my father.' Elsie's luscious lips pursed in a petulant little pout. 'So, when you do see Arthur, tell him I'm looking for him.'

'You're looking for trouble, and you'll get it if you hang about with our Arthur.'

10

'How can anybody get into trouble, just going for a walk?'
She shrugged her shoulders and rolled her eyes upwards in
mockery at his simplicity, then gave him a bewitching smile,
one he couldn't help returning. Her smile turned into something caressing, encouraging, almost seductive, and she raised
her shapely eyebrows for a fleeting second. His heart missed
a beat, and for one mad instant he thought he might have a
chance with her.

'Hm!' she said. 'That's better. I think that's the first time
I've ever seen you smile. I was beginning to think you
couldn't.' With a toss of her curls she turned a neat heel and
strutted away.

'You tell that son of yours to keep away from my Elsie –
she's no meat for the pitmen. We've got better prospects in
mind,' her father had told their mother the last time she'd been
in the shop. John liked him no better for the affront, and had
torn round to the shop the minute his mother arrived home, in
tears, to tell him of her belittlement before a shop full of
customers. John had succeeded in convincing His Lordship the
Flesh-Purveyor of Old Annsdale that that any messages intended
for Arthur should be given direct, but the butcher had so far not
found the time – Arthur said the guts. So the insult had served
only to strengthen Arthur's resolve to amuse himself with Elsie
as a deliberate goad to her father, and the butcher had retaliated
by sacking John's youngest sister, Sally, from her job as their
housemaid. Their mother now took her custom the further couple
of miles to the Co-op in Annsdale Colliery, despite the fact that
the Co-op's meat was supplied by Hartley's wholesale branch.

Now, John leaned against the door jamb and watched those
trim little feet walk that diminutive but voluptuous woman's
figure along the ancient village high street. And the way she
walked, he thought – like Venus in high heels. The apple of
her father's eye, and idol of most of the lads for miles around
was Elsie, and well she knew it. So confident was she of her
powers of seduction, she was well nigh uncontrollable, like a
headstrong child riding for a fall.

'I'm warning you, Elsie – don't go after him,' he called
after her. 'He's with a lot of other young fools and they're all
intent on trouble.'

11

She looked over her shoulder and gave him a laugh and a pretty wave, then continued on her path. Elsie would do precisely as Elsie liked. Fully aroused, fearful for her, and yet half amused, he wondered if she really understood the effect her teasing smiles and her caressing glances had on the men she came into contact with, and shook his head – a convent-educated eldest daughter with no brothers, how could she? He wondered how she would react when she did find out; would she be shocked, repelled ... or responsive? He fancied – strongly fancied – the latter, and in his mind's eye he took hold of her, began kissing her, squeezing her, caressing that soft flesh like a lover, gently running his hands over those beautiful breasts, that trim waist, those rounded haunches and ... and if he could have jumped into a cold bath at that very moment he would have set the water boiling.

He frowned. Some of the best lads for miles around were dashing themselves against the rocks of Elsie's allurements; but while better men were vying for her, Arthur was the one she favoured. Utterly and stupidly female, she had an unerring compulsion for a wrong 'un.

Women. He would never understand them.

'They'll ruin the strike before they've finished.' Martin Jude, pitman turned publican and married to John's sister Ginny, gave his opinion as he slowly pulled John a pint in the Cock Inn late that evening. John began to relax, the warmth and comfort of the place seeped into him, his eye resting on the lamps and coal fire whose gleam was reflected in the mahogany and polished brasses. Normally bursting at the seams with custom, the inn was barely half full, and few were spending much. Martin pushed John's glass towards him, and rang the money into the till. 'Racketing round the countryside smashing thing up and terrorizing people, the papers'll be full of it tomorrow, the whole country'll be told what a rabble the miners are. They'll get the union and everybody in it a bad name. Something's got to be done about Arthur, before he makes a mess of everything.'

'I can do nothing about him. I don't even know where he is,' said John.

'You could do nothing about him if you did know,' laughed one of Arthur's marrers, another young tearaway, who stood a bit further along the bar. 'He's twice the man you are. Arthur'll do what he wants, and he doesn't give a bugger whether it offends or pleases.'

John squared up to the young man, looked him up and down. 'Aye, you'll know, I suppose. You're as stupid as he is. You were with that pack threatening us in the pit yard.'

'Aye, that's right. Probably because you can afford a full pint, and here's the four of us, sharing one. You can expect a bit of ill-feeling when you're getting a wage, and we're not.'

'Most of my wage gets pooled into the strike fund, along with money from many another deputy and official that's still working. If I can afford a drink, it's because I save a bit when times are good, instead of spending everything in front of me.'

'That's easy for a feller that's got no wife and kids to keep. That's still living at home with his mammy, at twenty-five year old.'

'Well, bugger off to the club where the beer's cheaper, then. Or better still, go home and give the money to your wives you're complaining about having to keep. The way I look at you, the only way you'll keep her is to keep her bloody short.'

'Only of money, though. She goes short of nothing else,' the lad said, with a self-satisfied smirk. 'Naw, we came in to have a bit crack with Ginny, bring her the news, like, about what her little brother's been up to.'

Landlady of the Cock Inn and Martin's wife, Ginny grimaced and raised her shapely black eyebrows. 'I'd rather not know.'

'I'll tell you anyway. It might give you a laugh. We did a bit of racketing all right, we were all over the county. There must have been two hundred of us and we made a day of it. We lighted on Highlands Colliery and smashed every window we could see. Rickfield was the next target, but on the way we came on a hansom cab with a JP and the police superintendent in it.'

The young men with him began to laugh. He gave a broad grin and went on, '"Why this is too good a chance to miss," says your Arthur, "Lord Arsehole charges a toll for every ton of coal that passes over his land, and if toll-charging's good

13

enough for him, it's good enough for us," so he stops the cab, and tells 'em they're going nowhere until they've paid a sovereign, and he wouldn't let 'em, either. The JP was cursing him blind, and telling him he'd know him again, and next time he saw him he'd give him six months with hard labour. That didn't bother your Arthur. "We like to take our example from our betters," he told them, and then he said he thought it was a pity Lord Arsehole wasn't in the cab. He'd have charged him a heavy toll, as much as he charges, more than the whole bloody village has to live on in a dozen years. They didn't like it, but they paid up, and we let them go.'

'Aye, that sounds like our Arthur.' Ginny smiled in spite of herself.

The laughter was coming in gales by this time and all were looking towards the young speaker. Conscious now that every eye was on him, he played to his audience. 'At Rickfield, we smashed a few things up and burned the stables down. But they must have telegraphed Barham, because when we got near we spied the bobbies. I needn't tell you we didn't stop. We headed off towards Felscar, instead.

'On the way there we lit on a drayman, so we stopped him for a toll. He seemed to think that was funny, said we were welcome to all the beer, it wasn't his! Only would we please not smash the bottles? So we took him at his word. That put your Arthur in a good humour, and he started laughing. Then after we'd drunk up, while we were cutting across the country one lad fell down an old shaft, it must have been ten foot. When we pulled him out, he said he wouldn't have cared a damn if he hadn't scratched his best boots! Well, that creased Arthur, he was laughing so much he set us all off, so at Langwell we didn't do much damage, just had a bit fun, like, pushing the pit tubs down the hill. We'd set out on the rampage, and we finished laughing fit to bust!'

The young men standing with him were helpless at the memory of it, and some of the other customers were wiping the tears from their eyes.

John's expression soured. 'You're all idiots,' he said. 'If your brains were made of dynamite they couldn't blow your bloody caps off. Do you think they'll stomach that? There'll be a summons out already, and it won't be long before the place is full of army, and police, and a gang of imported black-legs.' Imported because no man could do a stint in the pit without his coal dust-blackened face, hands and legs betraying the fact that he had worked. Few local men would want to blackleg, and even fewer would dare.

'Just let 'em try it,' said one, all trace of good humour gone. 'We'll smash the pit and everything in it before we'll let anybody else work it.'

John looked at Martin, shaking his head. 'What can you do with 'em?' he asked, and turned again to the contingent of hotheads. 'Where's Arthur now, if he's not in the lock-up?'

The spokesman shrugged. 'How do I know? We were on the way back home when the butcher's lass came bouncing along the road. You know the way she walks, as if she were the Queen of Sheba.' He did a few strutting steps, in clumsy imitation, before continuing. '"Oh," says Arthur, "Elsie's dad thinks she's too good for the pitmen, but Elsie doesn't." "Oh, but I do think I'm too good," says Elsie, "for all the pitmen except one!" Arthur looked as pleased as punch, and he said, "Well, give us a kiss, then, Elsie," and she said, "Not here, Arthur," so he took her off towards Annsdale woods, and we gave 'em an almighty cheer.' He grinned. 'And she might have got more than a kiss, the mood your Arthur was in. He was drunk on victory, and as rampant as the butcher's dog.'

John's expression soured further. 'Aye, and tomorrow, when he's sober, he'll expect his family to bail him out of all the trouble he's caused,' he said. 'He'll have no bloody job to go back to after the strike, and he'll probably expect me to keep him, an' all.'

John stayed on after closing time for a quiet drink with his brothers-in-law. Wiry little Jimmy Hood, a winding-engineman and married to John's sister Emma, had been maimed in the disaster a few years back. 'Do the safety checks, man,' he encouraged. 'There's nobody that was living here six year ago would want you to stop doing them. I wish the last owners had been as keen; I'd still have me right leg. I have night-mares about that explosion to this day; I still wake up screaming

15

at times. Some of these young lads are too stupid to know their own danger.'

Martin, tall, fair and powerfully built, had been one of the rescuers. 'Aye. The new owners are a lot better than the old when it comes to mine safety, if only for the sake of preserving their property. I doubted there'd be anything of the pit left to work, after the last lot,' he said.

'Piggy in the middle. That's what this job is,' John told them. 'You can please nobody, men or management, and a lot of the men resent your authority. You've a foot in both camps and you belong to neither.'

In spite of their attempts at encouragement, John left the Cock more morose than he had ever felt in his life. He was a deputy, right enough, but his loyalties lay with the strikers. He was no bosses' man, and it hurt him to be divided from his own kind. 'He's twice the man you are,' they'd told him. He was sick of hearing his reckless brother's antics lauded and laughed at when all Arthur ever really achieved was to make matters worse for everybody. But Arthur would continue to enjoy the luxury of doing what he wanted, and not caring a bugger whether it pleased or offended. He had the adulation of his marrers, and Elsie Hartley, who was by common consent reckoned the belle of Annsdale, was never off their doorstep looking for him. Arthur'll always call the tune, and I'll always end up paying the piper, he thought, because he really doesn't care a bugger, about anybody. He's gone too far this time, though, and he can stew in it. I won't lift a finger to help him out of the mess he's in.

John felt trapped, oppressed, suffocated. Staying at home had been the worst decision he had made in his life, but he'd seen no alternative then, and could see none now. Playing the dutiful son had cost him his sweetheart and his chance to emigrate, but he had stayed to look after what was left of the family after his father's death and Ginny's and Emma's marriages. Hendrika and South Africa, he could hardly tell which he'd been the more in love with. He'd sacrificed both, and now headed a household composed of his mother, his sister Lizzie, almost seventeen, Sally, a year younger, and

Arthur. Full of regret for what might have been, he was sick of barbed comments and baiting about his single state, and he envied his brothers-in-law their happy married lives.

He was resolved on two points: he wanted a wife, and as soon as he could he wanted to emigrate, to better himself. Most stayed in the village because they knew nothing else, or they wouldn't be torn from friends and family. On John's return from sea he'd found that half of the lads he'd grown up with were dead, and Jimmy was maimed. He wasn't going to waste his life and his talents slaving for the owners, or helping them to keep others subjected to slavery. He walked on alone through the quiet streets of the ancient village, bitter lines of discontent and disappointment threatening to etch themselves permanently into his face.

The house was in darkness. Upstairs, his mother's and sisters' bedroom doors were closed and nothing stirred. Arthur was still out; the bed was empty. John threw off his shirt, dropped his trousers, and peeled off his socks, revealing well-shaped feet, muscular calves and sturdy thighs. He stretched, and rubbed his well-muscled torso and strong, sinewy arms, and a half remembered lesson of his schooldays came to mind. 'The Romans chose their fighting men of medium height, broad in the shoulder and narrow in the beam. They had strong arms and strong backs, just like the miners round here,' Miss Carr had told the class when he was about ten. She'd had them drawing pictures of the Romans and the forts they built along Hadrian's Wall, and John imagined himself with the perfect soldier physique, shield and sword in hand, defending his settlement, his hearth and home. For a time he could hardly wait to get to bed at night, so that he could dream his favourite dream about being a Roman soldier, going on marches, building forts, and rescuing the emperor's beautiful daughter from the barbarian hordes, through his own strength and valour. He'd convinced himself that he must be descended from a Roman soldier, because Miss Carr had said that when the army had finished with its fighting men, they usually got married and settled down with local women.

John still thought he would have made a good Roman soldier. He was proud of his body, its shapeliness and the strength

17

and iron hardness of its muscles. But at night, what use was a pair of strong arms with no bonny lass to hold? He climbed into his cold, barren bachelor's bed, pulled the blankets over his head and thought of Hendrika. Flaxen hair and blue eyes, a laughing mouth and freckles across her nose, her face was beginning to slip from his memory. He was losing even the memory of the girl who had loved him back. But Elsie Hartley's mocking, teasing little face was as clear as crystal.

Two

A banging like the crack of doom, then cries of alarm from his mother and sisters roused him from a sleep as deep as death. Still half stunned with it, John staggered out of bed and bumped into the wardrobe, blindly groping for the bedroom door. Barefoot and in his nightshirt he went downstairs to answer the summons. The women followed at a safe distance. He turned the key and pulled back the bolt, and the door was thrust wide open from the outside. Before he could utter a word of protest, John was pushed back into the hallway and pinned against the wall by two heavy, moustachioed policemen, while a third closed and bolted the door.

'Arthur Wilde, we've a warrant for your arrest. You're coming with us.'

Halfway down the stairs and with Lizzie behind her, his mother spoke up. 'That's not Arthur. That's John you've got. Arthur's not at home.' Lizzie ran back upstairs, but their mother, grey hair tumbling about her shoulders, faced the intruders with a quiet dignity.

The policemen looked at each other, and still keeping a grip on John while the sergeant held the lamp up to his face to inspect him. 'No, he doesn't answer the description,' he conceded. He nodded at the two constables. 'I'll keep a watch on this one, you search the house. You,' he addressed John's mother, 'light the mantles.'

With a coolness that surprised John, his mother did as she was told. One constable took a hurricane lamp into the kitchen to open the back door for the man posted outside. The banging of cupboard doors and the scraping of furniture along the floor signalled the dismantling and scrutinizing of everything in

19

their path as they worked their way through the downstairs rooms. Then they started up the stairs.

'Hey, hold still a minute. He's not here, she's told you.' John was wide awake by this time and furious. 'This is a private house. It belongs to my mother, not the owners, and you've no business tramping round in it before you've been asked.'

The sergeant brought his face so threateningly near to John's that their noses almost touched. 'You're a bit above yourself for a collier, aren't you? Who do you think you are, the Lord Chancellor? It doesn't matter whose house it is, we've got a warrant.'

John's mother was on the stairs, barring the constables' passage with one hand on the wall and the other on the banister rail. 'The only people up there are two young girls, in their nightclothes. I'm asking you to behave like gentlemen, and leave my house,' she said.

The men hesitated, but the sergeant urged them on. 'You can ignore the old woman. We've got a warrant. So if he is there, make sure you find him. He needs a lesson in good manners. Turn the place upside down, if you have to.'

They thrust John's mother out of the way and marched upstairs. Two seconds later Lizzie and Sally, both in their nightgowns, came running down again to huddle against her. The three of them walked downstairs and into the wrecked front room, their mother commenting quietly as they passed, 'You can let John go. He's not the one you want. And you're the one who needs the lesson in good manners.'

Let go, John followed the constables upstairs, to see them tearing clothes out of wardrobes, groping in and under beds, and, when everywhere else had been ransacked, pulling the drawers out of the girls' dressing table and flinging both drawers and contents onto the floor.

'What the hell are you doing that for?' John protested. 'He cannot hide in a bloody drawer.'

Neither deigned to reply, but the reason was manifest when they carried the table onto the landing and stood on it to search the loft space.

Finding nothing they returned downstairs with John following, and shook their heads at the sergeant.

'Nothing? All right, we'll have a look in your garden shed, missus.'

'If he was in the shed when you came, do you think he's still going to be there now?' asked John.

'Well, we'll just make sure he's not,' said the sergeant.

The empty shed was scrutinized, without bringing any Arthur to light, and the constables came back into the house. The sergeant fixed their mother with a menacing glare and warned, 'Your son's a ringleader. He's wanted for criminal damage, riot, affray, and demanding money with menaces. When he does come home, you tell him to give himself up, because we'll be back tomorrow night, and the night after, and every night until we've got him.'

John saw them out, and Lizzie came to stand beside him to see them go. Half the lights in the village were on, and a good many of the neighbours were at their doors, the better to enjoy the spectacle.

Lizzie shut the door, tears of anger and shame welling into her eyes. 'Oh, God,' she cried, 'why did I have to be born into a family like this?'

As soon as he got to work that morning John was summoned to see the manager. Mr Woolfe was seated at his desk attending to some correspondence and, although fully aware of John's presence, did not pay him the courtesy of any acknowledgement for several minutes. John stood rotating his cap in his hands, silently fuming, then apprehensive, then fuming again at the thought that this man's determination to establish his own superiority by humiliating him should make him feel such apprehension, then despising himself for his fear, and at the last disliking the manager for making him despise himself. No wonder that young men like Arthur went on the rampage, when all that reason and attention to duty earned was treatment bordering on contempt. When the manager did raise his head he leaned back in his well-upholstered green leather chair and kept John standing while he surveyed him. After a moment or two of this he said, 'You seem to have taken a bit of punishment.'

John nodded. 'I've no doubt you've heard all about it.'

'Do you know where your brother is?'

'No, I don't.'

'I hear the police were at your house last night, looking for him.'

'Aye, they were, four of 'em, all big lads and none of 'em local, but they wouldn't be, sent to do a job like they did,' John said, unable to conceal his anger. 'They just about tore the house apart. It'll take us a week to get straight again. They made as much racket as they could to make sure all the neighbours heard, and insulted me mother, and went storming into the bedrooms where me sisters were still in their nightclothes. They even ransacked their dressing table, tipped their clothes all over the bedroom, as if they were going to find our Arthur curled up in a drawer. He hasn't been home. We've no idea where he is, and we've been threatened with another visit tonight.'

The manager looked John full in the face, his expression softening not one whit. 'I'm sorry to hear that, but he's made some powerful enemies. I'm a self-made man, as you know, and no supporter of the aristocracy, but giving gratuitous offence to them, and getting on the wrong side of JPs is worse than stupid. If he thinks that'll help the miners' cause, he needs his head examined. I want to see Arthur locked up, out of the way, where he can't do any more damage. What I don't want is any repeat of yesterday's rampage.'

John opened his mouth to ask what he was supposed to do to stop it, but the manager's raised hand silenced him.

'That *will* be the day, when I let a rabble-rouser like Arthur Wilde decide what happens in my pit. I'm the major shareholder and the manager here. This is my pit, and I'll decide who works in it and who doesn't, and I'll decide how they work. So, my workers are going to work the new three-shift system, and they're going to work it at the old rates. If they won't, others will, and they'll need houses. So if the men won't return to work, there'll be some evictions in Annsdale Colliery, starting with the ringleaders.'

He paused for a moment, lips set and eyes like flint. John kept quiet, and the manager went on, 'You've shown a lot of promise. You're a good deputy, and you've got influence over the men. You've got a fair bit with management as well. Apply yourself and you could make overman before long, and then undermanager. If keeping you on doesn't prove more trouble than it's worth, that is. Your brother, Arthur – well.' He paused again, as if the phenomenon of Arthur baffled description. 'That brother of yours is a liability to us, and to you. He won't be working here again, and you'll be looking for another job as well, if we have any more trouble from him. Destroying property won't do their side any more good than ours in the long run.' He fixed John with a penetrating stare. 'So it's up to you to convince the rabble of that, and cool them down. I'm holding you responsible. Keep your brother under control, or suffer the consequences.' He gave a curt nod of dismissal, and returned his attention to the matters on his desk.

Aghast at the thought of losing his own employment, and infuriated at the injustice of it, John protested, 'It's hardly fair to talk about sacking me for what our Arthur does.'

'Life's not fair,' the manager said, tight lipped and implacable. 'You're old enough to know that. You've a bad pedigree, John, and it's not only Arthur. Your sister's married to that union sympathizer Jude, and they both do as much as they can to aid and abet every troublemaker for miles. It's time for you to decide where your loyalties lie. Are you with the management and me, or are you with certain members of your family and the strikers? There's a choice to be made, so make it, and quick.'

Arthur was already as good as sacked, and Sally was without a place. Lizzie had a decent job as an apprentice to the village tailor, but she didn't earn that much, and John wasn't going to give her any room to tell people she'd ever kept him. The loss of his job would be a disaster, both for the family and for that little miser's pile he'd been amassing for years, his South Africa savings fund – his hoard of hope. He left the office seething. Short of tying weights to Arthur's legs and dropping him in the Wear, there was nothing he could do about him. Same old story, he thought. Arthur has the time of his life, and I get saddled with the consequences.

He did his shift and set out for home. A horde of cheeky brats followed him, chanting:

Oh, the putter gets a shilling,
The hewer half a crown,
But the man with the stick gets seven and six
For walking up and down.

'I wish I had my stick this minute,' he said, suddenly rounding on them. 'I would lay it on you.' They scattered, laughing, then regrouped at a safe distance to sing him three-quarters of the way home.

He took refuge at the Cock that evening, expecting a quiet pint and a few words of commiseration from Ginny and Martin. Ginny pulled his beer for him, her expressive black eyes darting towards a couple of men in dark suits and darker expressions sitting at a corner table talking earnestly to Martin and glancing occasionally in John's direction.

'Somebody to see you,' she said, tucking an errant strand of black hair back into its fastenings.

'What's everybody looking at me for? I have nothing to do with our Arthur's antics. I thought I'd come here to get out of the road of that. I had to go and see the manager this morning. He had a face like thunder over it.'

'And you took the brunt of it. That cannot have been very pleasant.'

'It wasn't.'

She shot him a look of sympathy. 'You can take them upstairs, if you want privacy.'

'What the hell? We've none of that anyway; the world might as well know all our business. You heard about the visit we got last night, I suppose.'

'Our Lizzie's been in, telling us all about it. Two young lasses, it was enough to terrify them out of their wits, but you know our Lizzie; she was more churned up about the affront to her dignity. I doubt me mother'll ever hold her head up in the village again after it, either.'

'Aye, the neighbours were all out of their beds, getting a good eyeful. They'll have plenty to talk about for weeks to come when Arthur ends up in court, and months and maybe

24

years if he gets sent to jail. "These rough pitmen, not fit to live among decent people." I can just hear it. She'll die of shame then.'

Ginny sighed, her eyelids lowered until the black lashes almost swept her cheeks, her expression downcast. She'd bought the house in Old Annsdale for her mother six years ago, with money earned in the music halls. The rest of the pitmen and their families lived in Annsdale Colliery, a collection of jerry-built houses thrown up to accommodate mining families about sixty years back. Annsdale Colliery then had had the atmosphere and reputation of a lawless frontier town, but had become tamer over the years and was now a settled community. Separated from their fellow mineworkers by Ginny's largesse, Arthur and John had the distinction of being the only two men in the ancient mother village who returned home after a day's work covered in pit muck, and the stares of some of the villagers made John feel like an exhibit at a freak show.

He smiled at her, determined to avoid any hint of ingratitude for her generosity. 'Cheer up lass; we'll get over it. We've got over a lot worse.'

'I sometimes think I made a big mistake buying my mother that house. I don't think you've ever been happy there. You've lived there six year, and they still look down on you.'

'They're not all alike. People never are. A few of the natives are friendly. And come strike, lock-out or the sack, at least the owners cannot evict us; they cannot make us homeless. You've put that out of their power, and we might be glad of it before we've finished. He's not going to give anybody a penny more, and he intends to make this bloody three-shift system stick, Ginny man. He'll make us have it, if he can. He's talking about evictions and blacklegging now. Oh, and he's got doubts about me. How did he put it? I've got the wrong pedigree. He's not sure which side I'm on. I bloody am, but I daren't tell him which it is.'

Martin returned to the bar, and jerked his head in the direction of the men he'd just left. 'They'd like a word.'

John raised his eyebrows. 'Hepburn and Shaw. Two of the heaviest guns in the union. They must mean business.'

They stood up for a formal shaking of hands when John went over to join them, then with no further preliminary Mr Hepburn began. 'The executive never wanted this strike; you know that, don't you?'

'I know that, and a lot of people call the executive traitors and deceivers an' all, for making agreements nobody wants. A lot of people are asking themselves who you really represent, apart from yourselves. The owners have been coining money for the past six year, and we've never had a sniff of it. Prices are going up, and wages are not. And as for this three-shift system – well. Nobody wants it.'

Mr Hepburn frowned, and went on as if John hadn't spoken. 'There's something a lot bigger than this coming up. There'll be a national strike soon, the first in history, if the owners don't agree to the minimum wage. The whole country'll be out, and Arthur Wilde's getting us all a bad name. He's threatening the credibility of the union.'

'As far as a lot of people are concerned, you're the ones who're threatening the credibility of the union, not Arthur,' John said.

Mr Shaw's tones were conciliatory. 'We've agreed to back this strike, but we need tight discipline. And with Arthur Wilde on the loose, there's not much hope of that. He'll ruin it. It'd be better all round if he disappeared.'

'Am I my brother's keeper? He has bloody disappeared,' John said, 'and we'll never be rid of the boys in blue until he shows up.'

'It'll be better all round if he doesn't show up. When his case comes up, the papers will be full of it all again. It's bad publicity.'

'What do you want me to do?' asked John. 'Tie him in a sack and toss him in the Wear?'

They didn't sanction the suggestion, but made no objection to it either. Eventually, having laboured their point sufficiently, they rose and left, nodding in Martin's direction on the way out.

John returned to the bar irritated and disgruntled, yet again feeling the dead weight of responsibility. 'The worst of it is, they're right,' he admitted to Ginny and Martin. 'Coal stocks are lower than they've ever been, and the price is rising. The owners will want to settle before long, in their own interest. We could win this one. Something will have to be done about Arthur, and it looks as if I'm the one that's expected to do it.'

Down in the blacker-than-pitch depth of the mine, John stopped to set a flame for testing, carefully lowering the wick of his lamp until it was about an eighth of an inch high, where it showed a speck of yellow light, and on top of it that faint line of pale blue called the fuel-cap. He watched carefully for a larger blue triangle of flame to form above the testing flame, knowing that its size would increase with the proportion of murderous firedamp. None appeared; the cap stayed flat and faint. Satisfied, he raised the wick and moved on, loping with back stooped through low passages, to test the face, the ends of the face, the broken workings, every break hole and cavity in the roof, to test everywhere that methane-laden, combustible firedamp might bleed and accumulate.

There was plenty of stone dust in the passageways to stop any ignition of coal dust, plenty of air at the face, and a check of all the props and roof supports assured him that all was well as far as his district was concerned. When the lads returned to work, the fifty or so in his charge would be as safe from fire, explosion and roof falls as he could make them. He went to his kist to sit and make the report.

The cold of the worst winter they'd had for years came as a shock after the heat of the depth of the mine, and he drew a sharp breath then saw the vapour hang on the air as he exhaled. He started for home under a white sky and snow-laden branches, warming again as he walked, and inhaling gratefully the fresh, clean air.

There must have been at least a thousand gathered in the park when he passed by, with a dozen mounted policemen and as many on foot watching them. The union officials seemed to have changed their tune.

'So, the owners will let you back to work on the old rates, for a three-shift system of working that nobody wants – and that you came out on strike against weeks ago! By, isn't that bonny? Well, if you'll stand for that, you'll stand for anything, and I'll wash my hands of you!' Ben Shaw bellowed from the bandstand. There was a murmuring of agreement from the crowd.

'The price of coal's up by two and six a ton, but you've not seen an increase in pay for eight year! You want a fair day's pay for a fair day's work, and you're not getting it! You want a clean, comfortable home to come home to, and a wife that's not as worn out as you are! But you won't get it, if you don't stand up for yourselves like men! You did right to come out, and you'll do right to stay out, until they cave in. The thought of all the profit they're losing'll see to that! Stick it out; stick it out! Demand's high and stocks are low – they'll be begging you to go back before long, at any price.'

'Why, there speaks a man who's getting three square meals a day. I wish I could stand up there wi' me belly full, tellin' other folks to starve a bit longer! Well, I had enough of scratting round for a crust and queuing at bloody soup kitchens during the last strike, so how long's it going to go on this time?' demanded a young woman with a baby tied up in her shawl and a couple of skinny children hanging on to her skirts, all blue with the cold. John felt sympathy for her, but she was hooted down by others in the crowd, and he was stunned when his impassioned little spitfire of a sister leapt onto the bandstand.

'We want nothing but our rights,' Emma shouted, glaring at the last speaker. 'Managers, shareholders, the landed gentry, all can take a share of the wealth our men break their backs to produce. It's only our men who're robbed of the fruits of their labour and kept down by force. They call England a free country, but I say, free for *who*? Not for *us*, who are used worse than any black slaves. Our men have their daily toil, they risk their lives every day to make money for the bosses, and what do they get for it? Hardly enough to feed their families, while their lords and masters can risk thousands of pounds on the turn of a card! For doing what? For doing nothing! David beat Goliath, and if we stick together, we can beat them!'

'Aye, why, David wasn't a married man, and Goliath couldn't evict him with his wife and bairns!' came another voice from the crowd.

'I'm a wife, and I've got bairns,' Emma shrieked at the doubters, 'four of 'em, but I would rather starve and beg than give in when I know we can win. And what does this three-shift system mean for us women? Any woman with three men in the house all on different shifts will never see her bed – she'll be making meals and getting baths ready all times of the bloody day and night. Do you love your slavery so much you want *more* of it? Let's stick together, let's *never* lose heart and give in! We've had slavery enough; we'll have no more of tyrants *grinding* us!'

There were hearty cries of 'Hear, hear!' from the crowd, and a cheer went up. Stepping down with her cheeks flushed, Emma caught sight of John, and beckoned him to join them.

'You're a fraud, our Em,' he told her. 'That lass'll be getting nothing but strike pay, and what they can get at the soup kitchens and the Cock. Jimmy's an engineman, still getting a wage.'

'Aye, and a damned small wage it is,' she retorted, 'and the best part of it goes into the pool, just like yours does. I doubt I'm any better off than her. But if we stick this out, we'll both see the benefit, her and me an' all.'

Three

The parson's lad was laughing with head thrown back, and the riders gathered round him looked cheerful and exhilarated after their day's sport. Elsie's cheeks glowed with cold and exercise, but there was an expression of haughty disdain on her face, which was at odds with the merriment of her companions. Mounted on a chestnut mare, dressed in a black riding habit with black bowler and veil atop her mahogany curls, she sat apart from the others. Head erect and back straight in her side saddle, she made a picture no man could resist. Covered in filth from the pit, John paused and stared; but the last thing he expected was any acknowledgement from her.

She caught his eye and waved. 'Hello, John, hello!' This public recognition was something new, and his heart turned a somersault. She rode towards him and leaned down.

'It's the first time I've seen you out with the hounds, Elsie.'

'But it's not the first time I've been out. My father says he intends to make a huntswoman of me if it's the last thing he ever does,' she said, her eyes rolling upwards a little, her rosy lips turning grimly down for an instant. 'But there's something I've got to tell you, John. Listen for me tonight.' Then she was gone, to rejoin the rest of the returning hunt. It was evident from their faces that her open recognition of him was as much a surprise to them as it was to him, and not a welcome one. The parson's lad was no longer laughing, and gave John a look that would have turned milk sour, but Elsie was studiously ignoring him. So what did John care about the parson's lad? He pulled himself up to his full height and walked off homewards in his pit duds, with his heart racing, and a spring in his step, and a power in his limbs sufficient to knock a dozen parsons' sons right off their high horses; his pleasure marred only by the feeling that the something Elsie had to tell would concern Arthur.

'Are you not going to the Cock tonight, John?' his mother asked, after the meal had been eaten and everything washed and cleared away. A cosy fire glowed in the hearth and she and the two girls were settled at the quilting frame, busy with their needles.

'No. I think I'll get on with some studying. I'll have to get stuck into it, if I'm ever going to make a mining engineer.'

He spread his books out on the table, listening hard for a knock on the door, but it never came.

The following night, after his mother and sisters had gone to bed, came the long-awaited tapping on the door.

'John!' He heard the whisper, and his pulse began to race even before he saw her standing in the shadows. 'I saw the police here again when I came yesterday, so I went away. Arthur's been hiding in Mr Farr's barn, but he can't stop there much longer, because Mr Farr told my dad there are some strike-breakers coming. The manager's paying people in the village to take some of them in, but the rest are going to be staying in barns until there are houses for them.'

'Ah,' John nodded, the information sinking in, 'I wondered where they were going to billet them.'

'Arthur said to come and tell you, and you'd think of something to do.'

She gave him a look of wide-eyed appeal, and he answered with one of sheer exasperation. 'It's too late to do anything now, Elsie, and I couldn't go to the barn anyway. The police are keeping watch on the house, and they're not going to give up until they've got him. If I went to the barn I'd end up leading them right to him.'

'But, John, he'll freeze to death if somebody doesn't take him in.'

'Come in, Elsie, or you'll be the one freezing to death.' She stepped into the narrow hallway, so near to him that he brushed against her skirt as he closed the door. 'Bad enough he's caused all this trouble for us, without roping you in. I don't

31

doubt he *will* end up getting six months before he's finished, and he'll deserve it, too.'

'No, he won't,' she contradicted, with some spirit. 'He's only fighting for decent wages, to make the colliery company pay the men and boys properly, instead of giving them starvation wages for slavery.' Her mouth was set in a determined line. With a sigh, John went upstairs for a couple of pairs of thick socks and two blankets. She took them from him without a word, and her hands felt icy. He went into the kitchen and found a couple of stottie cakes and some cheese. Arthur was making use of her as well, with no thought about what trouble he might be causing for her, and she, little fool, was letting him. She should have sent him packing with the same disdain she'd shown the rest of her admirers. He put the food in a paper bag, and returned to the hallway. He wanted to take hold of Elsie and shake her out of these illusions she had about Arthur, make her understand what he was really like. He looked directly into her dark eyes as he handed her the bread-cakes and cheese, and his anger at Arthur boiled over.

'Take everything our Arthur says with a big pinch of salt, Elsie. He's made his own trouble, so don't let your sympathy run away with you. Do as your dad's told you, and send him packing. Tell him to find another bolt hole, or go to one of his marrers; he's got plenty. Whatever he does, he'd better not come here, or to any of his family, unless he wants to end up breaking rocks.'

'Well, somebody's got to help him,' Elsie protested, clutching her load to her chest.

Oh aye, we'll all help him, thought John. We'll all run after our Arthur's arse for evermore. Let's not spare ourselves to get him out of all the trouble he causes, and then he'll be able to bring us some more. Aloud, he said, 'I'll think of something. Watch out for me in the village. I'll let you know as soon as I can get him away.'

Some of the new workforce were casting apprehensive glances at the long, single wire rope suspending the cage. John read out the notice at the front of it: '"Strictly Prohibited. No candles, flints, matches, cigarettes or pipes, or any other combustible

32

material to be taken down the mine." So let's have it all now, if you've got any, before we all get blown to kingdom come.' He saw to it that every man turned out his pockets and gave over every bit of contraband to the banksman.

'All right now, you've been given two brass checks with your number on. Why, he wants one o' them, and when you come out of the pit, you hand the other one over. I don't suppose I need to explain why.'

Each man handed over a brass check, and at last all were in the cage and the gates slammed shut. The banksman rang the signal for the winding engineman, Jimmy Hood by name, to lower it. A few of the men were looking very edgy as the headgear span round and the cage whistled down. John's stomach lurched and the blood started pounding in his ears, but he was used to it, and most of them were not.

'It must be about eight year since that cable last broke,' he mused, as if to himself. 'That was just before I went away to sea. Come to think, this one's getting a bit worn, like.' He heard gasps and oaths, but his grin, and the expressions of terror he knew would be on their faces were alike concealed by blackness. A shrieking gale of hot air squealed past them as they hurtled downward, away from light and cold and into the darkness and heat at the bottom of the shaft, where the cage stopped with a violent crash and a jolt. Jimmy had given them the bumpiest landing he dared.

John was the first out, the familiar tang of the mine meeting his nostrils, of ponies, men, timber and coal, and when they set to work in earnest, the reek of powder would be added to the mix. 'For them who've never been down a pit before, mind your step and watch your head. The roof's very low in some parts. We've a long walk underground until we get to the district we're working. And keep your ears open. A pit's never still, and it's never silent. It's always moaning and groaning, like a thing alive. The roadway sometimes feels as if it's coming up to meet the roof coming down. If you hear a crack, you might have to run for the shaft – it could mean the roof supports are giving way, maybe a couple of ton of stone's loosened and going to come down on you. If that happens you might never get out of the pit again. Or it might be the knockers. And don't whistle anywhere near the mine. It upsets them.'

Allowing them no time for questions, he led the way, lamp in hand. What a crew they were; half of them the dross of the mining industry, the other half unskilled labour from pasture and ploughland. Most of them were half fed, the majority probably given to drink. They were no better adapted to mine work than babes in arms. They would be a danger to themselves and everybody around them. Anything he could do to deter them from staying would be better for all concerned, John thought. It was a crime that anybody should allow them down a pit, and a greater one to encourage them to come, because although the owners denigrated pit work and determinedly kept wages down by equating it to mere labouring, they knew as well as the pitmen that no other labour could be compared to it. No other labourer worked at such risk to life, limb and health; and none could be compared to the miner for backbreaking labour, or skill, or that instinct for the mine that alerted him instantly to danger. He doubted that these men had been brought here to do any serious work. They were here to bring a skilled but recalcitrant workforce to heel, to give them the ultimatum, work on my terms or see your livelihood given to strangers. Work on my terms or starve. Work on my terms or be thrown out of your homes so that you can cast yourselves on the mercy of your relatives, or the parish.

Big Jim seemed to have gained the status of an unelected leader. As soon as they reached the face he spoke for the rest of the blacklegs in a drawling, southerly accent, now tinged with apprehension. 'What are the knockers?'

'The knockers?' repeated John, innocently. 'Spirits of the mine. Old Nick's little demons. And there are scores of bodies still down here that we never found after the last explosion six year ago, and there were hundreds of men killed even before that. You can sometimes imagine you hear their ghosts knocking.' He raised an arm, and tapped his knuckles on the roof, tap, tap, tap. 'Knocking for somebody to come and find them. Some men have even heard them calling. So take heed and do exactly as you're told, or you might be joining them. We're next door to hell down here. Can you not feel the heat of it? One step in the wrong direction and the devil will claim his own. He'll come and snatch your soul away.'

John was a deputy, and a good one. He would keep these men safe, if humanly possible. For the most part they were driven by hunger and privation to do what they were doing, and there were better ways than violence to persuade people to leave. The mine was an eerie place, and some of the men were superstitious, Big Jim among them. Some, but not all.

'Soul? He can have *my* soul for a couple of pork chops,' a little fellow spat. His face looked cadaverous in the feeble lamplight.

Big Jim turned on him. 'Don't you be making no promises like that. You mind what you say, or you'll 'ave me to answer to.'

John shrugged. 'He's probably right. It's probably all just superstition. I never believe any of it when I'm up, and out in the light of day. But I believe it when I'm down here. You can hardly help it at times. See how smooth the coal looks at the face – just like glossy black ice with the lamplight on it, like a black mirror? It's the mirror of hell.' He rubbed the black band with his jacket sleeve, and held the lamp up to it. 'I once looked at the coalface like that and I nearly jumped out of my skin. I saw my own father staring back at me, along with the little pony driver that was killed with him. They both lost their lives in the explosion six year ago, and when we found them they were clasped in each other's arms, bloated stinking rotten, and half eaten by rats. That was a sight.' The light from the lamp illuminated John's face, and the expression on it gave the men a very good impression of what that sight had been, without need for a word more. 'Still,' he grimaced, 'I've got to admit, I had been on the beer the night before I saw them in the face, so maybe that was it. But that reminds me. Make sure you hang your bait up high, where the rats and mice cannot get it. If you don't, there'll be nothing left for you to eat when break time comes round. They'll have had it all.'

The lad was lying in the roadway, stretched full length, groaning. He'd spent hours stooped and cramped, trying to stop his head rubbing on the roof while he shovelled coal into a tub.

'Away up, man,' John insisted, lamp in hand and looking down on him. 'You're no bloody good to us if you cannot frame better than this.'

The lad looked down at the pulsating centre of his skinny ribs. 'Look at that,' he gasped, 'my heart's just about busting through my chest.'

There was no quarter given in a mine, and the sooner the lad learned that, the better. 'Aye, there's thousands like that,' said John, without sympathy, 'but you'll have to get on with it, like. If you don't, you won't earn enough to buy next week's bread and dripping, and neither will the men, and they'll not like that.'

After a minute or two the boy slowly dragged himself to his feet.

'That's a good lad. Not much longer, and your first day's work'll be done. Then plenty more to come,' John consoled him, watching him go back to his work.

A sardonic smile flitted across John's face as he remembered his own apprenticeship in the pit; the painful cramps that had attacked legs bent underneath him for hour after tortured hour, the aching arms that felt as heavy as lead, the pins and needles that had assaulted his flesh in agonizing spasms. And the combination of hard work and heat, which made him run with sweat and opened every pore to irritating coal dust. Then came excruciating backache and the feeling that he couldn't lift another shovelful of coal to save his soul. But he'd had to do it. 'There's only two kinds of work in a pit, lad – hard, and harder,' the men had told him, and they'd shown him little sympathy. But those men had been men of iron who could cut coal like demons. The men and boys in this crew were a softer proposition. They were just beginning to understand what they'd let themselves in for, and John wouldn't show any more sympathy for them than had been shown to him. Those who hadn't been brought up to mining would soon have a very clear idea of what it was, and the sane ones among them would leave. When you reckoned it all up, it would be better for their sakes, as well as everybody else's.

*   *   *

It was as much as the police could do to keep the crowd back when they got to the surface. John hung back to see how things fell out before making a move in the direction of home. He watched the police form a protective cordon round the black-legs, and begin to march them quickly back to their billets. A furious mob of strikers with their wives and children surrounded them, all banging pans and pot lids, set-pot covers, fire blazers and any other instrument of rough music they could lay hand to, all yelling and screaming out threats at the top of their lungs. The faces of the women were more determined, more ferocious than the men's as they banged out a rhythm on their instru-ments and shouted out their war chant, 'Blacklegs, blacklegs, dirty blacklegs!' and their actions were more reckless than the men's. They ran alongside the procession, some of them trying to thrust themselves between lines of police to lunge at the enemy. Success there was denied to them and in sheer exas-peration one woman began to bawl out a familiar song.

> Oh, Annsdale pit is a terrible place,
> They rub wet clay in the blackleg's face,
> And around the heaps they run a race
> To catch the blackleg miner.

Others soon took up the refrain:

> So divn't gan near the Annsdale mine,
> Across the way they stretch a line,
> To catch the throat and break the spine
> Of the dirty blackleg miner.

> They grab his duds and his pick as well,
> They hoy them down the pit of hell,
> Then down go you, and fare you well,
> You dirty blackleg miner.

Their ferocity made the hair stand up at the back of John's neck, and he wondered how far some in the crowd were prepared to go to rid the village of the pit's new workforce.

'The neighbours,' said Arthur, 'a set of bloody farmers' boys and tuppence ha'penny shop assistants who're all right up their own arses. Bugger the neighbours, we've been there six year, and they've never been neighbourly to us. I wish we'd never shifted out of Annsdale Colliery. We were among real neighbours there.'

They'd caught the train to Newcastle at the stop beyond Annsdale, hoping to avoid the watchful eyes of either policemen or informers. In his heart of hearts John knew the truth of Arthur's words but said, 'We might have had a chance of getting on with them if it hadn't been for you causing trouble everywhere you go. I don't wonder they look down on us, the sort of things you get up to. All me mam wants is to live a quiet respectable life. It's not too much to ask.'

'Away and shite. We've no chance of getting on with most of 'em, because they think they're a cut above us, and it's time you all stared that fact full in the face and made yoursel's content with your own kind. We could be the best people ever born and they still wouldn't give us the time o' day. Anyway, never mind me Mam, what about you? What do you want? To spend your life being looked down on by a set of nancy shopkeepers and forelock-pulling farm labourers who haven't a ha'penny to scratch their backsides with?'

'It's a bit late to be asking me what I want, like. I wanted South Africa and Hendrika, but I knew I wasn't going to get them when you started throwing your bloody weight about at home after me dad died.'

'There was nothing to stop you going back to South Africa. We were doing all right before you came back.'

The look of panic on his mother's face, the mute appeal in her eyes whenever he spoke of going flashed into John's mind. At thirteen, Arthur had already been beyond her control, and the girls were frightened of him. So John postponed his return to Hendrika, and sent letters to her asking her to wait, just a bit longer. She wrote back: her parents were glad to have the Englishman out of the way, she said, they didn't want her to marry an Englishman and kept introducing her to nice Afrikaner boys – he must hurry up and come back to South Africa. But before six months had passed, she'd lost hope he'd ever return, and was married to someone more to her parents' liking. He couldn't blame her. He couldn't blame his mother either; she'd never asked him to stay, never put it into words. He couldn't blame her, but he did, and he blamed Arthur even more; he blamed them for ruining his chances of a better life. But argument was futile, and despite his irritation John made no attempt at it.

After a few minutes' silence, Arthur said, 'And you haven't thanked me.'

John looked at him in open-mouthed disbelief. 'Thanked you? For what? What have you ever done for me?'

'I've stopped you getting a good thumping, that's all. It was me that shouted, "Run for it, lads, they've got the cavalry out!" You mind that? The bloody cavalry were nowhere near, man. But lucky for you, I made 'em all run.' Arthur laughed at the memory, sounding so pleased at his own craft that John smiled with him.

'Why, that was clever, Arthur, so thank you.'

'And another thing,' said Arthur, in a friendly tone, 'it's time you stopped breaking your heart about that South African lass, man – lasses are ten a penny. Get another one. There's plenty more where she came from, there's plenty more every-where else an' all. Bonny lasses you can have a bit fun with, like Kath Leigh, in Annsdale Colliery. She's fun alive, that one. And there's at least three I know of like the look of you, you could have 'em for the asking, though what they see in you beats me. There's that lass I've seen at the Cock with her brother a time or two an' all, the ones from the cycling club. I've seen her giving you the eye. You'd be all right there. I could eat me bait out o' her drawers an' all.'

'I'd be satisfied with Elsie, if I were you.'

Arthur gave a suggestive laugh. 'If you knew Elsie like I know her, you wouldn't keep her on that pedestal. Still, she did all right by me. More than all right, when you come to reckon up.' He gave a knowing laugh and paused, but John would not give him the satisfaction of seeming interested. He was tired of Arthur's lewd, adolescent boasting, and not inclined to hear any of it applied to Elsie. After an interval, Arthur continued, 'And she kept me well fed. Aye, she's done all right by me, but the trouble is, I'm not satisfied with her. There's too many other lasses giving me the glad eye, and I want 'em all. That's why I'll never go to sea. Not enough women about, like.'

Feelings of resentment and irritation returned in full force. John gave him a look, wondering how it was that a pearl like Elsie Hartley could lower herself so far as to be trampled in Arthur's trough. 'And if Elsie knew you like I know you,' he said, 'she wouldn't be able to get shot fast enough.'

Arthur laughed again, and winced. 'Why, you should see your face, man. Like sour tripe. Never bother. Don't think it'll break Elsie's heart. She's too busy being in love with hersel' to have any time left over to be in love with anybody else. And I don't see many women hanging round you for all your polite gentlemanly ways.'

Walking along by the rails leading to Newcastle Docks, John was in his element. He sucked the fresh salt air deeply into his lungs and smiled, savouring the scent and thrilling to the chill northerly breeze caressing his cheeks. The crying of the gulls, the sound of the sea, the shouts of the men and the creak and clank of crane and cargo as they loaded and unloaded the ships made him wistful. Life at sea was reputed to be hard, but he'd had a soft berth and an easy enough master on his merchant ship, and on a bright cold day like this, to sail out on the tide was his idea of heaven. He would never regret his three years at sea; it was the only chance the toiling classes ever got to see a bit of the world. Arthur, unmoved, thrust his hands deeply into his pockets as he strode along.

'I'll find you somewhere safe to hide and you'll get work enough to keep body and soul together until it all blows over, if you behave yourself, and show 'em you can put your back into it, that is.'

'Sounds all right,' Arthur frowned, 'for cap-doffers like you.'

John ignored the insult, sensing the nervousness underlying Arthur's bravado.

'Why, does six months with hard labour sound any better?' He smiled, taking a malicious delight in Arthur's anxiety.

Arthur was silent, and John nodded towards a dockside inn. 'You go in there and get a half. I'll away and see what I can find.'

Half an hour later he returned with a brisk, ruddy-faced man who bristled with energy, and swept across the room towards Arthur, whose temper had not been improved by the wait. 'All right, Johnny, this the lad? Why, let's see what he's made of. The *Enterprise* is due out on the tide, and there's still plenty of cargo wants loading. Away, lad, follow me.'

'Away then, Arthur,' John urged.

Arthur shot him a malevolent glance, reluctantly got to his feet, and wiped the froth from his mouth.

John shrugged. 'That, or six months. Your choice.'

'Come on, come on, lad. No time to waste,' called his taskmaster, already halfway towards the door. Arthur grabbed his cap and chased after him.

John got a beer and sat for a while congratulating himself on a job well done. Arthur had lost his job at Annsdale pit and, knowing the manager, he was probably blacklisted for miles around, so better he should earn his keep elsewhere. John certainly didn't want another mouth to feed out of his pay; he hadn't given up the idea of emigrating yet, and wanted to save as much as he could. They were set fair for victory now, his mother would have peace, and he would keep his job – he'd make sure of it. He looked at the clock above the bar, and then strolled out into the twilight, his steps taking him in the direction of the *Enterprise*. Her gangways and anchor were up, she was cast off and about half a dozen yards away from the quayside. John grinned as he looked skywards and saw two figures standing at the ship's side, his old ship-mate Jack erect and tranquil, Arthur leaning over the rail as if he were contemplating making a leap for the dock.

John cupped his hands around his mouth and yelled a challenge to Jack. 'Make a man of him – if you can!'

Arthur's reaction was everything John knew it would be. A stream of filthy invective assailed his ears until drowned by a blast from the ship's hooter. Jack was doubled up with laughter.

'Never bother, John. I'll bring him back with better

41

manners!' Jack waved, shouting above the roar of the engines.

John yelled again, 'Did I say a month or two, Arthur? With a bit of luck, it might be a year or two. Don't forget to write.' He turned and strode swiftly along the dock with the wind at his back, breathing in air like nectar, scanning the wide sky, feeling like a boy again with a hundredweight of responsibility lifted from his shoulders.

Freedom. Days, weeks and months free from argument. The look of relief he would see on his mother's face. The security of his job. Their almost certain victory in a justified dispute that men and their families had made sacrifices for. And something much better, something he hardly dared admit, even to himself. His walk became a run, and ended in a leap as he jumped and punched the air in pure jubilation. He almost skipped towards the railway station, relishing his last glimpse of Arthur's face.

Sunday was ominously quiet. The strike-breakers went to work the following day escorted by police, and after the shift they and John again arrived at the surface to the din of pans, blazers and set-pot covers being beaten hard. The people of Annsdale Colliery howled in protest as the blacklegs paraded through the streets, again surrounded by their helmeted, brass-buttoned protectors, every burly constable with an expression of grim determination on his face, and a stout truncheon hanging at his left side. Undeterred, a woman picked up a stone and hurled it at the group, seeming not to care whom it hit, as long as it hit somebody. Others soon followed suit. The police broke ranks and started to pursue some of the crowd, leaving their charges unguarded and open to attack, and skirmishes started. Some blacklegs ran in the direction of Old Annsdale, hotly pursued by the incensed crowd. John raced after them, fearing what mischief might be perpetrated in the village, but glad beyond words that whatever it might be, Arthur could have no part in it. Passions were rising to such a pitch that someone might be killed.

He saw Elsie step out of the tailor's shop, and straight into the path of a young fugitive. She fell full length, and her bag was dashed from her hand, scattering its contents. The lad reeled, recovered himself and raced off, the strikers and their sympathizers behind him. John stopped and hunkered down beside her.

'Are you hurt?'

She looked pale. He helped her to sit up, and he saw the dirty imprints of his hands on her blue coat.

'Sorry,' he said.

'It's not your fault.' She pulled off a glove, and showed him a graze on the heel of her hand. 'I've bumped my elbow, as well.'

'Do you think you can stand?'

She nodded, and taking his hand let him help her to her feet. The tailor came out of his door, closely followed by apprentice Lizzie, his round bespectacled face full of solicitude.

'Come back into the shop and sit down. Come on,' he urged her. 'Lizzie, make her a cup of tea.' Lizzie disappeared, and the tailor took Elsie's elbow, but let go when she winced.

'No. I'm all right, Mr Surtees,' she said, dismissing the tailor with some authority. 'John will get my things and see me home.'

The tailor retreated into his shop. John took the handbag and gathered up Elsie's things, a purse, a key, a tiny bottle of perfume, miraculously unbroken, and a snow-white handkerchief, which he replaced complete with his finger-marks. He handed the bag to her with a smile, and got a smile in return. He smiled again, a little ruefully, feeling at a sad disadvantage in his filthy pit duds, his cheeks growing warm under their covering of grime.

Elsie's expression became serious. 'I wanted them to go away so I could ask you about Arthur. You got him away, then?'

He gazed into her bright brown eyes. The arch of those quizzical eyebrows entranced him and the full, soft lips of that questioning mouth – so near he had an almost overpowering impulse to kiss it. But that mouth might easily run away with itself and give the game away, implicate him in Arthur's disappearance. Her father was keeping some very elevated company these days, company that would have no sympathy for miners, especially those who broke the law. The less Elsie knew, the less she could talk about. Far better that she should know nothing that could get either of them into trouble.

'Come and I'll walk you back home.'

'Better not. They all seem to have gone now.'

John nodded. The street was empty again, though the din could still be heard.

'You got him away, then?'

'There's no need to worry, Elsie.'

'So you did get him away.'

He hesitated. 'He's out of harm's way.'

She stopped and scrutinized his face, and her eyes narrowed. 'I don't know why you won't tell me. I wouldn't tell anybody. I wouldn't have helped him hide if I were going to do that.' With a little toss of her head she turned from him and walked off in a huff, not stopping to look back.

It was the longest conversation he'd ever had with Elsie, and he felt a pang of disappointment at the way it had ended. Still, he didn't want the sort of consequences he might have to face if the police heard he'd helped his brother evade the law. He'd keep looking out for Elsie whenever he was in the village. He'd stay friendly, and hope she'd do the same.

At home, John scrubbed his hands and forearms while his mother ironed him a clean white shirt on one end of the kitchen table and Lizzie put his dinner on the other. Sally was polishing his shoes. They, thankfully, had accepted his bald statement that Arthur would be working away for a while, and asked no questions about it, agreeing with him that it would be better to say nothing, at least until the police lost interest in looking for him.

His meal eaten, John lifted the heavy tin bath off the outside wall and left his mother and Lizzie to fill it while he read the paper and Sally cleared the table. Then the women retired to the front room, giving him privacy to strip and scrub the grime from skin and hair, and to shave.

Out then, fed, pressed, brushed and polished to a pristine gleam by the women of his family, leaving his mother to deal with a heap of dusty pit clothes, and Sally, who was still without a place, to clean his boots. Feeling and looking as good as any man in the world, he set out in the dark and strode away towards the Cock. Elsie would be at home now, by the fire, behind drawn curtains, nursing her sore hand and elbow. It still niggled him that they'd parted at odds with each other, more so than all the other trials of the day put together. He looked at his hands, now clean, with the nails scrubbed white. Remembering the marks he'd put on her coat and her handkerchief, he swore to himself with vexation. Why could she never fall into his path when he was bathed and dressed up, and fit to look at? Never mind. The year was on the turn, and the days were lengthening. He'd see more and more of her come spring and summer, and she'd see more of him.

John stepped into the Cock, and felt cheered and comforted as the pub wrapped itself round him like a blanket, enfolding him, as always, in warmth and congeniality. A fire was blazing in the hearth and its glow shone richly in the plentiful brass and copperware. Ginny had almost pulled his pint before he got to the bar, and she gave him a smile of welcome.

'Rough day?'

'Aye, and more of 'em to come. And likely to get rougher.'

'Maybe not. The union men will hold a meeting tomorrow. They'll make it known that anybody that breaks the law and hurts any of the blacklegs will get their strike pay docked. There's not many will want to risk that.'

'I hope that threat applies to anybody that hurts a deputy, an' all.' He raised his eyebrows, and gave her a nod. 'This is one o' the times I'm glad I'm not living in Annsdale Colliery.'

'You'll be a lot gladder before long. Have you heard about the eviction notices?'

John put his pint down. 'No.'

'Why, our Em and Jimmy have got one.'

'But Jimmy's still working.'

'He's not. He's got the sack.'

That image of his sister on the bandstand, haranguing the crowd, sprang immediately to John's mind. 'How long have they got?'

'A week. And they're not the only ones. There's Maudie

Goodliffe, that washes the pots for me, and others beside.'

John finished his pint, and walked down to Emma's.

She was kneeling in the kitchen on the clippy mat wrapping plates and teacups in newspaper and packing them in a tea chest.

'You're quick off the mark, Em,' John said. 'Surely you've got till the end of the week.'

'Aye, why, they want us out, and we're going, so no time like the present. I'm not waiting for the candymen to come, dragging and bashing me stuff about. We'll move it ourselves.'

The candymen, those scavengers who would give children a few sweets or toffees in exchange for rags and bones, were employed along with the scrapings from docks and dosshouses whenever muscle was needed by the owners, or muscle without brain or scruple, to be exact. They had no respect for themselves, or anybody or anything else.

'Who will you stop with, Em, our Ginny or us?' John asked. 'You know you'll have a welcome in either place.' At least Emma had a choice where she went, unlike some in the village.

'We're not likely to be welcome anywhere for long, not with four little lads running round, destroying the place and getting on everybody's nerves.'

'Away, hinny. That's not right. We'll help you all we can. It'll not go on for ever, and you'll be back in your own home before long.'

'Not if Mr Woolfe has anything to do with it.' Emma leaned back on her heels, and looked around her tiny cottage, her face so rigid John knew she was near to tears. 'Your own four walls. Your home. Something you grow to love. The place your bairns lay their heads, and they can take it all away from you at a week's notice, and through no fault of Jimmy's. And it's spite. Pure spite. There was nothing wrong with Jimmy's work before I stood up at that meeting. Now there's everything wrong with it, and they've sacked him, poor lad. And they've put us on the street. They'll crush the spirit out of us, if they can.'

'Have you not got room for Jimmy up there?' Emma asked, but the wagon was so well laden with everything they owned

46

that there was little room for any passenger, and Martin shook his head. 'Not unless he wants to do the driving.'

'If you're walking, I'm walking. We'll go together, Em. I'll be all right.' Jimmy lifted the youngest child and took the eldest by the hand, while Emma locked her door for the last time. John walked beside them, casting sidelong glances at Jimmy, limping gamely along on his false leg, but felt hesitant to suggest that he should carry the baby of the family. They made their progress in silence, through a village whose shale heaps and sooty blemishes were now covered in a blanket of white. At last John could bear it no longer.

'Give us hold of the bairn, man. It's time Uncle John had a cuddle.' He tickled the child under the chin, and he smiled and turned away, burying his face in his father's shoulder.

'Maybe in a few minutes. I'll just carry him for now.'

They lapsed again into silence, and walked until they came out onto the Annsdale Road. John dropped back a few paces and watched them, Jimmy struggling on with the baby, and Emma and the other little lads walking slowly beside him in dappled sunshine and shade, under snow-laden branches. Bundled up in scarves and woollens, they put John in mind of a pair of love-birds whose nest had been stolen, cast out into the cold hard world with their chicks.

Once Emma had seen all her furniture manhandled into the loft at the Cock, she collapsed onto a chair and burst into tears. Jimmy leaned down and put an arm round her. 'It's all right, hinny. We'll be all right. Down but not out, eh?'

'Oh, Jimmy man,' she choked. 'It's bad enough for us, but what do people without families do?'

Emma herself had said it. At least they had family who could help, and the world would not be as cruel for them as it was sure to be for some. John frowned, thinking of the nest-raider, and pictured Woolfe at that very moment sitting at his ease before a roaring fire in his own spacious, secure, well-furnished house, surrounded by his safe, warm, well-fed family.

It wasn't likely that anything would ever be any different in England. The only thing for a man with no money but plenty of enterprise to do was to get the hell out of it, John thought.

Four

When John called at the Cock the following evening, Emma had settled her boys for the night. Tears were done with, and in their place was steely determination.

'I wanted to be doing something,' she told him, 'so I went with Maudie and some of the other women up to the grocer's in Old Annsdale, and to Hartley's shop. They're the only ones that's been trading with the blacklegs, and we thought it was time to put a stop to it. "I'll sell my meat to who I like," Mr Hartley says, high and mighty, like. "Your new customers might be here a couple of weeks or so, not much more than that, the way I look at things," I said, "then when they've all gone, and this strike's over, the pitmen's wives will buy their meat from who *they* like. And if you carry on the way you are doing, they won't like *you*, and they won't be shopping here. They'll be telling the Co-op to find another supplier an' all, in this village and all the others." You should have seen the look on his face. I thought he'd burst a blood vessel he was that mad, but he got the message.'

John's heart sank at the news of another wedge between his family and the Hartleys. But there was nothing he could do, no protest he could justifiably make. The women had a right to protect their own interests.

'It did me good anyway; I came away laughing,' Maudie grinned, nodding her agreement.

'It did us both good,' said Emma, 'just to even the score a bit, and we'll keep on until we get our own way.'

'Aye – and you just wait till they try to evict me. They'll not get me out as easy as they did you, Em. I'll give 'em something to think about,' said Maudie. 'You watch.'

*   *   *

A couple of days later, John stood aside for a cart carrying a few women into Old Annsdale. It was escorted by ranks of police and followed by a large and threatening crowd of jeering miners' wives and daughters, with Emma and Maudie to the fore. Emma gave him a brief wave as he walked quickly on home, then the cart stopped at the grocer's and the catcalls and rough music rose to a crescendo as the women, pale with fright, were helped down by their protectors. The scene was compelling, and despite his better judgement, John stopped to look. They went inside the shop, but were out again before a minute had passed, and without the food they needed. The shopkeeper, as if wanting to make it abundantly clear to the crowd that he neither sought nor welcomed the strangers' patronage, ostentatiously shooed them off his premises, then closed and locked his door. A thin, lank-haired young girl, not much more than a child, fainted as she tried to get back into the cart. A couple of policemen lifted her in, to the drum of frying pans, shovels, set-pot covers and the like, and the hooting and braying of the crowd. The driver forced a passage to the baker's, where the would-be customers received the selfsame treatment. The poor girl fainted again and had to be bundled back into the cart with her companions.

Hartley himself came out as they approached his shop and shook his head at them. His eyes met John's for a fraction of a second before he retreated into his premises and closed his door, and John knew in that instant that all hopes of rebuilding cordial relations between their two families were obliterated. He had despised the miners before, though he had tried to conceal the fact for the sake of his trade. He would detest them after this humiliation – and because Emma had made herself conspicuous in it, most of his hatred would probably be focused on those nearest to him, his neighbours in Old Annsdale.

The cart and its escort passed on and out of the village, with the beat of the makeshift drums and cries of 'Blacklegs, blacklegs, we'll catch you,' following them, all the way.

The sight of terrified women cowering and huddling together like animals awaiting slaughter was pitiful, and John couldn't help but feel sorry for them. He wished to God he'd gone on home out of the way of it all, because Hartley would for ever associate him with the scene. Still, John smiled. Because for all his bluster, it was evident that Elsie's father was not so foolhardy that he dared defy the women he looked down upon.

Ginny's idea was to put as much of her pot-washer's stuff in the loft as they could, and leave the rest in the yard with a tarpaulin over it, until such time as Maudie could get somewhere else to live, or to store it. She got the loan of the dray from the brewery, and asked John to take it down to Annsdale Colliery on the day of the evictions to help Maudie with the furniture.

There were about a dozen candymen in the street when he got there, with as many police standing by to see that nobody interfered with them. Three or four of them to each house, they were working with a will, bursting into one targeted home after another to lift, throw or drag the contents out, and board the house up. John didn't wonder at the speed of the operation; they would want to have it done and be paid and off, back to Sunderland, or Hartlepool, or wherever the hell else they'd been dredged from. Cries for them to be careful with this hard-won table or that scrimped-and-saved-for dresser fell on deaf ears, and prized and polished pieces, the housewives' pride and joy, went crashing into the roadway along with the rest. John thought how wise Emma had been to save her poor bits of furniture from such rough handling. The pleas of the women, the tears of children, threats, insults and rough music, all left the candymen unmoved. Silently and systematically, they stripped one house after another of its contents, and chairs, tables, dressers, wardrobes, crockery, cutlery, dogs, cats, caged birds, men, women and children, all went tumbling through the doors.

Until they got to the last house. Maudie was hanging out of her bedroom window when they got there. 'I've locked the door,' she told them. 'You're not getting in here. You'll not get *my* stuff out, or me either.'

Maudie's mother and sisters were there to watch the proceedings, and judging by their expressions, they were expecting to see a bit of fun. People who were not too busy stacking their possessions onto carts and barrows of every description soon joined them.

The men made no reply, but produced a bunch of keys,

then discovered that Maudie had left her key in the lock so that they couldn't get theirs in.

'Aye, that's right, I've bolted it an' all,' she jeered, 'and the same at the back.'

'You're wasting your time and ours an' all, missus. Come and open up, before we knock the windowpane out.'

'Away and play with your – feet,' laughed Maudie.

The tinkle of splintering glass was her only answer, and one of the men was soon through the window to open the door and let the others in. Maudie's husband came quietly out, but Maudie and her boy refused to come down the stairs, so after throwing out the rest of the contents, the candymen went up after her.

Ned Goodliffe set to work with John, stacking their household goods on the dray. 'She's not bothered about the furniture; you can see we've got naught posh.' He laughed, and spat. 'They've got more of a job on than they think, getting her out. She's got a great big sea chest up the stairs, and she's been filling it with stones ever since we got the eviction notice. She's locked it, and her mother has the key. She's sitting on top if it now, with her arms folded, and you ought to see the look on her face, man. They'll have to carry her down the stairs, kicking hell out of them all the way, and then they'll have to go back for the chest. It'll probably break their backs.'

John watched with interest, while continuing to load the dray. Maudie's audience of friends and neighbours was not disappointed. She did indeed refuse to move, so two of the biggest, most muscular men went upstairs for her, to half drag and half carry her out, kicking and screaming and cursing them blind all the way down. They dumped her in the roadway, all three of them heaving and panting, Maudie's face puce with rage, theirs with exertion. Another went up after her six-year-old, and almost threw him at her when he got back.

'Go on, you bad little bugger, get to your bloody bitch of a mother.' He rubbed his hand angrily. 'The little swine's bitten me through to the bone.'

'Good lad, Harry,' Maudie said, wrapping a protective arm around her son. 'And I hope it goes bloody septic an' all,' she shouted. 'I hope you get blood poisoning. I hope your bloody arm drops off.'

He advanced towards her, fist raised, but a policeman stepped in to restrain him. 'That's enough. Just get the house boarded up, and we'll be away.'

Maudie stood up and turned to the crowd. 'So, the owners have got it their own way, and they've chucked us out of our houses. Well then, we ought to make them pay through the nose. We should all go up to the workhouse with our men and our bairns, and every living soul that depends on us – old Uncle Tom Cobley an' all – and make sure we put the bloody rates up. Let's make them find us something for our suppers, and let them find us a bed.'

John saw her late the same night, in the Cock. 'I see they wouldn't keep you in the workhouse, Maudie.'

'No. There were scores of us went up there, but they must have heard about it, because when we got there, there were dozens of police to stop anybody going in that didn't have orders, and none of us had, so we had to come away again. Nobody really wanted to be there anyway. Well, nobody would, unless they'd no choice.' Maudie paused to reflect. 'On second thoughts, though, I don't suppose there's much to choose between there and me mam's. That's where we've ended up.' She gave Emma a look of triumph. 'I told you they wouldn't get me out as easy as they did you, though, Em, and they didn't.'

'Aye, well I hope you didn't leave any stones in that stuff we've shoved in the loft for you. I think the bloody ceiling'll come down before we've finished,' said Ginny.

Jimmy sat at the piano, and Martin called to him, 'That one of Tommy Armstrong's, eh, Jimmy? In honour of Maudie, and the rest of you.' Jimmy gave a grim nod, and struck up with the first bars of 'The Oakey Strike Evictions'. Ginny took up the tune, with feeling.

It was in November and Aa nivvor will forget
How the polisses and the candymen at Oakey
   Houses met,
Johnny the bellman he was there squintin'
   roond aboot

And he put three men at ivvery door te torn
  the miners oot.

By this time all the customers and bar staff were singing with
her, and the chorus nearly brought the roof off.

And what wad Aa dee if Aa had the power mesel'?
Aa wad *hang* the twenty candymen – and Johnny whe carries
  the bell!

And next there came the Masters, and I think they should be
  shamed
For depriving wives and families of a comfortable home
And when they shift from where they are, Aa hope they go
  to Hell,
Along with the twenty candymen and Johnny whe carries the
  bell.
And what wad Aa dee if Aa had the power mesel'?
Aa wad *hang* the twenty candymen – and Johnny whe carries
  the bell!

There was no banging and rattling to accompany the blacklegs to and from work after the evictions. Instead there was
a silent, slow-paced crowd to the fore of the police to slow
their progress, and the low, unnerving hum of voices intoning
the Dead March. Many of the women were holding wreaths,
to hang around the necks of the strike-breakers.

After a couple of days, Big Jim sought John out. 'My wife
won't stay, she's terrified to set foot in either of the villages,
and I've no liking for the single life, so I'm going with her.
I can't say as I've any liking for coal mines either. I'll say
goodbye, John.' Big Jim held out his right hand. John grasped
it firmly, looking straight into his eyes.

'I wish I could say I'm sorry to see you go, Jim. Under
different circumstances, I would be.'

'Can't be helped, can it? Still, you've been as decent to us
as you could, so I'll wish you all the best. No hard feelings.'

'Aye, none here, either. And good luck to you an' all. I
hope you'll soon get something that'll suit you better.'

Jim walked on a few paces, then turned. 'We never wanted those people thrown out of their houses, you know.'

John nodded. 'It was bound to happen, Jim. Never bother, it'll probably turn out all right in the end.'

The Cock's concert room was carefully laid out with card tables, and was full of Ginny's carefully cultivated 'better class' customers, the ones whose money was keeping the inn afloat. She had organized a whist drive, to make a few pounds for the strike fund. John sat down with Jimmy, to play against a well-dressed young fellow partnered with one of the few women in the room.

'I'm Alice Peters, and this is my brother Tom,' she informed them, flashing John a smile while expertly shuffling the cards. 'Cut,' she ordered, offering the cards to Jimmy. Her pronunciation and manner would have placed her in the middle classes even if her appearance had not. Her face was rather square, her figure shapely though a little heavy. Not really a beauty, but vibrant and oozing confidence. She raised her green eyes to John's and smiled, revealing a deceptively childish dimple in her left cheek, which softened the effect of her high, starched collar. Her hair was a mousy brown, combed neatly back into a bun, but there was nothing mousy about the girl herself. She couldn't have been much more than twenty, but she dealt like a cardsharp. John and Jimmy exchanged a quick glance and sat up straight. Better watch this pair. But in spite of their best efforts, the couple seemed to have a real rapport, and won four games out of the five.

'See her?' muttered Jimmy when they passed on to the next table, 'slaps a master card down as if she's kicking you in the balls.'

John laughed. 'There's definitely something about her, though,' he grinned. 'Definitely.'

After Alice and Tom had collected their trophy bottle of whisky and been politely clapped, they stood at the bar alongside John and Jimmy, listening to talk about the strike.

'Aye, the labour unions seem to be posing a bit of a problem for the ruling classes lately. We're rattling the cage, and with a vengeance. We might be even more dangerous than they already think we are, if they push us to the limit,' swaggered Jimmy, the pint he'd drunk beginning to talk.

'What makes you think you have the right to strike against your masters?' Alice challenged.

Jimmy's jaw dropped. 'The right?' he asked, looking round the rest of the company with eyebrows raised, failing to see the point of such a question, a question too stupid to merit a serious answer, even if he were sober enough to give one. His wife was not so slow in snatching up the gauntlet.

'Our masters!' Emma exploded from the other side of the bar, leaning aggressively towards Alice. 'I've got no master! I'm as good as any of them! Slave drivers and robbers! What makes *them* think they own us, body and soul? You know one of the sins that cries to heaven for vengeance?'

Startled, Alice recoiled, and the place became so still that the dropping of a pin would have sounded like a lightning crack. Ginny and Martin, Maudie, Jimmy, Tom, and every-body else in the place had their eyes focused on Alice, awaiting her reply. Silently, slowly, she shook her head.

'Steady on, Emma, hinny. We don't want you giving any offence to our good custom,' Ginny protested.

But Emma was not to be stopped. 'Cheating a workman of his wages – that's what! It's committed against us every day of our lives, and heaven seems to be doing bugger all about it. So it's up to us to help ourselves, and we fully intend to do it.'

Too much taken aback to speak, Alice stared open-mouthed at Emma's flushed face and smouldering dark eyes.

Unlike Jimmy and Emma, John caught the real intent behind this middle-class lass's provocation at once, and was several jumps ahead in an argument that was running out of her control. He read the papers, and some of her comments while they'd been playing cards had raised his suspicions about her. 'I think you're one of Mrs Pankhurst's loyal followers, Miss Peters,' he said.

'Indeed I am, and proud of it.'

'And you seem surprised that anybody else can feel as strongly about their rights as you do about yours,' he observed, 'but our little local squabble is about a three-shift system which will mean more than sticking a bit of paper into a ballot box once every four year. It'll mean round-the-clock slavery for some of the women round here. And the big national fight that's just been called is for a minimum wage for the men who slave underground.'

'I already know that.'

John doubted she thoroughly understood the arguments, but rather than go into detail he smiled, and like a good music-hall stooge he gave her the cue she wanted, knowing full well where she would go with it.

'All right,' he began. 'To answer your question, then. Rights are like liberty, something you take, not something you wait to be given. Waiting to be given them marks you out as a slave and a fool, because you can never get them that way. We have the right to strike against our masters, as you please to call them, because although they'd like to treat us like slaves we're free men who know our own worth. We're denied a fair share of the wealth our labour produces. We don't get our due. We owe it to ourselves and our families to get our due.'

'Ha!' she pounced to trump his ace, just as he expected. 'You owe it to yourselves to get your due, you men. Well, what about us women? Where would you be without your wives? They work as hard as you, a lot harder in many cases. They're as intelligent as you. They owe it to themselves to get their due.'

There was laughter, and a chorus of protest about Alice's claim for the intelligence of women. She seemed to sense some sympathy from John, and looked to him for support.

'Don't look at me. I'm not married,' he laughed.

'We give our wives their due,' Jimmy protested.

'You do not.'

'They do,' John chimed in, for nothing but the love of verbal sparring. 'On the first of March a million of us will come out – the whole mining industry'll be at a standstill, and other industries all over the country will grind to a halt as a result. Pottery, glass, steel, bricks, the railways, shipping. How can they carry on without the pitman's labour? All the wheels will stop turning. They'll all be idle soon, and all because of a lot of avaricious mine owners and landowners who're determined to keep all the wealth we produce in their own pockets. We're rattling the cage so hard they'll have to give way. There'll be a new system in this country. We'll win this one, and when we do, everybody'll have their due, wives and families an' all.'

'But the wives won't have their due,' Alice persisted, 'because they won't have rights. They'll still be reliant on the grace and favour of men. How many of you working men, who make so much noise about your own rights, are pleased enough to play the despot in your homes? Husbands see nothing wrong in ruling their wives and daughters, and stopping them having any more security than what they see fit to provide. And if it pleases them to stop providing it, a woman is left with nothing, she's powerless to help herself. I accuse a lot of working men of hypocrisy. "I want decent treatment for myself and my class, but I insist on the right to keep my wife and daughters well under my heel," is what you're saying, when you argue against women having the vote.'

'Votes for women,' said a man further down the bar, his voice full of sarcasm. 'Just wrap it up there. We've heard enough.'

'They're all failures in the marriage market, and now they want to get their revenge by stirring all the married women up,' said his companion.

'The women are revolting!' came another comment.

Alice's brother raised his glass with a look of pure mischief in his eyes. 'It's got to come. These women are rattling their cage so hard they'll shake the bars out sooner or later. Can't keep them down for ever, and I say good luck to them.' He took a long draught of beer.

'I'll tell you what, then. My wife starts rattling any cages, and I'll bloody well rattle her, and she knows it,' came the rejoinder from the man further down the bar, with heavy emphasis.

'Then your wife will still get her vote,' Tom smiled at him, his voice maddeningly mild, 'through the exertions of other women. "The argument of the broken windowpane is the most valuable argument in modern politics," so Mrs Pankhurst says, and if Mrs Pankhurst says it, that means it's right. The

Government had better give in soon, or I doubt there'll be a pane of glass left whole in London. Better not argue too hard against them, or they might pay you a visit and make your house feel draughty. I feel deeply sorry for Mr Asquith. Our Prime Minister doesn't seem to be able to control anybody, miners, Irish Unionists, or suffragettes. He'll remember 1912 all right.'

Ginny and Emma stared for a moment at Tom, and then burst into laughter. 'The argument of the broken window-pane!' gasped Emma, holding a corner of her apron to her eyes. 'Well, if that doesn't beat the lot! Mrs Pankhurst must have been to the same school of politics as our Arthur.'

'The difference is that she'll be much more difficult to get rid of than him,' said Alice, 'and some of the most powerful people in the land have tried hard enough and failed, because she doesn't care a jot about going to prison. Men make a mistake when they take women for the weaker sex. We may be physically weaker, but morally, we're strong. And we'll win.'

'Well, I don't know of any man who's left his wife with nothing,' Jimmy muttered, still chewing on that accusation, and a few jumps behind in the argument.

Alice looked him straight in the eye. 'But you must know of wives and children who don't get their fair share. I hear of it, from time to time. I've heard of the famous "keepy-back", the half-crowns or more you men hide in your caps come Pay Friday. Most of you do it, and some keep their families half starved and badly clothed, while they squander housekeeping money on drink, or gambling.'

Jimmy said no more.

'No,' said Alice, 'what we women demand is as much political influence as you men have. Then we'll set about changing our conditions for the better, and no woman will have to rely on a man who ill-treats her. She'll either have a fair claim on their joint property, or be equipped to fend for herself.'

Some brows darkened in anger, but John was amused, and intrigued. Alice talked like no woman he had ever known before, challenging things that few he knew thought to question. The idea of separate spheres for men and women was strong in the colliery villages. From the cradle, the boys were reared like Spartans, to despise any sort of weakness and to demonstrate resilience and courage. Girls were taught the skills needed to nurture a man, body, mind and soul, and thus keep him at the coalface. The result was that the mining companies had a population of men who could work like slaves in inhuman conditions, and of women who could keep them fit for it. Naturally, the companies only paid the masculine half of this partnership, and the half of the partnership that got the wages considered it had a divine right to rule the other half.

Miss Peters knew the pitmen, right enough, or she knew enough of their ways to needle them. You couldn't accuse this young lady of being dull company. Out of mischief, and a wish to prolong the argument, John decided to prick the beautiful bubble she was blowing for her audience.

'I don't think Christabel Pankhurst or her mother care a lot about any hardships our women have to contend with, they're too far above the pitmen's wives. They're too fond of aristo-cratic company. They're only campaigning for votes for middle-class ladies like themselves, and their titled friends. They're not concerned with working people. You shouldn't come here and try to delude our women that the Pankhursts want to do anything for them, because they don't.'

Alice coloured. 'The Pankhursts and all the suffragettes want to smash the barrier that excludes women as a class from voting. Once we've done that, then we can begin to press for the vote for all women,' she protested.

'I think you're expecting over much o' the vote anyway,' he gave her a deliberately condescending, provoking smile. 'A lot of men have had the vote for long enough, but what working men find is that the only way to better their condi-tions or stop their rights being eroded is to withdraw their labour, and this strike proves it. It's the same with women – not women like you, Miss Peters, but women who exist on their own sweated labour like the women in Bermondsey in the East End of London. Did you ever hear tell of Mary MacArthur?'

'Of course I've heard of Mary MacArthur. She's the president of the National Federation of Women Workers.'

Alice's reply was impatient, almost aggressive.

Unprovoked, John went on, 'Well then, she's done a lot more for women like ours, and I mean working-class women slaving in sweated trades, than anything Mrs Pankhurst will ever do, or anybody like her. Those women workers managed to get themselves a good increase round about the time of the London Dock Strike last August, and that was without any votes. They downed tools and came out together, and their employers began to lose money.' He locked eyes with Alice, and repeated the word. 'Money. That's the top and bottom of everything with the employers, and it's a more convincing argument than shoving a bit of paper into a ballot box. At the end of the strike, some of those women came away with four times the pay they'd had before. Like I say, a lot of men have got the vote, but the Government always sides with capital. It doesn't do the working classes any favours, not until we start twisting balance sheets.'

Alice stood with her feet apart, chin tilted, eyes challenging, ready to take him on. 'The women here will never be able to do that, because there are no factories here and no jobs open to them except domestic service. Most of them work as hard for the pit as you do, in keeping you fed, and clean, and fit to work. How can they organize into unions and go on strike for better treatment? They work for *you*. *You* are their employers, and they've no choice but to take whatever you dole out to them.'

She'd made a point he couldn't answer, and for once John had to concede himself beaten in a political argument. He shrugged, and said nothing.

Alice pressed home her advantage. 'And I suppose you think so little of the vote you'd be willing to give up your right to choose your own Member of Parliament? It was your representatives in Parliament who restored your unions to the immunity they'd enjoyed before the Taff Vale Judgement.'

It was Martin who was goaded into protest this time. 'Aye, and look what happened a couple of years later,' he said. 'We got the Osbourne Judgement to disable the unions again. Wealth and Parliament and Law all go hand in hand against working people, and unity and solidarity are the only weapons they have. We've got to look after each other.'

'Be careful, Martin,' said John, recovering himself. 'Do not set yourself up against any militant suffragette. You must know Mrs Pankhurst and her friends all go about with little hammers now, because flints bounce off the best plate glass. You've got a lot of nice leaded windows here, some of them with bonny stained glass in 'em; and I wouldn't be surprised if Miss Peters had a handy little hammer in her bag!' The thought of Alice splintering the Cock's windows struck him as hilarious, and he spluttered into his beer.

Alice ignored him, and addressed herself to Martin. 'Wealth and Parliament won't go hand in hand when the Independent Labour Party gets more members elected. Since the ILP was formed you've had the Workmen's Compensation Act, the Miners' Eight Hours Act, and the Old Age Pensions Act. That's not bad going. You can't tell me none of that has bettered conditions for working people. Well, we women want the same. We want representation in Parliament so that we can end all discrimination against women.'

This woman, who spoke so far out of turn that she had stunned one half of the customers of the Cock and enraged the other half, had caused a tension that was almost palpable, and for a moment the whole place seemed to hold its breath.

'Aye, well, we'll take our share in heving the bairns, then!' one man declared at last, sticking his abdomen out and resting one hand on that, and the other in the small of his back, in the manner of a woman nine months gone. He had such an expression of agony on his face that the Cock erupted into laughter.

'And my wife can get my boots on and go down for a shift hewing the morn, while I turn over and have a lie-in,' another jeered.

John laughed as heartily as the rest, but he had enjoyed the argument with so robust and lucid an opponent, and was unwilling to let it end in ridicule. 'The Eight Hours Act didn't do us a lot of good; underground workers were already doing less than eight in Durham. And in spite of all those acts, prices kept going up, and wages didn't keep pace. Profits were all right, but we never saw the benefit.'

Emma was looking thoughtful, all aggression gone. Alice

faced her. 'Never mind what they say about the vote doing them no good, they wouldn't give it up, any of them. Yes, there will be a new system, and *all* women will have a say in it. We women are rattling our cages as hard as them, and the men will have to let us out. Off with the shackles, for us as well as for them. You wives will help win the strike, and in return, your men should help you win the vote.'

Emma said nothing, but Jimmy saw her expression. 'Not you an' all,' he protested. 'I don't understand it. We risk our lives to provide for our wives and bairns, and that should be enough for you, without wanting to take men's business over.'

'Why, she's right, man,' Emma flashed back at him. 'I've thought it for a long time. I'm as good a scholar as you are, if not better. I know as much as you, so why should I not have a vote? You've no need to bother, I'd be voting for the same party. It would be all the better for all of us.'

Maudie was busy washing beer mugs with her back turned to them all. 'Why, I wouldn't mind a vote. I would put some pepper and salt on it and fry it for me dinner,' she sneered, not bothering to turn round.

'Open your mouth when you can talk sense,' Martin laughed, flicking a bar cloth in her direction, 'and not until. And mind you don't chip any of the mugs.'

Five

Mr Woolfe called all the deputies and officials together on the first of March. He began without preamble. 'I want all those ponies brought to the surface, then this pit's closing. You've finally managed to get rid of my labour, so now you can join the rest of the strikers.'

John spoke up. 'I'm sorry to contradict, Mr Woolfe, but it wasn't us got rid of the labour. I think the blacklegs – I mean the labour, would write me a testimonial if I asked them, the way I looked after them. They left because their wives were frightened to go into the village like, and that was nothing to do with us.'

Mr Woolfe's eyes bored into John's face like twin gimlets. 'It was something to do with your nearest and dearest, though. I know for a fact that your sister was leading the rabble that terrorized them out of the place. Either you or her husband could have stopped her – if you'd wanted to.'

'Why, how could Jimmy do that?' John protested. 'He's not much bigger than her, and she's a lot fitter than he is. If it came to blows, I think he'd get the worst of it. And I can't interfere between man and wife. Women do as they like these days, they've got no respect for anybody, what with all these suffragettes racketing round the countryside, disputing with men and setting a bad example for all the other women. There's people in the Government cannot control them, so what chance have we got, like?'

The manager was silent for a moment or two.

'Is your wife in the WSPU, Mr Woolfe?' John asked, all innocence.

The manager bristled. 'What my wife's in, or what she isn't in, is none of your business. Just see to it that the drivers get the ponies out. I'm closing the pit.'

'It's a lock-out, then.'

'Yes. You've got your national strike now, and the rest of the owners have shut their pits. It's a lock-out.'

'Why, what about the safety checks? They'll have to be done, and we're the best men to do them.' John made the argument but did not really imagine that it would cut any ice with the irate Mr Woolfe. The response was what he expected.

'The best men will be the men I decide on, and that's not you. So carry out your orders, then go home.'

So, the long-awaited national strike had finally been declared. They had known it was on the cards since a few days before Christmas, when they'd been balloted on the question: 'Are you in favour of giving notice to establish a minimum wage for every man and boy working underground in the mines of Great Britain?' and they'd voted four to one in favour. Notices had been served in every district, and the owners had twisted and finally turned back to the September arguments they had previously rejected. They would now be prepared to discuss special terms for 'abnormal places', those parts of the mine which would not yield a hewer enough to feed his family after a week of slave labour – because the seam was thin, or crushed into meagrely priced small coal, or extra timbering was needed to keep the roof up, or the coal was full of stone, or the place was too wet or too dry.

Too late for that. Too much time had already been wasted in fruitless talk. The miners were intent on their minimum wage, and the unimaginable had happened. The whole mining industry was on strike, and the country would soon be at a standstill. The prospect of dipping into his savings was not pleasant, but John was certain that it wouldn't be for long, and so he determined make the best of it, and to enjoy the freedom of this unofficial holiday.

They were locked out. Well, apart from the money, that was all right. John would have a bath as soon as he got home, rub the coal dust from round his eyes and scrape it from under his fingernails. And whenever he went out, he'd be shaven and wearing a clean shirt and tie, in case he bumped into Elsie.

*   *   *

The change of environment made the ponies boisterous. John leaned on the five-bar gate, watching them for a while, whinnying and kicking and galloping round the field, and thought the March hares had nothing on them. He was soon joined by a few young pony drivers.

'Shouldn't you lads be in Sunday School, instead of kicking about the countryside?' he demanded.

'No. We're over big to be going to Sunday School. Have you ever ridden one, like?' one lad, about thirteen years old, asked him.

'Why, who hasn't? You see that little Galloway over there? Little Chance? He belonged to me when I started putting, years ago. I rode him for fun a few times when he was brought out of the pit for the holidays. Have you?'

'No. But I would like to have a go.'

'Would you like to be a jockey, and run in a race?'

The lad smiled, his eyes dancing. 'Why, aye, man. I would love it.'

John laughed. 'Well, maybe's we'll organize some pony races, and have a bit bet on you. I'll talk the idea over with the officials.'

If they could get enough interest in the event, it might raise an extra few coppers for the strike fund. He spied Elsie riding up the lane on her little mare, looking into the field at the ponies. He waited for her, and she stopped and dismounted. The lads made way and she stood beside John, resting her arms on the gate.

'Oh, look at them. Look at the way they're jumping and kicking. Sweet little things. They're like gambolling lambs!'

He smiled, pleased to have her beside him – pleased to be looking clean and well dressed, and clean-shaven. 'You wouldn't think some of them were so "sweet" if you had to make them pull tubs full of coal. They can be stubborn little beggars, and one or two of them are downright lazy.'

'Oh, the poor things. I think it's so cruel to make a pony work down a mine.'

'Aye, they certainly have a harder life than your bonny little mare.' He turned to Elsie's young horse and stroked her nose, murmuring a few admiring, encouraging words to her, while Elsie watched him, smiling.

After a minute or two, he went back to the gate, and turned his attention back to the pit ponies. 'But I'm not sure it's not cruel to bring them up. They're half blind when they first come to the surface; the light really hurts their eyes, especially in summer. And then some of them'll scour badly with eating fresh grass, until they get used to it, and some of them cannot graze, they've forgotten how, so they have to be hand-fed. And they'll feel the cold up here, after being in a nice warm pit.'

'But it's natural for them to be outside. And their coats look quite thick.'

'Aye, they don't seem to moult much underground. They'll be all right, once they get acclimatized.'

'They do look well cared for.'

'So they should. They're worth money, Elsie. They're a lot better looked after than the men are. If a pony and a man were injured together, which do you think the manager would ask about first?'

'Well, I don't know. The man, I should hope.'

'He wouldn't, though. He'd say, "How's the pony?" And as long as the pony was all right, he might remember to ask about the man.'

John's little Galloway separated himself from the group, and came over to nuzzle him. 'He remembers me,' said John, rubbing his nose, 'from our putting days together. How are you, Chance, my bonny lad? Do you know, Elsie, this pony saved my life once.'

'How was that?'

'Well, you know what a putter is, Elsie. He has to get the coal away from the face in tubs, using the pony to haul. The putter has to work hard, or he gets wrong from the hewers, and so he has to work the pony just as hard. Well, Chance was dragging a couple of tubs when he straightened his front legs and leaned back to let the tubs run into him, like a brake, you know. I was cussing because I had plenty of work to do, but I couldn't get him to move, and a minute or two later, the roof came down in front of us. I sometimes think they've got a sixth sense.' He looked at her for a moment or two, and smiled. 'If Chance hadn't refused to go on, why, I wouldn't be here talking to the bonniest lass in the two villages.'

Completely unabashed, Elsie returned his smile, and watched him with Chance for a minute or two. 'You must have been kind to him.'

'I was. It was him that wasn't kind to me, many a time. I used to beg a bit of carrot, or bread, or sometimes an apple from my mother, and take it for him in my jacket pocket. But it wasn't long before he learned to take treats without waiting to be given them. I soon saw I had to be careful and put my jacket right out of the way, because he got my bait a time or two, and ate the lot. Chewed right through the paper, and I was left to starve. And then I would sometimes want to work a bit longer, to make a bit more money, like, but Chance must have had a built-in clock, because he struck work on the dot. He was like a good union man – wouldn't work a minute past his time.'

'Clever little Chance. I'll bring you a treat tomorrow.' She rubbed his nose in a thoughtful fashion. 'Have you heard anything from Arthur, yet?'

Well, she was bound to ask, he thought, and now the police had all but disappeared and the whole nation was out on strike to keep them busy elsewhere, he might as well tell her. 'Why, no, Elsie, we haven't. He went to sea. He might be back in a month or two, or it might be a year. It depends whether he takes to the life, and where he gets to. I liked it. He might not. But whichever way it goes, I don't think he's the sort to be doing a lot of writing.'

'No, I don't suppose he is.' She shook her head slowly, and put her foot in the stirrup to remount, while John held the mare steady.

'You know, I think we'll organize some pony races, to raise a bit of money for the strike fund. Would you be willing to help?' he asked, to avoid Arthur being their final topic of conversation more than anything else.

'How could I help?'

He shrugged. 'I don't know, yet. Maybe you could ask your dad to put some posters in his shops.'

67

She rolled her eyes and pressed her lips together in a smile, and gathered up the reins.

He laughed. 'Well, if you cannot do that, maybe you can come and watch, maybe place a bet.'

'All right. I will.' She nodded, and rode away.

'Poor Sandie, man, poor Sandie, poor old dog,' Sam kept repeating, as John lay the howling greyhound on the kitchen floor. 'It looks all shapes. He'll never run again. I reckon it means putting him down.'

John knew a vet would be out of the question. He looked dubiously at the dog's crooked front leg, then at the owner. He'd helped Sam Hickey get a job in the lamp room after a back injury had made him unfit for underground work. He'd taken his own injury like a stoic, but now he had tears in his eyes. His wife looked on.

'Why, it's not gone compound, so he might be all right. We needn't give up yet, man,' John encouraged, sounding more confident than he felt. 'The skin's not broken. We could try putting a splint on. Give him a fighting chance. You've got some logs outside. You could easily cut a couple of splints, then all we have to do is smooth 'em down and pad 'em and bandage 'em on.'

'I couldn't. I know nothing about setting legs.'

'Well, I only know what we've done in the first aid classes, but the principle must be the same, man or dog. You just get the bones straightened, then you put the splint on. Once you start pulling you keep pulling, and you don't leave go until you've got the splints bandaged on tight. We could manage that between the three of us.'

'It'll hurt him, though,' Sam moaned, wincing on the dog's behalf.

'Oh, aye, it will hurt him,' John agreed, 'but you know what they say, Sam. You've sometimes got to be cruel to be kind. He's hurting now, and it'll get no better unless we do something. The only alternative's to put him out of his misery, and soon, if that's what you want?'

That wasn't what Sam wanted, so John set man and wife to helping him prepare makeshift splints, padding and bandages, then with Sam holding the howling dog still, and his wife pulling on its leg to keep it straight, he did the job.

Afterwards, the animal lay absolutely still and whimpering on the floor. Sweating a little himself, John watched the brutish-looking master wipe beads of perspiration from his brow and tears from his eyes, and would have been hard put to say which was in the greatest distress, man or dog.

When he'd recovered himself, Sam said, 'Thanks for what you've done. Will you come round now and again, to keep an eye on him, like? See he's doing all right?'

Mrs Hickey was in the house alone when he called the following day to keep his promise. While John looked at the dog, she filled the kettle, chattering to her caged canary, encouraging it to sing. When she turned to face him, blue eyes intense and wispy blonde curls framing her pink face, the top buttons of her blouse were undone.

'He wi' not sing,' she said, nodding towards the canary. 'He must know you're one of the buggers who take his relations down the pit to gas 'em.'

'Would you rather we gassed the men?' he asked, patting the dog's head. 'Sandie's no worse, anyway.'

She turned towards him and smiled, and he noticed that one of her corner teeth was a bit crooked. 'Sam said if he missed you, to thank you for everything you've done. Lucky you've done a few first aid classes, eh?'

'Aye, well, if we don't look after ourselves nobody else will; so we might as well learn as much as we can, whenever we get the chance.'

'Some haven't got the stomach for it, though. I know Sam wouldn't, he's too soft. He said to give you a cup of tea before you go.'

'If you're sure you can spare it?' John said. He had nothing pressing to do.

She nodded. 'Aye. The Co-op's letting people have credit to get what they want. I think they're frightened if they don't, we'll just go in and bloody take the stuff. Go and sit in the front room. It's tidier in there.'

He sat on a hard-backed dining chair and surveyed the

room, noting the heavy net curtains at the window, and the photograph of Sam in more prosperous days, receiving the cup at the pigeon fanciers' association. At last, Irene brought in the tea and leaned across him to place it on the table just beyond him, almost touching his face with her breasts. He caught a whiff of lavender water, and a couple more of her buttons seemed to have loosed themselves.

'Oh, pardon me.' He leaned far back in his chair.

'He'll not be back for hours,' she soothed, pressing nearer. 'He's gone to the pigeon fanciers, and he's always hours. Hours. And the old woman next door's as deaf as a post.'

She sighed, and pressed her ample bosom against him, then took his hand and put it inside her blouse. The soft fullness of her breast more than filled his hand. He smelled her scent and realized with a shock she had no corset on.

'Why, this is not right,' he protested. 'What about Sam?'

The dog looked at them from the kitchen with its mournful black eyes. She took John's hands and drew him away from its gaze towards the couch where she sat with her skirts lifted and her bare knees separated. 'I need something Sam's not been able to give us since he hurt his back,' she murmured, 'and it's a fair swap, for a cup of tea.'

Again, he protested. 'All the same, it's not right. It's not right.'

He kept on protesting. But neither he nor Irene Hickey could detect a shred of conviction in his voice.

'You know, Mother, people can get sick of porridge, and soup, and bread. I am. I'm sick of it. Can we not have something different?' Lizzie's voice had that aggrieved and plaintive quality that never failed to grate on John's nerves.

'You have had something different. You've had pan haggerty. You can only have what I can afford.'

'Well, I work all week. I'm working fifty hours a week, and I'm paying my share. I need some decent food.'

John snapped his newspaper shut. 'Leave me mother alone. You get decent food.' He knew what she was driving at. Lizzie was the only one bringing much money into the house, and she wanted to rub their noses in the fact. Next would come the question about why Sally couldn't get a place, and then how much was John getting in strike pay, and why couldn't he draw out more out of his savings to tide them over.

'Bread and soup, bread and marg, bread and dripping, bread and plum jam. And why is it always plum jam? Always plum, never anything for a change,' Lizzie went on. 'I would like some meat. We've had no meat for days.'

'Aye, well, think yourself lucky. Some people have had no meat for weeks. Some people get nothing but what the soup kitchens give them,' her mother said.

'But they're not working, are they?'

John cut in, 'Have you finished making those purse nets, Sal?' Sally nodded.

'Aye, well, the days are getting longer, and as we all know, I'm not working fifty hours a week, so I'll get out after tea and see what I can catch.'

He got out of the house immediately, and into the back garden to see to the ferrets – before Lizzie had the chance to ask why it had to be rabbits, and why they couldn't have some decent butcher's meat. If she started on that, he'd feel like slapping her.

The sun was sinking below the western horizon and setting the sky on fire as he left the house with Sally's purse nets in his pocket.

'Be careful, son. Don't get caught,' his mother warned, and he smiled. The admonition was never 'don't do it', – it was just 'don't get caught'. This good-living chapel woman thought like many another; that the Lord had filled the woods and fields with game to feed anybody who needed a meal, regardless of who owned the land. He went without the ferrets, and walked towards the farmland. The rabbits would all be producing young now, and it was not a time he liked to take them. Harvest time was better, you could get three-quarter-grown young ones then, and fully grown young ones by autumn. And they were beautiful. His mouth watered as he thought of his mother's fried rabbit, roast rabbit and rabbit pies, dished up with swede or carrots, and lovely fluffy dumplings. But at this time of year, he would have left the rabbits alone, had it not been for Lizzie's complaints.

71

Old Walter never minded a man catching a rabbit or two, or even a hare, to feed a hungry family, but the result of that was that there were very few rabbits to be caught on Walter's land. The Farrs' dealings with their poorer neighbours were less tolerant, so their farm would produce a richer yield. John debated with himself which way to turn – whether to go for an almost certain catch and run the risk of arrest and an appearance in court, or to set his nets in a place where he was almost sure to find them empty. After a few moments' indecision, he walked past Walter's land, and onto the Farrs'. He would peg the nets over the holes, and then beat it home, and come back at dawn to claim his catch before anyone else was out of bed. He would sort the rabbits out and release any pregnant or milky doe, and just take the bucks.

The task completed, he was walking back along by a hedge bordering a ploughed field, when he spotted a hare in the moonlight, crouching in one of the furrows. With a light wind blowing his scent away from the animal's sensitive nose, and knowing that anything directly in front of it would not be seen clearly, John hunkered down by the hedge at the end of the same furrow and applied the back of his hand to his pursed lips. The noise he emitted alerted the hare, which, ears back, then bounded like an arrow straight along the furrow, towards the sound of a distressed doe in the clutches of a jack, to do battle for her and gain her for himself.

Instead, he gained a speedy death, and John was almost back on Walter's land with his prize when he saw the gamekeeper and his bullmastiff coming over the fields towards him, and Elsie Hartley riding along the road from the other direction.

He was the quarry now, but if he made a dash for it, the gamekeeper would unleash the dog, and the agonizing thought of Elsie seeing him either in full flight or brought down by the dog paralysed him for a moment. A tawny owl derided him with a mocking tu-whoo, tu-whoo, what to do? What to do? He squared his shoulders, and sauntered towards Elsie, concealing the hare as best he could.

She was by his side long before the keeper, placing her mare between him and the keeper's line of vision. 'I saw you take it, John, and I think he did too,' she whispered. 'Give it to me, and I'll wait for you outside the Cock.' He gave a little laugh of relief as he handed her his catch, and with a wave to the keeper and a civil 'Good night, George,' she rode calmly away.

George's manner to John was vastly different to that shown to Elsie. 'I saw you take something on Mr Farr's land, you thieving collier. Let's see what you've got.'

'I've got nothing.'

The keeper was having none of it. 'Lift your arms up. Let's see your hands.'

With the dog sitting guarding him, John had little alternative. He spread his arms and revealed his empty hands.

'All right. Now open your jacket. You'll have some nice big pockets inside there, I've no doubt.'

With an expression of patient resignation, John did as he was told, and the keeper plunged his hands into his pockets. He snatched them out again in short order, with a look of fury on his face.

'Ouch, you bugger!'

'Why, what's the matter, man?' asked John.

'You've got your pockets full of nettles, you bugger.'

'Oh, yes,' said John, as if only just remembering the fact. 'Why, I'd forgotten all about them. I was out gathering them for my mother. She wants 'em for soup.'

'You're a hunter, too.' Elsie was waiting in the yard at the Cock, and the murmur of her voice made his pulse quicken.

He took the proffered hare from her and laughed. 'The only difference is that I hunt on my own two feet, and I eat what I kill. I don't know whether I dare go back to the nets tomorrow morning, though. Thanks, Elsie. Will you come inside? Our Ginny'll have a nice cup of tea for you.'

'No, thank you,' she turned to go, and then looked back. 'That was funny, though, John, wasn't it? I wish I could have seen his face when he couldn't find the hare.'

'I wish you could have seen his face when he found the nettles I had in my pockets. I wouldn't like you to have heard the language, though.'

Her laughter rang out on the night air like a peal of silver bells.

He grinned. 'Thanks, Elsie. I never thought in my wildest dreams you would do anything like that for me. You saved my bacon.'

'No. I saved your hare,' she laughed. 'But, John, I never realised you had wild dreams. I never would have guessed it to look at you. And I'm in them, am I?' Her face became mock-serious, her eyebrows arched enquiringly.

'Why, of course I have Wilde dreams, Elsie. I am a Wilde. But you're only in the wildest,' he grinned.

She burst into another peal of laughter, and he joined in. And, he thought, now you'll ruin it all by asking me about Arthur. But she bade him goodnight with never a mention of Arthur.

Such relief flooded over him as he carried the hare into the Cock. What relief. An appearance in court with all Farr's friends on the bench, judging his cause in his favour, secure in the knowledge that he would do the same for them should the need arise, would probably have got John transported – or as near to it as they could manage these days. He could hardly get over it, the way she'd rescued him. It had been grand of her, really grand. It just about took his breath away. And better still, they'd shared a joke together.

He went home in a jaunty mood. Half the thrill of poaching was putting one over on the landowner, redressing the balance in favour of the little man, even if only by a tiny fraction, and they'd done that tonight, he and Elsie. And she liked him, otherwise why would she have ridden to his rescue? But his pleasure was alloyed with a niggling feeling of dissatisfaction. Because it would have been so much better if it had been the other way about. He should have been the one playing the hero and doing the rescuing, and Elsie should have been the damsel in distress.

Six

Annsdale
Pit Pony Races
For the Benefit of the Distress Fund
Saturday 23 March
to be held in the big field between Annsdale Colliery and
Durham Road.
Races start at 2 p.m.
**The Colliery Band will play a selection in the field, and also
parade down the principal streets of Annsdale Colliery.**
Prizes donated by local gentlemen
Programmes 1d each.

The signs were displayed in school, club and chapel, and in
the Co-op and every other shop sympathetic to the miners,
and John went down to the Cock on Saturday morning to post
a couple up there.

Maudie Goodliffe was usually among the first to arrive in
the mornings to dish out the breakfasts, and was often the last
to leave, after all the clearing away and washing-up was done.
At weekends she brought her boy with her. This Saturday she
was late and alone.

'The kids came yesterday and told me Mr Woolfe had got
hold of Harry, and taken him to his house.' Maudie stood in
the Cock in front of a vat of porridge, brown hair uncombed
and dark circles under her eyes; her pale, broad-featured face
was a mixture of woe and fury. 'So I went up there with my
sister, and we banged on the door till he answered. When he
finally came, he said the bairns had been following him,
bashing tin cans, and Harry had chucked a stone at him that
hit him on the head, and he wasn't going to stand for it. He

75

wouldn't let Harry out, said he was going to hand him over to the police. I was that mad, I smacked his face, and he shut the door on me. So we started battering on it, and then throwing stones at the windows, but he still wouldn't answer. In the end we kicked the bloody door in, and I went and got my bairn.'

'Well, you've got him back then, Maudie, so that's all right,' Ginny soothed. 'Come on, lass, shape up, they're waiting,' she nodded towards the waiting queue of pitmen and their families.

'It's not all right,' Maudie wailed, wiping a tear away with the corner of her apron, 'because the bobbies came and I'm up in court next week for assault and damage to property. He says I've done ten bob's worth of damage to his door. If they fine me, I cannot pay it. And I cannot go to jail, there's nobody to look after Harry.'

Harry's father was dead, and it was no secret in the village that Maudie favoured her boy over her new husband. The lad was set to run wild, but she wouldn't let Ned, his stepfather, touch him.

'Why, your man can look after him while he's on strike,' John said, 'and a bit of discipline'll do him a power of good.'

Maudie turned her back to him. 'I sometimes wonder whose bloody side you're on,' she muttered.

Ginny gave her a sharp glance. 'That's enough of that, Maudie; he doesn't deserve it. John's on our side, or he wouldn't be here. The only difference is, he's got more sense than most, and he'll tell you the truth. And if I were you, I'd take his advice about that lad of yours, it'll be easier on you both in the long run.'

From no one but Ginny would Maudie have taken it, but 'Sorry, John,' she said, and not too sullenly.

Ginny nodded. 'All right, then. The cycling club's throwing a fancy-dress party here the week after the pony races, to raise a bit more for the distress fund, like. Come and give us a hand. It'll be a bit extra for you, and that never comes in wrong.'

*   *   *

76

The coalhouses were nearly empty, both in his mother's cottage and at the Cock, so John was glad when Sally offered to go with Emma and a few others to pick coal from the stacks. Elsie had already seen him take a hare and nearly get taken himself, and he wouldn't have liked her to see him grubbing for bits of coal, or carrying it home. Sally set off with a sack. He was hard at work in the garden when she returned, hours later, without it.

'Mr Woolfe's set a watchman on, and we had to run when he saw us. I'd picked a good bit of coal, and it took me ages, but it was too heavy to run with, so I had to leave it. That watchman tipped it all back over the stacks, and he pinched the bag an' all. I'm frozen to the bone, and it's all been for nothing.'

Her face was full of woe. 'I'm sorry, hinny,' said John, 'but the coal's nearly all gone. One of us will have to go back and try again.'

'I'll go, John, but not today. Somebody said the other watchman's not so keen. If he sees you he just waits till you've done, but he doesn't interfere with your bags, so you just go back and carry on with filling them. I'll have to make sure it's him and not the other one next time.'

John took his two eldest nephews by the hand. 'Come and we'll see if the pony drivers will give you a ride before the races start.' The five-year-old hung back a bit, but the four-year-old was dragging John forward, eager for the experience. 'Hold, hold on a bit,' John laughed. 'You'll pull me in two.'

The youngest looked up and laughed. 'Away, Uncle John, hurry up!'

One of the young pony drivers hoisted him up, and, excited and laughing, he looked down at his brother. 'Away, Jem, let's have a race.' Jem tightened his grip on John's hand, and shrinking behind him a little, shook his head.

'Come on, man. It's fun. You'll like it once you get on,' said another pony driver, attempting to grab the child.

'Aye, maybe's a bit later,' John told him. 'But he's going to stop here and keep me company for a bit, aren't you, Jem?' The child nodded, with evident relief.

His place was soon taken by Maudie's lad, Harry, running forward as fast as his legs would carry him. 'Can I have a go, mister? Can I have a go?' Soon all the kids in Annsdale Colliery and many from surrounding villages were thronging round, begging a ride, turning their wide eyes up to the pony drivers, and treating them as if they were gods. Soon every pony had a burden, and the children who'd been unlucky waited at the starting post hoping for their turn.

'Shall we go and find your mammy, then?' John asked.

Jem shook his head. 'No, I want a ride.'

John saw Emma come walking across the field to join them, slowly at first, then briskly, in time to a catchy tune coming from the musicians on a fairly creditable bandstand made of timber borrowed from the pit, and chairs borrowed from people's houses. Jem stuck his fingers in his ears.

'What's the matter, do you not like the music?' Emma laughed. 'I'll wait with him if you've got things to do, John.'

'Aye, all right. We'll be starting the races in a few minutes, and I'm the one that's got to start them. Somebody else is on the finishing line. Jem's just got time to get a bit ride, if he hasn't changed his mind again.' John turned to go, when he saw the Annsdale Colliery's schoolmistress advancing on them, slightly breathless, but smart and neat, and not one of her grey hairs out of place.

After the exchange of pleasantries, Emma asked her, 'Are you all right, Miss Carr? Only you look a bit whammy, like.'

'I haven't been well lately, Emma. I'm getting too old, and too slow, and I'll probably retire at the end of the year. I'm only sorry I'm not handing the school over to you. You were the best little scholar I ever had, or ever will have now.'

Emma blushed at the compliment. 'Aye, well, that's what I would have liked at one time, only I got something else instead.' Glowing with maternal pride, she glanced down at Jem, and across at her second child, Tommy, just being lifted down from the pony so that Jem could take his place. 'And I cannot say I'm sorry.'

'You've got a hard life, though, Emma. Not much money and now even driven out of your home.'

'Aye, it's bonny hard lines on everybody. Still, I've got

'plenty of love,' said Emma, and the flush on her cheeks deepened as she looked at the aging and solitary schoolteacher.

'I know, I know,' Miss Carr squeezed her arm. 'I wish you everything that's good, Emma, and all your family. You too, John.'

'And you, Miss Carr. You were always good to me,' said Emma.

John dropped the flag, and the ponies and their riders were off down the field, some with saddles, some without, one lad dressed in a jockey's riding clothes, and God only knew where he'd managed to get them, and another one done up like something out of the American Wild West. Some were laughing, others grim faced, but before they were halfway to the finishing post two of the jockeys were off. He caught sight of Elsie with her two sisters on either side of her, further down the track. With wings on his heels he sped towards her, and she greeted him with a laugh.

'I couldn't see anywhere to place my bet, John.'

'No. If anybody's making a book, they're doing it well out of sight. But I never really thought you'd come, Elsie, let alone bring your sisters. I hoped you would, though.'

'We're here as peace envoys, I think. Mother and Father couldn't come themselves. But you'll have the prize they sent for one of the pony races.'

'That was very kind of them, and I'm sure it's appreciated,' said John, his face very grave. 'I'll have to get back. We've got six races, and the next one will be starting soon.' It was on the tip of his tongue to suggest that the younger girls join in the sack races or three-legged races being held for the youngsters further down the field in the intervals between the pony races, but the looks on their faces persuaded him that such antics among the colliers' children might be a long way beneath the dignity of the younger Miss Hartleys. Instead, he said, 'Have a look at the stall the Women's Co-operative Guild have got over there. My mother's on that, and they've got some lovely stuff for sale, jams and pickled onions and cakes and biscuits and things. You might see something you'd like. And the Chapel Gardening Club are selling pots of bulbs and geranium cuttings, bedding plants and that kind of thing. You could get your ma a nice bowl of crocuses. Or if you want a peep into the future, we've got an old gypsy woman telling fortunes with a crystal ball, over there, in that tent.'

Elsie laughed. 'You make a good salesman.'

'Only if I can guarantee what's on sale, not otherwise. And it's all in a good cause,' he smiled. But his talent for selling was not as great as Elsie claimed, because as he turned to go he heard the middle sister say, 'We'll go and get our fortunes told, and then let's go home. We've shown our faces, like Father said. I'm sure he doesn't expect us to stay here until it finishes.'

His next chance to spend a few minutes with her came when the younger girls went into Martha the Gypsy's tent, leaving Elsie sitting on a bench outside. She looked up as he approached.

'Maybe it's just as well you couldn't place your bet. It looks as if Chance has slowed down a bit. You'd have lost your money.'

She shrugged, and then gave him a sly smile. 'Did you go back for your rabbits?'

'Shush,' he whispered, 'do not mention that. Walls have ears, especially canvas ones. But yes, I did. I was up and out and at the nets before the crack of dawn, and I had a couple of jacks gutted and back in me mother's kitchen before the gamekeeper was out of bed.'

She laughed, and he murmured, 'Thanks again for coming to my rescue. I hope I may do the same for you some day.'

'I hope I'm never in such danger that you have to.' She shivered. 'I'm glad you've got such a fine day for your races, but how cold it is.'

Cuddle up to me, he thought, but taking off his jacket, he said, 'I don't feel it myself, but the year's on the turn, and it'll soon be getting warmer. It's Easter in a couple of weeks.'

'It's cold now, though,' she said, but she shook her head when he proffered the jacket.

He put it on his knee. 'Aye, I suppose it is. That's why we organized some races for the kids and we've got a tug o' war for the men soon. We didn't think the ladies would want to race, so they have to stand about and get cold.' He stood up and offered her his hand. 'Come and we'll have a brisk walk round. It'll warm you up a bit.'

Elsie nodded, and rose to her feet, then sat down again. 'Oh,' she said, 'I felt a bit dizzy. I've had no breakfast, or lunch, either.'

'You're not one of these lasses that starves hersel' to death to get an eighteen-inch waist, are you? Yours cannot be much more than that now.'

She shook her head and took his hand to be helped up, refusing again his offer of the jacket. He slipped it on and gave her his arm.

'I don't suppose you've heard from Arthur,' she murmured, tucking her little hand into the crook of his elbow.

'No, and I don't suppose you have, either,' he said. 'The wind's blown our Arthur away, and he might never come back.' He licked a finger and held it up to the breeze. 'And the wind's just changed an' all, and maybe my luck'll change with it. Come for a walk with me, Elsie. I'm the one that's here beside you.'

She smiled, and he put his free hand on top of the one resting on his arm for a moment.

'There's the rector and his wife,' said John, nodding towards them. 'It's not often they make an appearance among the pitmen.'

It was Elsie who voiced surprise when they got near enough to speak to the rector and his lady. He looked round at the miners and their families. 'They are my parishioners, after all, even if only nominally. And they look a thriving, well-turned-out set of people, I must say. I hope they'll return to work before they've destroyed the country altogether.'

'Why, there's two sides to that question, like,' said John, 'and more than one party to any dispute.' He could have said that the clean and tidy surface appearance of the mining people who had dressed as well as they could for the day was an indication of pride, and not of prosperity. It masked a lot of poverty and privation that they chose to keep hidden.

It would have been futile to say anything, for the rector

appeared to think it beneath his dignity to enter into any discussion with John, and with a supercilious 'Oh, indeed?' he turned his enquiring gaze on Elsie.

She flushed a little. 'These people are my father's customers, and he says we must show them our support. I'm here with my sisters. My father gave a prize for one of the pony races. This is John Wilde. He organized it all. He's one of our neighbours in Old Annsdale.'

'Ah, yes, I believe I once saw you speaking to him after the hunt.' The rector looked down his nose at John. 'You're employed by the colliery company, I take it. I don't remember seeing you in church, young man.'

'It's not likely you would. I don't go,' said John.

'You attend one of the Wesleyan chapels, I dare say.'

'They don't see much of me there, either.'

The rector tut-tutted, and with a shake of his head, turned to go.

'Will Rupert be home for Easter?' Elsie suddenly asked. 'Or is he staying in Oxford?'

'He may be home. Or he may stay with friends,' the rector's wife replied.

'I would have thought he'd want to be here for the hunting.'

'Oh,' the rector smiled, tipping his hat, 'I've no doubt he'll be hunting, wherever he is. We'll say goodbye. Must get on. See you in church, Elsie.'

At the rector's departure the colour drained from Elsie's face. John looked into her deep, dark brown eyes and said, 'The roses have gone from your cheeks. I hope you haven't got what Miss Carr's got. She was saying she didn't feel well earlier on. Are you hungry?'

'Yes, a bit.'

'Why, let's take you to the tea tent. You'll be sheltered from the wind in there, and you can sit down. I'll get you a cup of tea and a bun, and Maudie or our Emma'll look after you till I get this next race started.'

'But wasn't it Maudie and Emma who threatened my father?'

He paused. 'Aye, I suppose it was, but your father's given us a peace offering since then, and we've accepted it, so it'll be all right. They will look after you.'

'No,' she said. 'Thank you, John, but I think I'll find my sisters, and go home with them.'

It was now or never. She would be off soon, and he couldn't miss his opportunity, so he held onto the hand linked in his for a few moments, while he had the chance. He knew Elsie's father wouldn't want her to be making any arrangements to see any pitmen, but people don't always do what their fathers want them to do. John would never have gone to sea if he'd done what his father wanted, and Elsie had already gone against her father's wishes in going out with Arthur. So nothing venture, nothing win. 'Elsie.' He hesitated. 'Will you let me take you for a walk? Tomorrow, maybe, or next Sunday?'

After the races, John threw himself with gusto into the tug o' war, elated at the prospect of his promised outing with Elsie. Different sets of marrers and officials, shopkeepers and even police grouped themselves at either end of the rope, with John and a couple of overmen acting as arbiters to ensure that the numbers were roughly even on both sides before joining the lines themselves. John took up a position to the fore on one side of the rope and, to his amazement, the rector suddenly threw his weight and muscle in on the other side, gripping onto the rope, digging his heels into the turf and, jaw clenched, heaving with all his might. The more dogged determination and aggression he displayed, the more tenacious and unyielding John became, and the heaving and pulling went on for several minutes until, inch by inch, John's side won the day, to his unbounded satisfaction. He held out his hand to the rector, and after a couple of seconds' hesitation the older man grasped it.

The bandsmen struck up 'The Blaydon Races' and marched round the field with some of the young girls skipping and dancing in front and one old fellow a bit the worse for drink among them, his face wreathed in smiles and arms raised, prancing and skipping and twirling with the best of them. Maudie's lad and some bigger boys tagged along at the rear. Safely out of the sight of the musicians, they began mimicking their marching and playing, thumbing their noses and making a mockery of them for devilment and the amusement of the onlookers. Harry passed by, aping the bandsmen's smart step and playing his imaginary trumpet in the most farcical way possible. John caught the little beggar's impish eye, and gave him a warning frown. Undeterred, Harry marched mischievously on. The rest of the crowd fell in and followed the band, shouting, singing and cheering, walking to the rhythm of the music, out of the gate and away, towards homes, clubs and pubs.

Ginny and Martin had already gone to open up, and Emma and Jimmy took the children back to the Cock. John, Sally and Lizzie, with their mother and the usual corps of volunteers were left to take down the tents and stalls, and carry them back. When everything had been put away or left ready for collection, they went through to the taproom and sat down at tables set out with plates of bread and cheese. Ginny and Emma were ready with large jugs of soup and began to pour it into an assortment of mugs and bowls.

The laughter and chatter and argument about who did well in the races and competitions and who could have done a lot better was soon replaced by the gentle clink of spoons against bowls, and the sipping of soup, with an occasional request for bread or salt or cheese, as a room full of hungry people fell to and ate. All was quiet until the air was rent by a series of noisy explosions, like rapid gunfire.

Everybody looked up, and all eyes fell on Harry. Stunned that such a rattle could come from so small a child, for a moment nobody spoke. Emma's laughter broke the silence.

'What a little rasper! I've never heard anything like it.'

Maudie cuffed Harry lightly round the ear. 'You dirty little bugger!'

He looked her straight in the eye, and protested loudly, 'You and Ned do it, worse ones than mine an' all. And then you say, "It's all this bloody pea soup. It makes everybody fart all the time." So what for are you blaming me, like?'

Never was an animal more assiduously cared for. John had found himself calling round to see to Sam Hickey's dog at least four or five times a week, usually when Sam was at the pigeon fanciers or the whippet racers' meeting. Irene Hickey was a well-built, warm and sensuous woman, generous in every way, and a good thirteen years his senior. He had been tense at the outset of their guilty liaison, on the alert for dreaded signs of possessiveness or love. Relief was mingled with a pang of disappointment when he realized he was in no danger. She wanted the act, not John himself, and had not lost the habit of loving her husband. John sometimes wondered if Sam realized what was going on, thought he must know, and guessed that he chose to turn a blind eye. He surmised that life with a placid woman whose temper had been sweetened by a lover might be preferable to life with a shrew, and soothed his conscience with that thought. 'You mind that song our Ginny sometimes sings, Irene?' he once asked her. '"If You Talk in Your Sleep, Don't Mention My Name".'

At their first couplings she'd been shameless, not willing to feign a climax to preserve a young man's pride, but selfish, and determined he should make her satisfaction real. 'No, there, just there,' she would say with an impatient gleam in her eyes. 'Not like that, like this,' and place his fingers on the most intimate parts of her ample flesh to demonstrate with utter concentration. Initially, he'd felt guilty and awkward as he'd fumbled with her, blushing in shame for her more than for himself. He was glad of her self-centredness in the end, for he was fast becoming an accomplished lover, knew where and how to touch to bring her into readiness. Usually she was melting moist in anticipation of him, but he had learned that teasing her a little, making her wait, increased her eagerness. He learned to master himself, to take her unbearably slowly, to make her frantic with desire then to enter her fully and keep her on the very edge of that rapture she sought from him for an agonizing age, watching the flush of her cheeks and neck, her erect nipples and her languorous eyes, listening as her breathing slowed and deepened then hearing her moans, glorying in his erotic power, his maleness, his complete masculine control of her. Quite deliberately he would choose the moment to bring her to her climax and then watch her paroxysms of pleasure with a forced detachment.

A second later he would withdraw, thoughts of Elsie flashing unbidden into his mind as release came in a euphoric surge.

Seven

H e couldn't quite put his finger on what it was that was so different about Elsie, but there was something. A sort of nervous gaiety seemed to have replaced her usual confident bounce and she kept looking at him expectantly, he supposed wondering if he were going to give her news of Arthur.

'I'm sorry,' John said. 'We haven't heard from him, if that's what you're wondering.'

Elsie shrugged. 'I suppose if he cared, he would write, and if he wanted to come back, he would.'

He wasn't going to contradict her, so said nothing, and they resumed their walk through Annsdale woods, following the course of the beck until John nodded towards a fallen tree. They sat down for a moment on the massive trunk and stared towards the water. 'Ooo-look, ooo-look,' a stock dove's call from a nest in a nearby tree hole filled the silence.

He pondered, and then decided that if Elsie wanted to talk about Arthur, then they would talk about him; and talk about him, and talk about him, until she got him right out of her system.

'What is it about our Arthur you like so much, Elsie? It's obvious your dad doesn't want you to have anything to do with him.'

'Oh, my dad. He doesn't want us to have anything to do with any of the mining people. He says they're a lot of underground savages.'

'Why do you then? Have anything to do with us, I mean.'

'I don't know.' She shrugged again, then thought for a moment. 'Yes, I do know. You remember when the disaster happened. Well, how could anybody forget it? I was about eleven then, not much younger than some of the boys who were killed. I cried for months, to see everybody else crying, and all those funerals, and so much grief, and the thought of all those poor trapped, burned boys. My dad said I was silly to take on like that. "It's a shame for them, but they brought it on themselves for disobeying orders and doing things they shouldn't have done, and anyway, they don't feel things the same way we would feel them, because they're a hardened sort of people." That's what he said.'

A profound dislike rose in John against Hartley for his ignorant, callous presumption, and his foul opinions. He made no comment, but watched Elsie's profile closely, and listened in silence.

'Anyway, I thought that however hardened they were, any people must feel pain if they were burned to death, and even the farmers' cows grieve for their calves when they're taken away, you know. So I knew those mothers must be grieving for their boys, and for a long time it seemed to take a hold of my mind. But gradually, everybody talked about it less, and thought about it less, and I forgot about it, until they put the Monument up on the hill, on the Durham Road.'

'The angel, taking flight to heaven with a dead miner in his arms.'

'Yes. I couldn't pass it without the tears coming to my eyes. Because I thought that however much some people despise them, God and the angels love the miners. It used to make me weep, but I was young then, you know.'

John smiled, and took hold of her hand. 'And you're getting old now,' he said. 'But you still haven't told me why you like our Arthur.'

A shaft of sunlight penetrated the trees and fell on the heart-shaped face she turned towards him, illuminating skin as smooth and flawless as a rose petal. It was with a pang that he saw tears standing now in those bitter-chocolate eyes.

'Why, because he looks so exactly like the young miner in the angel's arms, of course,' she said.

So that was it. Arthur was about the same age as some of the lads who'd been killed, and Elsie's romantic young girl's imagination had seen a likeness between him and a victim wrought in marble.

'But our Arthur's not the lad in the statue, Elsie. And he's no angel, either.'

She turned her face away from him. 'Oh, I know that now. I know that now,' she said.

There was a roaring fire in the grate at the Cock that night. 'Were you up at the stacks again, like?' he asked Emma, knowing it was not likely on a Sunday. With a glance towards Maudie, Emma shook her head and pressed her fingers to her lips. Maudie grinned, and crooked her finger at him. He craned forward.

'No,' she whispered. 'We were up at Woolfe's coalhouse with barrows last night, while they were all out for the evening visiting their fancy friends. We made quite a few journeys. Me mam's got enough coal to last two or three months now, and Ginny's got enough for a week or two. He's had me up in court and they've fined me, so it's up to me to get it all back the best way I can, and I'll get the full value from him before I've finished. Tit for tat, that's what I say. Look after the people who look after you.'

It was Monday. Lizzie was at work, and his mother and Sally were in the front room, busy quilting. With no work to go to himself, John soaked in peace for a full quarter of an hour in a hot bath before the kitchen fire, his mind bathed in pleasurable anticipation of his forthcoming meeting with Elsie. Then, with the water cooling rapidly, he started a vigorous scrubbing of his skin, paying particular attention to armpits, feet and nether parts. When satisfied he was as clean as any whistle, he grabbed the warm towel his mother had left before the fire for him, wrapped himself in it and got out, to sharpen his razor on the leather strop hanging by the sink. Scalding water from the kettle in his shaving mug, he lathered his face and gave himself the closest shave he had ever had in his life, until his chin was as smooth as a baby's bottom, just in case she gave him a kiss. The mere thought that it might happen thrilled him, and he smiled. Shave completed, he combed his hair carefully, seeing the nondescript brown of it, and frowning as he compared it to Arthur's thick, black curls. One lock wouldn't stay back, would keep dropping over his forehead, and he combed it back a dozen times, cursing in exasperation. Couldn't be helped, he'd have to be off, and he set out with a mixture of excitement, apprehension and sheer joy bubbling inside him.

He walked under greening branches, and his spirits soared at the sight of stark winter in full flight before spring. His eye was suddenly taken by a couple of hares, chasing across a field. They turned to face each other and started a mad sparring, a play-boxing, landing blows on each other, and only half in fun. Then one turned and leapt at his opponent, dealing him a vicious kick in the ribs, swift and unexpected. The other fell back, winded, and then rallied. Savage retaliation followed, and the pair pranced and kicked at each other in an earnest, bruising combat. At last one of them yielded and slunk away, half crippled, to take cover under the hedge. It seemed cruel, was cruel, but it was nature's way of weeding out the weak. There was doubtless some fair lady hare at the root of it, and faint heart wouldn't win her. John smiled a close-mouthed, secret smile. It was much the same when men competed for a darling, nature favoured strength in both intellect and physique. He passed a pond, not much bigger than a puddle, and it was plain to see that Froggy had been a-wooing; the pond was full of frogspawn. It seemed as if the whole world was wide awake, and mad with lust.

He got to the trysting place ten minutes before time. Naturally she wasn't there. He would have been upset if she had been. He looked at the watch he'd inherited from his father. He could expect her to be at least another twenty minutes or half an hour. It was a bonny day and fairly mild, so he sat on that fallen tree in Annsdale wood and waited. The woodland smelled of spring. The cooing and chirruping of nesting birds sounded sweeter than ever, and the beauty of the Lenten lilies gladdened his eye. The woods were full of the wonder of new life, but the prospect of seeing and touching Elsie was the most magical of all.

He looked at his watch. She was an hour late, and he was

beginning to feel chilled. He went back to the footpath and walked briskly up and down. He could set off and walk in the direction of her home, he'd probably bump into her on the way. No, he wouldn't do that, there was her father, and if anyone saw her meeting him it might cause trouble for her. There was nothing to do but wait. He went back to the fallen tree.

In a state of agitation, imagining every ill that could befall her or his suit with her, he waited for three hours, and then went home, searching the darkening landscape for her all the way, wondering what the matter was. Maybe she'd been taken ill. Maybe her father found out she was coming to meet him, and stopped her, or had she just not been able to get away? Worst of all, she might have changed her mind about him. He refused to think about that possibility.

He thought about it all night, but it was Wednesday before he could see her to ask her why she hadn't been there to meet him. She looked awkward and embarrassed, but before they'd exchanged two sentences John saw the parson's son looming up towards them.

With one eye on Rupert, Elsie shrugged, and gave John a brittle smile. 'It was only an April Fool,' she said. 'I never meant you to take it seriously.'

'Why, it's a funny way to treat anybody, Elsie,' he reproached her. 'I waited for you in the cold for over three hours.'

Her laughter sounded shrill. 'It is funny. That's the point.'

'Well, when shall I see you again?' John asked, with a foolish smile. 'Shall I take you for a walk on Good Friday, or Easter Sunday, or some time when it's not the first of April?'

'I can't see you again,' she said, and the knuckles were white on the little hand that clutched her coat. 'It was only an April Fool. Can't you take a joke?' The look she gave John pierced him like a knife, and the smile died on his lips. Rupert was almost upon them now. Elsie gave a shrug that lacked her usual carelessness, and her step as she walked away from him seemed to have lost its buoyancy. Rupert followed close on her heels. Elsie turned to look at John and hesitated for a

90

moment, as if she might say something more, but instead she turned again and almost ran away. Rupert strode after her, but after they'd exchanged a couple of words, he stopped and walked back, passing John as though he were invisible.

It made no sense. He stared after her, thinking back to the night she'd saved him and his hare from the clutches of the gamekeeper, and her laughter at the trick they'd played on him. Now she was laughing about a trick she'd played on John, and his sense of indebtedness to her had made him stand there grinning like an idiot when he should have been angry with her for keeping him standing freezing in the woods for no good reason. It was hard to believe she could treat him like that, after such warmth, such friendliness. But Elsie had a reputation for breaking hearts, and now he saw how well she had earned it. She could add his to her trophies. She had a strange sense of humour, and he'd been her silly, idiotic, grinning fool.

And such a fool. Devastated, he went home, and picked up the paper. The *Titanic* had left Belfast Lough for Southampton and thence her maiden voyage to New York. She was a floating palace, the most magnificent ship ever built, surpassing the best of the French by a mile. How he wished he were aboard her, going anywhere, anywhere but here. To the bottom, preferably.

Women, he thought. Let them go. There's no making them out, except to say they're cruel, faithless and capricious.

Hurt brewed in him, and cooked itself into an unreasoning stew of rage and rancour. Why had she led him on? Why single him out with her smiles and her come-hither looks? Why go out of her way to speak to him so publicly, and so evidently against the wishes of her own set, as if he were a favoured suitor? Arthur was right, she was too much in love with herself to have any love left over for anybody else, least of all one of the pitman race. She had just been making game of him. And yet, and yet . . . he had seen something in her face after her mockery had knocked the bottom out of his world – something that was neither joy nor triumph.

He was trying to delude himself, trying to drive himself mad with hope, and he was too old for that. She'd made a bloody fool of him, and that was the end of it. What was she, anyway? Nothing but a vain, conceited little vixen who fed her vanity on the hearts of her admirers. He wasn't the first she'd rejected, and he doubted very much that he would be the last.

Well, he wasn't going to curl up in a hole and lick his wounds, like a jilted lover. He wanted a wife and he wanted children by her. If it wasn't to be Elsie, he hardly cared who, but he wanted a wholesome, flesh-and-blood wife, a woman with a woman's heart. 'And when I get her, I'll love her,' he muttered to himself. 'I'll make me mind up to it.' He would go to the fancy-dress party with Lizzie, step out like a man. He would take the world by the throat and squeeze whatever pleasure he could from it and in the end he might find a pleasure that would take his mind off Elsie. He wanted to sing. He wanted to dance. He wanted to have a woman who was not years older than him and married to somebody else. He wanted to live. Above all, he wanted to get blindingly, leglessly, disgustingly drunk.

Such members of the mining community who could be trusted not to alienate their middle-class supporters had been invited to join the party and the more was indeed proving the merrier. Unable to stand or sit still, John threw himself into heaving barrels of beer up from the cellar, and dragging the long trestle tables from under the stage of Ginny's function room, which served for concerts, dances, dining, whist drives and union meetings. After he'd put the tables up, he was tempted to put his masculine prestige at hazard by helping the women with the lading of them, with boiled hams, roast sirloins, cheeses, pickles of every variety, breads, cakes and beer. He managed to restrain himself, but wanted to be doing something. The Cock was buzzing with laughter and chat. He threw himself into the crack, talking and laughing more loudly than ever before in his life.

In an oddly vicious mood, he amused himself by watching Lizzie, who in turn was eyeing one of the members of the cycling club. Lizzie was a girl who put some value on herself, and fortune had certainly smiled on her. She'd sidestepped the usual fate of the miner's daughter, being sent out to a 'place', to slave in somebody else's house. Lizzie was a promising apprentice tailoress, making hunting clothes and other attire for the gentry. She was quick on the uptake and clever with her needle. She looked quite the young lady tonight, in a soft lawn blouse and a blue serge skirt of her own making. Lizzie would be careful whom she loved, and it wouldn't be one of her own, he knew that. It would be nobody who worked anywhere near a mine.

John recognized his opponent at cards of a few nights ago, and could see what it was about him that so attracted her. Tom Peters was a self-assured, good-looking young fellow with a roguish twinkle in his eyes and a pair of well-turned calves shown to advantage by the knee-breeches which comprised part of his fairly nondescript fancy dress. He looked sleek and well to do, as one who had never suffered so much as an hour's privation or a day's hard labour. Just the sort to interest Lizzie.

'He's quite a few cuts above the pitmen, Lizzie,' he whispered. 'He's an articled clerk, and his uncle's a solicitor in Durham. Or that's what he told me and our Jimmy at the whist drive. He might even be good enough for you. I'll introduce you if you like.'

'What are you being so sarcastic about? What's got into you tonight? You're going to leave us all to go to South Africa, so don't blame me for trying to better myself. I had enough of our Arthur sneering and making nasty comments, and thank God he's gone, so no need for you to start.' She gave him a fleeting, disparaging glance before tilting her chin in Tom's direction. 'You wouldn't blame a man for going for the best job he could get, and a husband is a woman's job, so why shouldn't she try for the best on offer? I'll be seventeen soon. It's time I was on the look-out, and I don't want to miss an opportunity. So yes, I would like to be introduced, John, and I don't care what you think about it. And don't you dare say anything to show me up, either.'

After the meal the girls cleared the tables. John set to with a will, stowing the tables back under the stage, then sprinkling grated candle wax on the smooth wooden floor in preparation for the dancing. Tom's fingers were already flying over the strings of his banjo, and Jimmy was trying to pick up the foot-tapping tune on the piano.

When all was done, John watched Lizzie turn towards the mirror at the back of the bar and raise her arms to rearrange the pins in her black curls, then run her eyes critically over her reflection. She had a strong resemblance to Ginny, and they were a pair of good-looking lasses, no doubt about it. Lizzie sucked in her stomach and tucked her blouse tight into the nipped-in waist of her blue serge skirt then pulled the skirt straight and turned a determined eye on her quarry. Introduction proved unnecessary. John watched in fascination when, as if drawn to her by telepathy, Tom laid aside his banjo and came forward to ask Lizzie for the first dance. She gave him a shy smile and demurely dropped her gaze, allowing him to lead her onto the floor. What an actress.

A comely girl in a Pierrot costume, with two black teardrops painted on the white cheeks beneath her green eyes, put a hand on John's arm and boldly claimed a dance from him. The Pierrot had a familiar dimple in her left cheek, and he recognized his most redoubtable opponent, Miss Votes-for-Women. At least the conversation would not be tedious.

'This is the first time any woman's ever asked me for a dance,' he grinned, taking her hand and circling an arm round her waist to give her a bold and rather familiar squeeze. He looked so closely into her green eyes that he noticed the tiny blue flecks in them, and her eyes laughed back into his.

She was roughly the same height as John. There was an air of immense energy about her, and they danced well together. After ten minutes or so, he nodded towards the piano. 'Hope you can play,' he said. 'I cannot, and our Jimmy's already merry. One whiff of the barman's apron's usually enough to lay him out. You probably realized that the other night.'

'I know. I drank him under the table,' she boasted.

He smiled. 'That wouldn't take a lot of doing.'

'We've been here a few times, you know,' Alice continued. 'On the tandem. The Cock's a good place to stop.'

'I know. There's not many women come in the Cock, unless Ginny's doing a concert or a whist drive. I thought the cycling club was just for men an' all.'

'Nothing's going to be just for men for much longer.'

'I shouldn't think you'd want to be the only woman. I wouldn't like to be in any club if I was the only man.'

Alice laughed. 'That's different. What could you join as the only man, except a quilting club, or a rug brodding club, or the union of dutiful mothers, and who'd want to join them? The only clubs worth being in are the ones that won't have women – yet – and Parliament's the biggest and the best of them. But we'll make them change their minds.' She laughed again and he laughed along with her, but he knew she wasn't joking.

'You're making war on us all. You know you're nothing but a lot of ugly old maids venting your bitterness on men, don't you?'

She stood back from him, a look of outrage on her face. 'What? What did you say?'

'Why, it's not me that says it, Miss Peters. It's everybody else. The medical profession reckon you're something worse. The doctors say that women are unbalanced, and prone to hysteria, like. Not right in their heads, in other words.' He gave a wicked grin, and took her in his arms again to resume the dance, but she wouldn't move.

'Who says so?' she demanded.

'Why, one Sir Almroth Wright, in a letter to *The Times* at the end of last month. I read it at the Institute. Have you not heard of him? He seems to know all there is to know about women, and he speaks for the rest of his profession. Here, I asked for the paper after they'd done with it and I kept the cutting, in case I ever bumped into you again.' He reached a hand into his jacket pocket, took out the paper and handed it to her.

Alice read, '"These upsettings of her mental equilibrium are the things that a woman has the most cause to fear; and no doctor can ever lose sight of the fact that the mind of a woman is always threatened with danger from the reverberations of her physiological emergencies."' She paused to take it in, and said nothing for a moment.

'And if that doesn't convince people that women should never have the vote, nothing will,' John goaded her.

Alice's eyes narrowed. 'It's the minds of the medical profession that are unbalanced. They're the ones who are certifiable. They presume to know everything about everybody and everything, but the majority of them are no better than quacks and witch doctors, gone mad with conceit and arrogance.'

The sight of her pursed-mouth anger was exactly the reaction he had hoped for. John threw back his head and laughed. 'That's probably because most of them are men, Miss Peters.'

She softened and smiled. 'We will win, in the end,' she assured him, 'but you've had your victory already. The Government's made sure you got your minimum wage.'

'Aye, if you can call it a victory, although we had a minimum in this area before the national strike. But, we made the Prime Minister cry, and the dispute's gone out like a damp squib. I wish the Government had stayed out of it, though. The federation might have done a lot better in the end. The underground workers didn't get their five and two. When they balloted us again a lot of us were for staying out, and I believe they would have got it if we had.'

'But they've got the minimum wage – a fair day's pay for a fair day's work. You've made history.'

'They wouldn't want the country at a standstill for very long. Too much money to lose, so they've given just enough to make sure that doesn't happen. But the unions still have to negotiate with the owners about what the minimum's going to be. So we're not as happy as we thought we'd be. Like I said, half the men were for staying out, the half of them that realize just how much power they've got if they stick together. They could have brought the country to its knees, man. They could have destroyed the Establishment. It's frightening. It scares me, and I'm one of them. It'll never happen again, though. The powers that be will learn from this, and make certain they never leave themselves so wide open again.'

He danced more with Alice than any other girl in the room, and the talk never stopped. Most other girls he'd met would neither have known nor cared who the Prime Minister was, and their conversation never ranged beyond family and neighbours, but Alice was a ferment of ideas, up with the times, interested in what was going on in the world, and not frightened to give her own opinion. She was a girl you could have a decent conversation with, but well out of his class.

An hour later Jimmy was playing more and more wrong notes and losing tempo, and the dancing became farcical. Alice caught Tom's eye, and together they went and lifted him off the piano stool, and deposited him on one of the upholstered benches that lined the walls. Alice sat at the piano and flexed her fingers, and Tom took up his banjo.

John stood at her shoulder as they began a fast-paced rendition of 'Alexander's Ragtime Band'. 'By, you had every foot in the place tapping there,' John told them, as a cheer went up at the end of the tune.

'We'll play one especially for you now,' Alice said, and threw herself into 'The Lads of Wear and Tyne'.

'I never thought you'd know that song, Miss Peters! he exclaimed.

She laughed up at him. 'Alice. Call me Alice. Who could live anywhere in the North East and not know that? We have an interesting history, my family. There's a lot you don't know about us. Tell you what, John. You get the beer in. Bet I can hold mine better than you can yours.'

'Another Cushie Butterfield.' He gave a wry smile and went to the bar. Normally, he would never have accepted the challenge, would never have encouraged any girl to make a spectacle of herself, but in his present mood he threw off restraints of conscience and felt capable of anything. Besides, he was curious to know how far she really would go in her bid for female supremacy.

He put the beer on top of the piano. 'There's the first one, Alice.'

She nodded, and she and Tom played a couple more strike songs, then Alice stood up to down her beer. A couple of the men gave her a cheer as she put the glass down and wiped the froth from her lips, and she turned to give them a bow before sitting down again to rattle out an Irish jig. Tom went for the next round.

John turned to his sister. 'Come on then, Lizzie?' She shrugged and put a hand on his shoulder in a desultory fashion, making it obvious she'd far sooner be dancing with Tom.

In between the dances, Alice matched John pint for pint. After the fourth, Tom closed the piano lid. 'I think you need some fresh air, Alice. Take a walk outside with me.'

'It's all right, Tom,' John interposed. 'I'll look after her. If you leave, the dancing will have to stop. There's nobody else to play.'

She leaned on his arm, giggling, as he supported her along the road. 'Come on, a brisk walk and a bit of fresh air, it's too cold for a stroll,' he urged her, 'then we'll get back and have a warm by the fire.'

'Is it cold? I don't feel it.' She pulled him to a halt and still laughing put her lips close to his. 'Have you ever kissed a girl, John?'

'What for do you want to know that, like? Do you want me to kiss you?'

'If you like.'

He held her close, and brushed his lips against hers. Her lips opened and he felt her teeth against his tongue as he pressed his mouth against hers. She might be his for the taking. He might lure her into the shadows and take full advantage of her recklessness. His exploring, testing hand strayed from her waist to her breast to start a gentle, tender massage. She offered no resistance, but suddenly snorted and then shook with laughter, and laughed until her eyes ran. Her laughter was infectious, and he joined in, abandoning his evidently amusing attempts at seduction. It was not to be, or not tonight, at any rate.

'I'm surprised your mother and father let you roam about the way they do. You might get yourself into trouble,' he told her.

'Oh, my father probably hasn't noticed we've left London yet,' she said. 'He's a keen antiquarian. When he's not busy with the law, he never notices anything but his precious old books. They're his obsession. He lost interest in his practice years ago. He'd give it up and devote his life to his mouldy old books, if he could. That's why Tom chose to come and work with Uncle William.'

'What about your mother then? She must have noticed you've gone.'

'Not she. She ran off years ago with an architect who was doing some building work on Dad's chambers.' Alice laughed, with no sign of distress. 'She developed a passion for him about the same time father got one for old books. As father took less notice of her, he took a good deal, and she found she liked it.'

John could think of nothing to say to this, so held her arm over his shoulder and with his other arm around her waist he half walked and half carried her back to the inn.

In spite – or possibly because – of her intoxication Alice hadn't given up the contest. She wasn't beaten, wouldn't admit she was licked at any rate, in spite of Tom's and John's urging, and John refused to concede despite Tom's pleas. It might suit Tom to give in to his sister's every whim, but that didn't mean that John had to follow suit. Alice could concede, or she could drink her beer – like the man she'd challenged. His lips twisted in a wry smile as he brought back the seventh pint, put it in her hand, and raised his own glass. 'Good health,' he grinned.

Under the streaked white make-up, her face assumed a greenish cast. She put the drink down on the piano and went to lie on the seat at Jimmy's feet. John picked it up and followed her. 'You've forgotten your beer, Alice,' he taunted. She raised her hand in a gesture of refusal and defeat.

He held the drink close to her face. 'Why, just look, it's got a lovely head on it. And the smell . . . mmm. Surely you're going to drink it, now I've brought it for you?' The poor Pierrot shook her head – not too ill to look annoyed.

John enjoyed his victory, and enjoyed rubbing it in. 'Why, never bother, Alice,' he soothed. 'It'll not go to waste. I'll drink it for you, along with me own.'

She suddenly sat up, clamped a hand over her mouth and staggered towards the door, retching all the way. Tom started after her, and John put a restraining hand on his arm to detain him for a moment. 'She'll be all right. And you might not believe it, but I've done her a good turn. She'll never do that again.'

Eight

He'd lost Hendrika, and Elsie had no interest in him, but Alice liked him. After his treatment of her, it amazed him; and the fact that a well-heeled girl from the middle classes would openly show she liked him amazed him even more. Other women he knew were conditioned to wait until a man made the first move, but Alice was an irresistible force who, if she saw no good reason for a convention, would sweep the convention aside. He was flattered beyond words that she singled him out, flattered at her open and undisguised attraction to him, and he wondered how much of that was owing to the fact that he'd been so far from his usual restrained, deferential self on the night of the fancy-dress party that he'd hardly cared what he did, or what anybody thought about it. It seemed that Arthur was right. Polite, gentlemanly ways really did seem to be an impediment to success with women. From now on he would take a leaf out of Arthur's book. Whatever the way of it, being with Alice was like feeling the sun on his face after a half a lifetime in the Arctic. She was balm to his bruised pride.

She liked him, but she was a solicitor's daughter; and although he already had an exacting, responsible job and was studying to better himself and become a mining engineer, he still bore the stigma of the pit. What the hell did it matter, anyway? If Alice wanted to have a bit of fun with him, he was game. What was to stop him?

Mr Woolfe abandoned his insistence on a three-shift system for the time being, and the following day John and the other deputies and officials went down and spent a couple of shifts in making sure the pit was safe. After that the men were all back in their houses and back at work, and working furiously. While the pit had lain idle the vast weight of earth itself had laboured at loosening the coal in the seams, so that to begin with it was twice as easy to win. Empty coalhouses were replenished in a week. Production soared.

On Sunday morning Alice arrived at the Cock in her cycling outfit, with Tom beside her, in plus fours. John and Lizzie, more modestly dressed, went out as soon as they heard them in the yard.

'That's a spanker of a cycle you've got there, Alice,' John said. 'No need to ask what you're advertising. Come and look at this, Lizzie.'

The dimple pitted Alice's cheek and her lips parted in a smile. He bent to give the cycle a closer inspection, while Lizzie stood back a little. Enamelled in purple, white and emerald, the colours of the Women's Social and Political Union, it had the medallion of freedom on the gear-case. 'Elswick Cycles,' he read. 'Oh, I see. Made in Newcastle, that festering hotbed of women's suffrage. They've even got the manufacturers at it now. Aye, Ginny and Martin have Elswick cycles, but they're not half as smart as yours, Alice.'

'No, they're not,' she agreed. 'They're not the right colours. It's purple for justice, white for purity and green for hope; that's the fashion now. I wouldn't be seen dead with anything else.'

'Why, how much did you pay to be in the fashion, if it's not too cheeky to ask?' said Lizzie.

Alice smiled. 'It is, very cheeky, but I'll answer anyway. Ten guineas.'

Lizzie's eyebrows arched a little. John whistled. 'That's a lot of money.'

'But money well spent.'

Lizzie had practised bicycle riding all week, and looking well in her best skirt and jacket, she set off on Ginny's bike, as confident as Tom and Alice. John had nothing to cycle in except his second-best suit and a pair of borrowed bicycle clips. He wobbled uncertainly behind on a bicycle borrowed from Martin.

The day was fresh and cold and the peace perfect, the still-ness only broken by their own chat and the clamour of the birds trying to outdo each other in song, warning others off their territory. The four laboured and sweated up the hills, then like the birds, Alice and Tom went soaring down, with Lizzie and John following a little more cautiously. The air smelled of the countryside, moist and chill, feeling clean in his lungs.

After a journey of a couple of hours they stopped to rest on the crest of a hill, and surveyed the patchwork of farm-land spread out for them below in the clearness of the day. John propped his bike against the bank, confident he would soon be as good a cyclist as any. He went to climb a nearby oak and scan the horizon to the east.

'I thought so,' he called down to them, 'if you get high enough, you can just see the sea. It's marvellous, man.'

Alice left her bike and followed him. 'Help me up, Tom,' she called. 'I want to see it too.'

Tom followed her to the foot of the oak, clasped his hands together to give her a leg up. Agile and vigorous in her divided skirt, she climbed the rest herself.

'Do you want a lift up, Lizzie?' Lizzie shook her head, so Tom left her at the foot of the tree, and clambered up himself.

'Oh, be careful, Tom, be careful,' Lizzie warned. She'd shown no such concern about him, John noticed. Alice was now carefully shuffling along the branch to sit astride it behind him.

He turned towards her and she looked in the direction of his pointing finger. 'See, Alice? You can just make it out, over there. The North Sea. It's the start of anywhere you want to go. You can get a ship from Newcastle to just about anywhere in the world, but South Africa's the place, Alice man. I'd give my right arm to get there.' He looked at her as if in jest, with laughter in his eyes. 'Why don't you come with us? We'll get on a ship and sail away to Cape Town.'

Her dimple became evident, and her clear eyes returned his laughter. 'Because I'm already exactly where I want to be! Everything I care about is here, is happening here, in England. How can you think about leaving? These are times of change, exciting times, and I couldn't tear myself away for anything or anybody. The suffragette movement's my passion now, and I'll never give it up until we've won. Besides, I'm English, and I love England. Just open your eyes and look around you. I don't believe there can be a more beautiful country in the whole world.'

'You've never seen South Africa, Alice,' John said, but looking around him he silently agreed that on this bright April day, from this vantage point, his own land was as bonny as anywhere in the world.

'I see you don't deny it,' said Alice, after a few moments, 'and you could do some good here if you wanted to. You could do a little politicking, see if you can get into Parliament. You wouldn't be the first MP to rise from the ranks in a mining constituency, and you could do much more for the miners' interests as an MP than as a lowly deputy.'

'I thought I was doing all right when I got made a "lowly deputy", as you call it,' John said, tilting his head back, crossing his eyes and giving a self-deprecating little smile, as if reeling from a well-landed right hook. 'Anyway, it's not politics I'm interested in. It's mechanical engineering, mining engineering. That's what I want to do, in the end. Preferably in South Africa. I wouldn't know the first thing about being an MP.'

'You've got a good brain, and you could easily learn about being an MP. If you wanted to, that is. The first step would be to join the Independent Labour Party. Then to get yourself elected as a checkweighman. Most local candidates seem to have been selected from their ranks recently, or so my father says.'

'Then he must have told you that all the checkweighmen seem to be Methodists, and all the candidates selected by the Independent Labour Party up here are Methodists as well. I know what the routine is, Alice.'

'But your family are Methodists, aren't they?'

He laughed. 'Our Sal and me mam are. They go to chapel, and it's easy enough for them. But a man can either go to the chapel or go out and enjoy a pint and the crack with his marrers. You can be in the party that enjoys a drink, or you can be in the chapel party. You cannot belong to both. And I would far rather go for a pint. And there's another reason I cannot stand for Parliament, something you don't realize.'

'What's that?'

'I'm still living with my mother. I'm her main support, but as far as voting goes, I cannot get on the register – I don't fulfil the property qualification. There's a lot of men still haven't got the vote, Alice, and I've got no more right to vote than you have. And if I cannot vote, I cannot stand for Parliament.'

They cycled on for miles until they came to an old coaching inn where they stopped, quite famished. 'How many beers would you like, Alice?' John enquired, with mock solicitude, as they propped the bicycles against the wall.

'Why, as many as you – like she had the other night,' said Lizzie. The pose she adopted, with chin jutting and a dangerous gleam in her eyes was Alice to the life, and the impression she proceeded to give them of Alice's performance on the night of the fancy-dress party was larger than life. She mimed the placing an imaginary drink on an imaginary piano, and Alice's reluctance to take it, and finished by staggering towards the wooden bench at the entrance to the pub, and lying down on it. '"You've forgotten your beer, Alice,"' she jeered, in a creditable imitation of John's voice, then raised her hand in a gesture of defeat that was more Alice than Alice. '"Why, just look, it's got a lovely head on it. And the smell . . . mmm. Surely you're going to drink it, now I've brought it for you?"' she mocked, and shook her head after the words, with a face of suffering and irritation which was a near perfect replica of Alice's.

Tom laughed in astonishment at the performance. 'Bravo!' he exclaimed. 'You're good enough to be on the stage, Lizzie.'

'I know I am,' said Lizzie, sitting up and snapping back into her own persona, 'and that's where I ought to be, and would be now, if our Ginny had stayed in London, instead of coming back here to marry Martin.'

Alice laughed, but looked a little piqued. 'That was quite brilliant, Lizzie.'

John gave Alice no quarter, either. 'And you told me, "I'm

not like other women" – but you're just like other women when it comes to holding your drink, Alice. *Not as good as a man*, I mean.'

Alice gave a careless little shrug. 'Yes, it was all very funny. But if you're my friends, you'll forget about it now, and never speak of it again. It was quite out of character, and as I've been asked to fill the breach at the school in Annsdale Colliery now Miss Carr is ill, I'd rather not have it mentioned. It's evident that the school board haven't heard about it, or they wouldn't have offered me the job. I'd rather they didn't hear of it at all, if possible. What does it matter, anyway? Drinking's for idiots, so it's not surprising that men do more of it than women. I have much more important things to do, such as influencing young minds and getting votes for women. You must join us in the struggle, Lizzie.'

'I'll think it over,' said Lizzie, 'although I'm at work all day, you know, and with helping my mother, I don't get much spare time. And I have to earn my keep, so I certainly cannot run the risk of going to prison.'

'Oh, my God,' said John. 'The school's going to be turned into a training ground for suffragettes. I think a suffragette's a more dangerous teacher than a drinker. One of us should tell the school board what they've let themselves in for.'

'No need,' Tom grinned. 'They'll find out soon enough.'

It was getting dark when they left Tom and Alice, and cycled back to the Cock. Except for Ginny, the bar was empty, and as soon as the door was closed Lizzie seized hold of John, and squealing in excitement, dragged him violently round in a in a mad, exuberant polka.

'You enjoyed yourselves, then?' Ginny smiled.

'Oh, Ginny, it was perfect, man! We cycled for miles, and didn't get a drop of rain. There was hardly a cloud in the sky. I did a take-off of Alice, and you should have seen Tom's face! He couldn't get over how good it was; he said I ought to be on the stage. He's perfect, Ginny, perfect. He's everything I want.'

'Steady on,' warned John, smiling at her pleasure but not convinced that what Lizzie wanted was within her reach.

'Keep your feet on the ground. You've been on one outing. You haven't published the banns.'

She stopped, and pushed him away from her, frowning as though he were deliberately obstructing her. 'Oh, you Jeremiah. Well, you won't spoil it for me. You'll see.'

As soon as he got in from work that afternoon his mother nodded towards the table where the newspaper lay. 'Why, just look at that, John,' she said.

He could hardly believe his eyes. The *Titanic*? Gone to the bottom? Impossible. But it was so. The pride of the Belfast shipyard, the ship that had been vaunted unsinkable was sunk without trace. He skimmed the story, and then sat down.

'My God. Over one and a half thousand people lost, they think, Mother.'

She nodded, and without a word began to spoon hot food onto his plate.

'I cannot believe it.'

'I can. There's always some trouble for somebody. You'd better wash your hands.'

He tore his eyes away from the print just long enough to do so, and then sat down to eat. Hardly noticing what he ate, he read on.

The *Titanic* was sunk, with over twice as many people drowned as rescued. Only about seven hundred people had got into lifeboats, simply because there weren't enough of them. Unbelievable. The ship builders and ship owners had been so supremely confident that the ship was unsinkable, they'd provided only as many lifeboats as they thought they might need to rescue survivors from *other* shipwrecks.

'My God,' he repeated. 'What do you say, Mam? Man proposes and God disposes? He's disposed here, all right. Those poor beggars who were emigrating, hoping to make a better life! I bet there's a lot more than two-thirds of them drowned, travelling steerage. Probably more like nine-tenths, if not more. And the poor buggers in the engine room, they'll all be gone.' And then the thought struck him, and he glanced sharply at his mother. She'd put no food out for herself, and was sitting hugging herself, staring into the fire.

They still had heard nothing from Arthur. An unpleasant shiver ran down John's back before he determinedly dismissed the thought.

The nation was plunged into mourning. There was very little else talked about in the village all week, and very little else in the papers. On Sunday, the people in both villages were preparing to go to memorial services. Emma was going to the Catholic church with Jimmy and the bairns. John, his mother and the girls were getting ready to go to chapel when Lizzie suddenly announced, 'Tom and Alice are going to the rector's service here in the village. So that's where I'm going an' all.'

'Ooh, our Lizzie,' said Sally, 'it's bad enough our Emma talking about turning Catholic, without you changing. And the rector's high church an' all. Bells and candles and all that.'

Impervious to criticism, Lizzie stood in front of the mirror to put the finishing touches to her hair, and then carefully put on her hat and secured it with a large hatpin. 'I don't care. God's just the same everywhere, and Tom's going to St Aidan's, so that's where I'm going.' No sooner said than done, and Lizzie was out of the house and walking in the direction of the church.

'Why, I would never have thought our Lizzie would have done that. He's high church an' all, you know,' Sally repeated, her shock and disapproval obvious.

'Well, you might as well get used to the idea, Sal,' John said, taking Lizzie's place at the mirror to knot his tie. 'Our Lizzie's going to join the upper crust if she can, so she'd better get well in with the upper-crust God. She reminds me of a story Alice told me, when she was trying to convince me I ought to become a checkweighman and stand for Parliament. She said there was a certain Protestant called Henry of Navarre laid siege to Paris, and when he took the city over he was told he couldn't be crowned king if he wasn't a Catholic. So he said, "Paris is worth a mass," and he turned Catholic. Paris was worth a mass to him, and Tom Peters is worth a Church of England service to our Lizzie. It's the same thing – she wants him, and when you come to reckon up, if that's all she has to do to get him it'll be worth it for her. Good luck to her.'

'Well, I think it's awful,' said Sally, looking in their mother's direction and failing to catch her eye. Their mother made no comment.

'Me mam's thinking a catch like Tom Peters would be worth it an' all,' John said, 'and she's probably thinking, "At least he's not a Catholic without a ha'penny to scratch his behind with, and going to have her pregnant all the time." Isn't that right, Mam?'

'That's enough of that, John,' his mother frowned. 'Come on, or we'll be late.'

They walked out of the old village and on to Annsdale Colliery to join other people on their way to the Primitive Methodist Chapel. The place was packed, and the mood very sombre. A favourite lay preacher was at the pulpit.

'The hearts of the multitude have been touched, and their consciences have been aroused,' he began. John silently agreed with the first part of the proposition, but not with the second, and then he remembered Arthur, and wondered whether his conscience should be aroused. No, he told himself firmly. It was a million to one chance that Arthur was on that ship. Probably less chance than that. He could put it right out of his mind.

The hymns had been well chosen. 'Oh, God Our Help in Ages Past', 'Nearer My God to Thee', 'Give to the Winds Thy Fear'. All the old sorrows and miseries of the whole congregation seemed to be pooling themselves into that vast titanic grief, and finding expression. John sang with real feeling, surrendering to self-pity at Elsie's rejection of him. Looking round he saw sympathy on every face. His mother and Sally both had the tears trickling down their cheeks, and he wondered if they'd had the same thought as him, about Arthur. At last they got to the last three verses of the last hymn,

> God be with you till we meet again,
> When life's perils thick confound you,

108

Put his arms unfailing round you,
God be with you till we meet again.

Till we meet, till we meet,
Till we meet again at Jesus' feet,
Till we meet, till we meet,
God be with you till we meet again.

God be with you till we meet again,
Keep love's banner floating o'er you,
Smite death's threatening way before you,
God be with you till we meet again.

John suddenly saw Arthur as a little child, full of mischief, laughing up at him with his big black eyes alive with fun and devilment. Then another image flashed into his mind, of his brother's cold corpse with its open eyes death-dull, floating to the bottom of the ocean.

He was glad to step into that place that never failed to enhance his joys and soothe his sorrows, his refuge in times of trouble, his sanctuary – the Cock Inn. Ginny and Martin had closed for the day, and had invited the whole family for dinner, along with Tom and Alice. There was a roaring fire in the best room, and as there were fifteen of them, Ginny had decided to serve the meal in there

'Away, Philip, give us a hand to shift the tables,' said John, to Ginny's twelve-year-old stepson.

'I hope we're not having soup,' Jem piped up.

'That we're not,' said Ginny. 'It's Yorkshire puddings and onion gravy to start, then roast pork and crackling and stuffing and apple sauce. Come by, Jem. Let your Uncle John and Philip get these tables shoved together, then your mam can get the cloth and the cutlery on, and I can bring the dinner in.'

Soon the tables were butted together, laid with a couple of cloths, cutlery and condiments, and Ginny, Sally and their mother brought in the Yorkshire puddings on sizzling hot plates. Lizzie was seated at the table, engrossed in conversation with Tom, and John guessed that that was about as much effort as any of them could expect of her that day. When all were seated Tom opened the conversation.

'Today was the first time I've ever been in the church at Old Annsdale. The rector was telling us it was mentioned in the Domesday Book, and the tower was used as a watchtower against Scottish raiders. Apparently, it had a portcullis for defence and a room where stores could be laid in case of attack. It's a very impressive old church. He's inordinately proud of it.'

'Yes,' Lizzie enthused, 'and isn't it a nice picture of St George killing the dragon? It's really, really old.'

'Aye, it is. It's always been my favourite,' John agreed, although he'd neither been in the church nor ever laid eyes on the nice picture, and he knew for a fact that until today, neither had Lizzie.

'The church was packed,' said Alice, very smart in a new light green costume and a cream linen blouse. 'I was surprised to see so many people.'

'It was the same at the chapel. There were people in there who've never been to chapel for years. There were even some strong young men shedding tears before the service was over,' said John's mother, with a glance in his direction. Alice lifted her head and John felt her penetrating green eyes upon him, but she made no comment.

'Same with us,' said Jimmy, 'at the Catholic church.'

'It's amazing how a disaster like this sends everybody rushing back to God, whether they believe in him or not,' said John's mother. 'Pass me the salt, will you, Sally.'

'I bet there's been enough tears shed in this country today to float the *Titanic* again,' said Jimmy, 'but I think most of the people at our church were crying for themselves as much as for the people on board. It doesn't take a lot. Our own disaster's not that long ago.'

'I'm thankful that none of my friends or family were on that ship,' said Alice. 'I feel sorry for people whose were. They must be frantic.'

John looked across to Philip. 'I thought your gran and Matt might have been here, Phil.'

'No. They've gone to hith daughter'th.'

'Ah,' said John. 'She seems to spend a good bit of time there.'

'Aye,' said Philip, 'the getth on all right with them.'

'Your gran's never looked back since she married Matt,' said Ginny. 'She's got a new lease of life.'

It was true, thought John. Philip's grandmother had married again in her fifties, after she'd lost a husband and two sons to the pit, and a daughter to tuberculosis. After Martin had married again and taken Philip to live with him and Ginny, she had been completely alone, until Matt Smith walked into her house and her heart and brought her back to life. John looked at his mother and wondered how she would fare when Sally and Lizzie had husbands, and he had a wife. But it was easier to picture her as a solitary widow lost in the chapel and good works than a blushing bride of fifty.

'You've had two happy marriages, Martin. So what's the secret?' John asked, suddenly. 'What makes a marriage happy?'

'Picking the bonniest lass in the village,' Martin said, with a laugh in Ginny's direction, then seeing that John was serious, said, 'No, it's a lot more than that, for any man with a ha'p'orth of sense, that is. Your weal or woe for the rest of your life is set when you choose your wife. A bonny face isn't even a tenth of it. It's a woman, and I mean a grown-up woman – a real companion you want. Somebody who'll soothe your sorrows and lighten your joys, and help you in your life's work, bring your bairns up in the right way, and look after the whole family. And you have to want to do the same for her. Like people say, give and take. Respect each other. Really love each other. I can't explain it, except to say that when you've got a good wife, bad times aren't half as bad, and good times are more than twice as good. You'll know when you've got it.'

'What a speech!' laughed Ginny, her cheeks pink. 'You soft thing. Come on, who's going to help me bring the dinner in?' Emma and Sally followed her, and returned with the roast and the accompaniments.

'Does anybody want a fill-up?' asked Martin. Tom and

Jimmy nodded, and John went to the bar to fill a jug with beer, and another with water for the teetotallers. Martin stood up to carve the joint and share it out with crisp crackling.

'This lot must be costing you a bob or two,' murmured Emma, taking her seat again beside Ginny.

'We might as well enjoy it all while we can, with people we care about, while we've still got them round us,' said Ginny. 'You can't take it with you. If we don't know that now, we never will.'

'You could save it, and leave it to your descendants,' said Tom.

'Shall I pass you the stuffing, Tom?' asked Lizzie. He nodded, absently.

Helping herself to lashings of apple sauce, Ginny said, 'Some people have got no descendants, Tom, and some people's descendants are dead before they are. What then? What does it say in the bible? Take no heed for the morrow, or something? I suppose that's because there's no guarantee it'll come, so make the best of the day you've got, that's my motto.'

'Would you like some peas, Tom?' Lizzie again. Tom nodded.

'You're very quiet, John,' Alice remarked.

He caught her eye. 'I suppose I am. And I meant to ask you, how did you get on at the school last week?'

'Very well. I'm too busy feeling my feet to have managed any conversions yet, though,' she laughed.

'Well, they'd better all watch out when you do. You'll have them all chaining themselves to the railings,' he joked.

After the rice pudding was served and cleared away, John refilled all the glasses. and Martin stood up and raised his.

'I propose a toast, to Alice and Tom, for all their help during the strike,' he said.

'Hear, hear,' said Lizzie, the first to her feet.

'To Alice and Tom,' they all chorused.

'Thank you,' said Alice, her eyes shining. 'Getting involved in mining disputes is a tradition in our family. A distant relative of ours defended the miners in 1844. He won his case, and the miners carried him shoulder high through the streets of Durham! Of course, it's a long time ago, but Martin may have heard of him. The latest cause was very worthy, and I hope our efforts helped it along. Now, you must have a little fighting spirit left, and you need never lack a worthy cause until we've won votes for women. We need labourers for our field. I hope you'll help us, if you can.'

'Well, I will,' said Lizzie, looking at Tom. 'I'll help as much as ever I can.'

The women cleared the tables, and John and Philip put them back in their places. Jimmy sat at the piano and played a few hymn tunes, then closed the lid. The youngest two children began to get fractious, and Emma took them upstairs for a sleep.

Ginny and Sally and their mother went to make a cup of tea, leaving Alice and Lizzie and the men to read the papers.

'Oh, look, Alice, here's a suit, looks just like yours,' said Lizzie, scanning the adverts.

'Hmm? Oh, yes,' said Alice, 'but the report of suffragette outrages on the middle pages is much more interesting. Read about those.' Lizzie turned to the middle pages, and all was quiet until the tea arrived.

Tom took his cup and stood gazing out of the window. 'I think we must be off after this, Alice. It looks like rain.'

Lizzie looked up. 'Oh, no! You're not going so soon, surely. I'm sure it'll only be a shower. It will soon clear up again. Stay a bit longer. Give us a tune on the piano.'

'Another time, I think, Lizzie. We've heard enough hymns, and nobody's in the mood for jollity.'

'So play something that's not a hymn, and not jolly, then. Something nice and serious.'

He gave her a smile and put his cup down. 'If you insist. I'll play "The Lost Chord", if somebody will sing it.'

'I will, and Ginny,' said Lizzie.

So Tom played, and the girls sang, and after the performance Lizzie sighed. 'That was lovely, Tom.'

'And now we really must go. Are you ready, Alice?'

'Yes, I suppose so. I've lots to prepare for tomorrow's lessons. I think I must make the *Titanic* the theme of every one of them, from arithmetic to English. It's all the children will be interested in, anyway.'

Lizzie lingered at the door to wave them off long after the others had returned to the bar. Near to John, Sally picked up the paper and looked at the headlines again. 'Oh, I wish our Arthur would write,' she murmured.

Lizzie burst in and sped across to them to snatch the paper from Sally's hand and find the fashion adverts. She gave a howl of anguish. 'Did you see that suit she was wearing? Here it is, in the paper, the selfsame one. Marshall and Snellgrove, in London. Six guineas! Six guineas! And she had a new hat, and gloves, and shoes. She looks like a fashion plate. Where do people like her get the money, that's what I want to know.'

'From their parents, as a rule,' said Martin. 'They're born into it, and they usually invest it well in shares and education for their children, so they get the best jobs and stay in the middle classes, and the system perpetuates itself.'

'Aye, and there's a pile of pots to wash. That's a system that perpetuates itself an' all. So who's going to give us a hand to wash 'em, then?' asked Emma, looking at her mother and sisters.

Lizzie flung herself into a chair with the paper, to pore through the fashion adverts. With a sigh, Sally followed the rest of the women into the kitchen.

Nine

For the first time in his life, John went home to a dinner left in the oven between two plates for him. The fire was banked up with small coal, and he stirred it with the poker to bring it to life again, and then ate in solitude, with no cheering female presence to either soothe his worries, or minister to his physical needs. Dried-up meal finished, he put the dishes in the sink, lifted the tin bath off the wall and filled it himself. He got in, and discovered he'd forgotten the soap, brush and flannel. Pleased he'd remembered to close the curtains, he got out again to fetch them, leaving pools of water on mats and linoleum. The water was lukewarm, so he made short work of washing himself and scrubbed his back the best way he could, wishing his mother were there to do it for him. He'd forgotten to warm a towel, or even put it within reach, so undertook another cold, wet trek to find one. With a stab of sympathy he thought of that anti-suffragette poster entitled 'A Suffragette's Home', the one depicting a workingman arrived home from a day's labour with no wife to greet him and no meal ready, staring in despair at his comfortless home and his neglected children.

He found the towel and rubbed his hair dry. It's true, he thought. A house without a woman in it is a poor sort of a place, almost worse than a tomb. But Alice and Tom had supported the miners during the strike, and the time had come to settle the score. Alice had told them all that sacrifices had to be made if women were ever going to force the Government to give them the vote. She'd swept him along with her arguments, and like a fool he'd agreed with her. But it was a bit hard, he thought, that he should be making any sacrifices when he hadn't even got the vote himself. Nobody except

Sally seemed to see that, or care much about it. If this went on very long, he'd have to relearn all those skills of self-reliance he'd been happy to forget when he came out of the Merchant Navy.

Poor old Jimmy. He hadn't only his own meal and his own bath to get, he'd have to go and collect his four kids from his mother, and feed and look after them. John got dressed, emptied the bath and put it back on the outside wall, then went down to see how Jimmy was faring.

'I'm just about tearing my bloody hair out, man. These four are destroying me. It's bad enough when Em's here,' said Jimmy, dragging the two-year-old away from the coal scuttle. 'Now I'll have to wash him again, or he'll have muck all over everything, and I'll get wrong when she gets back.'

'All right. Jem, go and get your coats. Me and your da will take you all down to the Cock to see your uncle Martin for an hour,' said John. Jem did as he was told.

'This is not a man's job,' said Jimmy, rubbing the squirming two-year-old with a wet flannel. 'I'll tell you, John, me and Em have never fallen out yet, but we will if she keeps this up much longer.'

'We went to Alice's uncle's house, and she had some posters there, joined with straps, so you had one covering you at the front, from your neck to your knees, and another one the same size at your back. Then we went round the Town Hall and Market Place, down High Street and Saddler Street, over Elvet Bridge, back over the footbridge and up North Bailey and back along Saddler Street, and then we went round the Town Hall and Market Place again. Then Alice got up on a box in Market Place, and started talking to the crowd,' Sally told him, her face animated.

'What did she say?' asked John.

'Everything she's said before,' said their mother, hanging up her coat, drawing the hatpin out and removing her hat before collapsing into a chair. 'I'm exhausted. Put the kettle on, Lizzie. I'll make a meal when I've had a cup of tea.'

'Some of the people were shouting at her, telling her she

116

was a disgrace, and she ought to be at home getting her man's tea ready, and things like that, but she gave as good as she got, didn't she, Mam?' said Sally.

'Yes, and more beside. I got a bit frightened at one stage, us standing with the suffragette posters on us, as if we really were suffragettes, especially when the crowd started shouting. I don't think I'd like to do that again. I said to her, "I'm a bit too old to be carrying on like this, Alice." All she said to that was that I'm no older than Mrs Pankhurst, and she's been to prison for the cause, and that when we get the vote I'll be one of the first beneficiaries because I'm over the age of thirty and I'm a householder. It might be all right to have a vote, but I don't care that much that I'm willing to go to prison for it. And I shan't be tramping all over Durham wearing suffragette posters front and back again, either.'

'Yes, but what exactly did Alice say to the crowd?' asked John.

Lizzie filled the kettle and set it on the range 'Why, everything that was on the posters. How many women were in jail on hunger strike, and how many petitions had been presented to the King and Parliament, and how many false promises the Government had made, and that. And about women being forcibly fed, and about how men couldn't manage without women, so they should give them their rights. I'll agree with her there, but I shan't be helping the cause for a week or two. We've got too much to do at work. I'll be working late.'

'Some men started shouting about the suffragettes causing damage to property, and Alice said Sir Edward Carson was preaching sedition and arming rebels for civil war in Ireland, and nobody was doing anything about him. She said that's what men do, when they're determined to have their own way, and now women are taking a leaf out of their book. Oh, she can stand up and argue with the men, she really can,' said Sally. 'She blamed all the violence on a Mr Hobhouse, because he told Parliament they couldn't take the suffragettes seriously until they started burning and destroying things. And she said, "We've only just begun, and if the Government don't give us the vote we won't just be opposing the Liberals at by-elections. We'll rock the Liberal Government to its foundations."'

'Good heavens,' said John, 'it sounds as if she was starting the next civil war just about the time I was getting me own dinner out of the oven.'

'I've invited her and Tom to tea, next Sunday afternoon,' said his mother.

'You know what our Em said?' Sally went on, with eyes like saucers. 'She said she'd make just as good a speaker as Alice. And Alice said they could get her some practice if she liked, dealing with the ridicule and hostility you get from the crowd. So our Em said she'd talked to a crowd before, and she'd stirred them up, and she'd enjoyed it, and she'd be back there next Saturday to do it again!'

'Hmm,' said John, with great misgivings. 'That'll go down well with our Jimmy – I don't think.'

Sam opened the door and, tail wagging furiously, Sandy went lolloping over to lick John's hand. John stooped to rub his ears. 'You know me now, bonny lad. We're old friends, eh, Sandy? He's getting about a bit better, Sam.'

'Aye, thanks to you he is. Put the kettle on, Irene,' Sam called to his wife, 'we've got a visitor, like. Come in and sit down, John.'

'Aye, he's doing a bit better,' John stepped inside and nodded towards the dog, at a loss for anything else to say.

'Aye, he seems all right now. As good as he's going to get, probably. I don't think he'll ever run again.'

'No, I doubt he'll ever be fit to run. I think that'll bother you more than him, though Sam. Most animals are bone lazy. Just as happy to curl up in front of the fire as run. I might call in again, like. Just to have another look at him,' John said.

'Thanks, John. For all the trouble you've gone to.'

A deep and solemn gratitude was written on Sam's open, honest face, and John reached up to a collar that suddenly seemed too tight, to ease it a little with his forefinger. 'How are you going on with the pigeons, then, Sam?'

Sam's eyes lit up, and he grinned. 'Oh, champion. I've got a couple of little belters, they'll stand just as good a chance as anybody else's birds in the next race. They're a pair of little champions, man. And I built a better loft during the strike, with some old wood I had given. Come into the yard and have a look.'

Irene had the tea ready when they got back into the kitchen. John carefully avoided catching her eye, wondering whether she felt as guilty and awkward as he did. He drank his tea, and made conversation with Sam about the pigeons. When he got up to leave Sam pressed a bottle of Newcastle brown ale into his hands.

'I cannot take this, Sam.'

'Take it. It's not much. And you've earned it, and more besides.'

'But you're a teetotaller, Sam,' John protested. 'You never touch the stuff. You never buy beer.'

'Not for myself, I've signed the pledge, like. But I know you can take it without hurting anybody else, and you like a drop. So I got it for you, like.'

John took the proffered gift with a blush and an embarrassed glance in Irene's direction. He murmured his thanks and escaped from the house with a better opinion of Sam Hickey, and a poorer one of himself. It was time he finished things with Irene.

'So I said to her, "Why, who's going to be looking after these bairns, then?" and she said, "You are. They're yours as much as they're mine, so you take a turn." So I said, "I had enough of looking after them last Saturday after going to work, and it's not coming off again," but she put her bloody hat on and went, just as if I hadn't spoken. She would rather be addressing meetings than looking after her own bairns. I tell you, John, our Em's getting a right big head, all that rubbish them friends o' yours are pumping into it. All these big ideas seem to matter more to her than her own family.' Jimmy stood at the kitchen table, cutting slices from a large loaf. 'It took me ages to get them washed and dressed this morning, and I'll probably have hours of this afore she gets back.' He began to spread the bread with dripping, and then the kettle began to boil. Jimmy left the task to lift the kettle and make a pot of tea. The littlest one crawled over to the table and tugged at the cloth, bringing loaf, slices of bread, dripping, plates, cups and knives crashing to the floor. Jimmy's face reddened with anger and he swore and raised a hand, but seeing the child shrink from him he lowered it without striking. John helped him to clear the debris, salvage all the food and crockery that could be salvaged, and replace it on the table while the kettle boiled on unattended.

'Here, I'll get you a cup of tea,' said Jimmy, returning to the task of pouring scalding water on the tea leaves. 'There's no milk. She can spend money on a bloody train fare that gets us nothing, and she didn't even leave me enough money to go and get a gill of milk from the cart. You'll have to drink it without.'

'That's all right, man. Worse things happen at sea. Have you got any sugar?'

'It's in the cupboard.'

John put his tea on a stool and opened the cupboard door. An instant later he startled to piercing shrieks and turned round to see his two-year-old nephew jumping in agony, drenched in hot tea. John felt sick to his stomach.

'Bloody hell, John, man, he's pulled the tea all over himself!' Jimmy exclaimed.

'How's he done that? He was at the other side of the room! I'd hardly turned my bloody back!' said John, swiftly moving the chair out of his way to get to the child, and begin unfastening his clothes. 'Let's get his clothes off, man. I'll get them off him,' said John, above the child's stomach-churning shrieks and cries of 'Mammy, Mammy!'

'All right, Joe, all right, let's get these off and see where you're hurt.'

Jimmy started rummaging in a drawer and found a towel, then crossed to the sink and ran cold water over it. John had managed to get the shirt and trousers off the child, and took the wet cloth from Jimmy and applied it to the child's chest. 'We'll keep wetting it, try to take the heat out. You sit with him. I'll bring the tin bath in. If we can sit him in that, we can keep pouring cold water on the compress.'

John went out for the bath, and was followed into the house by the young woman who lived next door.

'What's happened? I heard the bairn screaming. The whole

street can hear him. So what's going on here, like?' she demanded.

Jimmy was sitting by the sweating, sobbing, blotchy-faced child, holding the tea towel in place. He looked up, red-faced and furious. 'What's happened? Bloody votes for women, that's what's bloody happened. She's gone cavorting in Durham and left me to struggle with the bairns. It's all right, Joe, you'll be all right,' he kept repeating, in an attempt to soothe his child.

John put the bath down and rummaged in the drawer for another tea towel. 'He's scalded himself with a cup of tea,' he explained briefly, crossing to the sink to soak the towel with cold water. 'It's my fault, but I only put it down for half a second. He must have been across the room like lightning.'

'You want to tell her where she gets off, leaving the bairns,' said the neighbour, placing her hands on her hips. 'My husband wouldn't put up with it. Do you want me to watch the other three till she gets back, like?'

Jimmy shot her a look of gratitude. 'You can take two of 'em, if you don't mind. Jem can stay.'

The woman lifted the littlest one, and took the other one by the hand, with something on her face, John thought, that was a cross between satisfaction at her own virtue, and a gloating pleasure at Emma's failings. He'd no doubt that she would have enough to talk about for a week or two to come, and with plenty of emphasis on her own creditable part in the affair.

Jem sat watching the proceedings with eyes like saucers, as, despite Joe's tears and protests, they sat him in the bath and kept pouring water over the cold compress, until he was shivering. Then, fearing to freeze him to death, they lifted him out onto a towel. Joe had exhausted himself, and his crying had subsided into sporadic sobs.

'She's got some Fenning's cooling powders in the cupboard. We'll give him some of that now he's a bit calmer. He likes them, he'll take it no bother,' said Jimmy.

John found them, doses of yellow powder folded in paper. He unwrapped one and mixed it with cold water. Joe took it without protest, and asked for another drink, then seemed to

121

settle. Jimmy removed the compress to reveal a reddened, blistered area covering half of Joe's chest.

'I bet it'll scar,' said John. 'Oh, Jimmy, man, it would never have happened if I hadn't turned my back on that tea. I feel terrible.'

'It would never have happened if our Em had stayed where she belongs. This is the last bloody time, though, or there'll be hell to pay.'

'I'll go down to the Co-op,' said John, 'and get a tin of Vaseline. We'll have to put some grease on his vest, or it'll stick to him. Find one of his vests, and put it in the oven on a plate. The first aid man says you can sterilize dressings like that.'

Joe wouldn't let them dress him but had just stopped crying when Emma stepped into the house a couple of hours later. At the sight of her, the child held his arms up to be lifted, and the dam of tears burst afresh. Emma paled at the sight of his blistered skin and rushed towards him, but stopped in her tracks, not daring to pick him up for fear of hurting him. His screams rose to a crescendo.

'Oh, my God,' she wailed, 'what the hell have you done to him? Can I not trust you with the bairns for one afternoon?'

The following day Alice stepped into the hallowed front room of John's mother's cottage for the very first time, and her eye was taken by a collection of watercolours hanging opposite the fireplace. The sight of this bonny girl with her green eyes and her dimple so completely absorbed in scrutinizing the paintings gave John an unexpected feeling of pleasure. He watched her lean over the polished mahogany table to get a better look at them; all views of whitewashed Cape Dutch houses, bathed in sunlight and set against sea and mountains.

'Your mother's got some beautiful watercolours,' she said.

He stood behind her with one arm round her waist, gazing where she gazed. 'Don't you wish we were there, on that beach together, Alice, strolling along, barefoot, hand in hand?' he asked. 'Isn't it beautiful? That's just outside Cape Town.'

'Tell her who painted them,' his mother insisted, glowing

with pride, and Alice turned towards him, eyes wide and eyebrows raised.

'A lad who was convalescing from the typhoid.'

'What was his name? He hasn't signed the pictures.'

John grinned. 'There was an old man who used to go out on the stoep and set his easel up. I showed an interest in what he was doing like, and he taught me a few of the tricks of the trade.'

Alice looked again at the pictures. 'They're very good,' she breathed. 'I'm impressed.'

'They're all right. All right for in here, at any rate,' John shrugged.

Alice and his mother exchanged a smile. 'He did one of them after he got home, from memory,' his mother told her, 'but our Lizzie and Arthur caught him just as he was finishing it, and they laughed at him and called him a Nance. So he put his paints and brushes away, and he's never touched them from that day to this.'

'If I had, everybody in the pit would have been calling me a Nance, and I wasn't having that,' John frowned.

'No, indeed,' said Alice, her face assuming a very serious expression, and though he looked very hard he detected only the faintest twitch at the corner of her mouth. Alice was quickly latching on to the fact that in a pit village, there were some things a man could do, and others he most definitely could not. He looked more intently at that face, and found it open, and wholesome. She would make a wife a man could respect, he thought. It felt good to have her in his home, and he suddenly pictured their children playing on the rug, or sitting under the quilting frame by Alice's feet, as he used to sit by his mother. He smiled at her. 'Give us a hold of your hat and coat. I'll hang them up.'

'Everything's ready. We're just waiting for Lizzie and Tom to get back from their cycle ride,' said his mother. 'I wish you and John could have gone with them, Alice. I was a bit doubtful about letting her go on her own.'

'Oh, I would have liked to, but the committee wanted to start on plans for the "Great Women from History" pageant in Newcastle. We're doing it jointly with the suffragists, and we've set the date for 6th July. I'm determined I'm going to be somebody like Boadicea or Joan of Arc, so I'll have to be at the meetings! Don't worry, Mrs Wilde. Lizzie will be quite safe with Tom, and the four of us can go out together next Sunday.' Alice pondered for a moment, then her eyes lit up with enthusiasm. 'I wonder whether Emma would like to be in the pageant. She's something of a Boadicea herself, you know. I wish you'd seen her yesterday. She'll make a wonderful speaker. She seems to know instinctively how to stir the crowd up, and get a lively discussion going. She's not frightened of them at all. In fact, she was getting some of the men *too* upset, and we had to restrain her in the end!'

John and his mother exchanged an apprehensive glance. 'I doubt she'll be coming again, Alice,' John said. 'There was an accident with one of the lads while she was out yesterday. Little Joe pulled a cup of hot tea over, and he got a bad scald.'

'I'm sorry to hear that. I hope he's all right.' Alice's face fell, and then brightened again. 'But accidents happen, you know, and it might just as easily have happened even if Emma had been at home.'

John nodded. 'I doubt it, and I don't think you'll manage to convince our Jimmy of that, or the bairn either. When he was hurt, he yelled for his mammy, and nobody else. And he kept on yelling for hours.'

'Oh dear. I'll call in to see them tomorrow afternoon.'

Knowing Jimmy's feelings about a certain suffragette who enticed men's wives away from their children, John opened his mouth to dissuade her; but Lizzie breezed in that same instant, rosy cheeked and bright eyed, with Tom in tow.

Their mother gave him a hearty, smiling welcome. 'Come in, Tom. Let me take your coat. Tea's ready, and as soon as Sally gets back from Emma's, we'll sit down.'

They hadn't long to wait. Sally was home before the kettle boiled.

'How's the little boy?' asked Alice.

Sally's young face was full of sympathy. 'Oh, it looks really bad,' she winced. 'They're trying to keep it covered up with his vest, but he keeps pulling at it. And he seemed a bit feverish.'

Alice frowned. 'Oh dear. I do hope he'll be all right.'

Tea might have been a very subdued affair, but nothing could dampen Lizzie's spirits, and her incessant chatter about her cycle ride with Tom lightened the atmosphere. After the meal, she suggested a game of whist, and their mother and Sally retired to the kitchen to wash up.

'Cheer up, Alice,' Lizzie reassured her, dealing the cards. 'It won't stop Emma coming to the suffragettes, now she's got the wind in her sails. She'll be telling Jimmy this very minute –' here Lizzie assumed Emma's expressions and mannerisms – '"They're your bairns as much as mine. You take a turn looking after them! What's sauce for the goose is sauce for the b— gander!" Won't she, John? I wish I'd been there yesterday to hear her, though, and I would have been, if Mr Surtees hadn't had so much work on. We've got quite a few red jackets to make for the hunting people. I've just finished one for Mr Hartley. He expects to get permission from the Master of the Hunt to wear it soon. And we've a lot of other work besides. He wants me to work late for the next few weeks, and I cannot very well refuse. I'd much rather be with you and the suffragettes, though. I bet Emma gave a good speech, did she?'

Alice nodded.

'Yes. She's quite clever. Miss Carr wanted her to go on and be a teacher, did you know that?'

'No,' Alice said, 'but I'm not surprised.'

They played hand after hand, sometimes changing partners: Wildes versus Peters, girls versus men, and Alice and John against Lizzie and Tom, but Lizzie seemed to be playing for Tom whoever she was partnered with.

Their mother and Sally came back into the front room and set up the quilting frame, to sit side by side in pleasant industry. The six of them spent a tranquil evening together, listening to Lizzie's ebullient chatter, and laughing at her mimicry.

After Alice and Tom had gone, Lizzie gave her mother a squeeze, with a smile on her lips and lovelight in her eyes. 'Thanks for inviting them, Ma. Isn't he a sweetheart? Isn't he a sweetheart? I don't know how anybody could resist him!'

Ten

'I've brought Miss Peters home, Uncle John,' said Jem, bursting with self-importance. 'Because I've done a really good picture.'

'Why, bring her in, then, and let's see it.' John smiled a welcome as he ushered Alice inside his sister's tiny cottage. She looked down at Jem. 'You like to come to school, don't you, Jem? And you're a good scholar. Show your mummy and daddy the picture you did.'

Jem held out his slate, with a drawing on it that was a barely recognizable representation of a boat. 'Tell them what it is, Jem,' Alice urged, with a glance at John.

'It's the *Titanic*,' Jem boasted. 'Miss Peters says it's a good picture, Dad.'

Jimmy had just thrown a few more coals on the fire. He replaced the coal scuttle, then took the slate and looked intently at it before placing it on the mantelpiece. 'Aye, it is a good picture, son. You've done well there. It's a shame you'll have to wipe it off again tomorrow.'

'Let's have a look, Dad! Let's have a look,' the four-year-old demanded. Jimmy handed him the picture, and Tommy scrutinized it. 'Oh, aye, that's the *Titanic* all right,' he pronounced. 'It is a good picture, Jem. It's all right, that, lad.'

Jimmy grinned, and took the slate from him, to replace it on the mantelpiece. 'I don't think the picture's the only thing Miss Peters has come to talk about, somehow,' he said.

'No, it isn't,' Alice confessed, crouching down until her eyes were level with Joe's, who, very subdued, was huddling against his mother on the sofa. 'John told me about Joe's accident yesterday. I came to ask how he is. How are you, Joe? Are you getting better?' The child shook his head.

126

Jimmy looked down on Alice from his place by the mantel, his face darkened by a frown. 'He'd be a lot better if his mother had been here looking after him,' he said. 'And she will be in future.'

Alice glanced up at him, crestfallen. 'But the way John described it, an accident like that could have happened just as easily with Emma at home. And if you'd heard her on Saturday, you'd have been proud of her. She can stand up to any amount of heckling from the men, and give as good as she gets.' John saw the two women's eyes meet, and he recognized a real affinity between the threadbare little engineman's wife with four raggy urchins at her knee, and the well-heeled daughter of the professional middle classes. They were both intelligent, with a strong sense of justice. They were both fighters. Alice was everything Emma could, and maybe should, have been.

'I'm not surprised she got heckling from the men, a lot of them wouldn't have had the vote either,' Jimmy protested. 'So what business have women got to get the vote over men? John's still living with his mother, so he cannot get on the register, but he's not making a song and dance about it.'

'That's because there aren't many men still living with their mammies at twenty-five year old for me to make a song and dance with,' said John, 'and I don't suppose the women are bound to wait till I get the vote before they ask for it themselves.'

'Why then, it's like Martin says,' argued Jimmy. 'Working people are better off with the Labour Party. They're for all adults having the vote, men and women alike, and they always have been. Mrs Pankhurst's Party is only concerned with getting the vote for women, and they'll be quite happy if it's only middle-class ladies like you, Miss Peters, so why should workingmen's wives sacrifice their families? There's nothing in it for them, anyway. They'll get a lot further working beside their own men for the Labour Party and votes for all adults.'

'But, Mr Hood, there aren't enough Labour MPs to make it happen, and there probably won't be for years and years. And you're mistaken about the Pankhursts. Their demand for votes for middle-class women is just the thin end of a very large wedge. As soon as we get that, we'll be pressing for the franchise to be extended, so that gradually all classes of women will have the vote. Emma's a brilliant speaker, and we have too few of them. The cause needs her.'

'Not as much as we do,' insisted Jimmy. 'Looking after bairns is a mother's job. It's not a man's work, and I'm not prepared to do any more of it.'

John said nothing, awaiting Emma's response, and when it came it made him proud of her.

She looked Alice straight in the eye, and expressed herself bluntly. 'I'm in a different class to the ladies you're used to associating with, Alice. I've no housemaids and nursemaids and cooks to do my work for me while I go out to make a noise in the world. If I had, I would love to work for the Women's Social and Political Union. But if my husband takes my work on, he does it on top of his own hard labour. If I ask neighbours to help me without helping them in return, it puts me further in their debt than I want to be. I cannot be away from home without doing hurt to my family, and it hurts me to hurt them. Look at this bairn's chest.' Emma pulled Joe's shirt up to reveal the scald. 'You're right, it might have happened even if I'd been at home, but at least I'd have been here to comfort him when he was crying for me. So that's the end of it. I'm not coming again.'

Jimmy's breath escaped in one long sigh of relief. 'You've seen sense at last, and not before time,' he said.

Alice looked deflated at the sight of the scald and the look of apprehension on the child's face. 'It does look very bad. I'm sorry about it, and I hope you're soon better, Joe. And Emma, I do understand. And we all thank you for the help you have been able to give us.'

John left with her, and Alice walked beside him, wheeling her bicycle.

'Well, I couldn't argue with that, could I?' she told him. 'It does look bad.'

'Imagine how I feel then. I was the cause of it.'

'Oh, John, it wasn't your fault. Accidents happen; they can't always be foreseen. I'm really sorry about losing Emma, though. She's a fiery little speaker. She would have been a real asset.'

'I'm sorry to say it, but I don't think you'll get many labourers for your vineyard in Annsdale Colliery, Alice. The women have got more than enough to do already, most of them.'

Lizzie was at work until six o'clock most Saturdays now, instead of finishing at noon, as she used to. To begin with, John was amazed at the cheerfulness with which she seemed to accept her employer's merciless sweating of her labour, but after a week or two he began to harbour deep suspicions about it. He challenged Mr Surtees one afternoon in the village.

'Exploit her?' the man protested. 'It's nothing of the sort. She works until six, I grant you, but she's not working for me. She coaxed a length of blue barathea out of me that had been lying about the shop for years, paid for by a customer who never came back to be measured. She's stayed late on Saturdays so she could use my cutting tables and my machines to make it up into a costume. I've even helped her with it.'

'Ah,' said John, the light dawning. 'And I bet she swore you to secrecy.'

'She did, but I shan't be keeping any secrets if she's going about telling people I'm exploiting her!'

'No, she hasn't said anything of the sort. She's kept the costume a secret from us, though. I'm sorry I said anything, Mr Surtees. I hope you'll forget it.'

John went home laughing. Working late! What a perfect excuse to dodge selling suffragette papers in Durham on Saturday afternoons, without giving offence to Alice. He was looking forward to seeing the blue costume, and wondered if it would be anything like Alice's six guinea green one.

He had a real rapport with Alice. He understood her, and there could hardly be a better basis for a marriage than that. He never ceased to wonder what she was doing with him, a man on a social plane so many pegs beneath her own. He had left school at the age of thirteen like all the other lads in the village, with the pit the only option open to them. Like the rest of them, John had finished school on the Friday, and had started work the following Monday, and had earned his own bread for the past twelve years. There was no family money at the back of him. The question of their future together perplexed him. He doubted that such disparity would allow for any, but Alice showed no sign of wanting to break off their friendship. He half guessed that being neither married nor having any firm engagement to be married left her free to be one of the wild women of the North East, free to harass the local MP and other worthies and put the fear God into all who opposed the suffragette movement, or dared to vote against their cause.

He was on the foreshift the following week, and started waiting for her outside school, so that they could go for a ride together, while Tom and Lizzie were still at work.

'Have you got a new bicycle?' she asked, the day he turned up on a bicycle that was not Martin's.

'New to me. I'll take it for a test run today, and if it's all right, I'll buy it for half the price of a new one. It'll be all right for going to work on an' all; and I should be able to sell it again without losing much on it when I emigrate,' he grinned.

'How did we ever start going out together, Alice?' John asked, chewing on a blade of grass as they lay taking a breather after a long uphill ride, looking at a clear blue sky full of fluffy white clouds, listening to a lark hovering high above, singing her heart out.

She propped herself up on one elbow to look at him. 'I beat you at a game of skill, remember? Then you weren't shy of beating me at drinking, which is a game of stupidity.' She frowned. 'I was a little cross about that, because the men in my family have always allowed me rather a lot of my own way. But then it intrigued me, just because it was different to what I'm used to. It seemed rather a challenge. But it was when we danced together. That was when I knew I really liked you, and I thought I wouldn't mind dancing with you for the rest of my life. You had a firm but gentle lead, and broad shoulders to rest my arms on. And your hands were – are, warm enough but not sweaty. And we enjoy our battles of wits. I put you in your place, and you put me in mine. You're the only man I've met who doesn't always give way to me. We're different as chalk and cheese in some things, and the

130

same in others. I think you're capable of doing something great. We interest each other.'

He was so near to her that their noses almost touched, and he saw a look in her blue-flecked green eyes that made him bold. 'If you really like me, Alice, we could move on now, to another game. The sort that only takes two players – one man and one woman.'

She leaned down, and planted a kiss on his lips.

'No, not like that, Alice, like this.' He took her in his arms and pulled her down beside him, to brush his lips lightly against hers, time and again. He made his kisses ever more open-lipped, searching, intrusive. She returned them, and allowed his exploring, caressing hand to ease the blouse out of her skirt and slide his hand underneath it, to cup her firm, full breasts, and with the lightest touch, stroke her erect nipple. Excited and eager at finding no resistance, he removed his hand to let it stray under her skirts and along her sturdy thighs, until at last his fingers found the soft, moist core of her. With a gasp, she thrust him away and uttered one word:

'No!'

No virgin's blush lay on her cheek, but her eyes told him that the refusal was absolute. 'That game has rather worse consequences for me than for you,' she said, after a moment or two, 'I like you, but I'd have to be a complete fool to allow it.'

'It wouldn't have any consequences for you, Alice. I'd make sure of it.'

'Hm, hm.' She made a grim little noise of derision and sat up, reciting.

> When lovely woman stoops to folly
> And finds too late that men betray,
> What charm can soothe her melancholy,
> What art can wash her guilt away?
>
> The only art her guilt to cover,
> To hide her shame from every eye,
> To give repentance to her lover
> And wring his bosom, is – to die.

She raised a handkerchief to her eyes, and turned her back to him.

He gave a short laugh. 'You are joking, aren't you?'

After a dramatic moment of mock grief she turned towards him with a smile, but her green eyes were serious. 'I most certainly am not. Those words are as true now as the day they were written. I take them as a warning, and you ought to know that I shall never stoop to such folly.'

'But you cannot think I'd do that to you, Alice. I would marry you.'

She was silent for a moment or two. 'No, I don't think you would betray, but you'll never be put to the test. I've been too well warned about the promises men make. I may be young, but I'm not naive, because my family have never shielded me from knowledge of the world.' She began tucking her blouse back into her skirt. 'I've sometimes been in court when some poor girl who's been seduced has tried to claim some main-tenance from the father of her child, only to see him bring forward two or three of his friends to testify that they have also . . . and in open court – and the poor shamed girl standing there for all to see! And then, of course, she gets no money to support the child. It's too appalling! That will never, ever happen to me.' She pressed her finger against his lips to silence the protest he was about to make, and pointed to her enamel brooch. 'You see that white band between the purple and the green? That stands for purity, and it's one of the reasons we want the vote, to get more even-handed treatment for women. We want to prevent sights like those on some disrep-utable streets late at night, and make sure that no woman has to degrade herself to exist. I should be a fine hypocrite if I failed to live up to the ideal in my own life.'

Not like her mother then, he thought, reaching out to pick a pink bird's eye primrose. He began pulling its petals with a sigh of disappointment. 'She loves me not. She loves me not. She'll never let her heart rule her head.'

She watched him for a while, then remarked, 'My head and heart work in partnership; neither rules. When I marry it will be from choice, without duress on either side, and with both my eyes open and my mind and heart engaged. My husband will have me as a virgin, whether it's you or anyone else.'

He plucked more petals. 'She loves me – maybe. And maybe she doesn't.' He threw the flower away and bringing the fingers of his right hand like a gun alongside his temple, made a noise like an explosion and feigned death.

She laughed. 'Yes, maybe I do, and maybe I don't, but I'll never make a good wife while the cause consumes me. I might never marry at all. I like you very much John, better than any man I've ever met, except those in my own family. But I'll be truthful. I could never accept the lot of the pitman's wife. If I'd any illusions about it before, I've none now. I've seen it too closely. But you could do better. Much, much better!'

'Cuckoo, cuckoo!' The bird announced that winter was well and truly gone, but the day was warm and bright enough to make the proclamation unnecessary. John caught sight of Elsie on the way home, looking so drab and downcast in a winter coat that he could hardly believe it really was her. Her face looked pale, like a blob of whitewash under the dark hat, and the spring was gone from her step. She reminded him of those women his mother accused of having 'let themselves go', and Alice now seemed to him the more attractive of the two. His anger towards her evaporated, and a flood of sympathy washed over him. He had an impulse to go to her, ask her what the trouble was, and tell her he would help her if he could. He saw that she had seen him, and hesitantly he walked towards her, but she hastened away. His company was spurned, his comfort unwanted. He should have known it would be.

So be it. At home, he changed out of his good clothes and sharpened the hoe, to get rid of a few weeds growing along the rows of vegetables, while he still had the light. Alice was honest anyway, he thought, not the sort to raise a man's hopes just to feed her own vanity and then dash them to the ground again. You knew exactly where you stood with her. Fair and square, that was Alice, and any children she had would be just the same – healthy and strong, and wise and witty, and brave and bonny, the best any man could hope for. He would be proud to be Alice's husband if it ever came to it, and over the moon to be the father of her children.

133

Neither did she seem to bear a grudge for his assault on her virtue, didn't seem to blame a man for trying. Her refusal went to prove the purity she believed in, he reasoned, and not any dislike of him, and it would make her a faithful wife. He sliced and uprooted weeds, thinking over and over again of the compliments she'd paid him: 'I thought I wouldn't mind dancing with you *for the rest of my life*. You had a firm but gentle lead, and broad shoulders to rest my arms on.' He flushed with pleasure and straightened up to lean on the hoe as he savoured the words, and then he imagined himself with Elsie in his arms, and his heart leapt at the thought that his broad shoulders and gentle lead might have the same effect on her. His pleasant mood was suddenly soured, tainted by guilt.

Eleven

'This has gone on far too long, you coming home late, and worn out,' said John, as they cycled past Surtees's shop the following Sunday. 'Fifty-six hours a week he's got you doing, and sometimes more. He ought to be ashamed of himself. What do you say, Tom?'

'I say he's a damned sweater, and you should have the law on him.'

'I will,' said John, 'but I'll have my law on him. It's a sight cheaper than yours. I'll be round at that shop as soon as I get loose from work tomorrow, and see what he's got to say for himself. He'll soon see reason, the way I'll put it to him.'

'Bravo,' said Tom.

Lizzie's face was a picture of consternation. 'No! You cannot do that. You'll lose me my job.'

He gave her his solemn assurance. 'Never bother about that. I'll just tell him it's not good enough.' John held up a fist. 'He'll soon see my point, then you'll have your Saturday after-noons back, and you'll be able to do a lot more to help Alice and the suffragettes.'

Lizzie's alarm subsided. Her eyes narrowed to slits, and she looked at him with a tight little smirk on her face.

'That would be marvellous,' said Alice. 'If all the women who can would do a little more, the few wouldn't have to do so much. If you were free next Saturday, Lizzie, you could help us sell a few copies of *Votes for Women*, in Durham. Or better still, as you're a tailoress, you could help us make the banners and the costumes for the pageant.'

'Isn't this marvellous?' Tom grinned, as they pedalled out of the village. 'Away from workrooms and classrooms and offices and pits for a few blessed hours, and out on the open

135

road. Absolute freedom. Perfect.' He bawled at the top of his voice, and not very tunefully.

> Here are the four of us out on the wheel,
> Happy as long as we go-oo,
> Life is a mixture but in it we feel
> Better the weal than the woe-oo!
>
> Happy are we as we peddle along,
> Scenting the breath of the May-ay ...

'Put a sock in it, Tom,' said Alice. 'There's a good boy.'

'If she thinks I'm wasting my time making banners and costumes for bloody pageants she can think again. If she wants banners, let her make them. She's got more time than me, and I've got better things to do.' Lizzie sat by the fire with her hair combed back into its bedtime plait, sipping her tea.

'Thanks, Mam,' said John, taking the proffered sultana scone. 'How's that bonny blue costume coming on, then, Lizzie?'

She looked at him, eyes smouldering. 'I knew you knew, you little swine. It didn't take me long to work that out.'

'That's enough of that, Lizzie,' their mother protested, pausing in her task of splitting and buttering another scone. 'Now you can apologize to John.'

'Yes, I think you should an' all. That wasn't called for,' said Sally.

'What did you say to him?' Lizzie demanded.

'I said he should let you off so you can go and help Alice with the suffragettes,' John laughed, raising his arms as if to fend off a blow.

'Well, I can tell you now, he's not going to. He's going to want me working as long as ever, and I'll have no time for any suffragette rubbish, and don't you stick your nose in again. I'd rather spend my spare time getting a new suit and a new blouse than any amount of votes, so they can keep their votes as far as I'm concerned. It's all right for her, she can go to London any time she likes with her purse full of her father's

136

money and get everything she wants, and think nothing of throwing six guineas over the counter for it. I'll get nothing unless I make shift to get it for myself.'

'Why, think about it, Lizzie,' John urged. 'Tom's all for the suffragettes, you know, and he might think you look bonny on a float, dressed up as one of the great women from history. You could cover yourself in glory there, bonny lass.'

Lizzie was quiet for a while. 'All right. I'll think about it,' she said. 'I might go, and see what they offer me. But if it's somebody ugly and old, I'm not doing it.'

'I can guarantee it won't be that. If you look at any of their posters you'll realize that dressed to the nines and looking like queens is more the Pankhursts' stamp. They only paint the men as ugly and old. And stupid, and drunk, and criminal.'

Lizzie ruminated for a time, then said, 'Thank God our Arthur's not here to make a mess of things. Can you see them still wanting to come and see us, if they'd met him? If he were at home we'd never see either of them again, Alice or Tom. I hope he never bloody comes back.'

'She really does seem to think a lot of you,' his mother told John after tea one evening, while he was poring over his books spread out on the front room table. His mother and Sally were seated companionably side by side at the quilting frame.

'Who does?' he asked, mind abstracted by the problem of pumping water from the mine.

'Why, who do you think? Alice, of course. She's here nearly as often as Hartley's daughter used to be, after our Arthur.'

He lifted his head. 'No, she's not round half as often as that.'

'She is. And what a nice girl she is. She's a lovely girl.'

'You used to say you didn't like the suffragettes. A lot of warped old maids with nothing better to occupy their minds, you called them.'

'Well, that was before I met any. I wouldn't really want to be a suffragette myself, but I do like Alice. She's not a warped old maid, and I don't think she ever will be. Some sharp young fellow will snap her up before long, and she'll be a good catch for anybody that gets her.'

137

'Aye, she will. But her dad and her uncle are solicitors, and her brother will be one before long an' all, and I work at the pit, so I doubt it'll be me. It's not likely to end in wedding bells, so don't start making any plans, Mam. We'll just see how things go.'

His mother frowned. 'I can't see why you bother with each other at all, if there's going to be nothing come of it.'

'Because I like her and she likes me, and it might never go any further than that. We'll just see how things go.'

His mother gave him an indulgent smile. 'She could go a lot further and do a lot worse than you, whether you work in the pit or not. And she says you could do better than the pit, if you set your mind to it. She seems to think you could go into Parliament. She says MPs get paid a wage now.'

'So I hear. But to get into Parliament you have to do a lot of campaigning, and you've got to be prepared to make a lot of speeches promising people the earth, so you can persuade them to vote for you. I don't think I'm cut out for it.'

There was a dreamy expression in his mother's eyes. 'Alice seems to think you are. She's got some great ideas for you. Maybe you need somebody like her, to give you a push. Give you a bit of inspiration. You never know what you can do till you try, and she knows a lot of people who might be able to help you.'

'They cannot help me with mining engineering, and that's what I'm concentrating on. Something I know I'm good at.' He didn't add, 'and something I know will get me a good start in South Africa'.

His mother seemed to read his mind, and stopped smiling. 'There's another thing I like about Alice,' she said, 'she's a girl who loves her own country and knows the value of her own people. She says there's no better place in the world than England.'

And she knows that, even though she's never been outside of it to see anywhere else, John thought, but he said nothing. Alice seemed to have a lot to say on every subject under the sun. She might have the edge on him when it came to money and education, but he had seen a bit of the world, and had something to compare England to. Alice hadn't.

*   *   *

138

She was proud to tell people her father and uncle were solicitors, and to let them know that Tom would soon be joining
her uncle's firm, and she wasn't shy of letting it be known
that she had gone to school until she was eighteen. But she
had told John, 'I'm *as intelligent* as you' – hadn't claimed
any superiority over him in that respect, neither was she was
ashamed to be seen with him. Alice took an interest in his
work in the mine, and would look over his books on engineering with a close attention, encouraging him yet constantly
putting forward her own idea of entry into politics as his better
option, as a means of advancing both himself and the cause
of the miners. However much he argued to the contrary, she
seemed to have the impression that all he had to do was ask
for a seat in Parliament, and somebody would give him one.
She brought the subject up again the Sunday after Whitsuntide,
as they sat on a grassy bank surveying the horizon after a
twelve-mile ride. Thoroughly tired of such heated political
arguments, Lizzie beckoned Tom, and they mounted their bicycles and fled some distance off.

'I'm not so sure the checkweighmen are all Methodists,
John,' Alice persisted. 'But even if they are, what of it? You
could easily join them, especially as you were brought up with
the chapel. You believe in God, don't you?'

'Which God? There's so many different ones to choose from.
The King and all our noble lords want everybody to listen to
the Church of England parson telling them what the Anglican
God says – that the rich man's got to be in his castle and the
poor man at the gate – because it serves their interests, so all
their retainers have to go and listen to that. But that's not the
God for men like our Mr Woolfe, who used to be poor – but
wouldn't stay at the gate. Men like him want their workers
going to the sort of chapels that preach their gospel – that the
workers should be happy to slave in the master's mine or
factory, and never take a drink so they can stay sober and earn
him a castle of his own, to compete with the aristocracy. The
mineworkers round here have got nothing, so some go to the
Primitive Methodists, and elect ranters from among themselves
who tell them that they're as good as the next, and God thinks
the wealth ought to be shared out among the people who produce

it. Obviously that's what the miners would like to see. Everybody picks the God that backs their own ideas.'

'You haven't mentioned the Catholics.'

'Why, they don't pick anything. They cannot even have an independent thought, but what they've got to go running to the priest to confess it. Put money onto the plate every Sunday and do everything the priest tells you to do, or we'll make sure our loving, merciful God leaves you to roast in Hell for evermore, that's the bargain the Catholics get from their church, and they're indoctrinated with it from the cradle.'

'But those Methodists who are in the union think for themselves. You've admitted that yourself. They believe that men have the right to the fruits of their labour, and they work towards that.'

'Aye, they do,' John said, 'but they still think they've got the right to sit in judgement on other people. We found that out, when our Ginny came back from London, with the whispering that went on because it came out that she'd lived with a man there. There weren't many of them thought twice about casting the first stone. They call themselves Christian, but they don't forget, and they don't forgive, a lot of them.'

'And yet a lot of people get comfort from religion.'

'Oh, aye, I'll grant you that. My mother among them, going around the house singing hymns after me dad was killed.' He sat up and started to sing in a fine baritone.

Rock of ages, cleft for me, let me hide myself in Thee,
Let the Water and the Blood from Thy riven side which
    flowed,
Be of sin the double cure, cleanse me from its guilt and
    power.

Not the labours of my hands can fulfil the law's demands
Could my zeal no respite know, could my tears for ever
    flow,
All for sin could not atone, Thou must save, and Thou alone.

140

'That was the main one, only she'd get to the bit about tears flowing, and her voice would start to falter, and the tears she was singing about would start running down her face, and she'd be so choked she could hardly finish it. She never hurt anybody in her life, and I'm tempted to say I don't know what she thought she was guilty of, but I do know.'

'What was it?'

John gathered his thoughts, then said, 'You know what the last local strike was about, Alice, a three-shift system. When a man's done his stint down the pit he needs a good meal, and it doesn't matter what time it is, so the women have to be there to get it ready, like. Not only that, but they get out of their beds at all hours of the night to warm their men's clothes and send them to work with a kiss and a few kind words. It's a tradition.'

'Yes,' Alice prompted him, 'I know. It's because there might be an accident. They're afraid he might never come home again.'

John nodded. 'Aye, or not alive, anyway. Well, when I was sixteen my dad gave me a belting because he thought I'd pinched something from a neighbour. I hadn't done it, and I was as mad as hell, so I decided I'd had enough. I thought I was over big to be taking hidings, so I went to sea, without telling my mother or anybody else except Jimmy. The day before my dad got killed, my mother had a telegram saying I was lost, presumed dead. So when he set off to work that morning, she turned away from him, wouldn't give him a kiss, wouldn't even speak to him.'

'And then it was too late.'

'Aye. For most of her married life he badly used her, but deep down she loved him, and funnily enough, at bottom, he loved her. So she's never forgiven herself. I think she even blames herself for the accident; she's got some superstitious idea that if she had kissed him, it would never have happened. But it was nothing to do with her, or anything she'd done. It was caused by people who already had plenty of money wanting plenty more; the sort of people who can never have enough. The sort who'll never grieve over any of us, or feel an atom of responsibility for any of the misery they've caused for us, in all their long and prosperous lives.'

'But at least her faith comforts her. And my uncle says that before the Methodist movement took root here, the mining villages were such brutal places that even the police hardly dared go into them.'

'And that's my point. If some of the pitmen were brutal it's because that's the way they were treated, and they still are. They had no education, and no choice about how they earned a living. They were bred like animals to produce wealth for other people and nothing else. Why should they care about other people's lives when nobody gave a tinker's cuss about theirs? Their lives were very hard and very short, more so then than now, so they lived hard, while they had the chance. They'd no guarantees they'd be alive the next day, because they counted for nothing with the owners, and they knew it. Most of the capitalist class are hymn-singing churchgoers, but some will expose poorer men to death and injury without a second thought if it'll squeeze them another copper out of their enterprises, because for all their religious prattle, profit's all they really care about. Oh, I don't doubt it suits them to have the miners tamed, and Wesley was the one who did it for them, but that doesn't prove the existence of God, or the goodness of his so-called servants. Your uncle's talking about social control, Alice, not truth.'

She gave him a broad smile, her dimple showing and her green eyes dancing in mockery. 'You are political, John. You're as political as I am, but your politics lie dormant, like a sleeping giant, waiting to be awoken.'

'Shut up, Alice, and come here. Nothing's ever going to alter, so it's a waste of time talking about it.' He pulled her towards him and stopped her mouth with long, sensuous kisses. 'God, you smell nice,' he murmured, and started to laugh.

'What's the matter?'

'I wish we could make that white band between the purple and green a lot narrower, that's all. The only sleeping giant that's starting to waken up round here is the one in my trousers. I wish you were as interested in doing something about that as you are in doing something about my so-called politics.'

But no. Alice left the question of what to do about *that* entirely to John.

He knew that he should stop going to see Irene, for many reasons; Alice, for one. It was beginning to seem possible that the friendship between them might blossom into a real courtship, after all. Marriage might be on the cards – it hadn't been ruled out. And Sam was a good-living man who had done him no wrong, and John was playing him foul, going behind his back and taking what didn't belong to him. The thought that in spite of all his care he might make Irene pregnant, that she might give birth to his child was not one he liked to dwell on, and he broke into a cold sweat whenever it caught him unawares.

He knew it was wrong, that if he visited the Hickeys' house at all he should go when Sam was in, and after every visit he resolved that he would, or stop going at all. But after a few days of celibacy he could easily convince himself that just once more wouldn't hurt. So he took care to go when Sam was out, because he wanted to keep taking what Irene was offering. He wanted to have her, to thrust himself into her and keep on thrusting, he wanted to see that look of primeval pleasure on her face, the look of a woman who has given herself up to a man, the look that told him he could do as he liked with her. During those moments he knew that nothing in the world could prevent her from opening herself to him, that she really couldn't help it. She'd abandoned herself to his will, and his control over her was absolute. Then the look on her face afterwards, when she'd had enough, and she looked satisfied, gorged almost – gorged on him. Then he could exult in his manhood, and his power as a man.

She'd started it. She had made herself his whore, and now he was using her as a whore; and the lust she had kindled in him was more powerful than dread of the consequences, for him or for anyone else.

Twelve

'We're determined to throw off those Victorian ideals of womanhood that have deluded and oppressed us for so long. We refuse to be mere "angels in the house". We'll forge a new identity, and ensure a higher place in society for women. That's why we take direct action – because it's the only way, and we do it for the sake of *all* the women of England,' Alice insisted, 'and you've got what most of us lack, Sally – spare time. You could do a lot to help the cause.'

John cut in. 'I've heard how suffragette women are treated in jail, and working-class women get the longest sentences and the worst treatment. You don't hear of them being in jail for a couple of days and then getting discharged on medical grounds like some members of the aristocracy do. Not that I'm saying they haven't suffered, and I'm not decrying anybody that's got the guts to stand up for what they believe in. But our Sal's got no friends in high places, so as far as the Government and the prison authorities are concerned she's nobody in particular, and she counts for nothing. So she's not doing it, Alice. They're your beliefs. You can do what you like about them, but our Sal's not going to be invalided over them.'

'Do you think that Sally herself might have an opinion on the subject?' Alice asked, looking dispassionately towards her.

Looking as uncomfortable as possible, Sally shrugged and blushed and spread her hands. 'I don't know. I don't know,' she said.

'Sally, it's very unlikely that you'd get caught.'

'Knowing our Sally, it's almost certain-sure she would. She could never carry anything like that off, and she could never stand a prison sentence. So she's not doing it. You'll be smashing no windows, Sally, and you'll be shoving nothing into post boxes except letters. So settle your mind to it.'

Alice faced John, chin tilted and eyes challenging. 'Sally has a mind of her own, and a right to choose what she does or doesn't do.'

John remained adamant. 'I'm the one that's looking after her, and she's a right to do what I tell her; and she's not doing anything that'll get her jailed.'

Alice stood up, directing her comments at Sally but still looking into John's eyes. 'I'll come back and see you another time, Sally. When we're not having our conversation commandeered by somebody else.'

'You can come any time and talk to her about anything, as long as it doesn't include breaking the law,' John insisted.

'I would never have believed you were such a caveman. Good afternoon, John.'

'Aye, well, now you know. Good afternoon, Alice.'

She went without another word, and closed the cottage door, leaving John alone with Sally.

'I think that's the first time you've fallen out with her, isn't it, John?'

'Aye, it is.'

'I'm sorry about that, but I'm glad you told her. I'd be too frightened to do anything like that. And it's not only that. I wouldn't like to go about destroying other people's things, even if I did get away with it. I don't think it's right.'

He gave her a fond look, this timid little rabbit of a sister of his. 'I knew that. But why didn't you tell her yourself, you silly lass?'

'Well, she's right about women having to make the Government sit up if they're ever going to get the vote, isn't she? And she's so strong. You don't feel as if you can say no to her,' she said.

Alice and her sister suffragettes knew that their chances of being admitted to hear the Cabinet minister speak in Durham the following Saturday were remote, so Alice was hunting for male representatives. To atone for his refusal to allow Sally to take part in any suffragette outrages, John let himself be persuaded to accompany Tom to the meeting. Hordes of well-dressed ladies were milling round the doors when they got to the hall, pressing to get in, but other than the minister's personal friends and Party followers, women were barred. Police had been set to guard every conceivable entrance to the hall; doors, windows – even the skylights and coal chutes had their defenders. The Government seemed to have learned its lesson about the dedication of the followers of the redoubtable Emmeline and Christabel. It no longer underestimated the suffragettes. Nothing seemed to have been forgotten – except that one thing. Namely that the women they imprisoned, criminalized, and barred from participation in public life had fathers, brothers, husbands and friends, and some of them were beginning to join in the fight.

'We won't be the only ones, you know,' Tom had said, with a twinkle in his eye. 'There'll be quite a few of us. It should be a very interesting meeting. You needn't worry about getting arrested. They can't arrest us all.'

Arrest! Alarm about a prison sentence and the effect that would have on his job and on his little miser's pile must have shown in John's eyes, because Tom seemed to be back pedalling as fast as he could, assuring him that arrest was out of the question – they would be doing nothing criminal. Nothing in the world that could warrant arrest. John silently resolved that he, at any rate, would do nothing that would warrant arrest.

With all the women locked outside to keep him safe from a barracking, the Minister launched into his speech. After a few minutes' silent attention his hopes of a smooth run and an easy passage appeared to be fulfilled, and streams of golden oratory flowed from his lips. He warmed to his theme, and made a joke about the months of hard labour he had completed on behalf of his listeners.

'What do you know about hard labour? What about the women you've locked up?' came a shout. Those members of the audience standing near to the challenger all turned their heads to look. Some stewards took the cue, and hastened towards him. A couple of them grasped him roughly by the arms and dragged him out of the hall. John watched their technique with interest.

146

The minister went on to speak about taxation, but a bellow of 'You ought to put a tax on stomach pumps!' cut him off mid-sentence. Other trusty stewards were soon on the spot to rough-handle the speaker out of the building.

Five minutes later, when the tumult had died down and all was quiet again, the minister continued his address. He got some way with it, until he remarked, 'There has been a great slump in . . .'

Tom cupped his hands around his mouth. 'There's been a worse slump in your reputation, because you torture women, you blackguards!' John watched two heavy, by now somewhat sweating and dishevelled bruisers move purposefully towards Tom, with looks of such ill intent that Tom sank down and crawled under the seats, to the great amusement of many of those standing nearby. The stewards found it impossible to extricate him, and called upon their colleagues for reinforcements. After considerable difficulty, they managed to drag him out, and one of them grasped his right arm and twisted it up his back, and almost lifting him off his feet by that and the seat of his trousers as they manhandled him from the hall.

Indignation had fast grown within John at the minister's refusal to acknowledge the protests at the Government's maltreatment of women, and this blatant repression of free speech, this travesty of any sort of democracy struck the steel in him. Unperturbed by the violence done at his behest, the minister took up the thread of his argument. 'Who is responsible,' he asked, 'for . . .'

'Why, who's responsible for force-feeding defenceless women in jail,' John cut in, his voice loud and clear, 'for shoving tubes down their noses and throats and pumping liquid into their stomachs that sometimes goes into their lungs so they end up with pleurisy, or heart attacks – that's what I want to know! But that's something you don't seem to care about!' The doormen nearest his section of the hall had not yet returned from their dealings with Tom, but others from further off began to advance on him. John grasped a nearby pillar and began to climb, putting himself well out of reach before they got to the spot. In looks and attitude they were identical to the candymen who'd carried out the evictions,

John thought; the same human dross that the powerful always employ to do their dirty work for them, thus keeping their own gentlemanly hands free from contamination. He'd had an open mind at the start of the meeting, but now he was beginning to loathe politician and henchman alike.

He faced the minister and loosed a torrent. 'Call yourself a representative of the people? I don't know how you dare. You represent nobody but yourselves and your own interests, none of you. You've promised the women the vote, and now you're torturing them for holding you to it, you hypocrites!'

The faces of many in the audience were upturned to John, and there were cries of 'Get down,' and 'Shut up.'

'Some of us have come to listen to the speech,' one furious man shouted. 'If you don't want to do the same, get out of the hall and leave it to people who do.'

'Why what for do you want to listen to him?' John demanded. 'Every word that comes out of his mouth is a lie, man, and as for free speech, it's a joke! They've done away with that, they've even censored every play that presents the women's case, and they've stopped every legal petition they've tried to present. They've incited them to violence, and they're using violence now, against anybody that dares to ask a civil question.' He saw two stewards advancing towards the pillar with long boathooks, but continued to harangue the minister. 'You're paying bully boys to do your dirty work for you . . .' He felt such a pull on his trousers that his grip on the pillar began to loosen, and he was dragged to the floor, to the cheers of some in the audience and the boos of others. The stewards heaved him to his feet and trounced him towards one of the exits.

'I suppose this is just another example of your Liberal principles, is it?' he shouted at the minister, while managing to land the roughest of his assailants a sound backhander. The largest of them, built like a prizefighter, took hold of John's ear in a nip as tight and vicious as a vice and dragged him out of the hall and towards the stairs by it, as if he were a naughty schoolboy. This was too much, and John managed to writhe free and get two of the stewards' necks encircled in his arms just as they got to the top of the stairs. A hefty kick dealt to the back of his knee sent all three reeling down together. A couple of policemen picked John from the heap of torsos, heads and limbs that landed at the bottom, and escorted him beyond the barricades, with a warning to stay away, unless he wanted a night in the cells. Bruised and sore, he spent the next hour searching, but neither Tom nor Alice were anywhere to be seen.

They had waited for at least half an hour in her uncle's drawing room, when Alice came down, rosy and sweet-smelling, with her hair still damp. She took Lizzie by both hands and stooped to kiss her cheek, and then grasped John's hands. 'If you'd come much earlier,' she said, sitting opposite them in an armchair, 'I wouldn't have been here. I was arrested, along with a few others, and we spent the night in the police cells.' She shuddered. 'They were filthy in the extreme. The place was infested with lice and fleas, and the stench of urine was abominable. The first thing I did when I got here was strip off my clothes and have a scalding hot bath. I don't think I shall ever wear any of them again.'

Lizzie's eyebrows lifted a fraction at that, but she said nothing.

'Why, what for did they lock you up, Alice?' asked John. 'They'd no call to do that.'

Alice gave a satisfied smile. 'I suppose they thought that my smashing the windscreen of the minister's Daimler with a hammer gave them sufficient "call". My uncle intervened this morning to secure our release, but I shall have to appear in court next week to answer a charge of criminal damage and disorderly behaviour.'

'Oh', said John, with a wry smile. 'Aye, I suppose they would think that hammering a Government minister's car was a good enough reason. Could you not have been satisfied with just waving your banners at them, Alice?'

'Certainly not.'

'Oh,' said Lizzie. 'What about Tom? Did he get locked up an' all?'

'No. An acquaintance of his came last night to tell my uncle that his arm had been broken. He's in hospital.'

'Oh, heavens!' Lizzie exclaimed.

'Aye, it was a lively meeting,' said John, 'I saw the way they twisted his arm up his back when they were pushing and shoving him out of the hall. They tried the same with me. I've suffered for "the cause" as well, you know. Look at the bruise on my ear.'

Alice obligingly inspected the dark blue bruising at the top of John's ear, and appeared deeply unimpressed. 'You're lucky that's all they did,' she said. 'We women dread those volunteer keepers of order far more than we dread the police. A policeman will often show some sympathy, will sometimes say something like: "I wish these politicians would do their own dirty work." But the voluntary stewards are a different breed. Most of them are that loathsome sort of man who enjoys the feeling of power that intimidating and bullying women gives him. Their insolence knows no bounds. They behave as if they've been given carte blanche to molest us, and try to drag skirts off, and do other, unspeakable things; the sort of things that no self-respecting woman would ever want to talk about.'

Lizzie turned pale. John grimaced. 'I'm not surprised at that either,' he said. 'But, if it's any consolation to you, they didn't have it all their own way. I managed to give one of 'em a good crack, and I took two of 'em tumbling down the steps with me when they kicked me out.'

'Oh,' Alice raised her eyebrows in mock surprise, 'and could you not have been satisfied with going quietly?'

He nodded, with a twinkle in his eye. 'That's just what I meant to do, and would have done if I'd had any sense, but they got my blood up, and I lost my head.'

Alice gave him an approving smile. 'Your mother's not expecting you back, is she? Stay to lunch, both of you. Then we'll go to the hospital and see Tom.'

John thought of the dinner they'd have to sacrifice to get that lunch – the culinary high point of their week: a mouthwatering meal of well-risen Yorkshire puddings, onion gravy, roast beef and roast potatoes, dished up with buttery mash and vegetables, and all brought to succulent perfection by his mother's skill and devotion. She would probably have made his favourite jam roly poly, as well.

150

Lizzie was willing, nay, eager, to miss all that. 'That's very kind of you, Alice,' she said, with a warning glance in John's direction. 'No, Mother's not expecting us back until this evening. We're free all day.'

So that was that. His lovely dinner would get cold, and be put on one side to be sliced and fried in dripping for him to eat after his shift tomorrow, and it would be good, but not half as good as if it had been eaten straight out of the oven today. They could easily have cycled home, and come back after dinners and lunches to go and see Tom, but John wasn't hardy enough to suggest it.

What a sight he looked, sitting up in bed, with his arm in an enormous plaster cast.

'Oh, Tom, what have they done to you?' Lizzie exclaimed, leaning across the bed to kiss him. He returned her greeting, and Alice's, but was far from his usual affable ironical self.

'They haven't heard the last of this, I promise you,' he assured them. 'I barracked the minister, that's all. I offered no violence to anybody, and by God, somebody's going to suffer for offering violence to me. They deliberately broke my arm.'

'They probably just got carried away. I doubt if they set out to do it,' said John.

'I tell you, they did. The pain was excruciating and I literally screamed at them to get off, but they wouldn't. It's lucky for me that your manager's wife was there. She knows Alice and she's seen me about Annsdale often enough to know who I am, so when she saw the condition I was in, she saw to it that I was brought to the hospital. The surgeon says I'll be lucky if they haven't damaged the radial nerve, or even the brachial artery. I could be permanently incapacitated. Oh, yes, I shall bring an action, by God I will, and I'll win my case. If they have maimed me, there'll be hell to pay. She's told me she'll stand up in court as a witness.'

'Aye, and so will I,' said John, 'and do you think you could bring one for me, while you're at it? I've been injured an' all. Why, just look at this, man.' With an aggrieved expression on his face, John stuck his damaged ear in Tom's line of vision.

Tom gave a slight chuckle at the sight of it, and his mood lightened somewhat. 'Certainly I will, but I'm not hopeful you'll get much in damages,' he said.

'It sounds as if your uncle's going to be a busy feller, what with you bringing actions, and Alice being had up for disorderly behaviour and criminal damage,' said John.

Tom's smile broadened. 'Oh, the old boy's a bit of a crusader. He loves a good scrap. And I'll be doing a fair bit of the work myself. You know, I always thought I was unlucky, being left handed, but perhaps it's just as well. Those louts have probably buggered my right arm for good. Excuse my language, ladies, but it still hurts like hell.'

'I wish we'd brought you something, Tom. Do you need anything?' asked Lizzie, looking at an enormous bowl of fruit by Tom's bed.

'Not that I can think of. Mrs Woolfe sent those. Wasn't that kind of her? And Uncle William brought everything else he thought I'd need yesterday evening.'

'Yes, he was a busy fellow yesterday evening,' said Alice. 'If it had been left to the police we would have had no bedding of any kind, but as soon as Uncle William heard of it, he sent friends with blankets. Of course, we couldn't sleep, for the filth and the stench, and the shouting and frightful noise when the drunks were being brought in. I'm told that's the usual thing on Saturday nights, and it went on until dawn. And they gave us no mattresses to lie on either. But thanks to Uncle William, at least we were warm.'

They parted company with Alice outside the hospital, and cycled on home.

'What did you think to the house?' Lizzie demanded.

'I think it was very big,' said John.

'It reminds me of that big house in London, where Ginny's songwriter lived when she worked on the music halls. I think you went to see them once, didn't you, Mr and Mrs Burns? I wonder if they're still there? It's a bit like their house, don't you think?'

'Aye, I do. It's a bit like a lot of folks' houses that have plenty of money, I suppose. But I wish you'd told the truth about my mother expecting us for dinner, Lizzie. We got a poor swap with that lunch.'

'Maybe we did, but me ma wouldn't have wanted us to miss the chance of getting to know their family a bit, I know that for a fact,' said Lizzie. 'She likes Alice, and she likes Tom, and I know she'd like to see something come of us going out with them.'

'Marriage, you mean?'

'Of course, marriage, I mean. We'll never have a better chance, either of us.'

'Hmm,' said John, and a picture sprang into his mind of dear uncle William standing in his silk waistcoat and long side whiskers carving the capon, smiling on them with a geniality that somehow seemed to underline his superiority, and speaking to them with an affability that in a strange and indefinable way served only to emphasize the distance between his world and the world of pit deputies and apprentice tailoresses. With sudden misgivings he said, 'Don't get too fond of him, Lizzie.'

She frowned. 'Why not? He's fond of me. Do you think he's too good for me? Well, he's not, and me ma doesn't think he is, either. They're not that much better off than some of her cousins. You won't be satisfied until you see me married to somebody who works in the pit, so I can work my fingers to the bone for the rest of my life, like our Emma, and never have a ha'penny to scratch my backside with.'

'Why, it's not that at all, Lizzie man,' John protested. 'I think you should just be careful, that's all.'

'And I'm going to be careful an' all; careful to get a good catch. Alice thinks that getting the vote is going to get the whole bloody world for women, but she's already got the whole world, if she did but know it, and it's her father and her uncle that's given her it. A woman can only get anything in this world by latching onto the right man, and Tom's the right man for me. And anyway, you're too late with your advice. I already am fond of him. More than fond.'

Thirteen

B eautifully dressed for the occasion in a purple-trimmed lilac costume with white blouse and a stunning purple and white hat, Alice was the third suffragette to be tried before the magistrate that day. Her bearing was erect, proud and unrepentant and at the end of the hearing she placed her immaculately gloved hands on the dock and inclined slightly towards him. Her words rang out clearly in the still court-room. 'Today, Sir Edward Carson and James Craig are openly stockpiling guns and ammunition and training men in Ulster with the express intention of preventing Irish Home Rule by armed insurrection – and nothing is done! Refusal of the demand for men's suffrage resulted in the burning of Nottingham Castle, the seat of the anti-suffrage Duke of Newcastle, and the seat of another anti-suffrage gentleman in the neighbourhood was also set on fire. The mistress of that house died of illness caused by the shock. It is remark-able that *not one arrest* was made in connection with these crimes! Instead, the Government gave in and passed the Reform Bill! Cabinet minister Mr Hobhouse tells us that such a "popular sentimental uprising" is necessary to persuade the Government that women want the vote!' Here Alice paused to let her words take effect, and looked slowly and deliber-ately round the court. 'The Government incites us to violence,' she resumed. 'I acted because the Government has blocked all legal protest. Words have failed, and now we say, "Deeds not words!" My action was political. I *demand* to be treated as a political prisoner.'

In appearance, bearing and argument she was magnificent, and John gazed at her with something like awe. The magis-trate took a more jaundiced view.

'Yes, you've got a very glib tongue, and you've enjoyed making a theatre of the court to show us all how clever you are.' He paused for several moments, looking at Alice over his half-moon glasses, his reptilian eyes utterly devoid of sympathy. 'Quite the lady barrister, but if you imagine that your connection with some members of the legal profession will protect you from the consequences of your crimes I fear you are mistaken, and I assure you that those consequences will be far less enjoyable than your appearance before us today.' He surveyed the court for several moments, his face like granite. 'It is,' he resumed, 'very hard to deal with those for whom arrest has no terrors and imprisonment no shame, but deal with them we must. I sentence you to three months' imprisonment. Take the lady away.'

As she left the court Alice turned her face towards John and Tom and waved, her green eyes shining with the light of battle, her expression undaunted.

'Three months! Three months in Newcastle jail,' said John, trying to visualize what horrors Alice would have undergone before he saw her again.

'Oh, yes,' said Tom, sitting beside him with his arm encased in plaster. 'Magistrates like to see humility and contrition, and plentiful repentance, but they'll look for it in vain with Alice. Most of Mrs Pankhurst's followers have a streak of the Joan of Arc in them.'

'Fair enough with Mrs Pankhurst, she's been to jail enough times herself, and with hard labour. It's the other one I cannot stomach, the one who sits nice and safe, directing operations from gay Paree, while her followers run all the risk.'

'Christabel, you mean. Well, she was the first one to go to jail, you know. And if the Government did get all the leaders, the Women's Social and Political Union might cease to exist.'

John said nothing, but privately he thought that that might be no bad thing. Tom seemed almost indifferent to the tortures that were probably in store for Alice, and John wasn't sure that the WSPU was achieving much by its militant tactics except to bring the wrath of the Government and public alike down on the suffragettes' heads.

He was sure of one thing, though. If it were any of his sisters, he wouldn't be taking it so calmly.

'Why, what else could they do, man?' asked Jimmy, limping back to his armchair by the fire. 'They couldn't have a convicted criminal teaching the bairns, now could they?'

'She shouldn't be a criminal. She should be a political prisoner,' said John.

'I don't think it's fair to call her a criminal, Jimmy,' Emma said. 'She didn't do it out of malice. She did it to make a political point – the Government have blocked all legal means for us women to get the vote, and we're not going to give up. So we have to resort to illegal means.'

'It's not fair that men have got the vote and women haven't, Dad,' Jem piped up, from his position on the clippy mat at his father's feet.

'And I'm fed up of hearing that from him an' all,' said Jimmy. 'That's what she's been teaching the kids ever since she came, and not much else. He comes home full of it. The bloody school board did right to sack her, and the first thing they got Miss Carr to instil in the bairns was that destroying other people's things is nothing brave and wonderful, it's wrong, and if any of them do it they'll deserve to get sent to prison. And they did right there an' all.'

'Aye, but destroying the mine owner's property is the first thing the pitmen talk about when the manager brings black-legs in to work it,' said Emma, her eyes burning as she looked at her husband. '*You* talk about direct action, and you don't see anything wrong in it then. There's no difference.'

'There's a bloody big difference. If any of us got jailed for doing something like she's done, there'd be no argument about us being political prisoners. We'd be bloody criminals, and that would be the end of it. Look at the way the police hounded and threatened your mother about our Arthur. We'd get precious little sympathy from anybody,' Jimmy retorted, looking at John in an appeal for confirmation. 'And I bet when she was teaching them about the *Titanic* she didn't find any fault with the idea of "women and children first", either. I bet she saw naught wrong wi' that.'

156

'And do you find any fault with it, like?' Emma demanded, with a dangerous glint in her eyes.

'No, I don't. All I'm saying is that men are called on to make a lot of sacrifices for women, and they shouldn't try to deny it, and paint us as black as they do.'

'Aye, but think on this, Jimmy,' said John, quietly. 'When we were on strike – when our backs were against the wall because we were fighting for something we thought we had a right to, Alice and her brother helped the strike fund as much as they could. They have got a strong sense of justice, man, and not only for themselves. And her uncle's defended many a miner in court. One good turn deserves another. Maybe we owe her something in return.'

Women must fight, and men must weep, in the present instance at least, thought John. It was a reversal of the natural state of affairs. He was too far away from the prison to be able to visit every day, and the days he did visit, he couldn't get in to see her. He missed Alice. He missed her vitality. He missed her outrageous opinions and the pungency with which she expressed them. He missed that lucidity of thought, which exhilarated him and spurred him to sharpen his own wits to keep pace with her, or just ahead, if he could, because Alice was not the sort to tolerate fools gladly. You could take her or leave her, but you could never mistake her. She left none of her views or intentions to be guessed at – except for that question of marriage. He was now beginning to accept the fact that he would never persuade her to emigrate, and he knew he would never see her sitting at a quilting frame either, or wasting her talents in that non-stop round of privation and drudgery that was the lot of the pit wife.

Before a fortnight had elapsed, they heard that Alice was to be released, on the grounds of ill health. Tom stayed at home waiting for a visit from the doctor because of pain in his arm, but John was there, waiting at the prison gates when she came out. Her altered appearance was a shock. She looked about seventy, and it almost broke his heart to see her once cheerful, animated face turned grey and gaunt, her once lively green eyes now dull, bloodshot and sunken.

'My God, Alice. What the hell have they done to you?' he asked, supporting her with an arm around her waist. She was nothing but skin and bone. 'We'll take care of you, bonny lass,' he choked, 'me and my mother and the lasses. Never fear. We'll soon have you right again.'

Alice shook her head. 'No. The Newcastle WSPU are here for me. Didn't Tom tell you they were coming?' She nodded towards a landau, decked out with purple, white and green ribbons.

'Aye, I thought they were supposed to be coming, but I wasn't going to risk them failing and you being here on your own, so I took a day off work.'

She looked into his eyes and smiled. 'That was kind. But I'll be all right. They'll want to do everything they can for me. And Tom and Uncle William would never have left me to manage alone, you know. If they hadn't been perfectly certain the WSPU would be here to look after me, they'd have come themselves.'

A group of fashionably dressed, capable middle-class ladies hastened across to them and surrounded Alice, clucking and exclaiming and uttering words of comfort, like protective hens round a chick. Two of them took her by the arms and supported her to the landau, and the rest followed.

John stood with his cloth cap in his hand, in his clean and tidy but markedly less fashionable suit and watched them go, unneeded and unheeded, helpless to help, redundant.

A few days later John opened the door to see her on the doorstep, with Tom. The redness was gone from her eyes, and she was a better colour. Calling to his mother to put the kettle on, he ushered them in, and sat Alice in the best chair, with a cushion at her back, and a stool for her feet. To his surprise, she accepted the fuss.

'Oh, Alice,' his mother and Sally chorused, both shocked at the sight of her.

'I refused all food for two days,' she explained, with a weak smile. Then on Saturday afternoon seven or eight wardresses came into my cell and forced me onto the bed and held me down while a couple of doctors rammed a tube down my neck and forcibly fed me. I can't describe how horrible that was – my eardrums seemed to be bursting, and there was a horrible pain in my throat and chest. When they pulled the tube out I was sick all over the bed and all over the one who'd rammed it down. He slapped my face!'

'Oh, Alice,' Sally repeated. John said nothing, but sat on the arm of her chair, and put a sympathetic hand on her shoulder. His mother shook her head, and lifted the kettle to pour scalding water on the tea leaves.

'I would never have believed that a doctor could behave in such a fashion, but I've had a rude awakening to the ways of the world – or the ways of some of those who wield power in it. I felt faint for ages afterwards, and I'd such a pain in my chest and my ears, and my nose was so sore. That happened day after day, with the tube going first down one nostril, then the other. I soon realized that struggling was useless; they'd get it down eventually, no matter how much I resisted. It was like rape. So I stopped resisting, and sat still while a wardress put it down. They couldn't stop me being sick afterwards, though. I was in a state of sheer nervous exhaustion.' She heaved a long sigh. 'At times, I thought my heart would give out.'

'Don't talk about it any more, Alice,' John's mother begged. 'Just try to forget it. Talk about something else.'

'I'll never forget it, and I want to talk about it. I want everybody to know exactly what goes on,' Alice insisted. 'Well, in the end I was so ill that they took me to the hospital. You got warm water there instead of cold, and the beds were softer. All I wanted was to lie down and shut my eyes, and give in. But about three o'clock I heard the most hideous moaning and shrieking it made my blood run cold. Then it stopped, and a few minutes later it started again. I wondered what they were doing to her – it was terrifying. I thought they must be torturing her, and I actually imagined I might be next.' Alice shuddered. 'Then it dawned on me.'

'Drink this,' his mother interrupted, handing her a cup of tea.

Alice took a couple of sips, and continued, 'It was horrifying. She was giving birth, in the next cell. Her baby was being born in Newcastle prison, and she was away from her home and all her family. Laws that were made by men, and that no woman ever had anything to do with, had put her in there, in that condition, and I found out the next day that she was *awaiting trial*! She hadn't even been convicted, and in the end her case was dismissed for lack of evidence.'

Alice was silent for a long time, then she said, 'I shall never forget what I suffered with the birth pains of that woman. I always knew we had justice on our side, but I'm doubly, trebly – even a hundred times more convinced of it now. I shall fight for the vote, and I shall keep on fighting, if it takes my last breath.'

The same evening, after Alice and Tom had gone, John went straight round to see Irene, to straighten things out with her. Venturing no further than the doorstep, he told her, 'I won't be coming to see you any more, Irene. I've been seeing a lass regularly for weeks, and she's going to need looking after. And it's not fair to her for me to keep coming here.'

Irene smiled and arched her eyebrows. 'Why, man, what she doesn't know won't hurt her.'

'I know that, but I won't come again. Then there'll be nothing for her to know.'

'You're courting strong, then?' said Irene.

To save argument, he answered, 'Aye, that's about it.'

'I've just been round the butcher's, John.' Ginny looked him up and down and waited. He looked back, also waiting, for something more to complete the sense of what she was saying, but nothing was forthcoming. Finally she said, 'Come upstairs with me.'

He followed her, through the private door and upstairs into her spacious, carpeted sitting room. She threw her coat over a chair and turned to face him. 'I know it's a lie, before I repeat it, but Elsie's father says he's coming round to see you, to ask you what you intend to do about the mess you've left his daughter in.'

John stared at her.

'She's pregnant. About five months, they think. And she's told him you're the father.'

He was silent for a moment or two, unable to take it in. 'She says I'm the father?' he said, wondering and disbelieving, just as Alice opened the door. 'She says I'm the father? I've never been nearer to her than I am to you just now! She's never given me a second glance.'

It was the last Friday in June, and they had celebrated Alice's rapid improvement in health by going out for a short cycle ride together, ending at the Cock, as usual. He turned to Alice, saw the shocked expression on her face. 'I swear to you, Alice, I've never been near enough to her to lay a hand on her.'

'I believe you,' she said.

Ginny cast her a glance of approval. 'Well, thank God for that, but others might not. What are you going to do, John?'

'Go and see him. Tell him the truth. What else can I do?'

'Who do you think he's going to believe, you or his own daughter?' asked Ginny.

Alice's intelligent green eyes were serious. 'I met Elsie, when I was canvassing for support for the suffragettes at Hartley's. He's an obnoxious little man, and his wife has nothing to say for herself. Nor had Elsie, or not on that occasion, at least. I came away thinking that there's only one opinion allowed in that house, and that's Hartley's.'

'Why, that'll be about right,' said John. 'I'd better get round there, this minute.'

Alice put a restraining hand on his arm. 'No. You stay here. I'll go. I have two advantages over you – I'm a woman, and because of my family I have a bit of legal nous. It'll be much better if I go.'

Not sure himself what to do for the best, John bowed to Alice's judgement and let her go, then left the Cock himself, with feelings in tumult. Too agitated to go straight home he walked rapidly towards the beck, and through that very part of the wood he'd waited in for Elsie, and waited in vain. He sped along its course towards the Wear, wondering why on earth he'd let Alice talk him into letting her go on an errand that should have been his. How could he have left a lass to deal with this sort of trouble, something that was between him and Elsie's father? That wasn't acting like a man, and he despised himself for it. He stopped short, and wondered whether Alice had gone to find out for herself where the truth lay. And would she believe him, or Elsie?

Elsie, he thought, what the hell's she playing at? The same sort of bloody games she'd played in April when she'd had him waiting about for hours for her amusement, so she could laugh at his foolishness and misery. Her having my bairn, he thought, mine! If thinking could have got her pregnant it might be mine, but I've hardly ever been within arm's reach of her, let alone near enough for that. Whoever the bloody father is, it's not me, and I'm not going to be saddled with the responsibility. Why me? Why should I? Why pick me? He stooped to lift a couple of stones and pitch them viciously into the water. A flock of geese scattered in a flurry of feathers and angry squawks. 'Any port in a storm, I suppose,' he shouted after them, 'and I'll do if there's none better. That's the game she's playing, and it's not coming off.'

That point established, he walked on, feeling a little calmer. No doubt in his mind who the father was. The lad she'd been calling round asking for, for weeks. Arthur. He was the one who'd left all this shite behind him. Arthur! How did he manage it? He was a bloody nuisance when he was at home, and he managed to be an even bloodier nuisance when he wasn't. And that was why Elsie'd accused him, because Arthur was gone, and there was nobody else.

He turned for home, hardly aware of his surroundings, his mind filled with black thoughts of Arthur and Elsie Hartley, his blood beginning to boil again. Arrogant miss, how dare she? Who in God's name did she think she was to play such a trick on him? Who did she think he was, if she thought she could make use of him like that? Did she think he had no self-respect, no pride? Darkness was falling when he veered from his course and drew near to Annsdale Colliery.

Friday evening, and Sam would be at the pigeon fanciers' meeting. The time was long past when he could have used the dog as an excuse for going there, but it was getting dark, and with a bit of luck, he wouldn't be seen. Seething with rage and muttering oaths and curses, John cast promises, care and caution to the four winds and sped with angry, predatory steps in the direction of Irene Hickey's.

'If I were a young lass, the look on your face would make me run for my life,' she said, when he landed on her doorstep.

'You've only got to shut the door, Irene.'

'Oh, no, I cannot do that,' she laughed. 'I don't know what's firing you, but I want to feel the heat of it.'

Fourteen

'So I said, "Where did it happen, Elsie, what was the date, and what o'clock was it?" I'm not a solicitor's daughter for nothing.'

The Sunday morning had turned out fine, and the four of them had cycled a little way into the country before stopping to let Alice rest for a while. She resumed her tale. '"Where did he meet you, how did he get you to a place private enough?" I asked her, and she went all colours, from white to pink to white again, and opened her mouth to say something, then shut it again and said nothing, which is the best course for any offender to take, so uncle William says. I had no doubt she'd been lying, so I said, "Think carefully about this, Elsie. You're accusing him of getting you with child and then abandoning you. You're accusing an innocent man of an evil deed, and you'll have to prove your accusations in court." Then she burst into tears, and all she kept saying was, "I've got to marry somebody, and I thought he liked me." Unbelievable, isn't it? It's beyond all understanding. As if any man would marry a girl who was expecting another man's child just because he once liked her.' Alice raised her eyebrows and shrugged and spread her hands in a gesture of incredulity, smiling round at them with something of her old vivacity returning to her eyes, and seeming to rejoice in her own ingenuity.

Tom shook his head, and looked towards John with sympathy. Lizzie laughed out loud, but her eyes narrowed. 'I think My Lady Elsie's had it all her own way in Annsdale for so long she can hardly believe he wouldn't.'

John's face moved not a muscle. He knew Alice wanted his approval for her cleverness in rescuing him, and she certainly deserved his gratitude, but he felt no joy in his deliverance. His sole concern was to turn the conversation in another direction entirely, but Elsie filled his thoughts, and no amount of dredging through the contents of his mind could produce any other topic.

Still uncertain whether he should go and see Hartley himself, John hesitated, and the decision was taken from him when Hartley alighted from his cart and knocked on the door of their mother's cottage, with a quiet and shaken Elsie at his side. After an angry exchange with John, Hartley stormed off, and left his daughter in the street. John's mother pulled him back into the house and shut the door, whereupon John picked up the newspaper and made a pretence of reading it for a few minutes, his mind a maelstrom of ferocity, pity and love.

He flung the paper aside, and stood at the window watching Elsie, motionless under the market cross, hugging her knees.

Lizzie peeped over his shoulder. 'Mm,' she said, 'the belle of Annsdale. Fallen right off her high horse, now, hasn't she? Right off her high horse, and right out of her tower. Ding dong.'

John turned on her, eyes blazing. 'Shut up. Shut your spiteful mouth, Lizzie. Mother, you go and fetch her in. We cannot leave her in the street. She's been there a full five minutes, for everybody to gawp at.'

'She's got a mother of her own. She'd better look after her.'

'Her mother's not much use to her if her father won't have her in the house. She's having your grandbairn, Mother.'

'I don't know that.'

He stared at her, unable to believe his ears. 'What? The number of times she was round here looking for Arthur? You go and fetch her in, Lizzie.' Lizzie, in perfect imitation of the Elsie of five months ago, looked him in the eye, tossed her head and strutted proudly out of the room and off upstairs.

He appealed to little Sally. 'Sal? Will you go?' Sally stole a glance towards their mother, and seeing the expression on her face, dithered, and did nothing.

Again he glanced through the window and saw her, looking at window after window for some sign from somebody as to what she should do. The darling of the village since baby-hood, now every door was shut tight against her.

'I cannot watch any more of this. She's coming in.' He walked into the hallway and wrenched the door open. 'He got her in this state, and if he was here he'd have to marry her, so you make her welcome, just like you would if they were married.'

'Don't you dare bring her in here, John. This is my house.'

'It is, and I pay the bills in it, so she's coming in. If there's an extra mouth to feed, I'll be the one feeding it. You and Lizzie can sleep together, and she can sleep with Sal.'

He left the house and walked over to her. 'Come on, Elsie.'

She shrank from him. He hadn't meant the words as they sounded – rough, like a command. Wide dark eyes stared out of her stark face, and he wondered that there were no tears in them. 'Come on, Elsie,' he repeated, softening his voice and taking hold of her hand, but she wouldn't move. He squeezed her hand and looked into her eyes. 'Come away in, bonny lass. I'll look after you. I'll look after you as if you were my own sister. Come away. We've given 'em all enough of a spectacle for one day.'

The great day had arrived, and John was glad to see that Alice was recovered enough from her ordeal to look every inch a Warrior Queen, but he wasn't sure she was fit for a full day of playing the part in the Great Suffrage Procession she had taken so much trouble about. 'Are you sure you're well enough for this, Alice?' he asked.

'Of course I am,' she insisted, 'and I wouldn't miss it for the world.'

The sixth of July had been a good choice. They stood in Newcastle cattle market under a blue sky among a large and motley gathering of 'Great Women from History'. Lizzie had elected to represent the beauty women have given to the world by joining the Greek maidens on their float; and she did look beautifully Greek with her curled black hair fastened by bands of narrow purple and white ribbon, and dressed in a Doric chiton held up at the shoulders by purple and green WSPU enamelled badges.

'Why, I'm glad it's as warm as it is, Lizzie,' their mother told her, looking uneasy about the amount of flesh her daughter's costume revealed. 'You wouldn't want much of a breeze on you, with your arms bare, like that.' With his arm still in plaster Tom could hardly take his eyes off Lizzie's, naked and shapely. When his gaze strayed from them, it fixed itself on her glossy black curls, her black, excited eyes, laughing mouth and her flushed cheeks.

An Abbess Hilda with her nuns, a Nightingale with her nurses and wounded soldiers, a Boadicea and her two daughters, a group of Modern Crusaders, prisoners decorated with broad arrows, a Grace Darling with the Cullercoates fisherwomen, several Greek maidens and an impressive Joan of Arc, all stood in one grand melee. The organizers began the task of gathering them into the proper groups for the procession, and order was produced from chaos.

But Lizzie was not happy. She looked towards Tom, now surrounded by those exemplars of women's power to help, heal and comfort, and John heard vexation in her voice when she whispered, 'I wish I'd been a nurse, now.'

'No, you don't. They're nowhere near as bonny as the Greek maidens,' he assured her, 'so they'll never manage to steal him away from you.' She gave him a quick, suspicious look, then seeming to decide that he really meant it flashed him a broad smile. Directed by the organizer, she went off to take her place on the float of the Beauties. John found his mother, and with Emma, Ginny and Sally, went to join the row upon row of onlookers lining the streets to see the procession pass by.

The pageant started. A brave and noble Joan of Arc on her resplendent white steed was a worthy leader of it, her graceful bearing and superb control of her white charger setting the tone of the pageant – grace, vigour and determination. Alice came next, an impressive Warrior Queen, aptly placed at the front of the prisoners' float. Boadicea and her daughters were at the rear of it. Abbess Hilda and her nuns were followed by Nightingale with her nurses and wounded, with Tom searching the crowd for them, and having seen them, waving frantically with his good arm.

But it was Grace Darling, and the representation by the Cullercoates fisherwomen of the famous rescue of the sinking ship, illustrating the most familiar tale in the region, that seemed to strike the deepest chord with the Northern onlookers. The vigour of the fishergirls in their picturesque costumes tugging at their ropes with the greatest goodwill made a stirring impression of womanly strength and valour. After they had passed, John, his mother and sisters fell in to follow the plainclothes members of the WSPU and their sympathizers, and the Church League. The cheers and encouragement of all the people along the route showed the feeling of the majority towards women's suffrage. 'Gan on, hinnies,' shouted an old man standing in the crowd. 'Gan on, gan on, we like you fine.'

The procession wound its way through Newcastle, and at last reached Town Moor, where thousands assembled to hear the speakers. When Alice's turn came, she spoke of the ordeal of prison for all women, suffragette, remand prisoner and convict alike, and the people in the crowd responded with applause and shouts of encouragement. Watching her, John was reminded of Archimedes' lever – give me an Alice, and I will move the world. Thing was, he wasn't sure which way it might roll when she'd prised it from its moorings. But as far as he could see, the question was 'when', and not 'if'. Alice was going to change the world, whether the world liked it or not – the response she was getting from this crowd was proof enough of that. At last she returned to her chair at the back of the platform, and apart from her green eyes, which glowed with suffragette fervour, looking utterly exhausted.

After Lizzie had changed out of her Greek maiden costume, they left Alice and Tom in Newcastle with the leading members of the WSPU, and boarded the train to Annsdale.

'Why, you made a grand Greek maiden, Lizzie,' said John, thinking of Elsie alone in the house, and doing his utmost to promote cordial relations on their return.

'Aye, and even though I don't agree with a lot of what the WSPU have done, I've got to say, it was Alice that stole the show when she made that speech,' said Ginny. 'She's right. There is a lot wrong with the way things are weighted against

168

women. I realized that more than ever when I lived in London. It's a man's world all right.'

'I reckon you could have given as good a speech as that, you know, Em,' said John, 'although I'm not taking anything away from Alice.'

'Maybe. It's been a grand day, but I'm glad to be getting back. I cannot settle for long away from the bairns since our Joe got that scald.'

'I'm sorry about that,' said John, for the thousandth time.

Emma gave his arm a squeeze. 'I wish you'd stop saying that. You paid for the doctor, and you did everything you could. I'm not blaming you. I just want to be back home, that's all.'

'Well, I think the day's been a resounding success,' their mother said. 'And thank goodness the weather held.'

John settled back in his seat and looked out of the window, aware of occasional furtive glances in his direction. There was one topic nobody was going to mention, or not while he was there, at any rate – the same topic they had skirted round all day: Elsie. The pageant had been a resounding success, and John's mind drifted back to the inspiring speeches, with Alice's the best among them, and then over all those exemplars of womanly virtue, the holy nuns and the nurses who healed and comforted, the beauties who inspired the world's art, and the courageous women who fought and made sacrifices to save life or country. It had been a breathtaking show, a reminder to any man who needed it of the debt he owed to women, and the majority of men in Newcastle had seemed more than ready to acknowledge that debt. John pondered deeply on it all, but couldn't help wondering just how much help the vote would be to an unmarried pregnant girl, cast out by her family and shunned by her village – or where she might have fitted into that glory parade.

Fifteen

'Shush, shush,' said Lizzie. 'What's that noise? It sounds like something squeaking.'

John paused and looked up, shoe brush in hand and one foot lifted onto a newspaper-swathed chair where he'd been polishing his shoe without going to the trouble of taking it off, in preparation for their outing with Tom and Alice.

Lizzie looked out of the front window. 'There is, there's something outside.' She went to the front door. 'Why, come and look at this, John.'

He followed, to see a couple of large, overfilled sacks lying against the house wall, stuffed with shoes, toys and clothes. Lizzie lifted a mewing, writhing drawstring bag off the door-knob and opened it to reveal a little tabby cat, its green eyes wide with terror. His brows drawn together in a frown, John took it from her, felt its fur dank with sweat.

'Cowardly little bugger. He dumps all this stuff before anybody's out of bed, hasn't even got the guts to face us. Nasty little bugger an' all. As far as he's concerned, Alice wants horsewhipping, our Arthur wants jailing, and his own daughter wants certifying.'

'I'll agree with him about the last two, anyway,' said Lizzie.

He gave her a look of disgust. 'And you want a bit of charity, and he wants drowning in a vat of yellow paint. Just the right bloody colour for him.' He thrust the cat towards her. 'Here, you look after this, go and give it some milk or something. God knows how long it's been tied up in that. I'll bring these in.'

No sooner had he brought the sacks into the hallway and closed the door than Elsie appeared, a dressing gown wrapped round her. She took the kitten from Lizzie and sat on the stair for a moment, stooped protectively over it, stroking its fur and soothing it.

'I'll have to go, John,' Lizzie said. 'I'll be late for the service if I don't get a move on, and Tom and Alice will go in without me. I'll see you outside the church, and don't be late. The rector doesn't make his sermons over long.' A contemptuous, fleeting glance in Elsie's direction and Lizzie was gone.

John lifted one of the sacks. 'Let's come by, bonny lass, and I'll get this lot upstairs.'

Carefully avoiding his gaze, she stood up with the cat in her arms to look into one sack, then into the other one, pick up an old china doll and replace it, then run her finger over a box of paints.

Eyes still downcast she murmured, 'He hasn't forgotten anything, has he?'

Lizzie was right. The rector certainly knew how to make short work of a sermon. John was outside that fine old Norman church within the hour, and only just in time to meet them coming out.

'I think we won't go far this morning,' said Alice. 'Of course Tom's arm is getting a lot better, and he's well able to cycle with no hands on smooth, straight runs, but there are times when two hands are better.'

'Yes. Struggling along with one wing in plaster and sticking out as stiff as a board is all right for a short ride, but not much fun for a long journey. I feel such a fool wearing shirts that are too big, just to be able to get them on. It's lucky it's warm, and I can get away without wearing a jacket. And we have to get back to Durham this afternoon.'

'But I thought you were going to come back home with us, for lunch and a few games of whist!' cried Lizzie, her face a picture of disappointment.

'Well, under the circumstances, you know, it might be better if we come another time,' said Tom. 'When I look a bit more presentable, if you don't mind. And when the present situation is resolved.'

Lizzie seemed unable to check herself, and came straight

171

out with it. 'You mean when Elsie Hartley's not there,' she said, a flush of anger rising to her cheeks. 'You should never have let her set foot in our house, John.'

'What else could I do?' he asked. 'Nobody else was going to take her in, and I couldn't leave her in the street. She's having our Arthur's bairn.'

'She *said* that she was having your baby, John,' Alice interposed, 'and if I were in your shoes, I should think I had good enough reason for doubting everything else she says.'

'Well, I don't. I believe it's our Arthur's, because she was head over heels in love with him before he went away, and he dropped hints as well.'

'And you've still heard nothing from him, I suppose?' said Tom.

'No, and neither has she,' said Lizzie. 'You'd think he'd at least have written to her, if he cared that much about her.'

'Oh, dear,' Alice sighed. 'I suppose the best that can be hoped for is that her father will relent. I suggest we cycle along the Durham Road for a little way, and when Tom gets tired we can stop somewhere to rest.'

'I saw a clump of gentians last time I passed this way,' Tom announced, after five minutes' rest. 'Come on, Lizzie. Let's see if we can find them. They might still be in flower.'

Lizzie got up and followed him, leaving Alice and John lying on the bank with their eyes closed, listening to the coo coo coo of a pigeon, the twittering of smaller birds and the hum and buzz of insects. John luxuriated in the warmth of the sun, and looked lazily towards it with his eyes closed, seeing its golden-red glow on the insides of his lids. Blindly he reached for Alice's hand.

'This will probably be my last Sunday as a free woman,' she sighed.

'I wish to God you'd leave the WSPU, Alice. I think Queen Christabel's going the wrong way about things altogether.'

'Nonsense. You saw how much support we had yesterday.'

'I did. We had a great day, and you gave the best speech of the lot, no doubt about that. You had people on your side entirely. But the more people suffer over votes for women,

172

the more people get their property damaged, the more they'll turn against it. It's only a matter of time until somebody gets killed. And if you want my opinion, breaking the law makes it harder for the Government to give in, not easier.'

'You caused a lot of damage, and you achieved your ends.'

'Aye, by sitting at home idle so that there was no coal to power anything – that was what did the damage. We didn't go about destroying people's property – or that wasn't the policy of the leaders, at any rate. The union leaders were careful to stay within the law, and discipline anybody who stepped outside it.'

'Let's not quarrel about it,' said Alice, much to his surprise. 'I can't expect to remain at liberty much longer. I'm getting too well. They'll be coming to take me back to prison soon.'

He breathed deeply of the sweet, summer-scented air, picturing her locked in a miserable cell in a gloomy prison, and wondered how she could bear it. He turned his head towards her, she hers to him, until their noses almost touched. He stroked her cheek, then kissed her forehead. 'Poor, silly lass.' And she was in no mood to argue, for her mouth sought his and found it, and he leaned protectively over her for one long, lingering and tender kiss. 'I wish I could stop it happening. I wish I could take you to South Africa, out of the way of them all. They'd never get a hold of you there,' he murmured.

'But you know I'd never go,' she said. 'And you'll do a lot more good by staying here, in your own country. I'll tell your fortune for you, John. You'll get married next year and become a householder. You'll get onto the Electoral Register, and then go into politics and get elected with an enormous majority, and take your seat in Parliament.'

'They should have been coming home with us,' said Lizzie, as they watched Alice and Tom ride away towards Durham. 'We should all have had a good dinner together then spent the afternoon maybe playing cards, or sitting in the garden talking for hours about the pageant, and Alice's wonderful speech.'

'And the bonny Greek maiden you made.'

173

'Aye, that an' all, but all we have talked about was bloody Elsie Hartley.'

'Why, Lizzie, she was hardly mentioned.'

'Well, if she's not all we've talked about, she's all anybody's thought about, then. And she's the reason they're not coming home with us.'

'I couldn't very well let her go to the workhouse, and her father was even talking about having her certified.'

'Aye, and you should have let him an' all,' said Lizzie, 'you stupid, soft bugger. Nobody decent will set foot in our house while she's there.'

Instead of taking the bicycles back to the Cock, they went straight home. Dinner was ready, and their mother and Sally served it in silence. Elsie sat quietly with her kitten on her lap until she was called to the table, and when she stood up John plainly saw how tight her skirt was beginning to look, stretched around her expanding figure. Apart from John's efforts at conversation and Sally's responses to them, the meal was eaten in silence, and every glance, sigh or gesture from either their mother or Lizzie seemed to be an unspoken criticism of Elsie, who sat at the table and hardly ate a thing.

He lay in bed that night and thought of Alice. She'd been in a strangely quiet and conciliatory mood, not ready for the sort of vigorous argument she usually enjoyed. Still, with the rest of her sentence looming, he could hardly expect her to be full of joy. But it was utterly unlike her to be mysterious, and the prediction she'd made. . . he hardly knew what to think of it, but he more than half believed that she thought they would be man and wife before much longer. But for that, he'd have to sacrifice South Africa. He sighed. It wasn't the same head-over-heels intoxication he had for Hendrika that he felt for Alice, or the erotic obsession he'd once had for Elsie. And whatever heat he felt for Alice, he had to acknowledge that there was something a bit cold blooded, even calculating about her. She would never let her heart rule her head, unlike some, but she would make the sort of wife that Martin had described, she would make an honourable marriage, and she could well be worth the sacrifice of his dreams about emigration. It was odd, though; he only felt passion for Alice when she was within reach, when he could smell her and feel the warmth of her. When he was away from her, thinking of Alice never stirred him in that way at all.

But before she was pregnant, the mere thought of Elsie Hartley could set him on fire. It was strange that he could lie in bed now and think of her without desire. And it was beyond strange to think she was just a step across the landing, within calling distance, almost within reach, her heart beating, her sweet breath on the air. She was here, lying beside Sally, safe in the house, one of his little family of women. The thought pleased him, gave him a curious sense of peace. He need never again look for her in the village. He could go to and from work without looking for her, knowing he'd find her at home.

Sixteen

E lsie watched Mrs Wilde set the flat irons on the hearth to heat, then clear the kitchen table and spread a thick blanket, covered by a scorched sheet, on top of it. She lifted a heavy basket full of clean and dampened linen awaiting ironing on to a kitchen chair by the table, and turned to her. 'Your mother taught you to iron, I hope?'

'No. My mother sends the washing out.' Her father hadn't educated her to be a washerwoman. Elsie could not help the instantaneous, reflex curl of her lip, that almost imperceptible expression of disdain.

Almost. Mrs Wilde's mouth tightened. 'I should have known. Yes, I suppose it's too much to expect the high and mighty Mrs Hartley to deal with her own dirty linen, any more than she deals with her own pregnant unmarried daughter. Well, I don't send the washing out. I'll probably be taking it in before long, with two extra mouths to feed, and you'll have to do your share. You can start with these shirts of John's.'

Elsie bit back the retort on the tip of her tongue, knowing herself in too weak a position to argue. Instead she said, 'But I've never ironed a shirt in my life before.'

'You start by lifting a shirt from the basket and putting it on the table,' said Mrs Wilde, looking at her determinedly and speaking to her as if she were an imbecile. Reluctantly, Elsie lifted a shirt from the basket, a blend of anger and humiliation bringing the heat to her cheeks.

'The next thing you do is pick the iron up and set it on its heel on the table,' said Mrs Wilde. Elsie picked up the iron and set it on its heel.

'Now you turn the shirt over and stretch the collar out, with the wrong side facing upwards.' Elsie did so.

'Now you test the iron on the ironing sheet, and if it doesn't scorch, you press the iron along the back of the collar.'

And so it went on. Elsie had no alternative but to subject herself to Mrs Wilde's domination, and listen to her explain the simplest processes in terms that an idiot two-year-old could have understood. At last the shirt was finished, and placed on the clothes horse to air by the fire. Mercifully, the lesson was interrupted by a knock on the door. On her way to answer it Mrs Wilde nodded towards the basket.

'There's at least three hours' more work there for you to get on with,' she said.

A plump woman with white hair and rosy cheeks followed her into the kitchen on her return. Mrs Wilde filled the kettle and set it on the range.

'You'll have seen Elsie in the village from time to time, Mam Smith. It looks as if she'll be staying with us for a while. You can hardly help noticing she's in an interesting condition, and her father's thrown her out because of it.'

Hot and miserable, Elsie blushed furiously, felt further humiliated by her blushes, and blushed all the more. Mam Smith raised her eyebrows, but said nothing. Mrs Wilde continued, 'Her mother's taught her nothing, so I've been showing her how to iron. Do you know how to make tea, Elsie?'

Elsie raised her eyes, and ground out a sullen 'Yes.'

'Well then, you be getting on with the ironing, and when the kettle's boiled, make the tea, and bring it out into the garden for us. We'll be out there quilting, me and Mrs Smith.'

After she'd made the tea, Elsie stood at the kitchen door, with a cup in either hand. The two older women were sitting in a pool of sunshine at the quilting frame with their backs to her. Sitting at their ease, doing easy, pleasant work that they enjoyed, while she was slaving.

'First of all she accused John, said it was his, and there can't be anybody in either village doesn't know that. Then when Alice Peters made sure she couldn't make that stick, she said it was Arthur's. So God knows whose it is, but it looks as if it's going to be dumped on me.'

'Aye, it's bonny hard lines for you, Mary Ann. Just when

everything should be going right for you, you with your own house now, and John and Lizzie in good jobs.'

'I know. I never thought our John would have put me to this. You'd have thought he'd send her packing, after what she tried to do to him.'

'He always was a good-hearted lad, John.'

'Good-hearted? Soft, you mean.'

'I know. Still, I suppose the poor lass has got to have somewhere to lay her head, if her own family'll have nothing to do with her.'

They knew she was there. Or if they didn't, they didn't care whether she overheard them or not. That woman was deliberately insulting her, deliberately rubbing her nose in things, like people rub a kitten's nose in its own mess. Elsie's shoulders stiffened, and she marched out with the teacups.

'That's right, Elsie. Just leave them there, on top of the cold frame,' Mrs Wilde said, not raising her eyes above Elsie's waistline. Mrs Smith's eyes seemed to have fixed themselves on the same spot.

'I've a headache,' Elsie said. 'I'll have to go and lie down.'

'You'll have a headache whether you're lying down or ironing. So you'd better be ironing. I've got a headache as well, and you're the one who gave it me. So just get on with the ironing, Elsie. You can lie down when it's all done.'

Elsie turned back to the house with tears stinging her eyes. She heard Mrs Wilde murmur something, and before she stepped over the threshold she heard stifled giggles from those two old harridans. She would never have believed that grey-haired old women could behave like nasty sniggering school-children, but they were. They were laughing at her.

This was her father's fault. He'd leave her for a day or two as a punishment, and then he'd be back for her; he wouldn't be able to resist. Then it would be her turn. He wouldn't leave her destitute, not his little princess – destitute. He couldn't keep it up much longer. He wouldn't bear to be parted from her for more than a week. She had a good mind to go into Durham and sell some of her things, and then when he came for her she'd tell him she'd had to raise money on the clothes he'd lavished on her, to pay Mrs Wilde for the extra mouth she had to feed. He'd have to buy all new again. That would be her revenge.

That horrible woman. Extra mouths to feed! Taking in washing indeed!

The week went by, and her father didn't come. And now, however hard she tried to squeeze herself into them, her own beautiful skirts and dresses just would not fasten, and Elsie had no alternative but to wear those disgusting rags John Wilde had begged from his sister Emma, the one who lived in the colliery village with her maimed husband and a swarm of children. Emma's things made her feel ugly and dowdy, gave her the taint of poverty. And she was sick, sick to her soul of Mrs Wilde's slave-driving and her nasty comments about mouths to feed, and Lizzie was even worse. A whole week, and still her father hadn't come for her.

'All right, then. I'll sell everything I can,' she muttered to herself. 'I'm not having that venomous old witch saying she's put the food in my mouth for one more day.'

Early the next morning Elsie took her two sacks, each containing as much as she could carry, and set out through the streets of Old Annsdale. A few short months ago, she would have attracted smiles and compliments and admiring glances. Now she looked at people and they averted their eyes as she passed. A couple of lads called after her, jeering and laughing, 'We know what you've been doing!' After that she kept her eyes focused straight ahead, and looked neither right nor left, choosing neither to see nor to hear anyone. Her own father and mother had cast her out. Her father had stripped every last vestige of dignity from her and exposed her to the mockery of the whole village and when she got back home she'd make him know he'd done wrong. She'd make him suffer for leaving her to the mercy of the village outcasts. One pitman and his mother, to be exact, and she couldn't look him in the eye, hardly dared speak to him. A hot, nauseating wave of pain, shame and humiliation surged through her, and her cheeks burned at the memory of her interview with his so-called lady friend.

She boarded the train for Durham. Blue skies and sun-drenched fields and hamlets passed unseen, so wrapped was she in hideous reverie. She was trapped in a nightmare. Living in it. At the mercy of people she despised and who despised her. At the mercy of a man she had wronged. There was no avoiding it. At the mercy of a man she'd falsely accused. She hated him.

And then the mother. Always talking about her son. Her son, thought Elsie. You'd think she'd only ever had the one. She never talked about Arthur, the one who'd be in jail breaking rocks this very minute if it hadn't been for Elsie. Where would her 'good name in the village' that she was always boasting about be then? As if she'd ever had a good name in the village!

At last the train screeched to a halt, and clutching her sacks Elsie alighted onto the platform, along with several young men. She looked into a few of their faces, but not one of them gave her a second glance. A few short months ago, they would have been falling over themselves to help her, to carry her burdens – but then, a few short months ago, she wouldn't have been dressed in old rags, she wouldn't have been struggling with two hessian sacks, and she would have had a figure worth looking at. Her gaze lowered as far as her bulging waistline, and the tears chased each other down her cheeks. Her beautiful figure, gone. She was trapped inside a body that did everything that she willed it not to do. From the depths of her soul she ordered it to stop, commanded it to resume its own shape, to restore itself to its former beauty, but the gross body would not obey. Every day it became more of an obscenity, mocking her and holding her up to mockery.

Beads of perspiration stood on her forehead and trickled down to sting her eyes, and she could feel the sweat running between her shoulder blades and her breasts as she struggled out of the station and through the town with her sacks, to find a street of Victorian villas. At last she found the address she'd seen advertised in the paper. She let go of the sacks and paused to rest for a few minutes to wipe the sweat from her brow. She was inhaling heat, not air. It half suffocated her. She tucked the handkerchief back into her sleeve and lifted the sacks, half carrying, half dragging them up the steep steps.

The door was answered by a dishevelled middle-aged

woman, who looked at Elsie's belly, then at the naked third finger of her left hand. She revealed half a mouthful of blackened teeth in a knowing smile, then led Elsie into a back room full of rack upon rack of second-hand clothes. At least it was cooler in there, out of the heat of the merciless sun.

'Why, come on in, hinny. Fallen on hard times, I see,' the woman said, looking pointedly again for the non-existent ring. Elsie flushed, as much in anger as embarrassment. Fallen on hard times indeed. She could never have imagined herself, a few short months ago, standing in a stinking hole like this, selling the toys of her childhood and her good, tailored clothes to a creature such as the one before her. But she owed this low market trader no explanations, and would give her none. Without a word she heaved one sack onto a table and turned everything out. The woman looked the items over, one by one.

'Aye, it's good enough quality,' she admitted, 'but a bit on the small size, like. You're smaller than the average.'

'What about the toys, and the paint box? And the hat would fit anybody, and the muff.'

The woman turned the things over one by one, looking dubious. 'Hat's small. And it's the wrong season for muffs. Next winter, they'll be out of fashion.'

As if her customers were likely to be in any position to keep up with the fashion! Elsie looked through her, sensing what the ploy was. 'If you give me a good price for these, I've other things I can bring you. Better things.'

'Clothes might not be easy to sell. There aren't many girls as small as you are.'

Elsie gave her a hard stare. 'I know plenty. And some who'd be glad of them, if I'm giving them away. So if they're no use to you, I'll take them back.'

After much astute bargaining, Elsie came away with a reasonable price for her two good tailored suits, which was hardly a tenth of the money her father had given for them. How upset he would be when he found out she'd sold them. She dwelt on that thought, with great satisfaction. Serve him right.

*   *   *

181

'What are we going to do if he never comes back? What are we going to do if he does come back and says it's not his and refuses to marry her? What if he refuses to marry her even if it is his? Are we going to end up keeping her, idling about the house for the rest of her life?'

His mother was at him as soon as he got in from work, while he was still covered in pit muck, before he'd even had a chance to scrub his hands and get his dinner. Sally stood up and went into the garden, out of the way of the argument.

'It is his, and if he comes back he will marry her. If he doesn't come back she'll have to get a job like the rest of us,' John said, turning on the kitchen tap and grasping soap and nailbrush.

'With a child? How can she?'

He turned to look at her.

'Oh, no. Don't look at me. I knew that would be coming. I've done my share of looking after babies, and I'm not going to be saddled with another one, even if it is my own grandchild.'

'You keep saying *if* it's your grandchild, Mother. It is. Arthur's the one she kept coming round looking for.'

'Arthur's the only one *we* saw her looking for, but that's not to say she wasn't calling round other places as well, or that other people weren't calling on her. Arthur wasn't the only one. There was more than our Arthur chasing after that piece. The parson's lad for one. And if she can lie about you, she can lie about Arthur.'

'For heaven's sake, Mother, Arthur was the only one. And you heard what her father said. If it had been the parson's lad, he'd have married her. She wouldn't have been dumped on us.'

'Yes, dumped is right.'

John dried his hands, and sat down at the table. 'For God's sake, Mother, give it a rest, will you?'

He had never spoken so disrespectfully to his mother in his life before, and her eyes showed him she was hurt at the slight. She put a huge, piping-hot dinner in front of him. The food looked appetizing, and it smelled good.

His mother called Sally for her meal, and persisted with her arguments. 'Besides, she's not been brought up to work.'

Mollified by the sight of the food, John said, gently, 'She could maybe train to be a tailoress, like our Lizzie.'

His mother set a plate down in front of Sally, and one for herself, and sat down. 'You seem to have forgotten that baby again. And where's she going to get a job like that? You have to wait for dead men's shoes to get into work like that. Our Lizzie was lucky to get in there, and there'll be no more work in that shop until she leaves to get married. And even if there were, there's a queue a mile long of girls waiting for the chance, girls who're a lot more willing to do a fair day's work than Elsie Hartley is, our Sally among them.'

'Where is Elsie, anyway?' John asked.

'She's gone out. Frightened she'll be given some work to do, I suppose.'

There was a knock on the door, and his mother went to open it. 'Come in. Don't just stand there. And don't knock on the door, having people chasing up and down to answer it. You live here.'

Elsie stepped into the kitchen with her sacks folded under her arm, looking hot and exhausted. She sank down onto a kitchen chair.

'You look tired, Elsie. Have you got a bit of dinner for her, Mother?'

His mother took a plate, and filled it with meat and vegetables, moistened it with gravy, and set it down in front of Elsie. Elsie reached in her pocket, and put a few pound notes and a handful of silver on the table.

'That's money for my keep.'

'Why, where did you get that, Elsie?' asked John.

'I sold a lot of my clothes.'

His mother exploded. '*Well* then, what are you going to wear once you've had the baby, *miss*? You'll not carry it more than another three months, the way I look at you. Then you'll have nothing to put on, will you, you silly little . . . ?'

Sally looked up in alarm, and protested, 'Mother!'

Elsie stiffened.

Carefully avoiding his mother's eye, John said, 'Why, that was a good thought, Elsie.' He divided the money, and picked half of it up. 'Look, that'll be plenty to keep you.' He pushed his chair back and stood up to put the money on the mantel-piece for his mother, then sat down again to push the rest of the coins across the table towards Elsie. 'And there's half of it back for your pocket, so no need to sell any more of your things. Have you ironed my best shirt, Mam?' he asked. 'Tomorrow's my Saturday off, so I'm away up to Newcastle with Tom, to see if we can see Alice.'

'And you're lucky Alice will still have anything to do with you, after some of the things that have been said about you,' his mother commented.

'I hope she's all right,' said Sally, pushing her plate away. 'I cannot sit down to a meal without thinking about her. I hope she's not gone on hunger strike again.'

Tom boarded the train at Durham, and took a seat directly opposite John.

'How's the court case going?' John asked, with a nod in the direction of Tom's arm.

'It's to be heard in September. Couldn't get an earlier date.'

'How much do you expect to get?'

'We'll ask for £300, and accept £150.'

John gave a low whistle. 'I wish I were suing somebody.'

'I'm afraid it's impossible, in your case. After all, you did hit a fellow in the mouth, and take two of them down the stairs with you.'

John expected a grin from Tom at that, but his manner seemed unusually constrained. Eventually he said, 'Look, John, I wouldn't be saying this if Alice were here – but you wouldn't be the first to have a girl and then think better of the association and deny it, especially if you had good reason to think the baby she was expecting wasn't yours. The courts are well used to dealing with such cases. So I'll ask you, man to man: might it be yours? How can you be certain it's not?'

'The same way you can be certain it's not yours, Tom. Because I've never been near enough to her for it to be mine.'

John regarded Tom in silence for a moment or two, wondering what was coming next. Tom looked him directly in the eyes.

'Look, John, I've heard you were seen with her a time or two, round about the time it must have happened.'

'She lives in the same village. I'm bound to bump into her from time to time. I took her for a walk, once, and I arranged to take her for another, but she didn't show up. And nobody's seen any more than that, because that's all that ever happened. Elsie's Arthur's lass. I'm just seeing she comes to no harm until he comes back.'

'And yet some people think you're showing more than ordinary concern for the girl, even if you do think your brother's the man responsible.'

'Some people think the moon's made of green cheese, but we know it's not.'

'Look, John,' said Tom, for the third time. 'My sister thinks you have a lot of promise, and she's beginning to like you a good deal. If I thought you . . .'

'I think a good deal of her an' all,' said John, 'and I'm not the father of Elsie's baby, Tom. If I were, I wouldn't deny it, and I wouldn't be on this train with you – I'd already be married to her. But I *am* the reason our Arthur's not here, so I intend to look after Elsie until he comes home.'

After four days of prison, the bonny girl he'd lain on the bank with and who hadn't wanted to quarrel with him was beginning to metamorphose into the ravaged martyr for the cause he'd met outside the prison gate. Suffrage was the right word for it, thought John. He gave Alice his mother's and sister's love, told her Sally could hardly eat a meal for thinking about her, and pleaded with her to stop it: stop the hunger strike before she took a hurt that could never be mended. He looked deep into her fast dulling eyes, saw a thin flame of invincibility in their depths, and knew that she would never be vanquished. As her body weakened, her spirit strengthened, she told them, and it truly seemed so. She would never give it up, never – not until the vote was won.

In the teeth of such fanaticism, John gave up the argument. 'Our Emma's sorry she cannot do more,' he said. 'Really sorry.'

'I bet her husband's not, though,' Alice gave a weak smile.

'No, I cannot say he is. He wouldn't want the bairns to lose a mother, and Alice, there'll be some lives lost if this carries on much longer.'

'Then they'll have to give in,' said Alice. 'What's Lizzie doing?'

'Oh, we're keeping her busy enough,' said Tom. 'I should think she's selling *Votes for Women* in Durham as we speak.'

'What's that woman made of – Christabel Pankhurst?' asked John, as he and Tom left the prison. 'It grieves me to think of her sending her orders out to women like Alice, so they can take all the punishment while she stays in her safe lodgings in Paris.'

'I know it does,' said Tom, 'but that's why the WSPU is such an effective organization. It has leaders who are like generals. Not afraid to assume command.'

'Not democratic, in other words,' said John.

'I fear not.'

'They even strike their own medals, and award them like self-appointed queens, to sweeten the suffering they cause,' said John, with a look of distaste on his face.

'They would say that the Government has caused the suffering, by its intransigence. And their followers wear the medals with pride.'

They went along in silence, until they were on board the train and halfway home, then, 'They're going to win, aren't they?' said John.

'Yes, I rather think they are,' Tom agreed.

'I'll tell you this, then. When they do, I'll never let an election pass but what my mother and my sisters will vote. I'll make them go out in a blizzard but what they'll vote, seeing what women like Alice are sacrificing to get it for them.'

'I think you rather miss the point,' Tom laughed, all suspicion gone, his manner now friendly and unreserved. 'The point is that women should be able to choose for themselves, rather than do what men decide they ought to do.'

Seventeen

'No, I'm not going cycling today. Alice'll not be there, obviously, and it's time I got stuck into some of this studying, or it'll be a bad job for me when the exams come round,' said John. 'I've wasted enough time, so I'll get on with it while it's quiet, like.'

Lizzie had gone off to meet Tom and the rest of the cycling club, and was likely to be out until teatime. Elsie was upstairs.

'Oh,' his mother said, casting her eyes upwards. 'Well, in that case, you'll have to go to chapel on your own, Sally. We can't very well take Elsie. In any case, she's not chapel.'

Sally shrugged. 'All right, Mam.'

John stared at the two of them, Sally putting her coat on, his mother, who had never missed chapel on Sunday morning within living memory, retreating into the kitchen to busy herself there, making it very obvious that she would be going nowhere.

It dawned on him. 'It's all right,' he said, 'I'll take me books and go round to our Ginny's. There'll be somewhere quiet there where I can work.'

He put his jacket on, gathered up his books and set forth, wondering why his mother thought that Elsie should need chaperoning with him, or he with her, for that matter.

On Monday he went home to see her standing at the poss tub, clumsily pounding the clothes.

He flung his dusty jacket and cap on the nail outside the door. 'All right, Elsie?' She glanced up at him, looking pale and drawn, but said nothing. He walked on into the house and washed his hands.

'Cannot somebody else do that?'

'What?' his mother asked.

187

'Wash the clothes.'

She raised her eyebrows. 'Why, who should wash them, then?'

'Our Lizzie, or Sally, or you.'

'Our Lizzie's out at work, bringing a wage in, you know that. Our Sally's not strong. And I'm nearly fifty year old. Elsie's bringing nothing in, and she's as fit to do the work as the rest of us. There'll be plenty more of that for her if she's going to be Arthur's wife, so the sooner she gets used to it, the better.'

'But she looks worn out, Mam, and she's expecting a bairn.'

'Have you never seen a worn-out, pregnant woman washing clothes before, then?' his mother asked, spooning mountains of shepherds pie onto a hot plate. 'I have, thousands of them. I was one, while I was expecting you and your brother and sisters. I'd been brought up just as soft as Elsie before I married your dad, and I had to get on with it. So will Elsie. This'll not be the last time she's worn out and pregnant and slaving over the poss tub, the life she's chosen.' She added peas and gravy to the meal and set it before him.

'Are you not having any dinner, then?'

'We've had ours.' Sally looked up from the stocking she was knitting, and gave him a smile. John smiled back and ate his meal in silence, then unhooked the tin bath from the back wall. Elsie was standing on tiptoe, stooping down to the tub to lift washing heavy enough to pull her guts out and hold it between the rollers of the weighty mangling machine, then make desperate efforts to turn the handle.

He brought the bath into the kitchen. 'Why, is nobody going to turn the mangle for her, then?'

'She'll manage,' said his mother. 'She'll have to learn.'

John paused, fighting down an impulse to go out and help her himself. For one thing, it would anger his mother and probably make things worse for Elsie in the long run. For another, the neighbours would surely see him, and his masculine prestige would be destroyed. He knew men who'd taken years to live down epithets like 'nappy washer', or 'pram pusher', applied with the utmost scorn, and more often by the women than the men. No, a man's standing as a man was

188

something that needed careful preservation and regular rein-
forcement, and he would reinforce his now, among all these
women.

'You go out and turn the mangle for her, Sal,' John ordered,
looking directly at his sister. 'It's an easier job with two.'

Sally carefully put down her knitting, and casting an apprehensive glance in her mother's direction, went out.

Elsie lay in bed that night listening to Sally's deep, regular
breathing, wishing, wishing she could sleep too because she
would be exhausted tomorrow, with that old witch working
her to death. If only she could turn the clock back, just four
and a half months, and do it all differently.

But there was no turning back, and nowhere else to go,
except the workhouse. But surely that couldn't be any worse
than having to live in the same house as the man you hoped
might marry you, after he's rejected you. It was almost a fate
worse than death. How could she have been so stupid, stupid,
stupid? But she had some pride left, and she would pay her
way, as long and as far as she could – until there was nothing
left. And then God only knew what she'd do. She was trapped,
trapped, trapped in this ugly body, in this disgusting house,
with these loathsome women, and there was no escape. Her
whole life had been destroyed in an instant. If she survived
this, she would never, ever, allow herself to be alone with a
man again. They could all look somewhere else for their 'bit
cuddle'.

He'd returned from work exhausted, and had luxuriated in a
rare hour of idleness, dozing on his bed after his meal and his
bath. Now the late afternoon sun shone brightly through the
window, urging him up. He arose and threw open his window
to look out on a still brilliant summer's day. The neighbour's
wife, with an apron on and a scarf wrapped tightly round her
head to cover her hair was just taking up a carpet beater to
start lashing a rug she'd thrown over the line.

At that moment Elsie came out of the netty, and walked
through clouds of dust towards the back door. With a little
laugh, she put her hands to her face and called over the low

hedge dividing the gardens, 'Oh, Sylvia, be careful. You'll spoil my complexion.'

The woman stopped her beating and, with hand on hip and expression scornful, stared pointedly at Elsie's expanding waistline. 'I think I'm a bit late in the day to spoil your complexion, miss. There's nothing left to spoil.'

Elsie said nothing, but the smile on her face froze, and was replaced by something like fear as she sped towards the house.

'And from now on, it's not Sylvia to you. It's Mrs Robson, and don't you forget it,' the woman called after her.

He heard a burst of laughter from Lizzie, and fuming, threw on his trousers and flew down the stairs. Elsie passed him, cheeks flushed and eyes unnaturally bright, closely followed by Sally. He would have liked to put a reassuring hand on her arm, tell her he would put a stop to such insults, but some impenetrable barrier stood like a glass shield between them. She averted her eyes and said nothing to him, but very erect and wrapped in her wounded pride, she walked upstairs.

'I've known her since I was a baby. She used to come and take me out,' he heard her tell Sally, 'but I never will call her Sylvia again. I'll never speak to her again.'

Lizzie was still grinning when he got to the kitchen. 'You think that's very funny, but you should be careful,' he told her. 'There's many a slip twixt the cup and the lip, and you're not out of the woods yourself yet.'

'I'll never be in the same woods she's in. Alice says she's a complete fool, and I believe she is,' she asserted.

John wasted no further words on her. Robson was friendly with Martin and Ginny and often enjoyed a pint at the Cock, and he would want to continue to do so. John had spoken to him many a time, and although pitmen rarely made close friendships with men who didn't work down the mine, Robson seemed a decent enough sort, and they got on all right. Without a word to his own family, John went and knocked on his door. 'I'd like a word with your husband, Sylvia,' he demanded, no neighbourly smile softening his features. 'You can guess what it's about.'

'I wish you'd control your wife's tongue, Matt,' he said, as soon as Robson appeared. 'She's been making a lot of nasty remarks to Elsie that aren't called for. It'll be better all round if she keeps her comments to herself.'

'Why, what's she been saying, like?'

John gave the briefest details, and came away from the encounter with a grim little smile on his face. There would be no more trouble from Sylvia.

'Look at that.' His mother was almost weeping as she showed him the half-finished Durham quilt, many of the threads pulled, and several torn. 'Weeks and weeks of work, and it's ruined. I'll never sell it now. Who's going to want to buy that now, scratched and pulled to ribbons?'

'Why, if we pull it gently, Mam, this way and that, we should be able to tease most of 'em back in,' said Sally.

John looked towards Elsie, sitting on a dining chair holding her back, as if it were aching. The only part of her that expanded was her belly, swelling with Arthur's child. The rest seemed to be wasting away. Her beautiful brown eyes looked enormous in her gaunt face, but there was a glint in them that was not regret, and an expression about her mouth that made him pause, and wonder. She said nothing.

Lizzie was ready with a splash of paraffin for the flames. 'How? They're all pulled, and half of them are broken with that cat of hers, sharpening its claws on it, pulling it to shreds. She never checks it, and you get no apology for all the mess it makes.'

'That animal, it's got no business to be in the house. I hate animals in the house. We've none of our own, and I don't see why we should have hers. It's as much trouble as she is, if not more.' His mother glared at Elsie. 'Well, it lives outside from now on, madam!' she added, glancing towards John.

So it was up to him. 'Why, can you not wrap the quilt in a thicker blanket when you put it away, Mam, so the cat cannot get her claws through to it?' he asked.

'Can the cat not live outside, so I don't have to turn the house upside down for it?' she countered, not willing to give an inch.

He sighed, hardly knowing what to do, but suspecting that Elsie would be made to pay in his absence for any partiality he showed her now. The more concern he showed for Elsie, the more his mother and Lizzie seemed to pick at her. 'All right, Mother. All right, Elsie, maybe that's for the best. I know somebody wants rid of a little dog kennel. I'll get that for it to sleep in. Your cat'll be all right in that, Elsie,' he said.

John stepped into Irene's kitchen and looked round. 'Where is he? Where's Sam?'

'He's just gone round to one of his marrer's, to help him make a pigeon loft. He'll be gone a while.'

'I see he's still got that little dog kennel he wanted rid of.'

'Aye. Are you going to get a dog, then? I thought your mother wouldn't have one.'

'She won't. And she won't have Elsie's kitten in the house any more. It'll have to live outside. Oh, Christ, it's awful, Irene. Elsie can do nothing right for me mam. She cannot wash right, she cannot cook right, she cannot iron and she cannot clean. Our Lizzie's always baiting her and making a mockery of her, and I hardly dare check her, because that makes her worse when I'm out, or so our Sal says. I would rather manage a thousand men in a pit than four women in a house.'

'You soft bugger,' said Irene, reaching for the kettle and filling it at the tap. 'I don't know why you took her in after what she did to you. Send her packing back to her mother, let her look after her.'

John pulled a kitchen chair from under the table and sat down. 'She wouldn't, that's the trouble. Our Sal had a place with them before we fell out, and she reckons it's probably more her than him that wanted rid of Elsie when she started to show. Sal says the mother pretends everything's his doing when it comes to checking the girls, but she's the power behind the throne. She's the one that primes him behind the scenes, stacks the bullets up for him to fire. We've gone past that, anyway. Elsie's with us, and she'll have to stop with us, because she's got nowhere else except the workhouse, and she's not going there. It's all my doing anyway, so I've only myself to blame.'

'Why, how do you make that out?' said Irene, coming to stand beside him and running her fingers through his hair.

John paused. 'I've never told anybody else this, and I never will.' He caught hold of her wrist and paused again. Irene sat on a nearby chair, and listened. 'It's because I thought that with our Arthur out of the way I might stand a chance with her. I could have got him a job on the docks like I told him I would, but I wanted him out of the way altogether. They'd probably be married and in their own house by now if I hadn't sent him on a cruise. But I stood no chance with Elsie, and now Arthur's wanted, he's not here.'

'You stood a good chance to get her when she named you the father.'

His brows came together in a bitter frown. 'Why, how would I want her then? For one thing she was lying. For another thing she was showing with somebody else's bairn, my own brother's. How could I want her after that? She wasn't clean.'

'Clean? How was she not clean?'

'You know very well how. She's had another man round her.'

'You cheeky pup! Am I not clean, then?'

He looked at her with wonder. 'Why, no, Irene, you're not. You know you're not.'

'How, then? How am I not clean?' she demanded, leaning towards him, a dangerous glint in her normally come-hither blue eyes.

Completely off guard, he told the truth he'd imbibed with his mother's milk, the only truth he knew. 'Why, you know very well how you're not clean. You're married to Sam, and you're entertaining me.'

'Was I clean before I started entertaining you?'

'Why, for aught I know you were.'

'So it's entertaining you that's made me unclean.'

'Aye, I suppose so.'

'So it's you made me unclean, and you couldn't have done that unless you were unclean yourself, could you?'

She was arguing for the sake of arguing, being deliberately stupid. He looked at her with some irritation. 'Of course I'm not unclean. It's different for men.'

193

'Oh, aye, it's different for men all right. Sam's clean, and you're clean. But although I've never been further than the two of you, I'm not. I don't know how you reckon that up.' She stood up and moved away from him, lifted the poker to jab it down into the coals.

No mistaking matters now. Irene was angry. He gave a helpless shrug. 'It's just the way it is, that's all. You know very well.'

'Aye, I do,' she said, still grasping the poker. 'Men can do what they like, and nobody's to pass judgement on them. But they can sit in judgement on a woman.'

'There's nobody worse for passing judgement on women than other women, as far as I can see,' John protested. 'The men have nothing on them. Anyway, I didn't come here to argue.' Wanting to placate her, he went and pulled her towards him, and pressing himself into her stopped her mouth with a kiss. 'Put that poker down. I've got one a lot harder than that,' he cajoled, 'an' it's red hot an' all.'

'Are you sure I'm clean enough? I ought to throw you out, after what you just said,' she flared, wrenching herself free and still gripping the fire-iron. Not trusting himself to say any more, he waited in silence. She wavered, and after a moment or two looked at him and added, 'But lucky for you I've never been one to cut my nose off to spite my face.' She replaced the poker in its holder.

He gave a low chuckle. 'Lucky for you an' all, Irene,' he murmured. 'Come here and let's have a hold of you, and I'll make you glad you let me stay.' He led her into the front room and pushed her down onto the couch, leaning heavily on her, nuzzling her ear. She smelled good. She was warm, and soft, and plump, and yielding. 'Because I've got something nice for you, my pet. Something that you'll like,' he whispered, undoing her buttons, freeing her breasts and caressing her erect nipples. 'You're a canny woman, Irene, and you're clean enough for me. You'll do very well. And I'll do just as well for you.'

Later on, pondering on what he'd said, John knew he'd told only half the truth. The thought that Elsie was sullied was less than half of it. Worse was the knowledge that she'd named him only because she couldn't have Arthur. It was this feeling, it was the certain knowledge that Elsie thought of him as some sort of shoddy consolation prize and not even second best that most wounded him. That he found so unbearable.

And he shouldn't be thinking of Elsie in that way at all. There was a far better lass locked up in Newcastle jail, being tortured at this very moment for all he knew, and he sickened at the thought.

'Oh, it's lucky you weren't here earlier, John,' Sally whispered when he got home. 'There's been hell's flames around the house. Me mam brought some wool and gave it to Elsie, to start knitting things for the bairn, and she just took one look at it and said, "I'm too young to be a mother," and I thought me mam would have hit her, she was that mad. "Yes, and I'm too old to be a mother, and too young to be a grandmother, as well," she told her, "only I had no say in it. You should have thought about that, madam, before you let any man . . ." and I daren't tell you what she said next, but I was that glad you weren't there, or you'd have been dragged into the middle of it, with me mam looking at you, expecting you to do I don't know what.'

'Where's Elsie now?' asked John, softly.

'She said she had a headache, and she's gone upstairs out the road. But she took the needles and the knitting wool with her. I don't think she dared leave it behind.'

John left the kennel in the back garden and went out of the road as well, to seek refuge in the Cock Inn. It was getting late and the pub was full, but Ginny was standing washing glasses.

'Why, where's Maudie?' John asked.

'Ned came round to tell her the bairn hadn't come in, and he'd looked all over for him, but he was nowhere to be found. She was in a right state, you know how much she thinks about that bairn. So she laid into Ned, and now they've both gone off to look for him. Here,' she said, tossing him an apron. 'You can put that on, and come and help Martin behind the bar.'

Eighteen

'Why, what for are you out of bed at this time, Elsie?' asked John, finding her sitting on the garden bench with her head bent over the kitten. 'It's four o'clock in the morning.'

She looked up at him, dark circles evident under her eyes. 'She was mewing,' she said. 'She's too young to be left on her own. I had to come down to her. She was crying for me.'

He went to work with a heavy heart, thinking of the night she'd ridden up to him on her little mare to rescue him from the gamekeeper, and the sound of her laughter when she'd met him in the yard of the Cock Inn afterwardzs. She'd doted on that animal too, it was evident from the way she used to pat it and pet it and talk about it, but Elsie hadn't mentioned Love me Long since she'd been in the house. He'd never seen such a change in anybody in his life before. He was troubled by her thinness and her pallor, and something ominous he couldn't quite define. Either he'd have to train that kitten to sleep in the kennel without complaining, or there'd be a row about it sleeping in the house, because he couldn't and wouldn't let her stay up all night with it.

He found a few clean pit rags when he got home from work, and went out into the back garden, where Elsie was taking dried washing off the line and putting it into the laundry basket. He put the rags in the bottom of the kennel to make a bed for the kitten, and spent the next ten minutes trying to train her to go into it, without much success. Finally, he let her go, and watched her for a few minutes, playing round Elsie's swollen ankles, jumping and taking swipes at elusive butterflies.

'Just keep trying with her, Elsie, she'll soon get used to it,' he said. Elsie nodded, and went into the kitchen with the basket full of washing, and came out again directly the kitten followed her in. She picked her pet up, and with a quick, furtive little smile at John, put her in the kennel, and, as he had done, spent the next few minutes repeating the action.

Mindful of his own ambitions, and Alice's ambitions for him, he spread his books out on the table after the women had cleared the tea things. He had to show Alice he was capable of a lot more than a deputy's job, even if he'd little inclination for the route of checkweighman and parliamentary candidate that she kept trying to steer him towards. Mining engineering, that's what he'd set his heart on, and he'd wasted far too much time already. He sat down to apply himself to his studies, but soon found himself stealing glances at Elsie. She had left her kitten asleep in the garden, and now sat there looking a picture of innocence with her head bent over her knitting. He watched her for a moment or two, speculating on what it might be about Arthur that so attracted her, whether Arthur's resemblance to the angel was the whole of it, and why he himself had fallen short. Arthur should have found his way home by now, but trust that bugger to be nowhere in sight when he was wanted. He wondered what their love-making had been like, what her kisses felt like, her skin, her hair . . .

He checked himself. She should be his sister-in-law by now. It was hardly unknown for girls to be pregnant when they walked down the aisle, but by the time Arthur got back, if he got back at all, it would probably be too late. The baby would have the name of bastard because of his meddling. Elsie mooned about the house getting more and more pregnant every day, looking as sexless as a faded Madonna, as if a lascivious thought had never entered her head. He wondered how he'd feel if the baby were his, and pictured himself with her in their own little cottage, with her listening for the rattle of his boots when his shift was finished, then taking his piping-hot meal from the oven to set on the table as soon as he opened the door, a good wife, ready for his return, glad to see him. He caught her eye, and smiled. Uncertain, she returned his smile and looked down again at the garment she was making. But the baby was not his, and he imagined Arthur returning from sea, to find him with his lass and his baby. That didn't bear thinking about. It would probably end in murder. And Elsie still loved Arthur, and Arthur would always have an excuse to come and see her, on the pretext of visiting his bairn. She could be married to John and entertaining Arthur when his back was turned, and then he would never be sure whether his bairns were his own or Arthur's. How could any man endure that? The thought of it was more than he could stand. Impossible.

He dragged his attention back to his books, and started to read a summary of the Mines Act of 1911. He got to the bottom of the page and realized he had taken none of it in. His eyes drifted back to Elsie's face, and he thought of her laughter after she'd helped him take the hare, and wondered why she'd let him take her for a walk, and then left him in the lurch when he'd gone to meet her again. She must have known she was pregnant by then. His eyes were forever wandering to her face, and his mind was forever trying to get into her mind, and he couldn't. She was as close as an oyster.

She was a distraction. He'd never get any work done with her in the same room, or even in the same house. He could never think straight with her anywhere near. He snapped the books shut, gathered them together and lifted them.

'I'm going down to the Institute. There's something I've got to look up.'

A day or two later John found Sally by the front door, pulling the dead heads off the climbing rose as far as she could reach, and throwing them onto a sheet of newspaper.

'Where's Elsie?' he asked.

'She's gone to the Co-op for me mam's messages.'

'She talks to you a lot, Sal, but she hardly says anything to me.'

'Well, she's a bit afraid of you, knowing what she's done, like. And you don't say much to her.'

'Does she ever say anything about me?'

'Why, no, but there's something I've noticed. If it gets past

198

the time for you to come home from your shift, she can hardly sit still. She's even worse than me mam for that, and me mam sees the state she's in. Then when she hears your boots on the path, she's all right. She's like a spring, unwinding. She usually goes upstairs then, before you come in.'

John was silent for a few moments. 'I wish she'd talk to me. You're the only one that's got a kind word for her, Sal,' he said.

'I know, but I know her from before, from when I worked in their house. She's not like she used to be then,' Sally said. 'She was always full of herself there, but not in a nasty way, you know. She was always kind to me. But she's not the same at all now. Something's gone out of her. She reminds me of Charles Kingsley's poem,' said Sally. 'I've a good memory for poems. You mind the one?' she asked, then began to recite.

> I once had a sweet little doll, dears,
> The prettiest doll in the world.
> Her cheeks were so red and so white, dears,
> And her hair was so charmingly curled.
> But I lost my poor little doll, dears,
> As I played on the heath one day,
> And I cried for her more than a week, dears,
> But I never could find where she lay.

'Aye, I remember it,' said John, 'and doesn't it go on about finding the doll trodden by a cow, or something?'
   'Yes,'

> I found my poor little doll, dears,
> As I played on the heath one day.
> Folks say she is terribly changed, dears,
> For her paint is all washed away,
> And her arms trodden off by the cows, dears,
> And her hair not the least bit curled.'

John joined his voice to Sally's and they recited the last two lines together.

Yet for old sake's sake she is still, dears,
The prettiest doll in the world.

'And do you think our Arthur'll think she's still the prettiest doll in the world?" asked John, his expression grim.

'No, I don't,' said Sally, and her face fell. 'It's funny you should say that. It puts me in mind of the other day. I said, "Did you ever feel sorry for any of the lads who broke their hearts over you, Elsie?" and she said, "No, why should I?" So I said, "Because they loved you." "They loved what I looked like," she said, "they loved a beautiful figure and a bonny face. And now, when they pass me in the street, they look the other way, most of them. One or two of them even jeer at me. That's not love, is it?" she said. And I had to admit, it's not.'

'Sally,' said John, 'there's four of us in this house, apart from Elsie, and two don't want her here. If you're all right with her, and I'm all right with her, that's two of us, two out of four.'

'So we'll be doubly all right, shall we? Just to even things up a bit, like?' Sally asked, and he nodded.

'But you're all right to her already, John,' Sally smiled. 'And she does notice it.'

John was beginning to feel a little apprehensive about his appearance before a judge, albeit only as a witness. 'This is the first time I've ever been in a court, you know,' he told Tom, 'and I know nothing at all about them, except I hope never to be in one again. I hope they don't start asking me anything about my carry-on, or I might be the one being sued.'

Tom was thoroughly at home in these surroundings, and showed no nerves whatever. 'I've got Judge Barker,' he said, 'couldn't hope for better. Don't worry; he won't let them get away with throwing any spanner in the works about your antics. That's quite irrelevant to my case, and it happened after my arm was broken. There are only three questions he'll want to establish: are you a credible witness – yes; and did you see those ruffians handling me with unreasonable and unnecessary violence in full view of the platform – yes, and have I got clean hands, did I offer any violence to them in other

200

words – no. You know, it's a jolly good thing that my case is going to be heard before I get this monstrous plaster off,' Tom said, for the first time regarding the now dirty and tatty shoulder-to-wrist plaster with favour. 'It should look pretty impressive in court, don't you think?'

John nodded, not entirely reassured.

'Don't worry,' said Mrs Woolfe, who was sitting with them. 'Just wait out here with me until they call you, and answer the questions as briefly as you can – don't volunteer any information you haven't been asked for. If they need to know any more, they'll ask you another question. It will be open and shut. They haven't a leg to stand on.'

'And we'll go down to the Cock and have a couple of pints to celebrate afterwards, and tomorrow I'll go to the hospital to get this bloody pot off.' Tom rose, and followed his barrister into the court.

'Have you ever been in court before, Mrs Woolfe?' asked John, turning to his beautiful and well-dressed companion, who displayed all the fashion sense and dynamism he had come to associate with militant suffragettes.

'Once or twice, but with others, not on my own account as yet,' she said.

'You've never been to prison, then.'

'You're thinking of Alice. What a fighter for justice she is. I saw her only yesterday, brave girl.'

'I wish I had. I can only get there once a week.'

'Have faith. She's quite indomitable. They won't break her.'

John was silent, wishing Alice were out of that hell hole, free to eat her meals when she liked and leave them when she didn't, free to breathe fresh air and roam and laugh and dispute with him under open skies, rather than be in any position where she needed to be indomitable. Were these women brave, he wondered, or were they insane?

'A hundred pounds,' Tom told Ginny and Martin that evening. 'That's all I got. I hoped for at least twice as much, but I suppose I ought to be satisfied. It was worth another two hundred to hear the minister cross-examined, and have to admit under oath that ejections from his meetings are often violent. And the rebuke he got from the judge was priceless. Cabinet Ministers evidently need a reminder that they're not above the law, after all; and he looked like an overgrown, naughty schoolboy swallowing a dose of very nasty medicine.'

'It should make him more careful what he puts his lackeys up to in future,' said John. 'Maybe people will be able to ask an awkward question without having their bones broken, or being kicked down flights of steps.'

'Why, that's the first time in my life I've ever heard of anybody going to court and coming away satisfied,' Martin said, as the beer he was pulling spurted into the glass. 'Here, I think that deserves a drink on the house for you both.'

Tom grinned. 'No, it isn't. You'll have heard of the time the miners carried a distant relation of mine shoulder high through the streets about sixty years ago, after he'd won a court case for them, a dispute about the bond, I think.'

Martin's eyes widened. 'Well, that does deserve a drink.'

'The law sometimes does deliver, Martin. I'd go as far as to say it often happens in Uncle's firm. He only starts the sort of fight he's sure he can win. If you ever need a legal advisor, come to William Peters & Co.'

'Only another six weeks, and we'll have something else to celebrate,' said John. 'Alice will be out of jail.' He gave a wry smile. 'And that's something I never thought I'd say about any woman I'd ever kept company with – that she'd soon be out of jail. We'll be off to see her on Saturday, eh, Tom?'

They stayed in the inn chatting all evening. At about half past ten Ned Goodliffe called in, looking for Maudie. Harry'd gone missing again.

'Why, where did you find him last time?' asked John.

'We didn't,' said Ned. 'He came sauntering in at midnight, and wouldn't say where he'd been, except he'd been with a lot of bigger lads in their den. I'd have liked to give him a good hiding, but she,' he nodded towards Maudie, who stood with her arms defiantly folded, 'wouldn't let me touch him, and this is what happens. He does as he likes.'

'Why, you'd better let Ned correct him, Maudie, or he'll lead you a dance before he's much older,' said Ginny.

'Ugh, that cat!' his mother shrieked. 'Get your bloody hairy arse off my table!'

John turned an amazed face towards her and saw her knock the cat down and start pouring pudding batter into tins of smoking fat. He'd never seen such temper or heard such bad language from his mother in his life before, and on the Sabbath Day.

'Mother!' Sally exclaimed.

'A cat hair! On one of the puddings! Oh, disgusting!' their mother shuddered. 'It's too late now.' She swiftly put the puddings in the oven and slammed the door. 'It'll have to wait until they come out.' She turned back to the table and gave a cry of outrage. 'And here's some more. That bloody cat!'

'Mother!' Sally, again.

'Mother nothing,' she said, wiping the table furiously, and thrusting the cloth under John's nose, challenging him to deny the evidence. 'If there's anything I can't stand, it's animals in the house, filthy things – and we'll be eating that one's muck now.' She grasped a pan of potatoes and set it on the fire.

'Steady on, Mother. It's only a cat hair. It's nobody's life,' John protested. Elsie stole out of the house and into the back garden, and Sally followed. Lizzie got up and began to set the table with a smug look on her face, and John disappeared behind his newspaper until the dinner was ready and they all sat round the table waiting for his mother to dish up.

'That one's for you,' his mother said, flinging the hair-polluted pudding onto Elsie's plate. With an oath John sprang to his feet, pierced the pudding with his fork and hurled it into the fire, then forked one of his own onto Elsie's plate. His mother looked at him as if he'd stuck the fork into her heart, and he sat down deflated, his anger gone. Elsie glanced at him, and looked away again.

The meal was eaten in an uncomfortable silence, with his mother white and quiet, Sally and Elsie keeping their heads down and only Lizzie smiling, appearing to derive any pleasure from the upset.

Never mind. What his mother had done hadn't been called for, and if he let her get away with that, she might subject the lass to even worse humiliation. John kept looking towards his mother, thinking he would like to tell her he was sorry, but her nasty treatment of Elsie had to be checked, and he wasn't going to put himself in the wrong for doing it. It was nothing but a storm in a teacup, anyway. It would soon blow over.

'I'm going out to have an hour or two with Mam Smith,' his mother announced after they'd finished the meal. 'You can help Elsie with the washing-up, Sally, and stay in till I get back. I suppose you'll be meeting your young man, Lizzie?'

Lizzie nodded confirmation.

'Yes, and it'll be a good job when Alice is back, stop John moping round the house so much.'

'You'd better take an umbrella, Mam. It looks as if it might come on to rain,' said John, quietly offering the olive branch. His mother nodded, with her lips compressed, then put on her coat, picked up the umbrella, and left.

'You're in trouble now, my lad,' Lizzie laughed, casting admiring glances at her reflection as she teased stray wisps of her hair into curls. She put on the jacket of her smart new costume, which set off her black hair, and looked every bit as professionally made as anything ever sold by Marshall and Snellgrove. Lizzie looked a picture, and she knew it.

John sat down with the newspaper, and ignored her. After she'd tripped jubilantly out of the house to keep her appointment with Tom, he put the paper down to watch the pot-washers. The kitten crept into the house and rubbed itself round Elsie's ankles. She gave John a pleading look.

'It's all right, Elsie,' he said. 'Just finish the pots, you two, and we'll all go and sit in the garden with her.'

Sally looked out of the window. 'I don't think we will. It's coming on to rain.'

'All right, then,' he said, 'but you'll have to keep her off the tops. And as soon as me mam comes home, she goes outside.'

He waited until the girls had gone to bed that night to try and make things right with his mother. She sat opposite him, stiff,

204

cold and silent, and refusing to meet his eyes. Her only reply to his claims that Elsie looked ill was a shrug.

'Mother, we'll have to let her keep it with her at night. I've come down at four o'clock in the morning, and she's in the garden with it nearly every day this week, because it's mewing. You've seen her yourself. It's a clean little cat, it doesn't make a mess in the house. Let her have it upstairs at night, and it can stay out all day.'

She looked him full in the face. 'You'll do as you like. I don't know why you bother asking me. I count for nothing in this house since she came into it.'

He saw her hurt, and it hurt him. 'I love you, Mam. I always have, and I always will, but I would never have thought you could be as hard on anybody as you are on Elsie. She's only young. She's got nobody else but us, now. Will you not just have a bit of patience?'

'You think she's nice, but she's not. She was overjoyed when that animal destroyed my quilt – she was bubbling with it, only she doesn't let you see that. Heaven knows why, but you still seem to think butter wouldn't melt in her mouth. Elsie's not what you think she is. She's a little vixen.'

Nineteen

'Mr Asquith's Prisoners Released' the banner on the landau proclaimed, and there were two others beside it, all decked out in the WSPU colours. John stood with Tom, Lizzie and Uncle William, much nearer to the prison gates. Alice was to be discharged along with three other prisoners, and John manoeuvred himself to the front of the gathering, impatient to be the first to see and speak to her.

At last they stepped out, one by one, all looking terribly ill, and all triumphant. Alice was the last, and John went to throw his arms round her. 'Never again, Alice,' he said, 'never again.'

She smiled, and kissed him. 'They've arranged a breakfast for us, at the Inns of Court Hotel,' she told him. 'You must come with us. I want you all there.'

Amid the porcelain and silver, and table decorations, he heard congratulatory speeches for the released prisoners, then with due fanfare and ceremony, each one of them was awarded the 'Boadicean brooch', with her name and the date of her imprisonment engraved on the back. John's outwardly displayed happiness for Alice was alloyed with a boiling but suppressed rage against that supreme puppet master, Christabel Pankhurst. He looked round the room at all the suffragettes, and every face shone with pleasure. But how could these supposedly intelligent women sacrifice freedom and health on the orders of somebody who kept herself safe and pampered in the luxurious Parisian home of the aristocratic Princesse de Polignac? It was absolutely beyond him. And for what? A bauble, and a few kind words.

Days later, John was late home from the backshift. He ate almost nothing, then sat by the fire, very quiet. Sensing his low mood, his mother had worked quietly round him, serving his meal and getting his bath ready, and Sally had followed her example.

After he had bathed, the kitchen was clean and tidy again and the three women sat round the bright fire waiting for the kettle to boil. His mother and Sally were busy knitting pit stockings, their fingers flying over the grey wool. Elsie's fingers laboured more slowly over a white baby coat, and he was aware of the quick, curious glances she darted at him from time to time. John sat at the table to read the paper and unwind before bed, enough to be able to sleep, if that were possible. But try as he would, he couldn't get his mind off the accident.

'One of the hewers took a hurt at work today,' he sighed at last. 'Eighteen year old. He got a pick point in his eye. Poor lad. They've taken him to the infirmary. It'll be a miracle if they manage to save it, though. I think he's had that.'

'Annsdale pit,' his mother said, 'it's a slaughterhouse.'

'Your husband was killed in the explosion there,' said Elsie, not looking up from her work.

'He was, and my sons brought him out, months and months afterwards.'

'I heard that he needn't have died.'

'You heard right,' said his mother. 'He could have got out, but he was with a little pony driver that was injured, and he wouldn't leave him.'

'That was Jimmy's brother Joe,' Sally told her. 'He was only fourteen. Our Emma says she sees Tom sitting beside the fire to this day, weeping over his bairn. Tell her how you found them, John.'

'Yes, tell her,' said his mother. 'She might as well know the sort of life she's got facing her.'

John said nothing for a while, remembering his father with young Joe in his arms, and both of them bloated and rotting. The stuff of nightmares, the sight would haunt him as long as he lived.

'He doesn't want to talk about it,' his mother said, and the girls were silent.

'No, I'll tell her. We shifted a fall of rock, and we saw them. They were lying clasped in each other's arms, the bairn with his head resting on me dad's shoulder – like this.' He demonstrated their postures and then stopped, at the sight of the tears that filled Elsie's eyes. She hurriedly bent her head to her work again.

'Why, are you not going to tell her the rest, then?' asked Sally.

'What's the use of going over all that again? It's best forgotten about.'

'I doubt if you could ever forget anything like that, John,' murmured Elsie, with her eyes fixed on her knitting.

'Tell her the rest,' said Sally.

'Tom said, "We cannot touch them, John, man" – as if I needed telling that. We had to go for protective clothing and we held camphor bags between our teeth, but we couldn't stop our stomachs heaving. We laid 'em on stretchers, and then we half dragged and half carried them for miles underground, and bent double most of the way. Tom and me, another lad, and our Arthur. He was nothing but a lad himself then. When we got 'em to the surface, you couldn't have told who they were, you couldn't really have identified 'em, but everybody knew it was me dad, and Tom Hood's lad. Poor Tom. It affected me badly, so God only knows what it did to him, his own bairn. We could eat nothing for days afterwards. I thought I'd never get the reek of them out of me nostrils.'

'He hasn't told you that their wages were short that fortnight, either,' said his mother.

'Why was that?' asked Elsie.

'Because the company pays men for winning coal – not corpses, Elsie,' said John. 'And Mr Woolfe certainly wasn't going to pay us for wasting our time bringing people out who were killed because of the previous owner. That was nothing to do with him. All he said was: "Don't forget to bring the stretchers back."' John took the cup of tea his mother handed him and stirred it slowly. 'That was when I decided to go to night school to learn about mine safety, and go for a deputy's job, to try and stop anything like it happening again. It didn't have that effect on our Arthur, though. He didn't like authority

208

before the explosion, but that, and the rescue, and then finding me father, it all made him worse, or gave him an excuse to be worse, I don't know which. It made him hate everybody in authority.' John raised his cup to his lips and took a mouthful of tea, then put it down and added, 'And I can't stop accidents, even though I am a deputy.'

His mother sprang to his defence. 'An accident with a pick's a long way away from an explosion; and you cannot be everywhere at once, with fifty men to see about.'

'Your sister's beginning to get on my nerves,' said Alice, her voice low. 'I hate the way she talks about the pitmen and their wives, in front of you, and Emma, and even her own mother. And I hate the way she makes up to my brother: "Shall I get you this, Tom – can I get you that, Tom – oh, be careful, Tom, you might break a fingernail." It makes me want to retch.'

The Cock was the venue for a musical evening, thrown to celebrate Alice's release and to raise a few shillings for the suffragette cause, and Ginny was giving them all the benefit of her new gramophone. Emma, John's mother, and all the other women in the place were listening in misty-eyed silence to Caruso, pouring out his soul in adoration of the heavenly Aida. Lizzie was leaning intimately against Tom with a rapt expression, near to the one John often saw on Irene Hickey's face – that picture of bliss brought on by a good . . .

'You're so used to ordering him about you're surprised another lass would want to make a fuss of him. And she annoys you because she sometimes mimics you,' he murmured.

'It's not just that. I wonder how much she really cares about him. Really cares about *him*? I wonder if Tom's just her ticket away from the mining village.'

'I might have said the same once, but not now. Look at her. I think she's over heels in love.'

'Well, whatever the reason is, she's getting on my nerves, in a thousand different ways. And she always seems to have a good reason not to do anything for the cause.'

John well knew that the current reason Lizzie was doing so little for the suffragettes was that the tailor had let her have a length of cashmere at cost, and she was busy poring over pattern books, intending to make herself another suit, the start of what she called her 'trousseau'. She seemed never to leave the shop except to eat, or sleep, or go out with Tom. Still, no need to mention that, John thought.

Colluding with Lizzie he said, 'Aye, that would annoy you. But she does work long hours, Alice. And she can't forgo the time she spends with Tom, now can she?'

Alice looked sceptical. 'Well, Ginny at least is doing something for us. It might mean more converts. "And they that walk in darkness shall see a great light,"' she quoted, with a little smile. 'What time is it?'

'Nine o'clock.'

'I've a letter I forgot to hand on to Mrs Woolfe. She was meant to have it today. I'll cycle up there now and give it to her. I'll be back in half an hour or so.'

'Aye, all right,' he said, and she was gone.

'Oh, play it again,' Lizzie breathed, and Ginny reverently replaced the needle at the starting point. Watching the women's faces as the strains of 'Celeste Aida' washed over them all, the image of a man he'd known in his seafaring days, the aptly nicknamed Donkey Dick, drifted into John's head, the first time he'd thought of him in years. Oh, he thought, to be breeched like him, and to sing like Caruso! He would have all the bonny women in the two villages at his feet, and not one of them would be able to help herself. Why, there would be none of them immune . . .

The record stopped, and with it his pleasant reverie. There was a dash for the bar. John got another pint, and settled down with Tom and Lizzie. Jimmy sat at the piano, and Ginny started to sing one of her old music hall numbers entitled 'My Old Flame'.

Then Alice's quotation hung before him in letters of fire. He looked at Tom, who seemed oblivious of any planned outrage, if any there were. John was not reassured. He was beginning to know Alice a little, and there had been something peculiar about that smile as she left. The memory of it gave him a bad feeling.

'I'll be off, as well,' he told them. 'I've got work in the morning. I think I'll turn in.'

He stepped out of the inn and looked about. 'Did you see Miss Peters walk past? Did you see which way she went?' he asked a passer-by.

'I saw her, aye, but I'm not sure which way she went. I think she was cycling towards the manager's house,' the lad said.

If she were in the manager's house all well and good, John thought, but he fancied he could just make out the tip of the tallest chimney of the old grange, which had stood empty ever since its last occupant had died, almost a dozen years ago. 'And they that walk in darkness shall see a great light,' he repeated. He was no longer in any doubt that he had to get to the old house as fast as he could, and by the shortest route. Once out of the village he cut diagonally across the stubble of Walter's five-acre field, thanking God that the harvest had long been gathered in. Over that, and across a meadow, and he could see more of the house, and his heart leapt into his mouth at the sight of a faint orange glow. His pace increased to a run, over a beck and across another field, and through the trees and he'd reached the thick hawthorn hedge that surrounded the grounds at the back of the house – and there stood the manager's motorcar. Some of the downstairs windows of the grange were glowing orange-red as he sought frantically for a gap in the tight-packed thorn. Something stirred further along, and he saw a figure crawl out of the hedge and stand up – a woman. He ran towards her.

'Mrs Woolfe! Where's Alice?'

'In there,' the manager's wife gasped, with a movement of her hand towards the house.

He crawled through the hedge, the thorn tearing at his hands and clothing, then ran towards the house, searching for Alice all the way. There was no Alice, but there were three young lads, aged about ten or eleven, standing near the house, and another one just shinning down a drainpipe. He knew them all, and he knew their families. They were lads from Annsdale Colliery, lads that Alice had taught, that he had given pony rides to.

'What the hell are you doing here?' John demanded. 'Just

wait till I see your fathers – they'll warm your bloody backsides for you.'

'Mammy, Mammy!' He heard a terrified screaming, and
looked up to a small window with the sash thrown up, and a
bairn standing at it.

'It's Harry, mister. He daren't get out. He cannot reach the
drainpipe.'

'Ooo, help! Help!' shrieked the boy, waving frantically,
John looked desperately about him. The fire had been started
in the west of the house, and was now progressing eastwards.
There was a fire escape at the extreme eastern end, a couple
of windows away from where Harry stood. A window on the
ground floor to the west suddenly shattered, spewing splin-
ters of glass into the yard, and long tongues of red and orange
flame shot out of the house and licked at the stonework.

'Mammy, Mammy,' the child screamed in terror.

John reached the pipe, grasped it with both hands and began
to climb, hearing its creaks and groans as he went. He'd be
lucky to get to the window without it coming away from the
wall. His fingers grasped at cracked paintwork on top of thick
plaques of rust on both pipe and brackets as he heaved himself
upwards. Black smoke billowed out of the ground-floor
windows as he got one arm over the windowsill, and the pipe
creaked alarmingly when he pushed himself off it and into a
bathroom.

'Ooo, Mammy, Mammy!' the boy gasped, quivering near
the closed door as John clambered over the washbasin and
down to the floor.

'Mammy,' said John, 'I'll give you Mammy when I get you
out of here, you little b—'

He could feel the heat of the fire through the floorboards.
Not fear, but rather a cold detachment took hold of him, and
time seemed to slow almost to a standstill. He turned all the
taps on, and trickles of rusty water ran unwillingly out.

So now what? Either go down the pipe with the bairn and
risk it coming away from the wall and breaking both their
necks, or make a dash for the room with the fire escape, and
risk being burned alive. They'd have to move one way or the
other, and before very much longer. If they could get further

along they'd come to the room leading to the fire escape, an easier way to safety – if the door wasn't locked.

He opened the bathroom door half an inch and heard a mighty whoosh and a noise like the cracking of a thousand whips, and the heat was intense. He shut it, fast. There was no time to investigate that avenue, and it wasn't worth the risk. He clambered into the basin and onto the windowsill and sat with his back to the boy, his legs dangling into the void. 'Come on, Harry,' he urged, 'you'll have to climb on my back, and hold on tight.'

Needing no further prompting Harry did as he was told, and with both arms free John gingerly manoeuvred them both out of the window. Little streamers of pink and red flame were licking round the inside of the bathroom door and blistering the paint as John grasped the pipe, to test it with both their weights. He launched himself and Harry off the sill and onto the pipe. With the child's grip on his neck near choking him and the pipe creaking, he got down as fast as he could, his hands and shoes slithering over rust and cracked paint.

He set Harry down at the bottom, and stood amazed to see the boy he'd found quivering in a corner two minutes ago begin to shriek and shake with laughter, and laugh fit to burst himself. His companions in devilment ran towards him, jumping and gesticulating, and whooping and shouting, and Harry would have run to meet them equally cock-a-hoop, had John not caught hold of his wrist. 'Listen, you,' he threatened, 'don't you ever come here again. You make sure you're in your house before eight o'clock every night, because if I catch you out, I'll clip your bloody ear, and I don't care what your mother says about it.' His threat must have sounded convincing enough, because the laughter stopped, and Harry ran, as quiet as a mouse, towards the hole in the hedge.

'You lads get on home,' John shouted, 'the lot of you, and make sure Harry gets home an' all. I'll be coming round to see all your fathers tomorrow.'

'We didn't set the fire, mister,' one of them stopped to protest.

'How do I know that?' John's tone was aggressive, and intended to put the fear of God into them. 'And how will the police know, if I tell them? I know who you are, and I'll go and tell them about you this minute, unless you sling your hooks – now.'

They all disappeared, but where was Alice? Nowhere that he could see. He walked the full length of the house, calling for her, and started back again. Then he saw her, illuminated by the fire, standing near the hedge, waving to him.

He ran like the blazes across to her, and followed her through the hedge. The car was gone, so they ran on through the trees and over the meadow, and then they heard the distant clanging of fire engines and stopped in the lane to look back. The grange had turned into a vast mushroom of orange-red flame.

A policeman rode towards them on his bicycle. John held Alice's hand and squeezed it, a signal to beware. He nodded towards the fire as the policeman approached, and had just enough breath to call,

'Why, what's going on over there, man?'

The constable slowed, and dismounted. 'That's just what we'd like to know. And what are you doing out, might I ask?'

'We were just going to set a few nets on Old Walter's land, when we saw the fire. The rabbits are lovely this time of year, nicely fattened. It's all right, he knows me. I've got permission,' John assured him, pulling a couple of purse nets out of his pocket.

'And what about your ladyfriend? She doesn't look the rabbit-catching sort.'

'I'm not,' said Alice. 'But it's a fine night for a walk, and I was curious to see how it's done.'

'Hmm,' the policeman grunted, but seeming satisfied he remounted his bicycle and rode away.

Alice's knees buckled, and John put an arm round her just in time to stop her falling. 'So whose idea was the fire, Alice?' he asked softly.

She was silent for a moment then said, 'Well, Christabel thinks that now we have the—'

'Christabel!' John exploded. 'She's like Moloch in the bible, that one, or that god of the Aztecs that people got their hearts torn out for – she's got you all bloody mesmerised. You risk your lives and other people's on her orders, while

214

she sits on her throne, waiting for her blood tribute. Well, she nearly got it tonight, with both me and Maudie Goodliffe's lad. Come on,' he said, 'there's something I've got to do.'

'What?'

'You'll see.'

'You see, what's happened is that we've got the Government in a lot of trouble with the insurance companies, and Christabel feels we must press our advantage by even greater militancy. If we intensify the pressure, we'll soon have Asquith on the ropes, and he'll have to give in to our demands,' Alice said. Both she and Mrs Woolfe were sitting on the sofa in the manager's drawing room, physically in a state of near collapse, but Alice's mind was as clear as ever.

'Arson!' the manager exclaimed. 'Is that what you mean by greater militancy?'

'I'm afraid it is,' his wife confirmed. 'We were asked to pay the price demanded of suffragettes, and we've paid it.'

'So now you know it all, Mr Woolfe,' John said. 'Christabel Pankhust sent them a message that they had to burn the grange down, so they went and did it, and they nearly killed a bairn in the process. You're my employer, I'm well aware of that, but I want a promise from your wife that she'll never do anything like it again, because if she intends carrying on like this, she should be locked up, before she does manage to kill somebody. If it had been any of those lads that had set the fire there'd be no question in anybody's mind – they'd be in the cells already.'

'Louisa!' the manager prompted his wife.

'All right, I promise,' she said, her voice plaintive. 'We were told the house was empty. We had no idea the children were there. The mere thought of it has completely shattered my nerves. The strain of the whole ugly business has made me feel ill. Yes, I promise. I'll never do anything like it again, and I wish now I never had.'

The manager saw John out, with an assurance that he would have Alice driven safely home in his motorcar. 'And I'd appreciate it if. . .'

The upper hand was definitely John's tonight. 'If I said nothing about your wife setting fires, Mr Woolfe?'

'Well, yes.'

'But that bairn might have died, you know. Are you sure she can be trusted to do nothing like it again?'

'By God, she can,' the manager vowed. 'You can be absolutely certain of that.'

His hands began to hurt where the skin was rubbed off, but he walked home laughing. His close call with danger had exhilarated him, almost electrified him with exhilaration, and having had the manager in his power, even if only for the moment, was even better; it tickled him beyond expression.

Striding along, going over the events of the evening in his mind, he suddenly realized that Alice had managed to evade his demand for her pledge never to set another fire, and he couldn't for the life of him remember how she had done it. She was a wily one when she wanted to be, as slippery as an eel. He became thoughtful, not at all convinced that she would never commit arson again – only that he would never find out about it.

Twenty

'Our Ginny and Emma came down this morning, to pass an hour with me mam after the oldest two lads had gone to school. Me mam was going on about the quilt again, so our Ginny said, "It's not that bad, Mam, I don't know what you're bothering about. Come on, we've got an hour or two; we can all do a bit. I'm not much good at sewing, so I'll thread all the needles, and you four can get cracking. I'll give you the money for the bloody quilt," she said – you know what our Ginny's like. "The sooner you get it off the frame the sooner you can forget about it, and start again with a new one," she said, and she made Elsie sit beside our Emma, and she threaded the needles for them, and me and me mam kept having a go as well, in between getting the kitchen cleaned and the dinner on. Then me mam started going on about the cat scratching the furniture, and pulling threads in the uphol-stery, and our Ginny and Emma just looked at Elsie, and you could fair see they felt sorry for her. It'll not be long before me mam's at you about it again,' Sally warned him, as soon as he got home from work.

Sally was right. John had to tell Elsie, in front of his mother, that she could have the cat in the bedroom with her at night, but she was to make sure it stayed outside during the day. After that he escaped, planning to stay in the Cock until bedtime.

A tall, tanned stranger was standing at the bar in the taproom, regaling everybody with his exploits in the navy.

'Arthur!' John was beside him in a moment, grasping him by the shoulders, relief in his face and tears in his eyes. 'Welcome home, bonny lad.'

'Why, what's up with you, man?' Arthur looked nonplussed,

and announced to all and sundry, 'Oh, this is the lad that sent me on me holidays, little short arse here. I promised myself I'd break his nose whenever I saw him again, but he looks that glad to see me, I've changed me mind.'

John turned to Ginny. 'Get him a pint, will you?'

'He's got them lined up,' she said. 'Everybody in the pub wants to buy him one.'

'You're not the only bugger who's been to South Africa now, man. I've been in Cape Town an' all. By, there's some warm lasses waits for the ships coming in there – and they were all asking had I brought John Wilde with me! I had something to live up to, all right,' Arthur laughed, winking at Ginny and Martin.

John laughed with him, and caught sight of himself in the glass at the back of the bar – smaller than Arthur, hair a nondescript brown, and in spite of his weekend bicycling excursions, ghost pale by comparison with the sunburned sailor. His mouth twisted in a wry smile. He certainly suffered by the contrast.

After eight pints, Arthur seemed to think it was hugely funny that he'd put one over on the butcher, and laughed so much he had to hold onto John for support. 'Why, let's go round and see him,' he suggested, when they were almost home, 'see if he's got a glass of whisky for the lad who's made him a granddad.'

'No, let's not, Arthur,' John said. 'It must be three months since he left her on our doorstep, and they've never once been to see her, or even asked how she is. So he's best left alone.'

Arthur's mood changed in an instant. He shook his fist vaguely in the direction of the butcher's shop. 'Aye, he's like my arse,' he shouted, his speech slurred, 'best out of sight. Best out of bloody sight. Just like my arse.'

'Come on, let's get on home,' said John, desperate to get Arthur back inside before he started any trouble.

'I knew he didn't fancy me as a son-in-law, but he thought the sun shone out of her backside,' Arthur continued. 'I never thought he'd have chucked her out, the old bastard.'

'You never thought at all. I doubt you bloody cared, either,' said John, his customary feelings of antagonism towards Arthur beginning to resurface.

'Of course I bloody cared,' Arthur protested. 'I didn't do it on purpose. Nobody lands a lass in a mess on purpose. And I'd be married to her now, if you hadn't got me out of the road.'

'Well, you're back in the road. So you'd better face up to it,' said John, as their mother opened the door. Her expression of surprise at the sight of Arthur was rapidly followed by one of relief, and then of apprehension.

Awake for the foreshift, John glanced across at his brother, at the arch of his black eyebrows, and the sweep of the black lashes that lay on his sunburned cheeks. Arthur was fast asleep. He was a bonny lad, and there was no denying it. John got out of bed, glad to see him alive and well, and full of kindly feelings for him that would last, he knew, as long as Arthur stayed asleep – and were certain to evaporate as soon as he woke up.

Arthur was still asleep when he got home from work, and didn't come downstairs until well after John had eaten and bathed. He was reading the paper and Elsie had just finished washing the pots when Arthur walked into the kitchen still stretching and yawning and rubbing his eyes. John raised his head and his heart contracted to see his brother's expression of disgust at the sight of this pasty little scarecrow with her stringy hair and gaunt face, her enormous belly and her stick-like, reddened arms poking out of her rolled-up sleeves. Sally stood still with a plate and a tea towel in her hands, and his mother looked up from the fire, and laid the poker aside.

'I suppose I'll have to marry you, then, Elsie,' Arthur said, his jaw tightening.

'It's what everybody's expecting,' she replied, rolling her sleeves down, 'but you haven't asked me yet.'

'I haven't, have I?'

'And I haven't said yes.'

'Aye, there's that an' all.'

Very cool, Elsie fastened her cuffs, not sparing him a glance. After a minute's silence, Arthur asked, 'Will you marry me, then, Elsie?'

'Well, I suppose I'll have to marry you, Arthur.'

The silence became ominous. Suddenly becalmed and uncertain what to do next, Arthur said, 'Oh,' put on his cap and walked out of the house, looking foolish, deflated and angry.

This was the reply John had least expected to hear from the girl who was besotted with Arthur, and who could only save herself and her child from the slur of illegitimacy by marriage to him, and he was astounded at it.

'You took the wind out of his sails there, Elsie.' Sally looked awed. Elsie took off her apron, pushed back a tendril of hair, and sat down with her knitting, her face giving nothing away. She had courage, without a doubt, but she was playing a dangerous game making Arthur the butt of her wit. If she carried on crossing him like that, she was laying up a store of beatings for herself, John thought. He decided he'd stay in. He needed to get some studying done, anyway.

He went into the front room and spread his books out on the table, and Elsie crept in after him and sat on the couch with her knitting. His mother followed, and sat in the armchair. The cat sidled in, to rub itself round Elsie's ankles. She gave his mother a guilty look, folded her knitting, and took the cat outside, whereupon his mother decided she had work to do in the kitchen.

He'd worked for half an hour, and then Sally came in, and set a cup of tea at his elbow. 'Hard at it, John?' she whispered.

'Aye,' he said, 'I think I've broken the back of it now.'

'Ee,' said Sally, 'I hope Elsie won't talk to our Arthur like that whenever they do get married. She doesn't know him like we do. He'll never keep his temper like he has today.'

John nodded. 'She won't be long learning though,' he said, 'whenever they do get married.'

Arthur came home in a jocular mood, just after Lizzie got in from work. 'I've been to see one of my old school friends,' he announced, 'Kath Leigh. Now there's a lass who knows how to make a lad welcome. She was always all right, Kath. A big, strong, bonny lass that likes a bit of fun.'

'Aye, well, Arthur, tell us all about your travels, then. What sort of things you saw, and how you liked life at sea,' prompted John, to deflect him from discussion of other women's merits while Elsie was present.

'Some of it was all right, I suppose, getting round and seeing different things, but it's like I said, not enough women about. The ones you do meet, though, phew!' He raised his eyebrows and gave John a knowing grin, with a sly look in his mother's direction. 'You'll mind Sweaty Betty and Suicide Lil in Cape Town, John – they both remember you all right. Aye, they both think the world of you. They can hardly wait for your next visit.'

'No, I don't mind Sweaty Betty and Suicide Lil, Arthur,' John laughed, 'and I doubt they'll mind me, because I never knew them. I had a different sort of a lass while I was there.'

'Well, I had all sorts – when we were in port, but we weren't in port often enough, like, and I didn't want any of the bloody substitutes for women you get on board ships,' said Arthur, puckering his mouth and thrusting his pelvis forward, with one hand on his hip and the other behind his ear.

John frowned. 'Let's change the subject, shall we, Arthur? To something that's fit for women to listen to, if you can manage that.'

'Aye, all right. Let's hear about you and our Lizzie, then. I've heard you're going out with the one who used to be the teacher here until she got locked up, for smashing somebody's motorcar. I'm looking forward to meeting her. I reckon we'd get on like a house on fire.'

'Like a house on fire?' John asked, eyebrows raised. 'I hope not.'

'Yes, and I'm keeping company with her brother, you'll have heard that, an' all,' Lizzie cut in. 'And you mind your Ps and Qs if you see me out with him. I don't want you coming away with your filthy language and your dirty stories, and showing me up.'

'Are you scared I'll frighten him off, like?'

'Just pretend to be civilized, that's all.'

'I'll have no need to frighten him off,' said Arthur.

'What do you mean by that?'

'If you had any bloody sense, you'd know what I mean by

that,' said Arthur, contemptuously. 'So that's that subject over with. The next subject is I need a job – round here. I doubt Woolfe'll give us one, though.'

'You never know,' said John. 'Why not go and ask him? It's a full seven months at least since you destroyed a lot of his property. He might have forgotten, or if he hasn't, maybe you can bring him round if you eat enough humble pie.'

'It depends how much is enough,' said Arthur, his expression sour. 'I soon get bellyache, wi' that stuff.'

'Ask him anyway, and I'll put a good word in for you,' said John.

Arthur slowly raised his eyebrows and opened his eyes wider. 'What? *You'll* put a good word in for *me*? Times have changed. And are you far enough up his arse for it to do any good, like?'

'Just ask him – nice and polite, like,' said John.

'Aye, all right.' Arthur looked at Elsie, and his face resumed its sour aspect. 'Well, are we putting the banns up, or what?'

'If you like.'

'Not if I like,' Arthur stressed. 'I bloody *don't* like. It's if *you* like. You're the one that's bloody pregnant, not me.'

Elsie shrugged, and Arthur copied and exaggerated the shrug, rolling his eyes at the rest of them and then towards Elsie. 'I hope you've got plenty of hot water, Mam. I want a bath. There's a bit of dancing on at the club, and I'm taking Kath, if she'll come. I might as well enjoy my freedom while I can, with somebody that's got a bit of life in her.'

A protest rose to John's lips, and then died away. After all, Arthur had made the offer, and only waited for a definite answer. John looked towards Elsie, but the little oyster was tight in her shell, and prising that apart was more than he could do.

'You'd better take the offer while it's there, madam,' said their mother. 'The banns will take three weeks, and the way I look at you, your time will come not long after.'

Elsie went to bed early, and pulled the covers over her head. Her nerves were all to pieces, and waves of panic and depression chased each other, washing her down a fearful spiral, ever downwards into a terrifying abyss. How much more had to be endured? It was all John's fault. Did he realize what he'd done to her? Why couldn't he have come and got Arthur away sooner, when she'd asked him to? What could have been more important than that? She should have left Arthur to freeze, and then none of this would ever have happened. She should have let him freeze to death, and then she would be safe at home with her own beautiful figure and her lovely clothes and Love me Long to love and to groom and to ride. Or she should have done as she'd intended and gone to meet John on April the first, and made an even bigger fool of him than he thought she had, and then he might have thought the baby was his. She'd liked him, but going in cold blood to try to make somebody do that to you was a far different thing to what had happened with Arthur, and when the time came, her heart had failed her.

If she'd done as her father had wanted, she could have been married to the parson's son, and living in that beautiful old rectory. Pity for her she didn't like the parson's son, or the parson or the parson's wife either.

And how Lizzie enjoyed letting her know what she was in for. 'Well, I'll never marry a pitman. They're usually filthy for one thing. They call themselves slaves, so what's that make the wife? I've got plans, and they don't include dadding the dust out of mucky pit clothes against some poky little cottage wall, and having meals ready at all times of the day and night for when he comes back from the pit, if he comes back at all. We know that some of them don't. And what does the pit wife do then, probably thrown out of her home, and with a gaggle of kids round her ankles and nothing to feed them on? You can keep your pitmen. If I cannot do better than that, I'll give up altogether.' If she'd heard that once, she'd heard it a thousand times, and always said with a smile in her direction.

How could she ever have imagined Arthur a romantic hero? He was handsome, very handsome – and crude, and insulting, and cruel and oafish – and he actually thought his disgusting comments were funny! And that look on his face when he first saw her at the sink! He could deal an insult without opening his mouth. The dirt was gone from Arthur's eyes and fingernails now, but listening to him, she understood what her father meant when he said that the miners were a lot of underground savages. And that was something else she sensed about him now, just under the surface, waiting to erupt, something violent and repellent, and if she married him she would become his subject slave, and have to live in a poky little house like Emma's, among all the other savages in Annsdale Colliery, breaking her back at the poss-tub and wearing drab clothes and having endless babies that would be fed into the pit to be killed before they were even grown up, like Jimmy's little brother. If only I could disappear off the face of the earth, she thought, and never have to see or be seen by anybody again. If only I could, if only I could.

But she couldn't disappear, and tomorrow she would have to endure ... She knew not what, and she dare not think about it.

'Why, that's all right, then. When do you start?' John asked.

'Monday morning, same shift as you, in your team,' said Arthur, with a look on his face that was not entirely one of pleasure. 'I suppose I ought to thank you.'

'Don't thank me,' said John. 'Thank Christabel Pankhurst.'

'What?'

'Never mind.' John gave a sardonic smile, thinking of Mrs Woolfe's fire raising, doubting that the manager would even have contemplated employing Arthur again had it not been for that little leverage John had.

'Christabel Pankhurst?' Arthur stared at him. 'What's she got to do with aught?'

'If you want to thank me, just get the coal out, and don't cause any bloody trouble,' John told him, 'and that'll be thanks enough.'

It was the manager who insisted that Arthur should work on John's team as far as possible, and he made it clear he was holding John responsible for him. The arrangement suited John well enough. Having them both on the same shift meant easier work for his mother, with only two sets of mealtimes, for them and for Lizzie, and it meant he could keep an eye on what was going on at home when Arthur was in. The fact that he and Arthur were vying to be first in the bath when they got home was a minor nuisance, but John gave way to Arthur more often than not, to get him out of the house with the least delay.

Nothing more had been said about marriage and John tackled him about it. 'I've told me mam, and now I'll tell you,' said Arthur. 'I've asked her twice, and I'll not be asking her again. She'll have to ask me if she wants the banns up, and she'd better be bloody sharp about it, or I might be married to Kath.'

'How can you think about marrying Kath, when you've got Elsie in the state she's in?'

'Easy. I'm not absolutely certain I'm responsible for the state she's in. I'm not certain she was a virgin, for one thing. For another, she's not all that pleased to see me back. And for another thing, she told everybody you were the one.'

'And you think I'm lying when I say I'm not.'

'If I really thought that, I would never have asked her a second time, and I did ask her. No, what I reckon is, she thought you were soft enough to stand for it. But Elsie'll never make a pitman's wife. Never in this wide world. Your clothes would never be warmed, your dinner would never be ready, and when it did come, it would be bad. She's not been brought up to hard work, and her father's made it clear there's no money comes with her either, even to get her a bit of a start, like it's supposed to do with women like her. Anybody that gets her will get the worst of both worlds, a woman who's got nothing useful and knows nothing useful. I would rather have a wife that knows how to run a house, and look after a man.'

'She needs a husband, and the bairn'll need a father, and she'll learn how to run a house.'

'I doubt it, but I'll tell you this much. If I marry her she'll learn, and she'd better learn fast, or it'll be a bloody bad job for her.'

John stopped going down to the Cock, and hardly went out at all, unless he was meeting Alice. Instead he took to sitting in the front room with his books, trying to study, to grapple with the problems of keeping mines ventilated, or free from flooding, or some other hazard, or to con the Mines and Quarries Acts. Instead, his mind would float off onto a track of its own – a constant fret about the treatment facing Elsie if she did marry Arthur, which it would be hard for anybody to interfere with once they were man and wife, and then about the stigma and hardship she would face if she didn't marry Arthur. For the life of him, he couldn't decide which was worse. He sometimes wished he'd made no protest when she'd accused him of being the father, and just let events take their course. It couldn't be much longer before they did put the banns up. Elsie couldn't shilly-shally for much longer.

One afternoon when they were alone in the front room, with his mother and Sally busy elsewhere, the question in his mind popped out without warning, seemingly of its own volition. It hung on the air, like something tangible, as much of a surprise to him as it was to her.

'Do you like me, Elsie?'

She looked up from her knitting with an expression of astonishment on her face. He caught her eye and held it for a moment before she looked down again, murmuring, 'Yes.' Then with a faint blush and her face perfectly serious she deliberately lifted her head to look him full in the face, and with a little smile to add, 'Very much.'

John returned the look and the smile, and turned back to his books, cursing the warmth that was rising to his own cheeks.

Twenty-One

'What's the matter, Elsie?' John asked. It was getting dark and they found her sitting on the kitchen steps when they got home from work. She kept still and silent, so Arthur went straight on, into the house. John looked more closely. She had the cat on her knee, and was stooped protectively over it, and he saw its blood on her clothes and her hands.

'Why, what's happened here?' he asked.

'It wasn't her fault. Poor little Fizzie.'

'She's dead, Elsie.'

'No,' said Elsie. 'She's still warm. I don't think she's dead.'

'Elsie, she's dead.' The cat was completely motionless, and as Elsie moved and turned her face up to him, half its entrails slid out.

'She loved me,' Elsie whispered. 'Poor little Fizzie.'

'Put her down, bonny lass, and come in and wash your hands. You'll have to change your clothes an' all. I'll bury her later.'

She shook her head, refusing to go in the house, nor would she let him bury the cat. She sat with it, and kept putting a protecting, testing hand on its body, as if she expected it to come to life again. He went into the house and rounded ferociously on Arthur. 'Did you let the bloody ferrets out?'

'No, I bloody didn't. I've been at bloody work all day, the same as you. Nothing changes in this house, does it? The ferrets get out and kill the bloody cat, so our Arthur must be the one to blame. Well, ask me mother.'

Their mother said nothing. One glance at her white face and her stony stare, and John had no need to ask. He knew. Sally was sitting knitting, looking very subdued. Even Lizzie had nothing to say.

His mother began to fill the bath, and John ate his meal in silence with Arthur. As soon as he'd finished, he went out again to Elsie. 'Come on, bonny lass, lay her on these rags, and we'll put her in the kennel for now. Come on in, before our Arthur gets in the bath, and you can sit in the front room with the lasses.'

She shook her head, and he stayed outside with her until Arthur was bathed, dressed and on his way out, and his mother called him for the bath. Then he determinedly took the cat from Elsie and ushered her into the house. After she'd washed the blood off, he saw bites on her hands.

'What happened there?'

'The ferrets bit them,' she said, 'when I tried to get Fizzie away from them.'

'Get a clean bowl of hot water, and plenty of soap,' he ordered his mother. 'They should have been cleaned as soon as it happened. She'll be lucky if she doesn't end up with blood poisoning. Get them well scrubbed, Elsie, then put some iodine on.'

John heard her several times during the night, going downstairs and out into the garden. He got up early for work. By that time the cat was stiff and cold, and it was impossible even for Elsie to deny that she was dead. He buried her before he left, with Elsie beside him. He expected her to shed a few tears, but her pinched little face was expressionless, and her eyes as dry as the desert sand.

After that, Elsie's eyes lacked all lustre. The gleam of them was gone, and in its place a vacant stare, which seemed always to gaze beyond the time and space she inhabited. She seemed to be shrinking further and further into her shell, cutting herself adrift from the world and everything in it.

'It doesn't look as if your dad's ever going to get permission to wear his scarlet coat, Elsie. It's been lying in the shop waiting for him to collect it for months,' said Lizzie, on her return from work one evening.

'What?' said Elsie. Lizzie repeated the remark.

'Hunting's a winter sport,' said Elsie. 'They won't be starting again until October.'

'It's October the first today,' Lizzie laughed. 'I've heard of people not knowing what day it is, but never not knowing what month it is.'

'All right, Lizzie,' said John. 'What's your point?'

'Nothing, except the Master of the Hunt was in the shop with the rector, and they were talking about Elsie's dad. They seem to think about as well of him as you and our Arthur do. I don't think he'll ever get permission to wear his scarlet coat. In fact, I don't think he'll be hunting very often, not with the Annsdale Hunt, at any rate. I think your Elsie's put paid to that for him, all right. But Mr Surtees says he'd better come and pay for the coat now it's made, or he'll be after him. I told him Tom might take the case on for him if it comes to court.'

'I doubt if Tom would be bothered with a petty dispute like that. And why ask Elsie whether her father'll be going hunting if you know for a fact he won't?' asked John, with ill-concealed disgust.

'She's useless, she's absolutely useless. You can't even leave her to watch the oven without she lets the stuff burn. Everything she touches, she makes a mess of. It's not enough for her she's made a mess of herself.'

'I'll go.' Elsie looked completely detached.

'You will not,' said John, 'and Mother, you'll remember she didn't get into this state on her own.'

His mother looked at Elsie with murder in her eyes before turning to John. 'You seem to think that gives her more right to live in this house than I've got,' she blazed. 'All right then, I'll go. I'll go and stay at Ginny's. See how you'll manage with her looking after you. You'll go hungry and dirty if you have to wait for her.'

Face grim, John slipped into deputy mode. 'There's neither of you going anywhere. You can both calm down and make your minds up to get on with it, and get on with each other. Elsie, you try a bit harder to remember what you're told. And Mother, you make some allowances for her age and condition, and have a bit of patience, for pity's sake.'

*   *   *

229

When he and Arthur returned from the backshift, there was no Elsie to be seen. His mother claimed she would soon be back, and tried to make conversation. Lizzie affected indifference.

Sally looked genuinely upset. 'Me mam told her off for boiling the peas out of their shells. Elsie put her coat on and went, and I ran after her. She told me it was all right, to go back to me mother and not to worry. She said, "I'm a real charity case now. I've no claim on anybody and no right to expect anything. I'm nothing but another mouth to feed – I can't bear any more of it," and she wouldn't come back. She didn't go back to her dad's either – she walked out of the village.'

'Where do you think she has gone, Sally?'

'I think she's gone to the workhouse. She said, "If I have to live on charity, it won't be private charity."'

John looked at Arthur. 'Well?'

'Well what?'

'Are you going to fetch her back?'

'No fear. She went under her own steam, and if she wants to come back she can come back the same way, because she doesn't want me, and I don't want her. You're the bugger she can't keep her eyes off, not me.'

Stung almost to murder, John rounded on Arthur, grasped him by his shirt and raised a fist ready to strike. Lizzie grabbed John's jacket, and tried to pull him away. Their mother tried to thrust herself between the two of them, shrieking,

'Stop it, stop it!'

Brother glared at brother, both boiling with wrath and resentment. Sally's hands flew to her face, and she gave a little sob of fear. With that, John pushed Arthur away and sent him staggering backwards, then snatched his jacket off the peg, and stormed away to Hartley's house.

Mrs Hartley affected terror of him, and he supposed himself a fearful sight, unwashed, wild eyed, and fists twitching with a demonic energy. Hartley came to the door, and stood there stony-faced, with the mother mute at the back of him. Neither offered to help search for Elsie, and neither seemed to care what might have happened to her. As far as her parents were concerned, Elsie belonged to whoever had helped her disgrace herself, and it was up to them to look after her. John's hands itched to take their two heads and dash them together hard enough to knock their brains out. He was not invited in. After a few heated words Hartley slammed the door in his face.

John went for his bicycle, and pedalled it hard. A proud girl daily humiliated until she could endure no more – Elsie's despairing little face filled his mind, and the idea that she might have destroyed herself laid a chill on his heart and filled him with foreboding. He hoped to God he would find her in the workhouse.

It was around midnight when he got there and began clanging the bell. The porter eventually opened a window.

'Get away. You're too late, coming here drunk at this time o' night. You should have been here before one o'clock in the . .'

John turned towards him. 'I don't want to come in. I want to know if somebody else has.'

'Nuisance vagrants. Get away, before I send for the police.'

'I'm not a vagrant,' John shouted, seizing his bicycle and shaking it for the man to see. 'Vagrants don't go about on bicycles, and they're not covered in pit muck, either. I want to know if a young woman's come in, they call Elsie Hartley.'

'You're too late for that an' all, so get off. Get away, and if you've got to come back at all, come back at the proper time.' The porter closed the window, and shut it fast, leaving John with no alternative other than to cycle home again, to pass a sleepless night.

At six o'clock the following morning, as soon as the workhouse came to life, he was outside it again, clanging the bell. The porter admitted him and left him in a side room, cold and sparsely furnished. John sat down on a wooden chair placed along the wall, between a long deal table and the fireplace, whose cold ashes were imprisoned by a stout fireguard of heavy wrought iron. Alone, he had nothing to do but sit twisting his cap in his hands, and stare at a clean wall of painted brick, with long, high, bare windows. He had never been in the place before, and was surprised to see it so spotlessly clean, but it was stark, and as cold as the charity it dispensed. He got up from time to time, to cross a floor of bare stone flags polished to a glassy shine, and open the door to see if he could find anybody in the corridor. Seeing nobody, he would traverse the floor back to his seat, and wonder at the gloss on it – produced, no doubt, with pauper elbow grease. It wouldn't be long before miles of shiny floor like that were breaking Elsie's back and knees, and making her poor skinny little arms ache, and her hands sore. And with that thought he would sit down again, and wait. He must have waited over three hours, and he knew he'd missed the late shift for that day.

At last she was shown in to him, dressed in a clean but shapeless tent of some coarse, unironed material that reached almost to her feet. Her hair was hidden by an equally coarse white cap, and on her feet a pair of shiny, badly fitting boots. He stood up.

'You cannot stay here, Elsie.'

She gave him a half smile. 'I've still got some pride left.' There was no other reference to the row, and no recrimination, and beyond the curve of her lips he sensed a blank uncaring apathy that struck at him worse than any show of grief.

'You cannot stay here, Elsie. Nobody stays in here.'

'None of you mining people do,' she murmured. 'You look after your own, but I'm not one of you. I've dreaded ending here since my father left me, dreaded it. It's funny, though, now I am here I've nothing left to dread, except one thing. And it'll be better for you, John. You won't be in the middle.'

'You cannot stay here, Elsie.'

She rested a hand on his sleeve, so white it looked translucent, the wrist so thin a handshake might snap it. Face impassive, she said, 'It's better this way, and there's something I want you to know. I've caused you a lot of trouble, and I know now you don't bear me a grudge. And I want to ask you something. Something big.'

He took hold of her hands and listened. She hesitated for a moment, then went on with a determined little tilt of her chin.

232

'I know I've done wrong, but I don't think my father should have thrown me out and made a public show of me. I couldn't do that to anybody I'd ever professed to love, and I know you couldn't. And I think my mother could at least have done or said something to try to help me, but she did nothing. So I think however bad I've been, they've done wrong by me. Still, if they come to see me now, while I'm in here, I'll forgive them.' She paused for a moment, and shuddered. 'But if they don't, John, and if I die having this baby, will you bury me? They give all the unclaimed bodies to the medical school.' Her eyes grew wider, and her voice lower. 'They've got a dissecting room here, did you know that?'

He could not trust himself to speak, but nodded.

'I can't bear the thought of anybody cutting us up, either me or my baby – or of lying in a pauper's grave, either.'

'That'll never happen, Elsie,' he choked.

She nodded. 'And when I'm dead, if my mother or father come to put flowers on my grave, promise me you'll take them off. Take them off, and burn them.'

He looked up, and his face was twisted with grief and wet with tears. But her eyes were dead, and as dry as ashes.

The thought had never occurred to him that she might die, and now he wondered why not. As many women died in child-birth as men died in the pits. And she was so young, and she looked so ill now, and this was her first.

She'd looked at his wet and grief-contorted face and remembered something; and the last fragments of that invisible barrier that had separated them slipped away. 'You've broken my dream,' she'd told him. 'I was dreaming the other night that I was in my coffin, looking like I used to when everybody called me the belle of Annsdale. They were all there. My mother and father, and all my family, and all yours, and Sylvia and her family, and the rector and his son, and they were all laughing and talking, but none of them were even looking at me, and you were the only one crying. And it seemed so real. Because it was true, and it will be like that, except that I won't look beautiful. You'll be the only one to mourn me, and you've got the least reason. I did something bad to you, John,

233

and I've caused you nothing but trouble since. It'll be better if we die, me and my baby. Better for everybody. Better for us.'

A workhouse was not a prison, that he knew, but he thought that Elsie's incarceration was worse than any that Alice had endured, because Alice endured with the love and loyalty and support of her family and friends and fellow suffragettes, and her imprisonment was a source of pride and of celebration and not of disgrace, and on her release she was treated as a heroine. She endured with hope and for a cause, and poor Elsie was without hope.

Irene's right, he thought. When it comes to dealings between men and women, women get the worst of it, right enough – but Elsie won't stay in that place, not while I can stop it.

He would have gone to Ginny earlier, but the choice to take Elsie in had been his, and so the responsibility was his, and he knew that the sight of Elsie's burgeoning pregnancy couldn't help but remind Ginny of her miscarriages, and that he had not wanted to do. Now he had no choice. He would go to her, and beg her to take Elsie in. Reluctant though he was, it was the only way.

He thought of Elsie in that place, and was put in mind of his pony putting days and the first day he'd seen his favourite, little Chance. Still barely more than a foal and plump and glossy on his mother's milk, he had been brought down to be broken to the shafts, taken out of the sunshine and condemned to a life of toil and darkness from which there is no escape, and which can only be made bearable by a kindly master. John had loved the little animal, had been as kind as he could. Even so, the work had to be done. Elsie had been brought to him just like that, to be broken to the harshest of the world's harsh realities, the fate of an unwed mother, whom the whole world felt entitled to judge and scapegoat and vilify. And now they had all broken her, and they had broken her spirit, and he would never forgive them for it.

'Aye, she can come. She can earn her keep doing a bit of cleaning, and once the bairn's born she can work in the bar,' Ginny said.

'Thanks, to both of you. You won't be out of pocket – I'll see to that.'

'You're taking a lot of trouble over your brother's lass,' Martin observed, giving him a long and thoughtful look.

'Only because nobody else will. I asked Arthur to go for her, and he wouldn't. I asked her father an' all, and neither would he.' John suddenly felt defensive about the trouble he was taking, and took a nonchalant draught of his beer, to hide the fact.

He'd had no breakfast, and no dinner, and no sleep, and now, with bulk of the business concluded, he went home. Lizzie and Arthur were both at work, and Sally had gone for the messages.

'Well? Is she there?' his mother demanded, as soon as he walked in the door.

'Aye, she's there. And she's not stopping. I'm famished. Have you got a bit of bread and cheese, or something?'

A look of relief passed over his mother's face then. Even so, she wouldn't forgo criticism of Elsie. 'You think you know her – you don't. Elsie's a wilful little madam,' she said, taking a loaf from the crock and putting it on the board. 'She's put herself into a pet because she's been corrected, and she needs correcting. I don't wonder her parents'll have nothing to do with her. You can go and tell that relieving officer she's not been thrown out and she's no business to be there, living on the parish. I didn't throw her out.'

He gave her a look, and she pointed the bread-knife at him, repeating, 'I didn't throw her out. I – did – not – throw – her – out.'

'Why did you let the ferrets out, to kill her cat?' he demanded.

She flushed. 'Because I was sick and tired of it scratching and pulling my furniture to shreds, and destroying my work, and trailing its muck all over the tops, and she'd do nothing to check it herself, and I'm not sorry. I'm glad to be rid of it, if you want to know. And now you can get a bit of bread and cheese without cat hairs all over it. And I still didn't throw her out.'

No, you drove her out, he thought, but he said only, 'Oh, Mother.'

'Oh, Mother? You can go to that relieving officer and tell him I didn't throw her out, if you want her back so badly. She must have told the workhouse master I did, or he would never have let her in. If she's in that place, she's in there out of her own choice and under false pretences.'

'You don't have to come back to me mam's, there's plenty of room for you at our Ginny's,' he said, 'and I've told the Master so, and he'll tell the relieving officer. So when the Board of Guardians meet, they won't let you stay. They *won't* let you stay, so you might as well come with me now, and I'll take you to the Cock.' He looked her determinedly in the eye. 'You're not staying here, Elsie.'

'John,' she said, 'it's hopeless. You'll never be my brother-in-law. Arthur wants Kath Leigh, and I don't want Arthur.'

'That's got nothing to do with it. You'll like our Ginny, I hope. There's plenty of room for you at the Cock, and that's where you're going.'

'They've got my clothes,' she said, with a helpless little shrug, and a smile that cheered him by being a bit more of a smile than the one he'd seen that morning. 'They took them away to be washed, and disinfected.'

He thrust a bundle of clothes at her, feeling a weight like a tombstone suddenly lifting from his chest. 'I know that. Me mam's sent you some more. To come out in.'

Twenty-Two

'Well, I could never have wished her in the workhouse, but I can't deny I'm glad to see the back of her, like. She didn't do her fair share of the work, and what she did, she made a mess of,' said Lizzie.

John felt ridiculously cheerful, silly with cheerfulness, and Lizzie's comments had as much effect on him as water on a duck's back, but Sally had something to say.

'Only because you two never stopped picking at her. She got that she hardly dare touch anything in the end, for fear it wouldn't be right for you. Both of you.' Sal looked at Lizzie, and then at their mother, with her lips pursed.

His mother's expression of surprise at criticism from timid little Sally struck John as comical. It subdued her, but no censure could put a damper on Lizzie's delight.

'Well, she's at our Ginny's now, so all's well that end's well. Maybe we can have Alice and Tom for tea on Sunday. It'll be lovely to get back to the way we used to be before she came,' she hesitated, then continued with a frown, 'or as near as we can get with our Arthur in the house. The sooner Elsie comes to her senses and marries him, the sooner we can get him out of our road and into a pit house in Annsdale Colliery. Then it'll be like it was when he was at sea. Bloody grand.'

John caught Sally's eye, and a look of complicity passed between them, but neither said any more.

The days were shortening rapidly, and now that Alice was no longer teaching at the school, their evening bicycle rides had ceased, and John saw much less of her during the week. She and Tom accepted the invitation to Sunday tea, and arrived at about four o'clock. Arthur, well warned by Lizzie, was dressed in his best suit.

'Oh, you're the suffragette, then.' Arthur gave Alice one of his most engaging smiles as he took her hand, then leaning towards her with a conspiratorial air he whispered, 'Have you started any good fires lately, like?'

Alice swiftly glanced at John, who gave a quick, furtive shake of his head. The little exchange was not lost on Arthur. He grinned. 'Why, you're courting the right lad to keep you out of trouble if you have. He'll chuck you on a ship and get you six months hard labour at sea instead of in jail. Isn't that right, John?'

'And Tom, this is Arthur. Arthur, Tom,' John said, giving his brother a warning look. Arthur and Tom solemnly shook hands.

'I wish I'd asked Kath to tea an' all,' Arthur said, 'if we're all going to be in-laws, like.'

Both Alice and Tom's eyebrows lifted slightly at that, but neither made any comment. Lizzie gave Arthur a look, their mother and Sally busied themselves with setting the table, and John was relieved to see Arthur managing a fair imperson-ation of a well-mannered man for the rest of the afternoon. He excused himself directly after tea, and went out. Their mother and Sally cleared the table and retired to the kitchen, leaving the two couples in the front room.

Lizzie took the cards from the drawer. 'Shall we have a hand or two of whist?'

'I'm game, if everybody else is,' said John, and meeting no protest he began to deal the cards, with Lizzie and Tom sitting either side of him and Alice directly opposite.

'Who's Kath?' Alice asked, as he dealt the last card.

Lizzie gave an exasperated little tut. 'A girl that lives in Annsdale Colliery, that our Arthur went to school with.'

'But I thought he was to marry Elsie.'

'He is,' Lizzie insisted, 'but he didn't ask her in quite the way she wanted to be asked – down on one knee with one hand on his heart and the other holding a diamond ring. So she's playing silly b—s and our Arthur's baiting her with Kath, tit for tat. It's all a pantomime, and he'll be married to

Elsie before much longer. She hasn't much choice, has she?'

'When's the Women's March from Edinburgh going to get into Newcastle, Alice?' John asked, to deflect her from the topic of Elsie and Arthur. 'We should all go and watch them; make a day of it like.'

Alice's eyes lit up in anticipation. 'Yes, as many of us as possible. We must give them a really good reception. Are you going to come, Lizzie?'

'I am if he'll give me the day off,' Lizzie smiled happily, 'but you know what a slave driver he is. When is it?'

'Later this month, I'm not sure yet of the exact date.'

'I'll work extra before the day, and do full days on Saturdays, and then he'll maybe let me go. Are you going to be there, Tom?'

'If at all possible. It depends on the day.'

'Let's finish this hand, then go down to the Cock before they get busy, and ask Ginny if she'll come as well, with Emma if she can. And perhaps your mother and Sally can come too,' said Alice.

Ginny broke off from her task of polishing the bar in the best room at the Cock. 'Why, I'll go. I wouldn't mind getting away from this place, having a change of scene for a few hours. I would love to see the women march into Newcastle. We'll have to have plenty of banners waving, Alice.'

'And I've no doubt they'll have some impressive ones of their own.' Alice looked round, in a mildly distracted fashion. 'Where's Elsie?'

'Making herself useful upstairs,' said Ginny. 'She's not in a state to be down here. Why don't you go and sit by the fire – I'll bring you a drink across.'

They needed no second invitation, but walked across the carpeted stone flags towards polished mahogany chairs beside a generous blaze, a welcome sight on a cold dark night.

'We'll just have one, and then Alice and I must be off. I have a busy day tomorrow,' Tom said. Lizzie pulled a face of disappointment.

'I must say, it's very good of Ginny to take Elsie in,' Alice observed.

'Our Ginny's got a heart of gold,' John said.

'She might have a good deal of trouble though. The baby must be almost ready to be born. I hope Elsie appreciates what's been done for her.'

'She sounds a very silly girl,' said Tom. 'Do you think she'll have the sense?'

'Who knows?' Alice shrugged. 'Inferior minds and inferior morals do have a tendency to go together, don't they?'

The comment surprised John. It was very like remarks he'd often heard women make about one another, even if more elegantly expressed. But Alice was not like most other women, and for her it seemed entirely out of character. Perhaps it was just the white band of idealized suffragette purity talking, making its claim to rank alongside purple justice and green hope in Alice's reckoning. He looked across at Lizzie for her reaction, and was amazed to see confusion on her face, rather than the pleasure in Elsie's humiliation he had expected to find.

Arthur gave him a nudge before he set out for the foreshift the following day. 'Did you have any luck with the suffragette, then?'

John nodded towards his mother, busy clearing the breakfast things, and didn't answer.

'No,' Arthur continued, 'of course you didn't. Alice with the cast-iron drawers, if I look at her right. That's what's wrong wi' these suffragettes, they want their bloomer legs feeling up, that's all. If they got that often enough they wouldn't bother about the vote. Her brother looks a bit lively, though. I wonder how he's getting on with our Lizzie?'

'If you can't say something pleasant, Arthur, just keep your comments to yourself, will you?' their mother asked.

'Aye, you're working hard at it, Mam, and I wish you may succeed, but if he marries her, I'll get the biggest surprise I've ever had in me life, I'll tell you that for nothing. I doubt very much that our John's the one for Alice, an' all. You've bred a pair here that fart above their arseholes, and all your hard work'll come to nothing in the end, as like as not.'

'You've got a crystal ball, have you, Arthur?' John's voice was heavy with sarcasm.

'Aye, I have – and it says I'll be married before either of you. So if Miss Elsie wants a husband she'd better hurry up, or I'll be off with Kath Leigh.'

'I've got some good news, John,' Sally told him on his return from work that night. 'I've got a place, at a doctor's house in Darlington. He knows Miss Carr, and he told her he was looking for a girl, and she recommended me! I start tomorrow. Can you believe it?'

'How much is he going to pay you?' John demanded.

'Five bob a week.'

'He's not over generous, is he? You're worth a lot more than that,' John laughed. 'Tell him your brother says you've got to have ten, or he's not letting you go. You're too useful to him.'

Sally laughed too. 'Get away. You're as glad as I am. I'll be able to help with the money, and you'll be able to save more for South Africa, not that I want you to go, like.'

'Will you clean that little kennel out for me before you go, Sal? I'll take it back to Sam Hickey's now the cat's gone,' said John.

'Why, there's some funny goings-on in your house, if what I hear's right,' Irene told him when he went round with the kennel. 'If your Arthur's the father to Elsie's baby, he's not acting like it. He's never off the Leighs' doorstep, from what I've seen.'

'Has he denied he's the father, then? Have you heard that from anybody?'

'Why no, I haven't.'

'Well then, people round here would do a lot better if they could mind their own business, instead of everybody else's. You can see everything that's going off at the Leighs' house, and you can pass comment on it an' all, and everybody in this street's the same. We've had a good run, me and you, Irene, and it's time we chalked it out, before they all start talking about us.'

'How are they going to talk about us? Our house is at the end of the row, and the door's at the side. Nobody in the street can see anybody either coming in or going out. Besides, you've always had a good reason for coming.'

'An excuse, you mean. The reason's not something either of us would really want to admit to. And I don't suppose people think I disappear into thin air when I get to the end of the row.'

She took his face in her hands, and stopped his mouth with a kiss, slow and sensuous, making little bites at his lips. He began to respond and she pressed her kisses harder, intruding her tongue into his mouth and dropping one hand to reach slowly down, feeling for him. He clamped his hand around her wrist.

'What's the matter?' she murmured, hardly pausing in her kisses, 'have you got something down there that's too good to share?'

'I'll share it all right, if that's what you want,' he said, 'I'll give you more than you can manage.'

Vain boast that was, he thought ruefully, pulling his trousers up over an hour later. He hoped he'd given her enough, but he suspected he could have given her a week's worth, and Irene would never have cried 'too much'.

She stood brushing her blonde hair, with laughter in her eyes. 'The nights are pulling in,' she soothed. 'Winter's coming on, and people are drawing their curtains earlier and earlier. There's even less chance of anybody seeing or hearing anything now than there was before. I don't know what you're fashing yoursel' about. Just look out there. There's not a house wi' the curtains open.'

He looked, but was not convinced. 'We've gone far enough with this, and it's time to give over, before something happens that we'll both regret.'

He dropped a kiss on her forehead and started for home, thinking that in spite of his misgivings, life was better than it had been in a while. He'd done his best for Elsie, and she was safe and well looked after. She was putting a bit of weight on, and beginning to look a lot happier, and he could go and see her at Ginny's whenever he wanted. He had peace at home; Arthur was hardly ever there. And he could start saving again now that Sally had a place and Arthur was tipping up. He had Alice to spice his life with witty conversation and intelligent argument, and Irene for what Irene enjoyed. A lot of men would have been happy to coast along like this for ever.

'We must go to see this moving picture from Australia. Animated photographs, you know. Alice and I have seen them before in London,' Tom had told them, as if they'd never seen one in their lives before; 'but this one's from Australia, and it's over an hour long. They're showing it in Durham. It's called *The Story of the Ned Kelly Gang*, about a gang of Australian cut-throats. I'm told it's been banned in some parts of Australia, so that ought to be recommendation enough. We can't miss it, can we? It must be worth seeing. '

Lizzie was home from work at four o'clock that Saturday instead of at six. She spent two hours curling her hair, polishing her shoes, and pressing her blue costume. Finally, looking at herself in the mirror, she put on her new hat and carefully skewered it in place with a large hatpin. Fully satisfied with her appearance, she gave herself a smile of approval and turned to John.

'Are we going, then?'

Polished to a gleam himself, he nodded, and they set out for the station, but when they arrived at the People's Palace in Court Lane, Alice was waiting alone. 'Tom sends his apologies,' she told them. 'Something to do with a client. Urgent business.'

Lizzie said nothing, but her face fell a mile. John shrugged, 'Well, I suppose it can't be helped.' He took a girl on either arm, and led them inside.

The film was like nothing John had ever seen before, something amazing. It was not only the moving picture; the subject matter was fascinating. He was goggle eyed as he watched the actor playing Kelly, supposedly dressed in the rebel's actual armour – a bulletproof helmet and jerkin fashioned from ploughshares. John couldn't forbear laughing, wondering how he ever managed to move about in it, and thinking he would almost rather be shot outright than have to go about in such a contraption. He looked like a man in a boiler.

'Tom says the picture recouped its costs within a week of being shown in Melbourne,' Alice told them, at the end of the showing.

'Aye, it's a marvellous thing. I reckon there'll be a lot of actors out of work before long, Alice,' John said, as they left the theatre. 'These fellers only have to do the play once, and it can be shown over and over again. I'm glad I'm not an actor. It'll only be any good for them that can get work in the moving pictures soon, and the rest will starve.'

Lizzie contributed nothing to the conversation, and soon they parted with Alice and started the journey home. John was quite elated until he saw the misery in his sister's face. She said little on the way back, except, 'I wonder what's happened to Tom. I've never heard of him having to see a client in the evening before.' The wonder of an hour-long moving picture seemed lost on her.

The following day they joined the cycling club for the usual Sunday outing. Again, Alice was there without Tom. 'He couldn't come,' she told Lizzie, looking a little embarrassed. 'I'm sure he'll explain when he sees you.'

Lizzie gave a little shrug, her face white. 'I'll be off home, then,' she said. 'Two's company, and I'm a crowd. I'll see you later, John.'

'No, come with us, Lizzie. We're not just two. There's the rest of the members as well,' John urged.

'Another day. But I think I'll go home just now. I've got a lot to do, now our Sally's got a place.'

'What's he playing at, Alice?' John asked, once Lizzie was out of earshot.

'He's not playing at anything,' she said. 'And I'll leave it to him to explain. But you asked when the suffrage March will get into Newcastle. We're pretty sure now it'll be the twenty-first.'

'That's a Monday, isn't it? I'll see if I can get off work, but it might not be an easy day for most people to get away.'

They heard nothing from Tom for days. Then Lizzie got the letter, and her affliction was terrible to watch.

'But I love him, Mother, I really love him, and he told me

he loved me,' she cried, collapsing into tears. Their mother took Lizzie in her arms and held her tight, as if she'd been a little child. John picked up the letter that fell from her hand and put it on the mantelpiece. He and Arthur left the house together.

'I thought I'd enjoy saying "I told you so",' said Arthur, as soon as they'd closed the door. 'But now I know I wouldn't. All the same, it makes me bloody mad. Me Mother says, "You can't blame her for wanting to better herself," and the message you get is that men like us are beneath her. We blame the likes of Elsie's dad for looking down their noses at us, but our own family does just the same.'

'I don't know, John,' Alice said, the next time they were out with the cycling club. 'I think she made him feel suffocated, trapped. He's not used to being smothered. He's getting engaged to a girl he's known for years, so obviously he won't be able to see Lizzie again.'

'He's not frightened of being trapped by the girl he's known for years, then.'

'Obviously not. Probably because she doesn't make him feel trapped.'

'He could have told her face to face,' John said. He almost added 'like a man', but checked himself, out of consideration for Alice's feelings.

She flushed anyway. 'What would have been the use of that? I think a letter's kinder, if anything.'

'Hmm,' said John, utterly unconvinced. As far as he was concerned, Tom was a coward who had taken the coward's way out. 'There's one thing for sure, though,' he said, 'he's broken her heart, whichever way he's done it.'

'From Edinburgh to London for Woman Suffrage' the glorious leading banner proclaimed. All the women's suffrage societies were participating in the march, but it was the Newcastle WSPU who joined them for their triumphal march into the city. After hearing of Tom's jilting Lizzie, the women in the family demonstrated their solidarity with her by staying at home, but John was there, for Alice's sake.

245

He would have guessed that most of the marchers were between twenty and thirty years old, and right bonny lasses they were. There were also a few much younger, and some much older. Alice's pride and pleasure at the sight of them was almost palpable.

'Aren't they magnificent?' she declared, rather than asked.

John grinned. 'Aye, they are.' He paused, then asked, 'Is Tom's new girl a suffragette?'

Alice nodded, most of her attention still on the marchers. 'But that wasn't the reason he ended it. He simply found he couldn't respect Lizzie.'

The contempt with which she said it chilled him. He could hardly ask why not, but he could guess.

'But you're different, John,' Alice went on. 'You're a man that people *can* respect. And I never properly thanked you for helping us on the night of the fire. You averted a tragedy, and we wouldn't have liked anybody ever to be able to say that human life had been taken in the name of women's suffrage. So thank you.'

'Alice, do the same as the Pethwick-Lawrences have, and break with the Pankhursts. They will get somebody killed before they've done, and they think nothing about putting women they pretend to care about in the way of years of hard labour. Barring Sylvia, they don't know the meaning of democracy, and they'll do nothing for working women. They're just the opposite, arch-Tories, if anything. There's plenty of other suffrage societies you could join. You could even join one that's trying to get the vote for all adults, for lads like me, as well as the women.'

'No,' she said, 'I'm with the WSPU.'

They marched on for a while in silence, then Alice said, 'You never asked me to marry you, John.'

'I'd an idea you would only say yes if I joined the chapel and became a checkweighman. And I might ask you yet.'

'Your present occupation would be a barrier, I admit, but you could do so much better, either in mining engineering or in politics. I've thought about it for a long time you know, and very seriously. But there's a much greater barrier than your occupation.'

246

'Why, what could be bigger than that?' John asked, with a wry smile.

She grasped his hand, and suddenly stopped, and the rest of the marchers parted to flow past them.

'It was you who went to the workhouse for Elsie, not Arthur. I didn't realize that until Lizzie told me. Tom had suspected for some time that you were much too fond of Elsie Hartley.' John saw pain in Alice's eyes, and he looked away.

'She'll bring you no happiness. You could spend your life pining for her, but you can't marry. It's wrong, John. Everything makes it wrong. It's too incestuous. She's as good as your brother's wife.'

Beaten, he said, 'That's an old-fashioned view for a modern girl, Alice.'

'Some things don't bend to fashion. You want to rehabilitate her, but it's an impossibility, for you or anybody else – except Arthur, perhaps, and she'll probably be delivered before she can get the banns read and get married, so it will soon be impossible even for him. It's a sheer impossibility, John.'

He felt as if his lamp had suddenly gone out in the blackness of the mine and left him engulfed in darkness and standing motionless, not daring to move, unsure of the road in front of him and the ground beneath his feet.

'You love her. Admit it.'

He looked into his heart and saw the corner that would for ever be occupied by Elsie. His feelings for her shifted from passion to savagery, from anger to tenderness. It was something he couldn't explain, even to himself. And now it was all mingled with the sort of sympathy that would make the worst man alive reach out to catch a child and stop it from tumbling down an old mine shaft, and once he had a hold of it, hold on to stop its fall. He made no answer at first, but Alice waited so long in perfect silence that it was forced from him.

'I cannot seem to help it, Alice. I've tried, but the feeling will not go away. She's in my pores, like coal dust, like an irritant. I don't know if that's love, or not. But I do love you, and I like you a lot more than I've liked Elsie at times.'

She sighed. 'I believe you, but I can't share, John. I would want all of you, and as I can't have all I'll take nothing.'

He could say nothing more. He looked into her blue-flecked green eyes and saw everything that was courageous, honourable, fair, open and wholesome. A mist of tears suddenly clouded them as she stood back from him. 'I'm sorry. I'm not such a snob as Lizzie, but no sane woman would marry lower than her class for a man who would only be half hers. And I'm more upset for you than I am for myself.'

Voice bleak, he said, 'This is the end of it, then.'

'Yes, it is. You don't like letters, John, so I'll tell you now. I'm going on without you, and tomorrow I shall join the march to London. We may never see each other again, so good luck.'

'Good luck to you an' all, Alice. All the luck in the world.'

Away she went, holding on to her dark green hat and running, almost flying away from him to catch up with her cause and her suffragettes. The best lass in the North was soon among the marchers and lost to his sight, and he cursed himself for a fool in losing her.

'It's finished between me and Alice,' he told Lizzie, as soon as he got home, but if he wanted any sympathy, there was none forthcoming.

She looked up, her face pale and her eyes dark-circled. 'I'm glad. I'm glad I'll never have to meet either of them again,' she said, 'because me and Tom, we'd still be together if it hadn't been for her. He was all right the last time we met, but she's been whispering in his ear and laying the poison down until she's finally got what she wanted. I'm not good enough for Lady Alice, and so she's destroyed me. I'd say I hate her, but that's too mild for what I feel for her. I wish her in hell.

'Do you know what I dream? I dream I've got her in my power, and she has no escape, and the more I hurt her the happier I am, until I've killed her, and then I'm overjoyed. I could murder her. That's the crime I would love to commit, and I would, if only I could be sure I'd never be found out.'

Twenty-Three

'Elsie's been in labour for hours,' Ginny told him, when he got to the Cock at about nine o'clock that night. 'She started at about three o'clock this morning. Mam Smith's upstairs with her now.'

'She's all right, isn't she? I mean, she will be all right?'

'She's taking a long time,' said Ginny. 'I'll go up in a minute and see what's happening. Where's our Arthur? Maybe's we should send for him. And what about her mother and father?'

John grimaced. 'I doubt very much they'll want to know. Our Arthur'll be either at Kath's, or at the club. Send for him if you like, but I'm not going, because I know what his answer will be.'

'And what's that?'

'It'll be: "Well, what can I do about it, like?"'

Ginny dispatched Maudie to find Arthur, and then went upstairs to see how Elsie was faring. After a couple of minutes she was down again, and shaking her head at him. Wanting some diversion, John went to stand beside Jimmy, who was playing a few bars on the piano.

'Away and have a game of cribbage with me instead.'

They'd played half-heartedly for over half an hour before Maudie returned, and came to gather the glasses.

'Did you find our Arthur?' John asked.

'Aye.'

'Is he coming, then?'

'No.'

'Did you tell the Hartleys?'

'Aye.'

'And they're not coming, I suppose.'

'You suppose right.'

At length, Ginny went upstairs, and came down only to signal Elsie's lack of progress by another shake of her head, before returning upstairs. They dealt the cards and played some more, until well after closing time.

'She's taking some time about it,' John said.

Jimmy put the cribbage board and the cards away. 'Aye, the women have the worst of it, right enough,' he said, getting to his feet and reaching for his jacket. 'It churns me up. Our Emma has bad labours, but she was never as long as Elsie.'

Martin shook his head. 'Ginny's third miscarriage was enough for me. I made sure there were no more babies after that. I lost one good wife to tuberculosis, and I wasn't going to lose another through childbirth.'

Jimmy gave John's shoulder a squeeze before setting off for home. 'I hope they'll be all right, lad,' he said, as if he were consoling the husband and father.

'Aye, me an' all.'

Upstairs, Mam Smith looked anything but hopeful. 'I don't think this bairn's going to come on its own, and its mother's about finished; she's too tired to push,' she said. 'I think it'll have to be fetched, wi' the forceps. I would have sent for the doctor hours ago, but he'll charge a sight more than I do, and Elsie's got no money to pay him so I'll be liable for his fee if I do call him in. I don't know exactly how much he'll want, but I know it'll be more than I can afford. It's cases like this put the midwife in the poorhouse. So what does everybody want to do, like?'

John put on his jacket. 'She cannot go on like this. I'll go and fetch him,' he said. 'It's all right, Mam Smith. He'll have to have what he wants for it. He can come to me for the money.'

Elsie lay half conscious, imagining herself adrift in an open boat, bobbing on waves of pain in a blood-red sea of agony. She was tired, so very, very tired that she was stunned with tiredness, but the pains would give her no oblivion. She remembered what Emma had told her – 'If you die in childbirth all your sins are forgiven and you go straight to heaven.' She

250

sensed her guardian angel hovering above her, waiting to carry her to heaven's gate, so near she felt his breath on her cheek, and opening her eyes she saw that he had John's face. 'Oh, God, let it be soon, let it be soon,' she said.

She became conscious of voices, felt her legs being lifted and held apart, and then searing pain, and the room was filled with screams and pleas for mercy.

Arthur whistled when John told him what the doctor wanted for using his forceps in the middle of the night. 'Well, I haven't got that much money to pay out all at once. I just haven't. I'll have to owe it you for a bit, like.'

'Aye, all right, Arthur.'

Arthur was silent for a moment, then he said, 'It's going to be a dear carry on if she has to have forceps with all her bairns. Suppose she has ten? Anybody that weds Elsie'll be working all his life to just to pay bloody doctors.'

'Aye. Maybe he will,' John agreed, 'if he lets her have ten. But any decent husband would make sure he didn't give her ten.'

'Hm,' Arthur grunted. 'Not much bloody fun in that, either.'

'She's still asleep, poor lass,' Ginny said, as soon as they walked in. 'She's suffered the pains of hell. The bairn's asleep an' all – he's just as tired as she is. Call round on your way back from work. She'll want to thank you for getting the doctor,' said Ginny, 'and I suppose the proud father'll want to have a look at his handiwork.'

She was sitting up in bed, and looking at her reflection in a hand-mirror when he peeped round the door. 'Third time lucky. I came yesterday, and the day before, but you were asleep. How are you, bonny lass?'

The hand-mirror rapidly disappeared under the covers, and he pretended not to notice it. 'I'm still alive. And I'm so surprised,' she said, her eyebrows raised as if to attest to the fact. 'I was so sure I wouldn't be.'

He gazed into her deep brown eyes. 'Why, you're not sorry, are you?'

'No, I'm not sorry,' she smiled, 'not since you brought me here. Everything's so calm, and easy. Nothing seems to be a trouble, and Ginny and Martin are goodness itself. And thank you for bringing the doctor. He said we would have died if you hadn't.' She leaned towards him, and her eyes brightened as she nodded towards the cradle. 'Have a look, John.'

Unwilling, John did as she asked, and there he lay – a triumphant little hobgoblin with Arthur's nose, who looked up at him with sly, flitting smiles that seemed to say, *You've lost, you fool. You never could have won, and you've lost.*

On the way home, John thought of Alice. Hard to believe she'd been absent from his thoughts for two whole days. He missed her, suddenly. A ferment of ideas, invigorating, dauntless, he could have done with the distraction of one of her political arguments at that very moment, to dispel his dreary thoughts. He missed her sense of purpose, her vigour, her sheer dynamism. Alice had never been dull company. And she was the only woman he had ever really understood.

He missed her, but he couldn't help thinking that he ought to be missing her more. He missed her, but he was not devastated by the loss of her, not like Lizzie was over losing Tom. Nothing like it. Nowhere near. It had been more an affair of the mind than the heart. They hadn't really been suited to each other in any other way. It hadn't been real love. He would never have been happy with Alice.

Stop lying to yourself, he thought. You did love Alice, and you admired her, and you could have been perfectly happy with her . . . if only you'd never laid eyes on Elsie Hartley.

The baby was asleep after his feed, and Elsie was out of bed and sitting on a low nursing chair. She looked quickly up when she felt a hand lift her hair, and the brush stroke through it.

'How long is it since you brushed this, Elsie?' Ginny asked.

Elsie shrugged.

'Why, keep still then,' said Ginny, and Elsie winced a little as she felt the tugging. 'By, you've got a lot of knots in it.'

'It'th bonny hair, ithn't it, Ginny?' said Philip, who had

252

seemed unable to stay away from Elsie since the baby was born.

'Aye, it is,' said Ginny.

'Ith brown, but when the thun thines on it, it'th got glintth in it, red and gold. It'th lovely and thilky.' Elsie smiled at the expression on his face, and thought Philip's blond hair so beautiful that it was strange he should admire anyone else's.

'Aye, my lad, but you shouldn't be in a lady's bedroom, you know. Go and see what your dad's doing. See if you can give him a bit hand.'

'All right. And I'll come and make you a cup of tea in a bit.'

'You know what your dad would say to that, Phil,' said Ginny.

'Aye, I do,' Philip laughed. 'He would thay, "You don't make tea for the women, Phil. They make tea for you." But I don't mind making the tea, Ginny.'

'All right, Phil. You put the kettle on and go and help your dad, and I'll shout you when it's ready.'

'Philip's nice,' said Elsie, watching him go.

'He is,' said Ginny. They lapsed into a companionable silence. The brush was now gliding more easily through Elsie's hair, and the gentle rhythm of its slow, easy strokes soothed her. She abandoned herself to the touch, and had a strange fancy that the knots in her heart might unravel as easily as the knots in her hair, if only someone would help her tease them out.

'Short pleasure, long repentance,' she murmured. 'That's what my mother kept saying to me. Mam Smith said it as well, when I was in labour. But you've never said anything like that, Ginny.'

'Why, what would be the point in me saying anything like that?'

'There's no point in it,' said Elsie, 'except the pleasure it gives some people to say such things. And I had no pleasure, and it's too late to mend it now, even if I had.'

The brushing continued, with no break in the rhythm.

'What happened, Elsie?'

Elsie sighed. 'You remember when the police were

253

looking for Arthur? Well, he was hiding in Mr Farr's barn, only he couldn't stay there, because of the blacklegs coming. John said I had to tell him to go to his marrers, but when I did, he said he had no marrers who'd risk taking him in, and he was going to freeze to death, and he really did look as if he was dying of the cold. I felt sorry for him.'

The brushing slowed, and paused, and then resumed the rhythm. 'So you took him into your dad's house?'

Elsie nodded. 'And then it was a question of where to hide him. I couldn't let any of them see him, because they'd have turned him over to the police. So I had to hide him in my room, and it didn't seem a bad thing at the time. I told him to lie on the rug with his blankets, and he did for a while, and then he came creeping into bed beside me, telling me he was cold, and we'd both be warmer if we cuddled up together, and I got angry and tried to push him out. My dad heard us, and I nearly died of fright when he started shouting, asking what the commotion was. It wasn't until then that it came home to me what it would look like to other people, and what they would say if they came in and found Arthur in my room. I had to shout and tell my dad it was the cat jumping about.'

'I can imagine the rest,' said Ginny.

But Elsie went on. 'And then Arthur knew I daren't make a sound, and he was behind me, kissing my neck and squeezing me, and kissing my ear, and whispering things, and even though I was terrified because of my mother and father, and sisters, I wanted to laugh – nerves, you know. It was then he got his hands under my nightie, and I daren't push him away for fear of making any more noise.' She paused, and gave Ginny a wicked little smile. 'Then the thought came into my head – I thought: oh, well, this will be one in the eye for Rupert, at any rate.'

'Did Rupert deserve one in the eye?'

'Whether he did or not, I didn't like him. He was arrogant, and he thought he owned me, just because my father wanted to be in with the Hunt and his father had the power to say aye or nay to him. The first time I went hunting I laughed at him when he came a cropper, and he got his revenge by rubbing the fox's brush in my face, and it was rank. It nearly made me sick. I didn't like hunting, either. I thought it was cruel and pointless, but Rupert and my father, they both had a mania for it. They loved it, and they always had to be in at the kill – Rupert's mother and father, too. I thought if I did marry him I'd have to spend half of my life going foxhunting, and the other half listening to people talking about it.'

The long, slow strokes of the brush went on, and on. Elsie's smile died, and her eyes misted. 'But my poor little Love me Long. I still miss her. I see my sisters riding her sometimes, and it's hateful. I suppose they'll make good huntswomen, if my father manages to stay in with the hunt, that is. But it's hateful, Ginny. It's really hateful.'

'Did Arthur promise to marry you, Elsie?' Ginny asked, after an interval.

'Why no,' said Elsie. 'It wasn't like that at all. It was as if it was nothing that mattered at all. It was nothing but a lark to him – he said, "It's just a bit cuddle, like. Just a kiss and a cuddle, just a bit fun." And I was laughing – but it was nerves, you know.'

'I know. Only it's not often fun for the woman. Not in the long run, anyway.'

'No, and not even in the short run. But I don't know why I'm telling you all this, Ginny. I would never tell anybody else – I'd be too ashamed. I wonder why I'm telling you?' Elsie said, with a self-conscious little laugh.

'But Arthur took something he never should have taken.' Ginny's voice sounded hard. Turning towards her, Elsie saw her eyes were sad, and her mouth turned down.

'He did,' she replied, 'but what was the use of my complaining about it then, afterwards, when I'd deliberately taken him into my own bedroom? I daren't say anything about it to a living soul. Who'd have believed me if I'd told them I never thought he'd do such a thing, and never wanted him to?'

'I would. But not many other people, I'll grant you that.'

The belief in Ginny's voice brought tears to Elsie's eyes. She felt Ginny's fingers lift her hair, and then more long, soothing strokes of the brush. She settled back, and made an effort to turn the conversation before Ginny got onto the topic

255

of her shameful treatment of John. She still felt like dying at the humiliation of that.

'It's witchcraft. That's what it is. You've cast a spell on me, to make me tell you all my secrets. It's so different being here, Ginny, to your mother's. Nobody cares much if I get anything wrong, and nobody talks about mouths to feed.'

'It's still there, though, Elsie. You've dropped into a class that gets nothing without hard work, and the women have to work as hard as the men, if not harder.'

Well, she could work as well as the next, Elsie thought. Her father had, and he'd built a thriving business. But before she could reply there was a knock on the door, and Philip put his head round. 'The kettle's boiled.'

Ginny went to make the tea. Elsie lifted her baby, and went with Philip into the sitting room.

'What are you going to call him?' he asked.

'I don't know.'

'He'th a lovely baby, ithn't he?' Philip sighed, standing very close to Elsie, and stroking the baby on his cheek. 'Emma wouldn't call any of her babieth Philip. Nobody call'th their babieth after me, becauth I've got a lithp.'

Elsie looked at his downcast face and said, 'He's Philip, and you can be his godfather.'

Philip beamed from ear to ear, and Elsie looked from him to the baby in her arms. With his mop of dark hair, he was as different to his namesake as could be, but Philip he would be. The name would suit him; he would grow into it. She thought about a christening, and her face fell. Who would do that now, and what sort of a Christening would it be? Not the happy gathering with grandparents from both sides that she would once have expected, and she could hardly ask the rector.

'Anybody at home?' came a voice from the staircase. Arthur's voice. All thoughts of rectors and christenings went out of Elsie's head as Arthur strode through the door, like a man with a purpose, and one he wants to have done with.

'Ginny, Ginny,' called Elsie, and putting the baby in Philip's arms, she fled to fetch her.

When they got back with the tea, and an extra cup for

Arthur, he was cradling the baby in his arms, inspecting him closely. Elsie stood back, watching Arthur as minutely.

'Well, he's mine, then. I don't suppose there's any point denying it. He's a chip off the old block, all right.' He turned to Elsie, his manner abrupt. 'Well, you've made me a daddy, and I suppose I'd better make you a wife. So what about it, then? Are we going to make a go of it, or not?'

Elsie's lip curled a mere fraction. 'I don't know.'

Arthur caught the barely perceptible expression of scorn, and his brows came together in a frown. He thrust the baby into Elsie's arms, and his black eyes bored into hers. 'Still playing that game. Well, if you don't know, no bugger else does. You'd better hurry up and make your mind up, though, because this is the last time I'll ever ask you.' Arthur left his tea and went without another word, his boots thundering down the stairs.

Elsie stood in front of the long mirror in Ginny's bedroom, wearing one of Ginny's old silk dresses, casting a critical eye over herself.

'I know,' said Ginny. 'It fits where it touches. But it's not too small. And it's hardly been worn. Brown never suited me. I don't know why ever I bought it, but it does something for you; it brings out the colour of your eyes, and your hair – it brings you to life. You look a dazzler in it. Maybe's our Lizzie would alter it for you. She only wants your measurements, and she can take it up at the waist, and up at the hem, and maybe take it in a bit. It should do, then.'

Elsie gave her a look, and grimaced.

'I suppose that means she wouldn't do it for you. But she will if I ask her,' said Ginny.

The baby began to wail, and Elsie started struggling out of the dress, knowing her milk would begin to drip at the sound of him. Ginny helped her, and went to hang it up. Elsie lifted little Philip from his cradle and sat down in the low chair, lifting her camisole and freeing her breast. She winced as the eager little mouth sought her nipple and latched on, then sighed and relaxed into the chair as the child began to milk her, and the pain in her breast subsided. She smiled up at Ginny, who was pushing a footstool towards her feet.

257

'You're better to me than my own mother.'

'Oh, Elsie,' Ginny sighed, then said, 'I was just going to say, you don't know how lucky you are, with such a bonny bairn, but that would be stupid, the way you're placed.'

'John told me about you losing your babies.'

'Aye,' said Ginny, 'and then Martin said there would be no more. So that was the end of my hopes of being a mother.'

Elsie caught the expression in Ginny's eyes, and thought that Martin was too cruel. 'Philip calls you mother,' she said.

'He does, and I couldn't love him any better if he were mine, but he was six when we got married, and I would have liked to sit and feed my baby, just like you're doing now,' she said, and added, 'And now who's the witch, getting people's secrets out?'

'It's funny, Ginny, but this little Philip looks more like you than he does me.'

'Aye, well, if he looks like our Arthur, he'll look like me. Anybody would know Arthur's my brother, our Lizzie's an' all.'

'I think I'll call him Pip. It's too confusing, two Philips in the same house.'

Martin called up from the bottom of the stairs, 'Ginny, here's your mother and your Lizzie to see you.'

Ginny left the bedroom, and Elsie heard her greet the visitors. 'I suppose you've come to have a look at the bairn?'

'Yes,' Mrs Wilde replied, 'and I don't suppose her own mother or father have been yet?'

Elsie shrank back in her chair, wishing to God that they would go away and leave her in peace. They'd never wanted her in their house, so why did that horrible pair come here, and disturb her during the time she loved best? Ginny made some reply, but her voice was too low and indistinct to hear properly.

'Well, I think Philip's a lovely name. I doubted she'd call it Arthur. I'm just glad she's not called it John. That would have been something else to fill people's mouths,' came Lizzie's voice. And then all their voices became more and more indistinct. They'd gone off into the kitchen.

Elsie sighed and reached out a foot to kick the door shut.

258

She would shut out the world for half an hour and sit alone with her child in one of those blessed islands of peace in the sea of troubles that surrounded them, Pip's feeding time. She relaxed, smiling indulgently at her greedy boy, at his beautiful, beautiful hair, and his pretty mouth clamped firmly around her nipple, sensuously sucking sustenance from her, a sensation she loved. He would soon be as fat as a cherub on her milk, and she almost laughed with delight at the thought. A frown passed over her face, and cleared. Perhaps by the time he'd finished they would have tired of waiting, and be gone.

Half an hour later, Elsie looked into Mrs Wilde's face, pale and taut, her lips compressed in that too-familiar line of disapproval. 'Well, Elsie, and are you going to let us have a look at him?'

It had been a forlorn hope that she could avoid this meeting, so the sooner it was over the better. Elsie returned to the bedroom to lift her gorged and sleeping son from his cradle, and take him for inspection.

Mrs Wilde took him from her and held him gently in her arms, gazing at him, her face softening. 'He's beautiful,' she sighed, 'and he's Arthur's double. It's just like looking at one of my own.' She raised her eyes to Elsie. 'It's a sin you won't marry Arthur, and give this poor innocent baby a name.'

'Arthur doesn't want to marry me,' Elsie replied.

'What's that got to do with it, when you've got a child? He's willing to marry you. That should be enough.'

Elsie lifted her chin and turned away. 'He's so willing he takes every opportunity to let me know I'm not the one he wants. I don't want to live with a man I don't love, and who doesn't love me.'

'I suppose this little lad would want to have a father, though, instead of having the name of a bastard.'

'Well, I wouldn't get married to somebody who was always pushing his antics with other women in my face, either,' said Lizzie.

'Lizzie!' Mrs Wilde exclaimed, and Elsie stared at her in shock. This was support from an entirely unexpected quarter.

'Well, I wouldn't,' said Lizzie, looking first at her mother, and then at Elsie. 'I don't blame you.'

A flush rose to Mrs Wilde's cheeks. 'You two, you don't know what you're talking about. It's a terrible thing for a child, not to have a father. And there's something else, as well. This pride of yours has a price, Elsie, and it's not you that's paying it, or your family, either.'

Twenty-Four

'It's going to be a hard road to tread, Elsie. A man might be able to work himself out of a mess, he can go to sea, or emigrate, or a hundred other things a woman can't, not when she's got a child, not unless she leaves it with somebody else. And chances of marriage are slim. You'll find more lovers than husbands with a baby in tow, and there's no security in that.'

Ginny meant well, and Elsie supposed she'd seen enough of the world to know, but every fibre revolted at the thought of marriage to Arthur, and it must have shown in her eyes.

Ginny raised her eyebrows, a wry expression on her face. 'Tell him straight out, then, once and for all – then we'll all know what we're doing. Me mam won't be very pleased, but she'll get used to the idea – she's got used to a lot more. And ask our Lizzie if she's finished altering that frock while you're at it. We'll get you done up to the nines, see if you can attract a bit more custom for us, bring a bit more tin rattling into the till. Men like to see a bonny lass behind a bar, and you're getting bonnier by the day. When you're earning your own keep, you can be as proud as you like,' Ginny told her.

Elsie set out that evening, to carry out her instructions. It was the first time she'd set foot in Mrs Wilde's house since she'd left for the workhouse. She knocked on the door with some trepidation, holding herself very erect in spite of it. There was a slight awkwardness when Mrs Wilde opened the door and led her into the kitchen. John's eyes lit up at the sight of her, bright, brown and intelligent. He smiled, but said nothing. She gave him a fleeting smile, and turned to Arthur.

He was looking in the mirror, carefully combing his black hair. He turned and gave her a cool nod and resumed his preening. Elsie stared at his back. There was no affection here, not even the pretence of affection, and hers for him had died the night she saved him from the cold. She tried to remember what the etiquette books said on declining an offer of marriage. Though fully aware that polite convention would be wasted on him, she wanted to do it properly, formally and with dignity. She took a deep breath. 'Thank you for your generous offer of marriage, Arthur. I've thought it over very carefully, and I have decided to refuse you, absolutely. I hope this will not give you very much pain.'

She was talking to his back. She had rescued this disgusting oaf in his hour of need, and she had borne his child, and he hadn't the common courtesy to face her when she spoke to him. She felt the colour rise to her cheeks, and etiquette was thrown out of the window. Her brown eyes flashed fire as she drew herself up to her full five feet and gave tongue to her contempt: 'And I doubt very much that it will, since you've been rubbing my nose in your admiration for Miss Leigh ever since you came home. I wonder if she realizes what a prize she's won? I doubt it, and I pity her, from the bottom of my heart. You're rude, boorish and vain, and worse, and I wouldn't marry you if you were the last man on earth and I were starving in the gutter. So there's your answer.' She had descended to his level, and felt her face glowing with anger.

At last she'd made some impression on him, and Arthur turned to look her up and down for a moment or two. He shrugged. 'Oh, well, that's it, then. Now we know.'

She was conscious of John's eyes still on her, and of his face brightening further. He gave a snort of something like mirth, and quickly suppressed it. Mrs Wilde threw up her hands in exasperation.

Lizzie looked up from her sewing as if nothing had taken place. 'I've nearly finished, Elsie. I've left enough ease in it. I can see you've put a bit of meat on. If you'll sit and have a cup of tea, it'll be done before you've drunk it, and you can take it with you.'

John got up and pulled out a chair for her. 'Aye. Sit and have a cup of tea, Elsie.'

Elsie looked at the man who had rescued her from the work-house, and maintained her for months past, and anger drained away. Her knees felt weak as she sank into the chair he held for her. He loved her, she was sure of it. She'd known it the night she caught him poaching, and when she walked in the woods with him. Before then, even. He was a pitman with dirt round his fingernails, and she had been the belle of Annsdale, the most beautiful girl in the two villages, and in her panic and her arrogance she had hoped that was enough to make him glad to save her from the consequences of her own worse-than-folly and marry her, not reckoning that he also might have some pride.

And there stood the hateful obstacle to their happiness, admiring himself in front of the mirror, while the other, beloved impediment lay innocent in his cradle in the Cock Inn, waiting for her.

'Why, Elsie, hinny, you do the place no harm, looking like that. We'll soon have you behind the bar in the best room. I'll tell you what, John; you want a pint. You can show her how to pull it for you,' Martin said.

John came to stand behind her, and Elsie felt his hand on top of hers on the pump, and its pressure as he drew the lever down. She felt his eyes on her décolletage, and looked up into his face. He didn't look pleased, but said nothing except, 'Keep the glass steady.'

'It's very stiff, isn't it?' Elsie said.

To her amazement Maudie suddenly exploded. 'I bet it's stiff an' all, eh, John?' she burst out, and laughed until her eyes watered. Even Martin and Ginny were smiling, and Elsie stared at them all, utterly perplexed. John looked more displeased than ever.

'She's already got a couple of admirers, you know, and that's just collecting the glasses in her old frock,' said Maudie, once she'd got her breath back.

'Have I? Who?' Elsie laughed, blushing a little at the looks Maudie was directing at John.

'I don't know what they call them, but they look as if they're not short of a shilling or two. I can see they like the look of you, though, Elsie. Both of them. Their eyes were never off the place John's were on, just then.'

John went home in a black mood, angry with Ginny and Martin for getting Elsie up like that, not much better than some street girl with her goods on display for men to slaver over, and all in the name of attracting custom. All the more annoying because he daren't say anything about it, for fear of offending them. Not that they'd send Elsie packing, he knew they wouldn't, but all the same, Ginny shouldn't egg her on to dress like that. There was something about Ginny that . . . well, saucy was the polite word, and bawdy was the exact one. He used to think it was funny, and laugh along with the rest, but now the joke had gone stale as far as he was concerned. He visualized Elsie dressed as he would like, with a decent high neckline – they were in fashion, after all. But he could imagine what Ginny would say if he suggested it – 'She's working in a pub, not a bloody convent. And the customers like something a little bit – you know.'

Aye, he did know. And he didn't like it.

His mother was still up when he got in, sitting at the quilting frame.

'Where's our Arthur?'

She put her hands in the air and stretched, easing her shoulders. 'At the club, or Kath's. One or the other. I can't understand that girl, encouraging him when she knows he's got a baby to somebody else, and I can't understand her family, letting her. But he spends more time there than he does here, and they harbour him.' She got up and stretched again. 'The kettle's just boiled. We'll have a cup of tea in no time. How's our Ginny and Martin?'

'All right.'

'And how's Elsie?'

'All right.'

'All right?' His mother looked intently at him.

'Aye, all right.'

'And how's the baby?'

'I don't know, I hardly ever see her with him. I think

our Ginny and Phil do the best part of the looking after.'

'That girl. She's about as much use as a mother as she is at everything else. And our Arthur says that boy of Martin's wants watching. He'll go the wrong way if they're not careful,' his mother said.

John ignored the remarks and nodded towards the frame. 'What have you got on the go this time, Mam?'

'It's a quilt for the baby's cot. Whenever he gets into a cot. Poor little mite. It's nearly finished. I'll take it down as soon as it's done.'

'Aye, it looks nice,' John said. 'She'll like that. Where's our Lizzie?'

'Why, in bed, at this time. She spends most of her time in bed these days, breaking her heart over Tom Peters. You'd know, if you were ever at home yourself. And she's earlier back from work these days, as well. She'd started a lovely cashmere suit just before he jilted her, a bonny, rich brick-red colour, but that's gone by the board. It's still in the shop, with only the skirt half made, and now it's all rolled into a bundle, and she hasn't the heart to touch it. Mr Surtees called me in and showed it me the other day. He wanted to tell me how low she is. "She's making herself ill, Mrs Wilde," he said, as if I didn't already know. What a waste of lovely stuff, though.'

'Our poor Lizzie,' murmured John, overcome by sympathy for her misery. 'We're not very lucky in love, are we, me and our Liz?'

> Saw a moose run up the waal,
> Pit lie idle, pit lie idle,
> Saw its arse and that wes aal
> Pit lie idle O!

He pushed open the door and paused when he saw her sitting in an armchair, laughing and crooning a lullaby over a drowsy little Pip. Poor Ginny, she would have made a canny mother. He'd seen her suffer the grief of miscarriage after miscarriage, and now other people's babies were the only ones she'd ever nurse. John felt a lump begin to form in his throat, and the tears start to his eyes. He hardly knew what was the matter with him lately; he was like a mawkish old woman. He cleared his throat and straightened up, pulled his shoulders back, put a smile on his face and then stepped into the room, followed by his mother.

'All right, bonny lass?' His voice was brisk, jocular.

She looked up, with a welcome on her face, and put her fingers to her lips.

'Shh,' she whispered. 'Will you go and put the kettle on, Mam? I don't want to disturb him before he's asleep.'

His mother put the little quilt down beside her, and went into the kitchen.

'Where's Elsie?' he asked.

'Did you not see her? She's downstairs, in the taproom, with Martin and Jimmy.'

'I'll just go and tell her me mam's here, with something for the bairn.'

She was standing behind the bar with Martin, learning the measures and the prices of the spirits, decently dressed this time in a long-sleeved cotton blouse and a black skirt.

'Aal reet, John man?' she greeted him. 'Hes thoo come for thi pint, like?'

He gave a short laugh. 'Wey, Elsie, Aa reckon some o' these lowp-heeded lads have been teachin' thoo a bit o' Durham pitmatic. The've got nee mair sense.'

'The hev,' she contradicted. 'Aa knaa now what thy job is. Thoo hes te be in afore the men, an' keek at the flo-or en the roof, when yan heaves or tother lowers, en mek sure the props is areet, en check the gannin boards, en test fer gas, en mebbe lay a bit o' roadway or fettle an aud sexshun, en dee half the manager's job, checking the lads' work tallies, and orderin' em aboot. An gannin te thi kist fer te fetch the stuff te patch 'em up wi' if the feuls hort theirsels, cos the hevn't the sense the were born wi'.' She tilted her chin, and gave him a triumphant smile.

He gazed at her, wide eyed, and chuckled. 'Aye, thet's aboot reet. But I'm glad whoever taught you that didn't teach you any of the swear words that usually go with it, Elsie. I'm glad we can leave them in the pit, at least.'

'It was Martin and Jimmy,' she grinned. 'They were talking a language I could hardly understand at times, and pitmatic's the language of the taproom, so I had to learn, didn't I? Feel my hand,' she said, proudly stretching out her right arm. 'I'm a real barmaid now.'

He took the proffered hand in his, and felt the calluses beginning to form on her palm.

'Aye,' he said, holding on to her hand, 'you must have pulled a few pints to get them, right enough.' And still he held on, still gazing into her eyes. 'Come on upstairs. Me mam's brought something for the bairn.'

There was a bit of awkwardness when John brought Elsie face to face with his mother. It was not allowed to last long, however. It seemed to be Ginny's policy to be brisk and cheerful, and deliberately insensible of the tension in the air.

'Why, sit down, Elsie. Pour her a cup of tea, Mam, and then you can show her what you've brought.'

His mother obediently lifted the teapot.

'Isn't Elsie looking well, Mam?' Ginny ran on. 'She's getting a bit fatter, and she's nearly got her figure back. She'll soon be able to claim her old title again, the Belle of Annsdale.'

Elsie blushed, and the blush transformed beauty into radiance. John ached to take her in his arms and hold her tight, and cover those hot cheeks with kisses. Instead, he stared, and she blushed more deeply, and averted her eyes. 'Oh, I don't think so, Ginny,' she said, 'not now. Not now I'm a mother, you know.' Her voice trailed off to a whisper.

'Rubbish,' said Ginny. 'That's got nothing to do with whether you're bonny or not. And you are bonny. You're beginning to look really well. You'll soon be glowing with health, won't she, Mam?'

His mother had little alternative but to agree 'Yes, I think she will, but stop it, Ginny, you're embarrassing her.'

'All right, then. Show her what you've brought.'

His mother placed the exquisitely wrought, snow-white quilt on Elsie's knee. 'It's for his cot,' she said.

'Oh,' Elsie exclaimed, 'it's lovely.'

Her admiration was genuine. Mollified, his mother said, 'It'll keep him warm, these cold nights.'

'It will. Thank you very much.' Elsie hesitated, then added, 'I'm sorry about your other quilt.'

His mother nodded. 'And I'm sorry about your little cat, Elsie. I'm very sorry.'

He'd seen them in the Cock before, talking to her, looking at her. He'd seen the looks on their faces. He hated them all, leering at her. Because they thought she was defenceless, easy prey, a barmaid with an illegitimate baby, disowned by her own family. John's fingers contracted into his fists, and his shoulders hunched. He could deck them for looking at her. He could punch the leering, living daylights out of them. He could choke the life out of them and think he'd done nothing wrong, just for the looks on their faces. He saw a flush rise to her cheeks, and her look of confusion. They were making her squirm. Well, he'd make them squirm. He'd show them he was wide awake to their game. He was wide, wide awake to it, and they'd have him to deal with if they tried to play it out.

With a predatory step he strode towards the bar, thrust a shoulder between the two of them, then squared himself to face her, prising them apart. They staggered back and looked at him. He spared them not a glance, but stared straight ahead as if they were invisible, daring them to start something. Wishing they would.

'The usual, please, Elsie,' he ordered. He saw the relief on her face as she pulled his pint, and felt a surge of pure elation. 'Go upstairs and tell Martin I want a word with him, bonny lass. Don't worry about the bar. I'll look after it.'

She went, and with low mutterings between themselves, her two admirers moved away and took a seat near the fire. He turned and leaned against the bar, looking openly at them. He knew that Ginny allowed her customers a lot of bawdy chat, but Ginny was quick off the mark if they went too far, and could easily slap them down with a witticism. And there was something about Emma that kept the customers at a distance.

Those two needed little protection. They could fend for themselves. Not like Elsie.

It wasn't Martin who came down, but Ginny, her face questioning. John nodded towards the two men, not troubling to conceal the gesture.

'Keep them two away from Elsie, will you?'

'What for?'

'I don't like the way they look at her. And I don't like the way they talk to her. And she doesn't like it either.'

'Lower your voice, John,' Ginny hissed, throwing a placatory smile in the direction of her offended patrons. 'We cannot afford to have our best custom driven away. We've a lot of profit to make up, after what we lost during the strike. And you needn't worry about Elsie. She lives here, we're always within shouting distance, and she never has to leave the pub. They cannot get at her, unless she wants them to.'

John flushed with anger. 'Of course she doesn't.'

Ginny raised an eyebrow. 'How do you know that? One of them's offered to set her up in a house, with the bairn.'

Through clenched teeth, John hissed, 'What? As a kept woman? Which one? Which one said that to her? Who the hell does he think he is?'

Ginny sighed, looking at the taller of the pair. 'That one. He thinks he's a surgeon in Durham, and everybody else seems to think so an' all. He's got plenty of money, whatever he is, and he seems all right. He's made her a good offer, and it might be the best one she'll ever get, the way she's fixed.'

John could hardly believe his ears. 'It's not the best she'll get, and it's not good enough. She wants marriage, marriage or nothing. What does he think she is? I bet that bugger's married already. Trying to take advantage of a young lass. He wants a bloody good hiding, and I'll give him one, if he's not careful.'

Ginny gave him a long, appraising look, then said very softly, with the slightest, slyest of smiles on her face, 'Well, he won't expect to have to marry a lass that's got no money and already has a baby, now will he? That's not the way things work, and Elsie understands that, now. And you're right, he is married, but he's not the only bugger that marriage isn't enough for, is he? What about Mrs Hickey, then?'

John started back, the colour draining from his face. 'What?'

'I said, what about Mrs Hickey? I hear you're round there now and again, making yourself useful.'

'I go to look after the dog.'

'Aye, you went a couple of times to look after the dog, and now you go to look after her.'

'Who told you that?'

'You're telling me this minute, by the look on your face. You don't make a very good liar, John. And Irene told me. I'm no prude, as you well know, and a lot of people tell me things they wouldn't tell anybody else. I don't repeat them as a rule, but just this once I will. I've known how things were with her husband for a long time. I don't blame her, and I don't blame you, but people in glass houses, you know, John? So mind your step, or you might be the one getting the good hiding. And another thing I'll tell you – what one of the customers said about Irene – "she's like a big juicy spider, spreading her web out for the tastiest flies". So she's getting a name. You might not be the only visitor there. And you know what I think? I think it's nature. She's got to that time of life when a woman with no children begins to get desperate. You know what I mean, John? Desperate for a bairn, I mean. I know what I'm talking about because I've felt like that meself and I'm nowhere near her age – and she'd never be able to pass it off as Sam's, now would she? So just mind your step, that's all.'

'Here,' Ginny handed her a copper jug covered in a thin layer of Brasso. 'Rub it with that cloth until you can see your face in it. Give it plenty of elbow grease.'

Elsie took the jug, and began to rub hard. Ginny shook another dab of Brasso onto her cloth, and began to smear it on another of the copper and brass ornaments lined up on the newspaper. 'Aye,' she went on, 'me mam's had a hard life. I've seen the time me dad's beaten her black and blue, before she was left a widow. And then both me and our Em turned out to be a disappointment. She could never do anything with

270

Arthur, but she'd high hopes for our Lizzie and John, and they've come to nothing an' all.'

'I don't see how you could be a disappointment to anybody,' Elsie protested, pausing in her task of polishing. 'She really wanted John to marry Alice, though, didn't she?' She looked intently at the jug, and a distorted reflection returned her stare. She slowly resumed her rubbing.

'The top and bottom of it is our John's been itching to get back to South Africa for years, and she doesn't want him to go. He's been a good son to her, and she's clung on to him since me dad was killed. The main reason me mam wanted him and Alice together was because Alice will never leave England. But there's no Alice now, and there comes a time when mothers have to leave go, and it's long past the time with her and our John. He wants to go to South Africa, and she shouldn't stand in his way.'

A sad, sinking sensation overwhelmed Elsie, and stopped her rubbing. 'Do you think he will go, now?' she asked.

'I don't know, but he should. He loved it there, and it's been his dream ever since he came back.'

She turned to face him from her seat by the fire, peering at him through puffed and blackened eyes.

'My God, Irene! What the hell's happened to your face?' John stood rooted at the kitchen door, shocked at the sight.

'You can see what's happened to me face, John. It's had somebody's fists in it.' The bruising and swelling of her mouth, and the split in her lip made her speech indistinct.

'Sam's found out.'

She gave a strangled laugh, and put a hand up to her head. He saw her scalp, reddened and bald where a handful of her fair hair had been torn out. 'You don't think Sam could do a thing like this? He's never raised a hand to me all our married life.'

'Well, who?'

'Somebody who'd seen you visiting, and decided he wanted some of the same. Never bother, I never told. I swore blind there was nothing between us. I thought he was all right, but then he turned nasty and – he did this.' Irene shuddered, and

271

tears sprang to her eyes. 'I thought he was going to kill me.'

'Irene man, who was it? Tell us, and I'll make him wish he'd never been born. I bet he'll never lay a hand on another woman after I've finished with him.'

She gave a short laugh, dabbing away the tears that were now oozing onto her cheeks. 'No. If you did, he'd know for sure about us, and so would Sam. Anyway, you're too late. Sam's gone out with my brothers, looking for him.' She blew her nose, and went on, a little more composed. 'I haven't said a word about you, so don't you say anything, either. But you'll have to go, John. Go away, and never come back.'

John put out a hand to comfort her, but she shook her head, eager to get him out of the house. 'Go on, get away. And make sure nobody sees you.'

John went; full of anger at the perpetrator, and at himself for his helplessness to avenge Irene, but wondering how much Irene had left out of her tale about the man she'd thought was 'all right'. He pondered on that comment made to Ginny. Maybe having tried it, Irene had acquired the taste for adultery, and had been unlucky enough to tangle with one who liked it rough. He hadn't gone far when a hand reached out from the shadows and grasped his shoulder. He turned, but the faces were barely discernible in the darkness.

'It's true, then, John. What that bugger said.' It was Sam's voice and John could hear the hurt in it.

Not knowing what to say, he said nothing.

'Why, I never thought you would have done aught like that,' Sam choked. 'I'm sorry about this, like, but you should have left her alone, John man.'

Three solid punches to his nose and jaw, and John lay on the cobbles. A hefty boot made painful contact with his ribs, and then he heard Sam's voice again. 'That's enough. That's enough. Leave him alone now.'

They were gone. Holding onto his ribs, John dragged himself to his feet. His chest hurt like hell, but it could have been a deal worse. He'd been let off with a token beating, a lot less than he deserved. Maybe he owed his lighter punishment to past favours, or maybe Sam thought he was less to blame than Irene. Whatever the reason, honour seemed to be satisfied.

John stood up as straight as he could and tried to inhale. Painful – but he felt lucky to have got away so lightly.

Elsie stood behind the bar watching the clock, anxiously biting her lip. 'John hasn't been in for the past two nights,' she commented to Martin. 'Do you think something's happened to him?'

Martin grinned. 'You're beginning to know him too well, Elsie, and you're right. It takes a lot to make John miss his pint.' His face became serious. 'But he stayed away so as not to upset anybody, like. I might as well tell you, you'll probably find out anyway. He's been in a bit argument, and it's spoiled his good looks. That's why he's stopping at home for a bit.'

Elsie gasped, her fingers flying to her mouth. 'How bad is it? Is he – will he be all right?'

'Aye,' Martin grinned, 'he's taken no real hurt. Just a bit bruised, you know.'

'What sort of argument? What was it about?'

Elsie caught a look of confusion on his face. It was gone in an instant, but she hadn't been mistaken.

'Why, I cannot say. Something and nothing, I suppose. Men can find anything to fight about if they're that way out. Probably something that's gone off at the pit.'

She opened her mouth to ask something more, but he was gone, down to the cellar, and Elsie knew why. John had got into a fight over her, and Martin wanted to avoid any more of her questions. She thought of the night the doctors had been in, making their propositions, and her heart had leapt at the sight of John's jealousy, his open aggression and determination to shield her from them. She had been right all along. He loved her, and now he'd fought in her defence and been so badly hurt he kept away rather than let her see.

She couldn't stand in the bar any longer; she felt such a pain in her chest. She went through the door to the living quarters and sat at the bottom of the stairs, remembering the expression on his face when he'd first seen little Pip. Elsie's head sank into her hands, and she groaned. It was impossible, impossible. He loved her, but he would never, could never marry her. Not now she had Arthur's child.

Twenty-Five

'Christmas is coming; the goose is getting fat. I think we'll go out and cut some trees, and see if we can find a bit holly and mistletoe today, Martin – get the pub done up tomorrow; deck the halls, like. We'll have plenty custom on Christmas Eve and we want the place looking festive.'

John looked at his sister, standing there with Elsie's bairn in her arms, looking happy, doing what she liked best – getting them all organized for good times.

'Why, Ginny man, it's the shortest day today; it'll be dark before we set off. Can we not go tomorrow morning? We'll have plenty of time to get the place decorated in the afternoon,' Martin said.

'I would rather go today, while we can all go, while our John and Lizzie are off work. It'll make a nice walk together in the fresh air, and it's nearly a full moon tonight, so there'll be plenty of light. I love going for the tree. I love everything to do with Christmas. We'll call by Old Walter's and ask him for the lend of his wagon, so we'll get a ride back with it, like.'

'Yes, let's. I could do with some fresh air,' Lizzie agreed.

John laughed. Such was the logic of women. 'Aye, and then one of us'll have to take it all the way back to the farm, and then walk back again. And that'll not be any of you women, will it?'

'No, it'll not,' Jimmy agreed, 'but you'd better let them have it their own way. There'll be no peace until you do.'

Martin gave in. 'Well, go on, then, Ginny. Get cracking, if we're going. Get the Sunday dinner on the table, and let's get a move on.'

'The dinner's all right,' said Ginny, cooing and laughing at the baby. 'Elsie's fettling it. Our Emma's helping her.'

Walter answered the door, and took the bottle of rum Martin proffered, his old eyes lighting up at the sight, his wizened face wreathed in such smiles that John smiled at the sight of him. He left his prize in the farmhouse kitchen, and crossed the yard with Martin, to hitch the horse to the wagon. John stood with his sisters, and waited.

'Why don't you go to South Africa, John?' Ginny suddenly asked. 'You'll never get a better chance. You've no ties now Alice is gone.'

He supposed she was right. He really had no reason not to go now, and he would have been off like a shot if it hadn't been for . . . but he could hardly put Elsie forward as an excuse. 'Well, funds are a bit low at the moment, like, what with one thing and another. I'll have to save up again. I want to have enough money to get a proper start.'

Ginny must have read his mind. 'Don't fash yoursel' about Elsie. Dr de Mornay's not a bad feller. He's all right. She'll be all right with him.'

'How do you know? You only know what he's like in the pub, and that's bad enough. And he's that much all right he wants to start a harem,' John scowled, all good humour suddenly evaporated. 'I don't call that all right. And I don't like the way that other one sniffs round her, either. I get the feeling Elsie might be a joint enterprise between the pair of them – and I'm surprised you don't see it, after the education you got in London.' His tone was caustic. He regretted the words as soon as they were spoken, and the unintended insult they dealt to the best sister a man ever had.

If Ginny was offended, it didn't show. 'Oh, well,' she said, 'Let's leave things to sort themselves out, and just have a good Christmas.'

'Troubles don't go away just because it's Christmas.' There was an edge of desperation in Lizzie's voice.

Ginny sighed. 'I know that, Lizzie, but troubles pass, and there's more fish in the sea than ever came out of it, although I don't expect you to believe that just now.'

Lizzie put her fingers to her temples, and shook her head. 'Oh, if you could feel even half the pain I feel, you couldn't say a thing like that to me.' She looked up. 'Believe! I would never have believed he'd do this to me – leave without a word. If you'd heard the way he used to talk! He'd never seen such bonny black eyes, I had lips as sweet as honey, he could die for my kisses! I believed all that, and I loved him, and I could deny him nothing. Stupid, stupid, stupid me! And now he's gone, and left me with the sort of trouble that won't pass. So how will I ever believe anything again, after that?'

They stared at her, at a loss for words, and her grief turned to anger, directed at John. 'And you needn't look at me like that,' she said. 'I told you I'd never be in the same boat as Elsie, and I don't intend to be.'

Before he could open his mouth to protest Martin came round with Walter and the wagon, and conversation ceased.

'What about that one, then, Martin? A bonny fir tree, and not too big for the best room,' said Ginny, pointing from the wagon, after they'd driven a little way into the wood. 'And there's a little one. That'll do for our front room. And there's a couple more, over there, for our Em and me mam.'

'Aye, all right. If they're the ones you want, they're the ones we'll have to cut,' Martin said, and with a 'Whoa, whoa,' he pulled the horse to a halt.

John jumped down and picked up the axes, and Martin helped the women down. 'We'll go and see if we can find a bit holly, and maybe some mistletoe, if we're lucky. Give us a shout when you're ready,' Ginny said.

They were no sooner out of earshot than Martin asked, 'What's up wi' you and Lizzie? Anybody'd think we were getting ready for a funeral, instead of Christmas.'

'Our Lizzie? It sounds as if Tom Peters has left her something to remember him by. Something that'll want its nappies changing before long.'

'What! He's not, has he? I always thought he was all right.'

'Aye, and so did I. And so did she.'

They came to a halt beside the chosen tree. 'Does he know?' Martin asked. John shrugged.

'Why, what's she going to do, like? Go to court for a main-tenance order?'

'I don't know.' They took off their jackets and tossed them over a nearby branch.

'I'll take this one,' said John. 'You take the little one.'

Incensed at Tom Peters's treachery, John began to swing his axe against the trunk, chopping with a will, lopping out wedges of wood until the tree creaked and groaned. He stepped smartly out of the way a second before it crashed to the ground, and surveyed it with stern satisfaction. Vanquished. He set about a second tree, glowering at its dark green needles, grimly wishing it were Tom Peters's neck in the way of his axe – or that bloody surgeon's.

Four trees cut, they carried one each back to the wagon.

'Well now,' said Martin, continuing the conversation where they'd left it. 'That's what's wrong with Lizzie. So now what's wrong with you?'

'Me? I'm all right, man. There's nothing the matter with me.'

They threw the axes into the wagon, and the trees after them, and were turning to fetch the other two when Martin paused, his face perfectly serious. 'You did right to stop with your mam, just after the accident,' he said. 'She needed you. But that's six year ago, John, and if you wanted to go away to make a life of your own, she'd still have us.' He stressed the words: 'You wouldn't have to worry about her.'

He spied them some time before they saw him, and leaned against a tree to watch them walking along in the moonlight, their hands full of holly branches. Lizzie's voice carried in the stillness of the night, clear and plaintive.

'You know, Ginny, you never have anything good to say about that man, but if it hadn't been for him, you'd never have made the money you've made, and you wouldn't have the canny sitting down you've got in the Cock, either.'

'Aye, and he took his payment in full, and it's because of him I haven't got a swarm of bonny bairns round my ankles, like our Em. I'd swap the Cock for that, any day.'

'Well, I cannot let the grass grow under my feet. Something's got to be done quick, and he's the one who knows somebody who can do it.'

This was a conversation not intended for his ears, and John wanted to hear no more. 'Come on, lasses,' he shouted, 'get a move on. We've had the trees cut ages ago, and found a big clump of mistletoe an' all. Martin's waiting with the wagon.'

'That's right, lass. Rub the fat into the flour, until it looks like breadcrumbs.'

The fire blazed, and the oven was hot. The kitchen reeked of mincemeat, fruity and rummy. How easy Ginny seemed to make it all, Elsie thought. With her to teach, the task was pleasant, something to enjoy.

'That's right. Now take it to the sink and turn the tap on until it's just a tiny dribble, and hold the bowl under for half a second. Now mix that drop of water in. Now another drop. You want just enough to make the pastry stick together, and no more, or it'll be hard.'

Elsie worked with utter concentration and was rewarded with Ginny's approval.

'Right. Now flour your board, and knead the pastry into a flat cake, and roll it out, as thin as you can.'

Elsie went back to the table, and did as she was bid. Suddenly light of heart, she turned to Ginny and laughed. 'And we'll soon have some bonny mince pies,' she said.

'Aye, we will.'

The sheet of pastry was eventually thin, and flat, and even, and Elsie surveyed it with some pride.

Ginny handed her the cutters. 'You know, Elsie,' she murmured, 'if you're anything like me, one bugger destroys your life, and a better man tries to patch it up for you as best he can. Never mind what people say, or what they think. Don't forgo your better man. Everybody can see you love our John, and he's over heels in love with you. The sin is to deny it. You're free to marry who you like, and if you've any sense, you will.'

Elsie's face fell, and her heart sank to her shoes. 'John hasn't asked me to marry him, Ginny, and I couldn't, without my father's permission. And I don't want to ask him for anything.'

'Go to Scotland, then, and you won't have to.'

'There's something else, though, Ginny. John doesn't love Pip. He wouldn't want him. I know he wouldn't.'

> Wassail! Wassail! All over the town,
> Our bread it is white and our ale it is brown,
> Our bowl it is made of the green maple tree,
> With the wassail bowl, we'll drink unto thee!

Eight o'clock on Christmas Eve, and the Cock was already full of customers. Dr de Mornay and his friend stood by the piano, both looking in Elsie's direction, both pointedly lifting their glasses to her as they sang.

She'd seen that look before, on many men's faces, but never so bold, and so free, and so – threatening. Their eyes were still on her, making her feel hot, and ashamed – ashamed to be looked at like that. Those looks upon her made her feel mired, unclean. She flushed and looked away, and saw them out of her eye-corner, laughing. Oh, God, where was John?

Martin had said at the outset they couldn't have her at the Cock forever. There were too many people needing a living out of it already. John would never marry her, and she supposed she must find a keeper who would be willing to accept her with her baby, and stop burdening her friends. A pang of fear shot through her like an arrow.

> Then here's to the maid in the lily-white smock,
> Who trips to the door and pulls back the lock,
> Who trips to the door, and pulls back the pin
> For to let these jolly wassailers in!

They burst out laughing, their eyes still on her, ogling shamelessly. She answered with a nervous little smile.

He tucked in his shirt and pulled his braces up, then answered the tap on the bedroom door. 'Here you are, John. This is for Elsie, from me.' Lizzie hung her burden on the door and gazed at it for a moment or two, before meeting his eyes. 'I started it in love and hope, to go away in after we were married, Tom and me. I finished it in grief and despair. There's grief in every stitch, but she doesn't have to know that. Take it for her, and tell her I wish I'd been kinder to her, while she was here.'

John looked at the beautifully tailored brick-red cashmere costume. 'Why, you can't give that away, Lizzie man, not after all your hard work.'

'Well, I can't wear it. It's made to Elsie's measurements, not mine. And I would never want to, that's a certainty.' She fondled the material, and gave a rueful little laugh. 'I would have left it in the shop, but the stuff's over good to waste.'

He put an arm round her, and hugged her to him. 'What are you going to do, Liz?'

'I know what I'd like to do. I feel like committing a dreadful crime.'

'I'll do it for you. I'll go and give that bugger a good hiding.'

'No, you mustn't. He's a lawyer, John. They deal with things differently from us – you'd probably end up in jail. I thought I'd go to court, but our Ginny reckons I'll come off worst if I back him into a corner – he'll have seen all this sort of thing before, and he'll be up to all the tricks in the book. She says I might be better just asking him to do what's right. But I'm not doing that. I'm not going cap in hand to him for anything. It's been a bloody hard lesson for me, but I've learned it well, and I'm going to be all right, never bother about that.'

'Come with us. Come with me and me mam to the Cock. You don't want to be in on your own, on Christmas Eve.'

'Maybe later.'

So the two of them walked on without her, his mother with her hair waved and a new frock on under her old coat, John close-shaved and in his best suit with Lizzie's carefully folded gift in a carrier bag.

'I won't stay long. I'll just wish them all a merry Christmas, and then I'll come back and sit with our Lizzie.'

'Aye, all right, Mam.'

'John.' His mother paused. 'It won't be long before you go to South Africa.'

'Why, what makes you think that? I've got no plans to go.'

She hesitated. 'If it's money you're short of, you can have my savings.'

He gave an incredulous laugh. 'What? What do you take me for, Mam? I wouldn't touch your savings. And I wouldn't need to, anyway. I've got just about enough to get me there, if I decide I'm going.' After a short pause, he added, 'But this is a bit of a change. You've never wanted me to go before.'

'I don't want you to go now, but it's breaking my heart to see you and our Lizzie so miserable. I want you to have a happy life, with a wife and children – and South Africa as well, if that's what you want.'

'I do. But it's not because I don't care about you, Mam. You've been a good mother to me. I've always loved you, and I always will.'

Ginny caught sight of them as they walked in, and waved. John steered his mother through the throng to get to the bar where Ginny stood holding out a plate decorated with a couple of sprigs of holly, and piled high with well-filled mince pies, sugar crusted and still warm from the oven.

'Try one of these,' she laughed, 'and tell me what you think.'

'Why, there's no plate, Ginny. It'll make crumbs all over the floor,' his mother protested.

'Bugger the crumbs,' Ginny exclaimed. 'We'll worry about them tomorrow. Have one. Elsie made 'em. I'm giving 'em to all the special customers.'

John took a pie, and bit into it. 'Mmm, it's nice,' he said, then caught sight of the doctors. He inclined his head towards them. 'Have they had one?'

'Not yet,' said Ginny, with a sly smile.

John frowned. 'Well, don't bloody give 'em any, then.'

Ginny laughed. 'Give us a bit hand behind the bar, John. Martin's gone down the cellar to fetch another barrel up, and Elsie's going to play us a couple of carols on the piano by special request, give our Jimmy a rest, like. Our Emma's upstairs, settling the lads to sleep, Mam. She'll make you a cup of tea, if you want to go up. I know it's no use offering you a drink down here.'

His mother went upstairs, and John took his place behind the bar, to begin serving the customers, as fast as he could. 'I didn't even know Elsie could play the piano,' he said. Soon, the hubbub of the inn melded into the strains of 'The Holly and The Ivy', as most of the customers began to join the singing. Through narrowed eyes, John watched the surgeon and his friend, leaning either side of the piano, holding their drinks and singing. When they came to the end of the carol Dr de Mornay leaned down, and with his lips almost touching her cheek, whispered something in Elsie's ear, while turning over the sheet music. Outraged, he watched Elsie nod, and begin to play 'The Twelve Days of Christmas'.

Well, that was a song that was going to go on for long enough. John scowled and turned to Ginny. 'Why, how much of a rest does our Jimmy want?' he demanded. 'We could do with Elsie behind the bar, helping us.'

'Keep your hair on,' she grinned. 'He'll be back in a minute. You'll have to go and collect some glasses soon, Maudie. We'll soon have run out.' Maudie nodded, drying her hands on her apron as she went. 'Jimmy's just gone to kiss the lads goodnight. They're over excited – Christmas, you know, and staying here,' Ginny continued.

John grunted, pulling pints and changing money as fast as he could, casting frequent glances in the direction of the piano. As soon as the company started bawling about twelve lords aleaping John leapt round the bar and pushed his way across to the piano.

'You'll have to leave the piano-playing there, Elsie,' he said, firmly closing the piano lid as soon as the carol finished. 'Come on. There's over many customers waiting to be served.'

Elsie stood up, and with an apologetic, fleeting smile to the doctor, began threading her way through the crowd.

'But the landlord's back behind the bar. Let her stay,' the doctor protested. 'Season of goodwill, you know. Season of goodwill.'

'Aye,' John agreed, 'and Elsie's wanted, to pour it into

glasses. And here's your regular pianist back an' all. He'll play whatever you like.'

John stayed behind the bar, next to Elsie, keeping a wary eye on the doctors, and Ginny decided that with so much help she could go and talk to Lizzie, and persuade her to come back to the Cock.

The night wore on, with singing and jollity unabated. John began to relax, and to enjoy a joke with some of the customers. At last Ginny walked in, under the mistletoe hung over the door, and one of the customers caught hold of her and gave her a peck. She laughed, and after a good-humoured exchange with him took up her place behind the bar. With her back to help, John might have time to enjoy a pint himself, and he began to pull one, but the pump spluttered and failed before it was half full.

'Beer's off, Martin,' Ginny said, and Martin went grumbling down to the cellar. 'Try the other pump, John. You go and collect the glasses, Elsie, Maudie's washing them as fast as she can. I wish I could have got our Lizzie to come. It would have done her good to get out of the house, and stop fretting about that bugger. Poor little lass. She was all right for a season, but not for life.'

A good many of the customers were gone, and John was looking forward to seeing the back of them all and drawing the heavy curtains to start the private, family party. Elsie was returning with her tray laden when John saw the surgeon's friend take it from her, laughing as Dr de Mornay lifted her and whirled her in the direction of the mistletoe.

He felt Ginny's eyes on him, and heard her say, 'Me and Martin have talked it over, John. We'll look after the bairn, if he's what's in your way . . .'

Heedless, John lifted the bar counter and crossed the room. The doctor was holding Elsie in a bear hug and silencing her protests with a kiss that looked likely to suffocate her.

His eyes now level with the greying curls on the back of the surgeon's collar, John tapped him smartly on the shoulder. Jimmy stopped playing and a hush fell, as the whole company watched and waited. The surgeon turned, and something in

283

John's expression prompted him to release Elsie, and step back. Wiping her mouth on the back of her hand, Elsie moved in the direction of the bar, but John stood in her way, put his hands on her waist and looked deep into her bitter-chocolate eyes. She returned his gaze and held it for long moments and then he pulled her close. Cupping her head in his right hand he pressed his lips against hers in a sweet and tender kiss which became ever more searching and sensuous, an attempt to invade her, body and soul. He looked again into those brown eyes, saw those rosy lips form words of regret:

'I'm sorry it can never be.'

And then he heard his own voice, loud and aggressive, demanding, 'Why cannot it?'

Twenty-Six

Jubilant, John drew the Cock's thick curtains and turned to watch Elsie wiping the last of the tables. He and Martin butted a couple of them together and set some chairs round. Ginny brought a supper tray, full of pies, sandwiches and pickles, cakes and tea. At last all was done, and they sat down together – Emma and Jimmy, Maudie and Ned, Ginny and Martin, and John and Elsie. Unable to resist, John reached out and took Elsie's hand.

Maudie nudged Ned, and gave a suggestive smile. 'Better get a move on wi' that wedding,' she commented.

'Aye. I think so an' all,' John laughed, feasting his eyes on Elsie, his heart gladdened by her smiles. 'We're going to get married in Gretna Green. You can't beat that for romance, can you? We'll stay overnight in Scotland, and then we'll get the train back to Newcastle.'

'We've got some good friends there, that keep a good inn,' Martin said. 'They'll look after you until you board the ship, and it'll cost you nothing. They owe us a favour. Ginny'll write to them, and let them know you're coming.'

'Then you'll have to get Pip on the bottle, Ginny. That's not a long job,' said Maudie. 'Don't bother buying one o' them fancy bottles. I just stuck a teat on the end of a brown ale bottle when I was feeding Harry, and it did just as well.' She looked round at them all and laughed. 'I did drink the ale first, though, and I filled the bottle up wi' milk, in case you were wondering.'

He slept at the Cock that night, and in the small hours when everyone was asleep, he heard a tap on his door. He opened it to find Elsie standing before him. Without a word, he took her by the hand and led her to his bed. She lay beside him, rested her head on his naked, broad shoulder and he felt her shiver, felt the tension in her muscles. Sensing her fear, he began to soothe her, to stroke her hair, speak gently about anything and everything, determined to go no further with her until he'd won her trust. He murmured softly on and on, told her about his time in South Africa, how he had typhoid and got better, how he'd loved it there, had driven in a pony cart along the garden route. 'Oh, I can't wait to show it all to you. It's lovely, Elsie, but not half as lovely as you, my bonny little lass. My belle of Annsdale.'

Little by little her muscles softened, the weight of her head became heavier on his shoulder and her breathing slowed and deepened. Hours later he pulled her heavy, relaxed body closer to him and allowed his hand to travel down her smooth neck, over the mound of her breast, gently towards her navel, then up again. He cupped her breast in his hand, the nipple flat. She was sleeping like a baby.

Slowly he eased his aching shoulder from under her head, leaned on one elbow and looked down at her, trying to make out her features in the darkness. He stole out of bed, and quietly lit the lamp to gloat with the thrill of possession over the arch of those dark eyebrows, the matching lashes thickly fringing the lids and resting on her cheeks, the curve of those cheeks, the shape of the soft baby mouth. He suppressed an impulse to cover the pretty throat and beautiful breasts with kisses. He wouldn't touch her, because he wanted her as mad with love and as hot with lust for him as he was for her.

Patience, patience. He would not risk waking her. Morning would come soon enough, but his desire for her was over-powering, his urgency too great to contain as imagination broke its bonds and dwelt on the soft-lipped, open-mouthed kisses which would soon be his, on those breasts whose nipples would harden at his touch, and on that darker mouth between her thighs that would swell and moisten in eagerness for his penetration.

Elsie slept, and dreamed. She was standing on a ship, and looking over the side she saw her little son at the bottom of the vast ocean beneath her. Tendrils of seaweed were floating between his fingers and in his baby hair, and he was breathing the cold, salt water. She was watching him drown, but she couldn't swim. She wanted to jump over the side to save him, but an intense fear gripped her and she knew that if she did, it would be the death of both of them. So she stood alone and powerless, with icy fingers clutching at her heart, looking at the child she loved and should never have had, and praying for someone stronger than she to rescue him.

'Oh, oh!' She opened her eyes with a gasp and a sob, and her face was covered with salt tears. John lay sound asleep beside her. Shaken, she lay in bed for many minutes before dragging herself up to go and wash her face, but try as she might, she could not wash away the horror of that dream.

The night before they left was crisp, and the sunset brilliant. John set out for a stroll round the villages with Martin and Jimmy, to call in on all his old marrers and say his goodbyes. They knocked on the Leighs' door, and had a word with Arthur.

'Elsie's got what she wanted, then,' he said.

'I hope so. I've got what I want, anyway.'

Arthur put an arm round the girl at his side. 'Why, she's got you, and I've got Kath, and our Ginny's got a bairn. Everybody's happy.'

'No hard feelings, then? About either Elsie or the bairn?'

'No fear,' grinned Arthur. 'If she marries you, she'll not be taking me to court for maintenance. It'll be better all round. Kath wants a fresh start, and so do I, truth be known.'

John felt a pang as they passed Irene's door. God love her, if he could have said a private goodbye he would have done it, but it was impossible. Better left alone. He'd leave Ginny to say his goodbye for him.

'Oh, you do right,' Jimmy said. 'I'd go if I got the chance. No struggling against bosses and their starvation wages. Beautiful country, lovely climate. Plenty of hard work for a year or two, and you won't be sailing, man. You'll be flying.'

John laughed. 'Aye, it's what I've worked and saved for for the past six year. And now it's here. We're off, finally.'

'Aye. I envy you. But this country's all we'll ever know,

so we'll have to like it, like,' said Jimmy, 'and it's all right, you know. Look at that.' He nodded towards the sunset.

'Aye, and look at that,' John laughed in gentle derision, turning to look towards the winding gear.

They raised their eyes and saw a couple of miners, stopped on a gantry to exchange a word, two black silhouettes against a sky of fire. The image sank deep into John's soul, an impression of sadness and grandeur that pulled at his heartstrings. He looked at Martin and Jimmy, aware as never before that he loved them, and loved nigh on everything he was soon to leave behind. All three were quiet for a minute, then they turned and resumed their banter, all the way back to the Cock.

As might have been expected from friends of Ginny and Martin, the landlord and landlady of the Fox and Hounds spent the evening plying John and Elsie with food, drink and conviviality. Thoroughly at ease, they sat talking until midnight, when John stood up.

'Aye, well, we've had a busy couple of days, what with chasing to Gretna Green to get married, and then getting the train back here. Elsie's tired, so we'll be getting to bed.'

The landlord laughed. 'Aye, the honeymoon couple will want to get to bed, all right. And you'll be out with the morning tide, eh, lass?' He looked towards Elsie, beaming from ear to ear.

'A strong tide and a fair wind, to blow us all the way to South Africa, that's all we want now,' said John.

'And if it doesn't, a steamship will get you there just the same,' smiled the landlady. 'I'm always up early. I'll give you a shout, never bother. You can get the Corporation Tram. You'll be there in plenty of time.'

John slid down the bed, and wrapped his arms around his wife. She smiled sleepily, shyly stroking the hairs on his chest, quiet for a while as he gazed at her.

'What?' she asked.

'What? I love you to distraction, that's what.'

He hadn't had a woman for weeks, and now the one who'd been his obsession for years lay in his arms on the second

288

night of their unconsummated marriage. She's yours – take her, he thought. Take her and enjoy her, all his male nature prompted, and yet he hesitated, fearing to be too sudden and brutal. He must be patient, take things slowly, ignite a flame of desire in her, and when he saw its first flickering he would guard it from rough gusts and breathe it gently into life, taking care not to extinguish it before it took a hold and burned with hot lust – for him.

Slowly, gently, patiently, with all his heart and all his art he loved her, but she gave him back only his patience, and sad smiles, and a resigned, compliant passivity he did not want. She was closed in her little oyster shell, untouched by his caresses, his idolatry. Unreachable. Unknowable.

Devastated, he turned away from her with tears in his eyes. She saw the tears and gathered him into her arms, rocking him like a baby. 'What's wrong, John, what's wrong?'

He couldn't tell her, couldn't say the simple, childish words searing themselves into his mind: 'You don't love me. You never loved me,' and so he lay awake beside her, staring at a picture of the suffering Christ on the wall, knocking on the weed-choked door of the human heart, until he put the lamp out. He'd had more pain than pleasure from his lovemaking, but the knot was tied and he wouldn't slip it, the course set and he would not veer from it. And married or not, he knew he could never have dislodged her from either his heart or his mind. Upon this day he'd set his lifetime's weal or woe, and it was to be woe, woe, woe, just as Alice had predicted. Worse woe, to have mastery over her body and be driven mad because he was shut out of her heart. Woe without end, Amen.

'I have forsaken him.'

Christ with his sad face below his crown of thorns came to John in his dreams, drawing all the suffering wretches of the world to His own suffering self. But the voice was wrong, and it should have been 'Why hast thou forsaken me?'

'Are you awake, John?' Surfacing from sleep, he realized it was Elsie who spoke. Did she mean she had forsaken him? She was here. Forsaken. He pondered on the word and felt it bite into his heart.

'Are you awake, John?'

'Aye, I'm awake, Elsie.'

'I might never see him again. Will he forgive me, do you think?'

She was talking about her baby, not about John. She had forsaken her baby.

It was a long time before he answered her. 'Of course he will. Ginny loves him. He'll know no other mother. He'll worship her, just like Philip does. And Martin's a good man. He'll love him for her sake, if not for himself. They'll be good to him.'

'Ginny loves him,' repeated Elsie, 'I know she does. She's taken better care of him than I have. And he looks like her more than he looks like me.' Again, John was silent, unsure what she wanted him to say. They both knew damned fine who he looked like. He was the model of Arthur.

'But what will he think when he finds out Ginny's not his real mother? When he really understands? When he knows his real mother abandoned him?'

Impossible to imagine such a discovery, and John was silent for a long time before he spoke. 'I only know,' he said, 'they'll explain as well as they can. And they won't blame anybody. They're not that kind. But Elsie, you told us you were too young to be a mother. You wanted Ginny to take the bairn. And now she does love him, just as if he were her own.'

'She loves him, and she'll look after him,' said Elsie, her voice sounding hollow. 'But he's not the child she really wants. The only child she really wants is Martin's child, not mine. And I didn't want to get too fond of him because I knew you couldn't love him, because you don't like Arthur, so how could you love him? I knew you didn't like him.'

Amazed at the discovery of such thoughts running through her head John protested, 'I don't dislike him. How can anybody dislike a bairn?'

'You did.' She met his look of shock, and repeated, 'You did, though. You said, "Aye, he's got Arthur's nose right enough," and you didn't look pleased. And you hate Arthur.'

He turned towards her, propping himself on his elbow. 'I

290

don't hate Arthur. I could kill him at times, but I don't hate him. He's my brother.'

'And you all say he looks like your dad, and you all tell stories about the hiding you got off him, the one that made you run off, and the way he used to knock you all about.'

John recalled looking through the mirror at his back after that legendary belting, but the anger that used to accompany the memory had died the day he'd brought his father's remains out of the mine. 'I long since forgave me dad for every wrong he ever did us, and I only wish I could tell him so,' he said, 'and I do like the bairn, Elsie. He's a canny little lad.'

A stifled groan escaped her. 'What have I done? What have I done? It's too late now. Will he understand that I had no choice? I thought I had no choice.'

'He'll understand when he's older,' John said, with more certainty than he felt.

'When he's older. What while he's still a child? He'll wonder why I left him. He'll think I didn't love him. And the other children will taunt him, and call him names . . . for not having . . . Just like they called me names for having him and not being married.'

'There's a lot of people are not like that.'

'But a lot are. More than you imagine, and not always the ones you'd think.'

'He'll have to fight.'

'I don't want him to have to fight. And I don't want him to hate me. I don't want him to despise me.'

'He's Arthur's lad,' John said, 'he'll like fighting, and he'll be good at it.' He held her in his arms, helplessly stroking her hair. 'Oh, Elsie, Elsie, I wish – I wish you'd told me sooner, while there was still time.'

'I daren't tell you. I was sure you didn't like him. My little boy. What have I done? What have I done?'

He comforted her until she fell asleep, but had no answers to her questions: will he blame me? Will he be unhappy? Will I ever see him again? What if he's ill, what if he dies, what if I never have the chance to hold him again, to be told that he forgives me? Never, never have the chance?

He had no answers for her. It was too late. There was no

time to go back for him before the ship left, and with it all the hoping and working and saving that bought the passage. And what about the job he had waiting for him? He couldn't write to the mine manager and say he wouldn't be starting – the man was relying on him. It wasn't likely he'd ever get another job there, if he did a trick like that. Were his dreams to be sacrificed again, his ambition thwarted by ties of love, and not even ties of his own making?

Besides, he reasoned, it would ruin Ginny's happiness if they took the bairn from her now. After all the disappointment of her miscarriages, she was happy. She thought he was hers, and she loved him. Ginny would make a much better mother than Elsie. The bairn would have a better chance with her. She had so much more to give, more maturity, more experience, more money.

But not more love. There was something sacred in the bond between mother and child. He gave the ghost of a smile as he remembered Maudie's lad, Harry, screeching for his mammy on the night of the fire. Mammy, Mammy! And Emma's bairn, after that scald. Even that poor little bugger who'd had the pick-point in his eye, they all screamed for mammy. God might be everything the church people said he was, but in the pit, when men – even old, gnarled men – were trapped or hurt or terrified it was their mothers they cried for, most of them – not God.

Dawn was breaking through the flimsy curtains, heralding the leaving of their old life, and the starting of the new. He could see her face, pale in the half-light. He lifted her sleep-limp hand, soft and smooth. In South Africa she'd have everything she was used to, people to wait on her, someone to cook peas without boiling them out of their shells, someone to clean; as many cats with hairy arses as she liked, a nanny for any more bairns. Arthur was right. She'd never make a pitman's wife. Would she?

He got out of bed, and filled the basin at the washstand. He stared at himself in the mirror, thinking Elsie'd parted from her child for his sake. And it was easy to see why she thought he didn't like the child. He was a reminder that another man had possessed her, and John's jealousy had overwhelmed him. He knew he'd let it show.

At their leave-taking at the Cock, Ginny had brought the bairn down and put him in Elsie's arms for the last time. He'd smiled and gurgled at her, a wide, wet, toothless smile, and they had sat, oblivious to everybody else in the room, devouring each other with their big brown eyes. The rest of them had begun to get restless and John was like a cat on hot bricks for fear of missing the train. He'd finally said, 'Away, bonny lass, it's time we went,' and she'd looked at him with something in her eyes he hadn't recognized, that he'd refused to recognize. He soaped his face, and took up his razor.

A plea. Her eyes had been pleading with him, imploring him to let her keep her child, and he was so selfishly blind and so dead to her feelings he hadn't seen what was as plain as the nose on his face. She loved her bairn, wanted him, need never have been separated from him at all if she'd taken Arthur's or the surgeon's offer. But she'd chosen him.

'Mammy, Mammy.' Awful for a child never to know his own mother, for a man never to have kissed his own mother's face. Why couldn't she have told him she wanted her baby? It would have been so simple to bring him with them, to start a new life where he'd pass for John's child and no questions asked.

She might love John, but she hadn't been with him during his lovemaking. How could she? She'd been in Ginny's cosy sitting room, still tearing herself away from her firstborn son, the baby she loved with a mother's depthless love. For no matter how fond Ginny was of him, he was Elsie's bairn, and there was a bond between mother and son it would be sacrilege to break.

He dried his face and rinsed his razor, swilling all the dark shavings and water into the bucket. She'd feared losing him, to Alice, or some other lass, as he'd feared losing her. He caught hold of the towel and dried his face. With a pang of guilt he recognized that she'd been showing him that she loved her child, even while she was trying to make it appear she didn't. She had tried to make him understand, without words.

He looked at himself in the mirror. 'If you take her away from him you'll tear her heart out, and give her a wound that'll never heal,' he told his reflection. Time they both stopped playing this long, sad game of hide and seek with love.

The landlady came to wake them, but he sent her away, and didn't change out of his nightshirt.

He climbed back into bed beside her, and closed his eyes. He should have been in South Africa now, this very minute, married to Hendrika. Why wasn't he? He saw her in front of him so solidly now he could almost have reached out and touched her, and his eyes snapped open. He could never have been truly happy with Hendrika. Hendrika had a large and doting family to guard and protect her. She'd loved him, but she hadn't needed him. Neither had Alice. Alice needed no protection, would not have had it at any price. He wanted to lay tribute at his mistress's feet, and Alice could neither understand nor meet this need of his. She had been intent on showing him the bigger trophies she could capture for herself. She relished fighting her own battles, and she would vanquish all who stood in her path. 'I'll lay money she's hardly noticed I've gone,' he murmured.

Elsie did need him; she would sink without him. He was essential to her, and so she was to him. Her sheer defencelessness commanded all his love and his protection, his shield and his sword, his trophies and his tribute. Her tyranny was that of the weak over the strong.

He closed his eyes, his dark night of the soul over. He would give her the best tribute of all.

He felt her shaking his shoulder. 'Wake up, John, wake up. We're late. I've been down to see the landlady, and it's only twenty minutes to the ship leaving!'

He opened one eye and watched her for a moment, frantically gathering things together, and stuffing them into the bag.

'I wasn't asleep.'

'Well, why are you not getting dressed, then?'

He sat up and looked her full in the face. 'I was thinking, if you didn't want to live in a beautiful country that's just like heaven, full of sunshine and flowers and mountains, and everything made easy, if you'd rather have a life of drudgery as a pitman's wife, and you know how hard that is . . . we could go back and get the bairn, and stop here.'

She sat heavily on the bed beside him. 'But you don't love him.'

He brushed her cheek with the back of his hand, and lifted a tress of hair off her face. 'You know that priest that's round at our Emma's sometimes? He once said that love can be an act of will. It can be a practical thing, something you decide to do; it doesn't have to be a feeling. Loving kindness, that's what he called it. You can decide that you'll always treat somebody in a kind and loving way. You can show it by your actions. You can make your mind up to it, and I have. And it won't be hard, Elsie.'

She was silent, listening.

'I will love him, in that way at first, and when he gets to know me, he'll love me, because bairns do, then I'll love him all the more for that, then he'll love me more, and so it'll go on, because he is a canny little lad. I'll be a good dad to him, Elsie, as good as Martin could be, and probably a lot better than our Arthur. I'll guide him up in the right way, so he'll have the respect of everybody that knows him. We could stay in Annsdale and brazen it out. Our Ginny did, and half of them accept her, and half of them don't. It'll be the same for us. If you can't face that, there's other villages; and if they're not far enough off, there's other coalfields.'

'But you've always wanted to go to South Africa, John. You've dreamed of it for years.'

'I know I have, and maybe we'll be able to save a bit, and go in a couple of years, but maybe I should leave it as a dream. And maybe I've been deliberately blind about South Africa. There's slavery there and all, and the slaves are black, like us. The only difference is that their blackness doesn't wash off when they've done their stint. So you decide whether we go, or whether we stay. There's some things matter a lot more than dreams.'

'What?' she whispered.

He dropped a kiss on her forehead. 'Why, canny wives and bonny bairns.'

With a little sob she put her arms around him and covered

his face in kisses, then laid her head against his chest, and he hardly would have believed she had such strength, she so nearly squeezed the life out of him. When at last she lifted her head and looked into his eyes her cheeks were flushed and her face shone as if a hundred lamps had ignited inside. Pools of melted crystal glistened in her deep brown eyes and on her silky lashes, spilling onto that well-loved face, that radiant complexion of rose and ivory.

His throat tightened, and his own eyes moistened as he fished about in the pocket of his nightshirt and handed her a clean handkerchief. 'You know, Elsie, I think this is the first time I've seen you cry.'

'I'm so happy,' she choked. 'Happy I'm not going to be parted from him, because I couldn't bear it. I love him, John, and I love you.'

'I'll have to go and ask Mr Woolfe for me job back, and now I'm married, I'll get a house. And then I'll get the vote!' He raised one eyebrow and laughed, and gave her a little squeeze. 'And you know what we'll do as soon as we get a home, Elsie? We'll get our family photo taken – Mammy, Daddy and the bairn. A big one, that'll go over the mantelpiece.'

She bent her head to dab her eyes and blow her nose, then gave a little grunt to clear her throat. 'Before we do,' she whispered, 'we'll just lie in bed for a few minutes.' She stood up, and his heart leapt as she took off her bonny brick-red jacket and shyly unbuttoned her skirt and blouse. They fell unheeded to the floor and she sat quietly on the bed with her back to him, to remove her stockings. He lifted her long hair out of the way to expose the fastenings on her corset and with strong, impatient fingers loosed her from her prison of whalebone and laces.

She turned towards him, and her lips were parted in a smile that thrilled him with its glow, as bonny as a rainbow through a shower. A flash of recognition kindled in his eyes and he caught his breath as he saw her clearly for the very first time.

She was his canny, loving lass. His own, his Elsie. True mother, and true wife.